A Curse So Dark and Lonely

Also by Brigid Kemmerer

Letters to the Lost
More Than We Can Tell
Call It What You Want

A Heart So Fierce and Broken
A Vow So Bold and Deadly

Storm
Spark
Spirit
Secret
Sacrifice

Thicker Than Water

A CURSE SO DARK AND LONELY

BRIGID KEMMERER

BLOOMSBURY
NEW YORK LONDON OXFORD NEW DELHI SYDNEY

BLOOMSBURY YA
Bloomsbury Publishing Inc., part of Bloomsbury Publishing Plc
1385 Broadway, New York, NY 10018
29 Earlsfort Terrace, Dublin 2, Ireland

BLOOMSBURY and the Diana logo are trademarks of Bloomsbury Publishing Plc

First published in the United States of America in January 2019
by Bloomsbury YA

Library of Congress Cataloging-in-Publication Data
Names: Kemmerer, Brigid, author.
Title: A curse so dark and lonely / by Brigid Kemmerer.
Description: New York : Bloomsbury, 2019.
Summary: Eighteen for the three hundred twenty-seventh time, Prince Rhen despairs of breaking the curse that turns him into a beast at the end of each season—until feisty Harper enters his life.
Identifiers: LCCN 2018010847 (print) | LCCN 2018017988 (e-book)
ISBN 978-1-68119-508-7 (hardcover) • ISBN 978-1-68119-509-4 (e-book)
Subjects: | CYAC: Blessing and cursing—Fiction. | Magic—Fiction. | Cerebral palsy—Fiction. | People with disabilities—Fiction. | Fairy tales.
Classification: LCC PZ8.K374 Cur 2019 (print) | LCC PZ8.K374 (e-book) | DDC [Fic]—dc23
LC record available at https://lccn.loc.gov/2018010847

Book design by Jeanette Levy
Typeset by Westchester Publishing Services
Printed in Great Britain by CPI (UK) Ltd, Croydon CR0 4YY
13 15 17 19 20 18 16 14

To find out more about our authors and books visit www.bloomsbury.com
and sign up for our newsletters.

To my new family at Stone Forge CrossFit
Thank you for showing me how much stronger I could be

IISHELLASA ICE FOREST
THE FROZEN RIVER
SYHL SHALLOW
WILDTHORNE VALLEY
BLACKROCK PLAINS

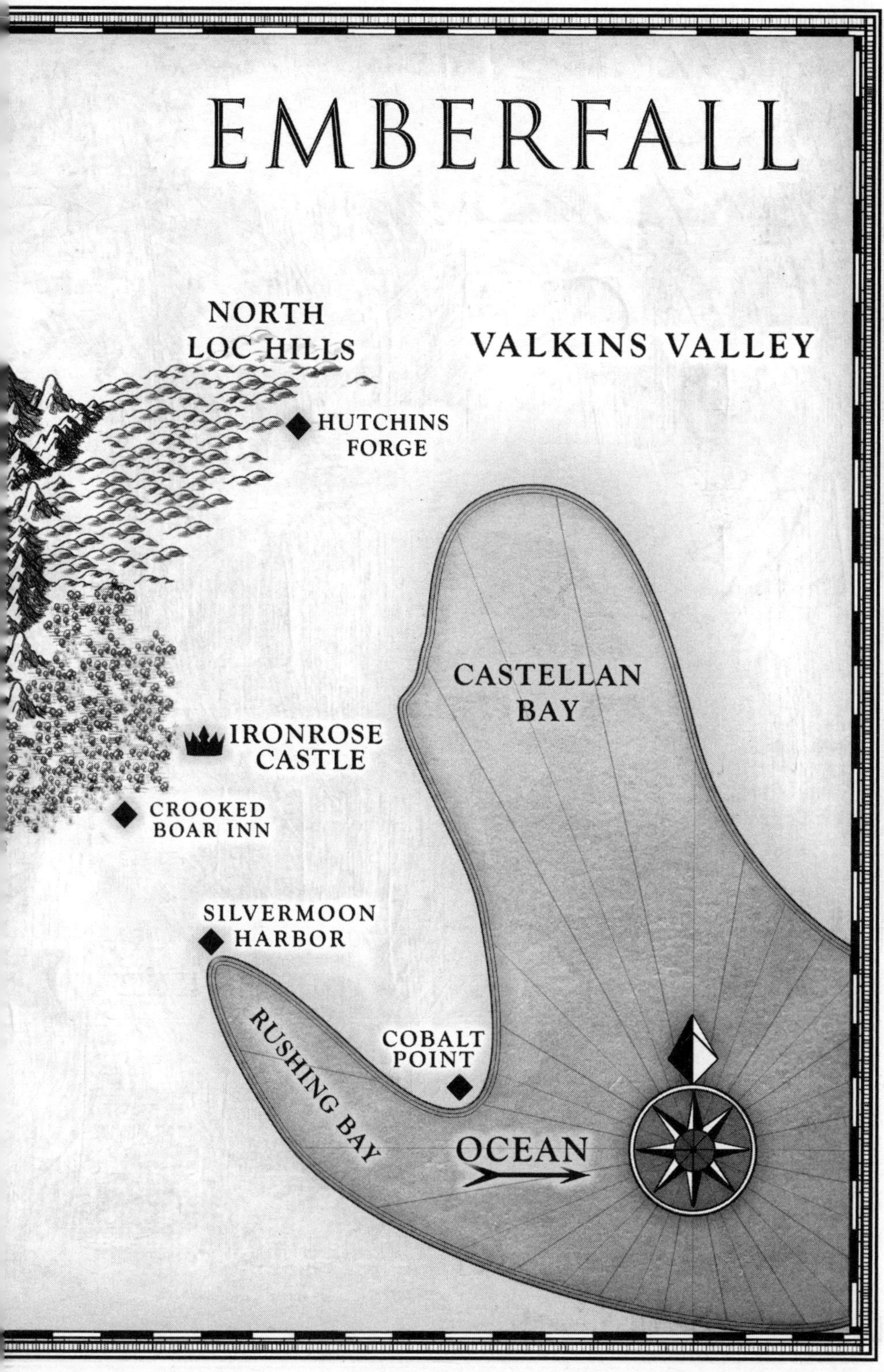
EMBERFALL
NORTH LOC HILLS
VALKINS VALLEY
HUTCHINS FORGE
CASTELLAN BAY
IRONROSE CASTLE
CROOKED BOAR INN
SILVERMOON HARBOR
RUSHING BAY
COBALT POINT
OCEAN

A Curse So Dark and Lonely

CHAPTER ONE

RHEN

There is blood under my fingernails. I wonder how many of my people I've killed this time.

I thrust my hands into the barrel beside the stables. The ice-cold water bites at my skin, but the blood clings. I shouldn't bother, because it will all be gone in an hour anyway, but I hate this. The blood. The not knowing.

Hooves ring against the cobblestones somewhere behind me, followed by the jingle of a horse's bridle.

I don't need to look. My guard commander always follows at a safe distance until the transition is complete.

Guard commander. As if Grey has men left to command.

As if he didn't earn the title by default.

I swipe the water from my hands and turn. Grey stands a few yards back, holding the reins of Ironheart, the fastest horse in the stables. The animal is blowing hard, its chest and flanks damp with sweat despite the early-morning chill.

For as long as we've been trapped here, Grey's appearance is somehow a continual surprise. He looks as young as the day he earned a position in the elite Royal Guard, his dark hair slightly unkempt, his face unlined. His uniform still fits him well, every buckle and strap perfectly arranged, every weapon shining in the near darkness.

He once carried a gleam of eagerness in his eye, a spark for adventure. For challenge.

That gleam has long since gone dark, the only aspect of his appearance that is never remade by the curse.

I wonder if my unchanged appearance startles him, too.

"How many?" I say.

"None. All of your people are safe this time."

This time. I should be relieved. I am not. My people will be at risk again soon enough. "And the girl?"

"Gone. As always."

I look back at the blood staining my hands, and a familiar tightness wraps around my rib cage. I turn back to the barrel and bury my hands in the water. It's so cold it nearly steals my breath.

"I'm covered in blood, Commander." A lick of anger curls through my chest. "I killed *something.*"

As if sensing danger, his horse stomps and dances at the end of the reins. Grey puts out a hand to calm the animal.

Once there would have been a stablehand rushing to take his horse, especially upon hearing my tone. Once there was a castle full of courtiers and historians and advisers who would have turned over a coin for a bit of gossip about Prince Rhen, heir to the throne of Emberfall.

Once there was a royal family that would have frowned on my antics.

Now there is me, and there is Grey.

"I left a trail of human blood on the path out of the forest," he says, unaffected by my anger. He's used to this. "The horse led a good chase, until you fell on a herd of deer in the southernmost part of your lands. We stayed well away from the villages."

That explains the condition of the animal. We traveled far tonight.

"I'll take the horse," I say. "The sun will be up soon."

Grey hands over the reins. This final hour is always the hardest. Full of regret for my failure once again. As always, I just want to get this over with.

"Any special requests, my lord?"

In the beginning, I was frivolous enough to say yes. I'd specify blondes or brunettes. Big breasts, or long legs, or tiny waists. I'd wine them and woo them and when they did not love me, another was easily found. The first time, the curse had seemed like a game.

Find me one you *like, Grey*, I'd said, laughing, as if finding women for his prince was a privilege.

Then I changed, and the monster tore through the castle, leaving a bloodbath.

When the season began again, I had no family left. No servants. Only six guardsmen, two of whom were badly injured.

By the third season, I had one.

Grey is still waiting for a response. I meet his eyes. "No, Commander. Anyone is fine." I sigh and begin leading the horse toward the stables, but then stop and turn. "Whose blood made the trail?"

Grey raises an arm and draws his sleeve back. A long knife wound still bleeds down into his hand, a slow trickle of crimson.

I'd order him to bind it, but the wound will be gone in an hour, when the sun is fully up.

So will the blood on my hands and the sweat on the horse's flanks. The cobblestones will be warm with early-fall sunlight, and my breath will no longer fog in the morning air.

The girl will be gone, and the season will begin again.

I'll be newly eighteen.

For the three hundred twenty-seventh time.

CHAPTER TWO

HARPER

Washington, DC, is so cold it should be illegal.

I pull up the hood of my sweatshirt, but the material is practically threadbare, and it doesn't do much good. I hate being out here playing lookout, but my brother has the worse end of this job, so I try not to complain.

Somewhere down the street, a man shouts and a car horn blares. I bite back a shiver and suck more tightly into the shadows. I found an old tire iron near the curb earlier, and I twist my fingers against the rusted metal, but whoever it was seems far away.

A glance at the timer on Jake's phone tells me he has another thirteen minutes. Thirteen minutes, and he'll be done, and we can go buy a cup of coffee.

We don't really have money to spend, but Jake always needs time to unwind, and he says coffee helps. It ratchets me up so I can't sleep, which means I don't crash until four in the morning and then I miss school. I've missed enough days of my senior year that it probably doesn't matter anymore. I sure don't have any friends who'll miss me.

So Jake and I will sit in a corner booth of the all-night diner, and his hands will tremble on the mug for a few minutes. Then he'll tell me what he had to do. It's never good.

I had to threaten to break his arm. I twisted it up behind his back. I think I almost dislocated it. His kids were there. It was awful.

I had to punch him. Told him I was going to hit him until a tooth came loose. He found the money real quick.

This guy was a musician. I threatened to smash a finger.

I don't want to hear the ways he shakes them down for cash. My brother is tall and built like a linebacker, but he's always been gentle and soft-spoken and kind. When Mom first got sick, when Dad got involved with Lawrence and his men, Jake would look out for me. He'd let me sleep in his room or sneak me out of the house for ice cream. That was when Dad was around, when Dad was the one getting threatened by Lawrence's "bill collectors," the men who'd come to our door to reclaim the money Dad had borrowed.

Now Dad's gone. And Jake's playing "bill collector" just to keep them off our backs.

Guilt twists my insides. If it were just me, I wouldn't let him do it.

But it's not just me. It's Mom, too.

Jake thinks he could do more for Lawrence. Buy us more time. But that would mean actually *doing* the things he's only threatening to do. It would mean truly hurting people.

It would break him. I can already see how even this is changing him. Sometimes I wish he'd drink his coffee in silence.

I told him that once, and he got mad. "You think it's hard to *listen*? I have to *do it*." His voice was tight and hard and almost broke. "You're lucky, Harper. You're lucky you just have to *hear* about it."

Yeah. I feel super lucky.

But then I felt selfish, because he's right. I'm not quick, and I'm not strong. Playing lookout is the only way he'll let me help. So now, when he needs to talk about these near-atrocities, I keep my mouth shut. I can't fight, but I can listen.

I glance at the phone. Twelve minutes. If his time runs out, it means the job went bad, and I'm supposed to run. To get Mom out. To hide.

We've gotten down to three minutes before. Two minutes. But he always appears, breathing hard and sometimes speckled with blood.

I'm not worried yet.

Rust flakes under my fingertips as I twist the ice-cold tire iron in my hand. Sunrise isn't far off, but I'll probably be too frozen by then to even notice.

A light feminine laugh carries in the air nearby, and I peek from the doorway. Two people stand alone by the corner, just at the edge of the circle of light cast by the streetlamp. The girl's hair shines like a shampoo commercial, swinging as she staggers a little. The bars all closed at three a.m., but she clearly didn't stop. Her micro-mini and open denim jacket make my sweatshirt feel like a parka.

The man is more suitably dressed, in dark clothes, with a long coat. I'm trying to decide if this is a cop busting a hooker or a john picking up a date, when the guy turns his head. I duck back into the doorway.

Her laughter rings through the street again. Either he's hilarious or this girl is hammered.

The laugh cuts short with a gasp. Like someone yanked a plug.

I hold my breath. The silence is sudden and absolute.

I can't risk looking.

I can't risk *not* looking.

Jake would be so pissed. I have one job here. I imagine him yelling. *Don't get involved, Harper! You're already vulnerable!*

He's right, but cerebral palsy doesn't mean my curiosity is broken. I peek out around the edge of the doorway.

The blonde has collapsed in the man's arms like a marionette, her head flopped to the side. His arm is hooked under her knees, and he keeps glancing up and down the street.

Jake will lose his mind if I call the cops. It's not like what *he's* doing is legal. If the police come around, Jake is at risk. I'm at risk. Mom's at risk.

I keep staring at that waving blond hair, at the limp arm dragging the ground. He could be a trafficker. She could be dead—or close. I can't do *nothing.*

I slip out of my sneakers so my stupid left foot won't make a dragging noise against the pavement. I can move quickly when I want to, but quiet is tough to master. I rush forward and raise the bar.

He turns at the last second, which probably saves his life. The bar comes down across his shoulders instead of his head. He grunts and stumbles forward. The girl goes sprawling onto the pavement.

I raise the bar to hit him again, but the man retaliates faster than I'm ready for. He blocks my swing and drives an elbow into my chest, hooking my ankle with his own. I'm falling before I realize it. My body slams into the concrete.

He's suddenly right there, almost on top of me. I start swinging. I can't reach his head, but I catch him across the hip. Then his ribs.

He seizes my wrist, then smacks my arm down to the pavement. I squeal and twist away from him, but it feels like he's kneeling on my right thigh. His free arm pins my chest. It hurts. A lot.

"Release the weapon." He's got an accent, but I can't place it. And now that his face is on top of mine, I realize he's young, not much older than Jake.

I clench my fingers even tighter around the bar. My breath makes huge panicked clouds between us. I beat at him with my free hand, but I might as well be striking a statue. He tightens his hold on my wrist, until I genuinely think the bones are rubbing together.

A whimper escapes my throat, but I grit my teeth and hold on.

"Release it," he says again, his tone thickening with anger.

"Jake!" I scream, hoping enough time has passed that he might be heading back. The pavement stabs daggers of ice into my back. Every muscle hurts, but I keep fighting. "Jake! Someone help me!"

I try to claw at his eyes, but the man's grip tightens in response. His gaze meets mine and there's no hesitation there. My wrist is going to break.

A siren kicks up somewhere nearby, but it'll be too late. I try to claw at his face again, but I catch his neck instead. Blood blossoms under my nails, and his eyes turn murderous. The sky lightens fractionally behind him, turning pink with streaks of orange.

His free hand lifts and I don't know if he's going to hit me or strangle me or break my neck. It doesn't matter. This is it. My last sight will be a glorious sunrise.

I'm wrong. His hand never strikes.

Instead, the sky disappears altogether.

CHAPTER THREE

RHEN

Sunlight gilds the fixtures in my sitting room, throwing shadows along the hand-sewn tapestries and the velvet chairs my parents once occupied. Sometimes, if I sit here long enough, I can imagine their presence. I can hear my father's brusque voice, full of admonishment and lectures. My mother's quiet disapproval.

I can remember my own arrogance.

I want to walk out of the castle and fling myself off a cliff.

That doesn't work. I've tried. More than once.

I always wake here, in this room, waiting in the sunlight. The fire always burns low, just as it is now, the flames crackling in a familiar pattern. The stone floor appears freshly swept, wine and goblets sitting ready on a side table. Grey's weapons hang on the opposite chair, waiting for his return.

Everything is always the same.

Except for the dead. They never come back.

The fire pops, a bit of kindling sliding to the base of the fireplace. Right on schedule. Grey will reappear soon.

I sigh. Practiced words wait on my tongue, though sometimes it takes the girls a while to awaken from the sleeping ether Grey gives them. They're always frightened at first, but I've learned how to ease their fears, to charm and coax them into trusting me.

Only to destroy that trust when autumn slides into winter. When they see me change.

The air flickers, and I straighten. As much as I hate the curse, the never-ending repetition of my life here, the girls are the one spot of change. Despite myself, I'm curious to see what motionless beauty will hang in Grey's arms today.

But when Grey appears, he's pinning a girl to the floor.

She's not a motionless beauty. She's scrawny and shoeless and digging her nails into the side of his neck.

Grey swears and knocks her hand away. Blood appears in lines across his throat.

I rise from the chair, nearly losing a moment to the sheer novelty of it all. "Commander! Release her."

He flings himself back and finds his feet. The girl scrambles away from him, clutching a rusted weapon of some sort. Her movement is labored and clumsy.

"What is this?" She gets a hand on the wall and staggers to her feet. "What did you do?"

Grey grabs his sword from the chair, pulling it free from the scabbard with a fierceness I haven't seen in . . . in *ages*. "Have no worries, my lord. This may be the shortest season yet."

The girl raises the rusted bar as if that will provide any kind of defense against a trained swordsman. Dark curls spill out of the hood of her clothing, and her face is tired, drawn, and dusty. I wonder if Grey injured her, the way she keeps her weight off her left leg.

"Try it." She glances between him and me. "I know a good spot I haven't hit with this yet."

"I will." Grey lifts his weapon and steps forward. "I know a good spot I haven't hit with *this* yet."

"Enough." I've never seen Grey go after one of the girls, but when he shows no intention of stopping, I sharpen my tone. "That is an *order*, Commander."

He stops, but his sword remains in his hand and he doesn't take his eyes off the girl. "Do not think," he tells her, his voice fierce, "that this means I will allow you to attack me again."

"Don't worry," she snaps. "I'm sure I'll get another chance."

"She attacked you?" My eyebrows rise. "Grey. She is half your size."

"She makes up for it in temperament. She most assuredly was not my first choice."

"Where am I?" The girl's eyes keep flicking from me to him to the sword in his hand—and then to the doorway behind us. Her knuckles are white where they grip the bar. "What did you do?"

I glance at Grey and lower my voice. "Put up your sword. You're frightening her."

The Royal Guard is trained to obey without hesitation and Grey is no exception. He slides his weapon into its sheath, but strings the sword belt around his waist.

I cannot remember the last time he was fully armed on the first day of the season. Probably not since there were men to command and threats to deflect.

But removing the weapon has drained some of the tension from the room. I put out a hand and keep my voice gentle, the way I speak to skittish horses in the stables. "You are safe here. May I have your weapon?"

Her eyes slide to Grey, to where his hand remains on the hilt of his sword. "No way."

"You fear Grey? Easily solved." I look at him. "Commander. You are ordered to not harm this girl."

He takes a step back and folds his arms.

The girl watches this exchange and then she draws a long breath and takes a tentative step forward, the bar held in front of her.

At least she can be tamed as easily as the others. I extend my hand and give her an encouraging look.

She takes another step—but then her expression shifts, her eyes darken, and she swings.

Hard steel slams into my waist, just below my rib cage. Silver hell, it *hurts.* I double over and barely have time to react before she's swinging for my head.

Luckily, my training is nearly as thorough as Grey's. I duck and catch the bar before she makes contact.

Now I understand why Grey grabbed his sword.

Her eyes flare, burning with defiance. I jerk her forward, ready to wrestle the bar out of her grasp.

Instead, she lets go, forcing me to fall back. She stumbles toward the door, limping into the hallway, her breathing ragged.

I let her go. The iron bar drops to the carpet and I press a hand to my side.

Grey hasn't moved. He's standing there, arms folded. "Do you still wish for me to leave her unharmed?"

There was a time when he wouldn't have dared to question me.

There was a time when I might have cared.

I sigh, then wince as my lungs expand into the already-forming bruise on my side. What began as a novelty now simply hurts. If she fights to run so fiercely now, there is little hope for later.

The shadows have shifted a bit, tracing their familiar path. I've watched it hundreds of times.

When this season ends in failure, I'll watch it again.

"She is injured," says Grey. "She cannot get far."

He is right. I am wasting time.

As if I don't have *time* in spades.

"Go," I say. "Bring her back."

CHAPTER FOUR

HARPER

I'm running down a long hallway, my breath roaring in my ears. This has to be a museum or some kind of historical building. My socks fight to grip the velvet carpeting that lines the marble floor. Wood paneling covers the walls, with stone masonry climbing to a ceiling that arches high above. Heavy wooden doors with wrought-iron handles sit at uneven intervals along the hallway, but none are open.

I don't stop to try any. I just run. I need to find another person or get out of here.

As I round a curve in the hallway, I'm met by a massive, sweeping, sunlit staircase that descends into a grand entranceway. The space is the size of my high school gymnasium, with a dark slate floor, massive stained glass windows, and a pair of iron doors. Tapestries hang from the walls, threaded with purples and greens and reds, shot through with strands of gold and silver that sparkle in the light. Tables sit along the side, laid out with cakes and pastries and dozens of champagne glasses. Half a dozen gilded white chairs wait in the corner, musical instruments sitting ready.

The place looks prepped for a wedding. Or a party. But definitely not a kidnapping.

I'm so confused—but at least I've found a door.

A sudden beeping pierces the silence.

Jake's timer.

I dig the phone out of my pocket, staring at the flashing zeroes. My throat closes up. I don't know if he made it out.

I need to get myself together. I'm standing in the open and tears won't give me anything but a wet face. Once I find somewhere safe, I can call 911.

I grip the banister and rush down the steps. My left leg is clumsy and about to give way, but I mentally threaten to cut it off if it doesn't get me out of here. It listens.

As I pass the corner, the instruments lift from the chairs in unison.

I startle and duck right, ready for one to come flying at me—but then, without warning, the instruments begin to play. Symphonic music fills the hall, a rich song filled with flutes and trumpets and violins.

This has to be a trick. An optical illusion. Like at a theme park, somehow triggered by my motion.

I reach out and grab a flute, expecting it to be fixed in place with thin wires or subtle plastic.

But it's not. My hand closes on the metal like I'm picking it up from a shelf. The steel is vibrating as if someone is playing. There's no weight to it—no batteries. No speaker. Nothing.

When I move it close to my ear, the sound is coming from inside the tube.

I take a step back and fling it away from me.

The flute snaps right back into place, levitating above the chair as though an invisible musician stood there holding it. The keys depress and release.

I swallow hard. This is a dream. I'm drugged. Something.

I'm wasting time. I need to get out of here.

I hurry for the door, prepared for it to be locked—but it's not. I stumble out onto a marble platform, and warm air swirls around me. Stone walls stretch to either side, and steps lead down to a cobblestone path. Acres of trimmed grass stretch as far as I can see, dappled by randomly spaced trees. Flower beds. A massive fountain spraying water into the air. In the distance is a dense forest, thick with vibrant greenery.

No paved road that I can see.

The door swings closed behind me, clanking into place, choking the music into silence. There's no railing here, so I ease down the steps and onto the cobblestones. The building towers over me, large cream-colored bricks spaced by blocks of marble and stone.

This isn't a museum. It's a castle. A big one.

And still, no people. No one *anywhere*—and I can see for acres. The silence is all-consuming. No cars. No buzzing power lines. No airplanes.

I jerk the phone out of my pocket and start punching in the numbers 911.

The phone beeps at me in protest. *No service.*

I shake it, like that's somehow going to help. Everything across the top is grayed out.

No cell towers. No Wi-Fi. No Bluetooth.

A whimper escapes my chest.

Those instruments were playing themselves.

I can't reason that out. It's too tangled up with my very real worry for my brother.

A new thought hits me, piling more worry on top. If something happened to Jake, no one is there to help Mom. I imagine her lying in bed, coughing wetly from the cancer that crowds her lungs. Needing food. Medicine. Needing someone to bring her to the bathroom.

Without warning, my eyes blur. I swipe at my cheeks and force my legs to run. Sweat collects inside my sweatshirt.

Wait. Sweat. It's warm.

It was freezing in DC.

All that sweat goes cold.

Panic later. I need to move.

A large outbuilding sits directly behind the castle, just beyond a sprawling courtyard lined with more cobblestones. Flowers bloom everywhere, spilling down wooden trellises, bursting from massive planters, blooming along hedges and in gardens. Still no people.

My muscles are tight and fatigued, and sweat runs a line down the side of my face. I pray for this to be some kind of garage, because I'm going to need an alternate form of transportation soon. I can't keep running forever. I flatten against the far wall of the castle, breathing hard, waiting. Listening.

When I hear nothing, I head for the building across the courtyard, my left foot dragging and begging for a break. I stumble through the doorway, slipping a little in my damp socks.

Three horses throw up their heads and snort.

Oh wow. Not a garage. A *stable.*

This is almost better. I don't know how to hot-wire a car, but I *do* know how to ride.

Back before our lives fell apart, when Dad had a job and a reputation, I rode horses. It had started as a therapeutic activity after all the cerebral palsy–related surgeries—but it turned into a passion. A freedom, as equine legs lent me strength and power. I worked at the stables in exchange for riding time for years, until we needed to move to the city.

Of everything we've had to give up, I miss the horses the most.

Thirty stalls flank each side of the aisle, made of richly stained boards leading halfway to the ceiling, topped with iron bars. Well-kept horses gleam in the sunlight that creeps through the skylights. Bridles hang at regular intervals along the wall, their bits and buckles sparkling, the leather carrying a rich shine. No wisps of hay lie in the aisle, no swarming flies collect on spilled grain. Every inch of these stables is perfection.

A buckskin stretches out his nose to blow puffs at my hand. He's tied to a ring inside his stall, and he's already saddled. He didn't jump when I came sliding into the aisle, and even now regards me calmly. He's big and solid, with a tan-colored coat and a black mane and tail. A hammered gold sign on the front of his stall reads *Ironwill.*

I run a hand down the buckskin's face. "I'll just call you Will."

A small closet beside his stall door houses boots and cloaks—and a dagger strung along a belt.

A real weapon. *Yes.*

I loop it around my waist and cinch it tight. The boots are too big, but they lace up my calves almost to my knees, giving my ankles some extra support.

I ease into the stall and bolt the door closed behind me. Will accepts a bridle readily, despite my shaking hands jerking at his mouth when I have to tighten the buckles.

"Sorry," I whisper, stroking him on the cheek. "Out of practice."

Then I hear the footstep, the rough rasp of a boot on stone.

I freeze—then duck to the far side of the horse, dragging him into a shadowed corner of the stall. His reins have gone slick in my palm, but I keep a tight hold so he blocks me here.

Someone clucks to each horse, making his way through the stables. A soft word, a pat on the neck. Another pause, then more footsteps.

Whoever it is, he's checking the stalls.

A wooden shelf runs along the side of the stall, probably for hay or feed. I fold my body onto it, then shimmy up and get to my hands and knees. It's an awkward position for mounting, but there's no way I can do it from the ground. I have to concentrate to maneuver my foot into the stirrup. Sweat courses down my back now, but I grab hold of the saddle.

It takes everything I have not to whimper. This is the world's most patient animal, because he stands absolutely still as I haul myself onto his back.

But I'm up here. I'm on.

I'm so exhausted I'm ready to cry. No, I *am* crying. Silent tears roll down my cheeks. I have to get out of here. I *have* to.

Footsteps, then a soft gasp of surprise. The bolt is thrown. I catch a glimpse of dark hair and see a flash of steel as the man draws a sword. The stall door begins to swing open.

I slam my heels into Will's flanks, screaming in rage for good measure. The horse is terrified—with reason. I'm terrifying myself. But he springs forward, slamming the door wide, knocking the armed man out of the way.

"Go!" I cry. "Please, Will! Go!" I dig my heels into his sides.

Will leaps across the aisle, finds purchase, and bolts.

Tears blur my vision, but sight won't help me stay on. I've lost both stirrups already, and we're careening over cobblestones. The fingers of my left hand tangle in Will's mane, and my other hand has wrapped around his neck. When we hit the grass, the horse is like a pumping oil rig, slamming me up and down with each stride.

A sharp whistle cuts the air behind me, three short chirps of sound.

Will digs in his hooves, skids to a stop, and whirls. I don't have a chance. I go flying over his shoulder and crash into the turf.

For a moment, I don't know which way is up. My head spins.

So close. *So close.*

Those men are coming after me. They're a blur in the sunlight, whether from tears or a head injury. I need to get to my feet. I need to run.

I manage to get myself upright, but my legs don't want to work quickly. The blond man is already there, reaching to grab me. The dark-haired swordsman is just behind him.

"No!" A small sound squeaks free of my chest. I stagger away from him and draw the dagger.

The swordsman begins to pull his weapon.

I backpedal farther, trip over my own feet, and sit down hard in the grass.

"Commander. Stop," the blond man says. He puts his hands up. "Be at ease. I will not harm you."

"You *chased* me."

"It's what we do to horse thieves," the swordsman says.

"Grey." The blond man cuts a sharp look his way, then extends a hand to me. "Please. You have nothing to fear."

He must be kidding.

I didn't get a good look at him before, but I do now. His profile is striking, with high cheekbones and an angular jaw. Rich brown eyes. No freckles, but enough time in the sun to stop anyone from describing him as pale. He wears a white shirt under a high-collared blue jacket accented with leather trim and detailed gold stitching. Gold buckles cross his chest and a dagger is belted to his hip.

He's staring down at me as if he faces half-crazed girls all the time.

I keep my dagger brandished in front of me. "Tell me where I am."

"You are on the grounds of Ironrose Castle, in the heart of Emberfall."

I rack my brain, trying to think of any attractions with those names that could be reasonably close to DC. This castle is *huge*. I would have heard of it. And Jake's ticking timer is the one puzzle piece that refuses to fit. There is literally *nowhere* the swordsman could have taken me so quickly. I wet my lips. "What's the closest city?"

"Silvermoon Harbor." He hesitates, then steps closer. "You're confused. Please—allow me to help you."

"No." I thrust the dagger up at him and he stops. "I'm getting out of here. I'm going home."

"You cannot find your way home from here."

I glare at the armed man behind him. "He got me here. There has to be a way back."

The swordsman's expression is inscrutable, lacking any of the charm of the man in front of me. "There is not."

I glare up at him. "There has to be."

His face does not change. "There. Is. Not."

"Enough." The blond man extends a hand again. "We will not argue this point in the courtyard. Come. I will show you to a room. Are you hungry?"

I can't decide if they're crazy—or if I am. I adjust my grip on the dagger. "I'm not going *anywhere* with you."

"I understand your reluctance, but I cannot allow you to leave the castle grounds. It is unsafe. I have no soldiers to patrol the King's Highway."

"The King's Highway," I repeat numbly. Everything he says sounds so *logical*. Not like he's trying to cajole me into following him. More like he's surprised I would consider anything else.

I can't make sense of any of this.

"Please," he says more gently. "Surely you know we could take you by force."

My heart skips a beat in my chest. I do know that. I don't know what's worse—being taken by force, or going willingly. "Don't you threaten me."

"Threaten you?" His eyebrows go up. "You think I intend to *threaten* you by offering safety and comfort and food?"

He sounds offended. I know men who take what they want. They don't act like this.

I don't know where I am, but my body already hurts. I'm not entirely sure I can get off the ground unaided. I definitely can't run again.

He's right: they *could* take me by force. I should conserve my energy.

I can rest. I can eat. I'll find a way out.

I hold my breath and slide the dagger into its sheath. I expect the men to protest my keeping the weapon, but they don't.

Despite my determination, this feels like giving up. I wonder what Jake would say.

Oh, Jake. I don't know if he's okay. I don't know what to do.

I can survive this. I have to.

So I grit my teeth, lock down my emotions, and reach up to take his hand.

CHAPTER FIVE

RHEN

After we return Ironwill to the stables, the girl walks quietly beside me, her gait uneven enough to tell me she's truly injured. She's keeping her distance from both me and Grey, her arms wrapped tightly around her abdomen, one hand resting on the hilt of her dagger.

I'm impressed that she found a weapon—and more so that she went for the stables as a means of escape. Most of the girls Grey drags from her world won't touch a blade or a bridle, and instead gravitate to the finery found within the lushly outfitted wardrobes inside Ironrose Castle. This early in the season, the other girls would sit by the hearth and gaze at me over crystal goblets, while I'd pour wine and tell stories with just enough devilishness to make them blush.

If I put a crystal goblet in this one's hand, she'd likely smash it and use the shards to cut me.

"I feel you looking at me," she says. Sunlight gleams in her night-dark curls. "Stop it."

Half a dozen compliments leap to my tongue, but she's not the type to swoon for pretty lies. "I was wondering if you would share your name."

She hesitates, like she's weighing the ramifications of the question. "Harper."

Ah. Of course. No Annabeth or Isabella for this one. A name with edges.

"Harper." I give her a nod. "I am very pleased to make your acquaintance, my lady."

She looks like she thinks I'm mocking her. "And who are you?"

"My name is Rhen." To my left, Grey glances at me, but I ignore him. At one time, I would have used titles to my advantage, dazzling girls with the promise of wealth and power. But as time has passed and my kingdom has fallen into poverty and terror, I have little pride left in who I am.

"You live in a castle," Harper says. "I'm thinking there's more than just 'Rhen.' "

"Would a list of titles impress you?" I add a shred of practiced intrigue to my voice, but it takes more effort than it once did. "I'm certain there's more than just 'Harper.' "

She ignores that and glances away, her eyes finding Grey. "And him?"

"Grey of Wildthorne Valley," I say. "Commander of the Royal Guard."

Grey gives her a nod. "My lady."

"Commander. That means there should be people to command." Her eyes are narrow and calculating. I have no idea where Grey found her, but her distrust runs deeper than in any of the other girls he's brought here. "Where are they?"

Many fled and many more died, but I do not say that. "Gone. We are alone."

"There's no one else here?"

"You sound skeptical. I assure you, you will find no one else on the property."

I expect more questions, but she seems to withdraw farther. She's so determined to keep space between us that she's practically walking on the narrow edge of the path.

"Do not torment yourself to keep your distance," I say to her. "You have nothing to fear from me."

Well. She has nothing to fear *now*.

"Oh yeah?" Her glare is sharp. "Why don't you tell me what you were going to do with that woman Commander Grey *meant* to kidnap?"

"I would not have harmed her." At least not at first, and not intentionally. Grey is well practiced in keeping them safe once the change overtakes me and violence is inevitable.

"She wasn't conscious. She wasn't going willingly." Her words are fierce. "And for the record, I'm not either."

I have to look away. Once, this coiled tightness in my chest would have been arrogance. Now it is shame.

I remember a time when my people feared the day I would come to lead—because I was seen as spoiled and selfish and not half the man my father was.

Now I am spoiled and selfish in another way, and no better fit to rule.

We've reached the castle steps, and I offer a hand, but she ignores me to limp up the steps on her own. Grey strides ahead of her, reaching for the ornate gold handle. As he swings the door wide, lively music pours out from the Great Hall.

Harper stops short.

"It is only music," I tell her. "I admit, I once found it wondrous as well."

Now I hate all of it.

Usually the girls are charmed, even delighted, but Harper looks like she wants to turn and walk right back out of here.

She must steel her nerve, because she moves into the room and peers at the instruments. She places her fingers over the vibrating strings of a violin. "This has to be a trick."

"You can throw them into the hearth. Beat them into splinters. Nothing stops the music. Believe me, I've tried."

Her eyebrows go up. "You've thrown musical instruments . . . into the *fireplace*?"

"I have." In truth, I've burned the entire castle to the ground. More than once. The music continues to play from the ash and rubble.

It was actually quite fascinating the first time.

I gesture toward the staircase before she can ask more questions. "Your room, my lady?"

Grey waits behind as Harper follows me up the main staircase and down the west hall. I always take them to Arabella's room because my eldest sister's tastes were calm and inviting: flowers and butterflies and lace. Arabella would have slept half the day away if her tutors had allowed it, so food always waits on her side table: honeyed biscuits, jam and sliced cheese, a pot of tea, and a pitcher of water. A small crock of butter will be half-melted beside the biscuits.

I unlock the door and swing it wide, then nod toward the back of the room. "Through that door, you'll find a hot bath. Through the other, a dressing room." I glance down at her ragged, sweat-dampened attire. "You should be able to find clothes, if that . . . suits your fancy."

"And you'll leave me alone?"

She sounds doubtful, but I nod. "If that is what you wish."

Harper eases through the doorway slowly, looking around. A finger traces the length of the side table, pausing for just a moment by the food—though she takes nothing.

I frown and glance at her feet, her legs now encased in the too-large boots of a livery boy. Her left ankle appears crooked, making her steps uneven. "Are you certain I cannot provide assistance of some sort?"

She turns in surprise. "What?"

"You are clearly injured in some way."

"I am not . . ." She hesitates. "I'm fine."

I cannot tell whether this is pride or fear or some combination of the two. While I am trying to puzzle it out, she says, "You told me I could be alone."

"As you wish, my lady." I give her a nod.

"Wait."

I stop with my hand on the door, surprised. "Yes?"

She bites her lip, then gazes around at the lush offerings of Arabella's chambers. "This place. The music. Is this all some kind of . . ." Her voice trails off and her expression turns sheepish. "Never mind."

"Enchantment?" I suggest, then raise an eyebrow.

She inhales almost hopefully—but then her expression darkens into a scowl. "You're mocking me. Forget it. Leave me alone."

"As you wish. I will return at midday." I pull the door closed, but I do not move from in front of it. This season has gone so terribly wrong. She will never trust me.

I will fail again.

I put my hand against the door. She has not moved from the other side. "I was not mocking you, my lady." I pause, but she says nothing. "Ironrose is not enchanted."

She speaks from just on the other side of the wood. "Fine. Then what is it?"

"Cursed."

With that, I turn the lock and take the key.

As usual, I take out my frustrations on Grey.

Or maybe he takes his out on me. I'm good with a sword, but he's better.

We're in the training arena, and clashing steel sings through the rafters. I see an opening and swing for his midsection, but he steps out of the path of the blade, twisting to parry and deflect. His attacks are quick and nearly lethal—which is good, because I need something to require my full attention.

Grey's sword slams into mine, driving me back a step. We've been at this for an hour and sweat threads through my hair. I recover enough to counterattack, my boots cutting neatly through the dust of the arena. I swing hard and fast, hoping to put him on the defensive.

It works at first, and he gives ground, backing away. But I know better than to think I have an advantage. He's not yielding; he's waiting for an opening.

His patience is always endless. I envy that.

I remember the day he was first assigned to my personal guard, though I'm not sure why. I barely gave any of them a glance then.

Just another subject, swearing to lay down his life. If something happened to one, another would be along shortly.

But Grey had been eager to prove himself. I think that's what I remember most clearly: the eagerness.

I quickly destroyed that, just like I destroyed everything else.

In the arena, Grey feigns an attack. I think I see an opening and I swing hard, the blade arcing wide. Grey ducks and bolts forward to drive his sword hilt into my stomach. He follows with a shoulder.

I go down. My sword skitters away in the dirt.

"Quite the demonstration, Your Highness." A feminine voice speaks from the railing at the side of the arena, accented by slowly clapping hands. For a wild, crazy moment, I think Harper must have found her way down here.

But it's not Harper. It is Lilith. The last—the *only*—enchantress in Emberfall. My father banished them from the kingdom once upon a time.

I was too stupid to know I should have done the same.

I fetch my sword and roll to my feet as Lilith steps into the arena. Not even the dust dares to cling to her skirts.

I force myself to sheathe my weapon instead of raising the blade and plunging it into her chest.

I've tried that before. It never ends well.

I bow low as she approaches, taking her hand to brush a kiss against her knuckles. I infuse my voice with false charm. "Good day to you, Lady Lilith. The morning light favors you, as always."

At the very least, that is true. Soft skin, pink cheeks, rose-colored lips that always seem to be keeping a secret. Hair the color of a raven's wing, perfect curls falling over her shoulder. An emerald silk dress clings to every curve, accentuating her narrow waist, the soft rise of her breasts. The color brings out the green in her eyes. In the sunlight pouring through the windows overhead, she's exquisite. She turned my head once, for all the wrong reasons.

"Such manners," she says, a faint trace of mockery in her voice. "One would think you'd been raised as royalty."

I know better than to let her bait me, but it's an ever-growing challenge. "One would think," I agree. "Perhaps some lessons take longer to learn than others."

Lilith glances at Grey, who stands silently behind me. "Did Commander Grey honestly think that scrap of a girl would be the one to break your curse?"

"From what I understand, she was not his first choice."

"Yet you throw away an opportunity by leaving her to languish alone?"

"She refused my company. I will not force myself on an unwilling girl."

"How chivalrous." She sounds as though she doesn't think it's chivalrous at all.

"I have played your game for well over three hundred seasons. If I allow one to *languish*, as you say, another will be along eventually."

She frowned. "That is not *playing*. That is giving up. Are you truly so tired of our little dance?"

Yes. I am. So terribly tired.

"Never," I say. "I find each season more enjoyable than the last, my lady."

She is not easily fooled. "For five years, your kingdom has been falling into poverty. Your people live in terror of the fierce creature that steals lives with horrifying regularity. And yet you abuse a chance to save them all?"

Five years. Somehow both longer and shorter than I thought—not that I have any means to track the intricacies of her magic. I knew time had passed outside the grounds of Ironrose. I knew my people were suffering. I hadn't realized how much.

Fury sharpens my words against my will. "I will not take full blame for casting my people into poverty and terror."

"You should, my prince. One must wonder how many opportunities to save them fate will grant you." She glances at Grey. "Do you tire of your gift, Commander? Perhaps the ability to cross to the other side at the start of each season is wasted on you."

I freeze. Her words always carry an element of threat. Once, I was too foolish to see that, but I can clearly read between the lines now.

"I never tire of the opportunity to serve the prince, my lady." His voice is emotionless. Grey is well practiced at never answering more than what is asked, at never offering an opportunity to start trouble.

He likely learned it from serving me.

"Commander Grey is grateful for your generosity," I say, trying to appeal to her vanity. If she removes his band, he will have no way to cross over. My chance of breaking this curse will be even more dire than it is now. "I have heard him remark often on your magnanimity and grace."

"You are such a pretty liar, Rhen." She reaches up to pat my cheek.

I flinch—and she smiles. She lives for this moment, the space between fear and action. I all but hold my breath, ready for my skin to split and blood to spill.

Her eyes shift past me, though, and she frowns, turning to face

Grey. "What happened to your neck?" She lifts a hand, but hesitates with her fingers an inch away from his throat.

He holds absolutely still. "An unfortunate misunderstanding."

"A misunderstanding?" She traces a finger along the uppermost scratch, and as her finger moves, the cut turns bright red. A trickle of blood spills down his neck. "Did that girl do this?"

He does not move, not even a twitch of muscle along his jaw. "Yes, my lady."

I am frozen, wanting to stop her, knowing that would likely end up worse for him.

She glides closer. "If she drew blood from the great Commander Grey, I believe I like her a bit more." She traces another line, her finger glowing red this time. More blood flows.

Grey still doesn't move, but he's not breathing. His eyes are hard.

I clench my jaw. I once thought the monstrous destruction was the worst part of the curse, but I've long since learned that it's not. It's this, the repeated humiliation and punishment. The powerlessness to reclaim what is mine. Being forced to watch as every dignity is stripped away.

She traces her finger along his neck a third time, her expression one of intrigue.

Grey flinches and hisses a breath. I smell burning flesh.

Lilith smiles.

I step forward and grab her wrist. "You will stop this."

Her eyebrows go up and she looks delighted. "Prince Rhen! Such spirit. One would think you have some *concern* for your subjects."

"You leave me with one man to command, and I will not have him harmed. If you must play, play with me."

"Very well." She swipes her free hand across the front of my abdomen.

I don't feel her nails. I don't feel anything.

And then I feel the pain, as if she sliced into me with pure fire.

Spots fill my vision, and my knees hit the dirt floor. I'm distantly aware of Grey trying to catch me. I clutch an arm to my stomach, but this injury is infused by magic and nothing I do will stop it. Fire burns through my veins now. The rafters spin overhead.

I wish for darkness to overtake me. I wish for oblivion. I wish to *die.*

I kneel, barely held upright by Grey's grip on my shoulder, molten lava surging through my veins.

Draw your sword, Commander, I want to say to him. *End it.*

It would not work. I'd wake back in that cursed room, waiting for Grey to return with a new girl.

Lilith speaks from above me. "Are you truly so tired, my dear prince? Do you wish for me to end your torment?"

"Yes, my lady." My voice is barely a whisper. The words are a plea. A prayer. Even if the end to my torment means the end of *me*, it would mean an end to the suffering my people have endured. It would mean freedom for Grey.

"I *am* generous, Prince Rhen. I will have mercy on you. This shall be your final season. Your days will march in tandem with the rest of Emberfall. Once this season expires, Ironrose will return to its former state."

Relief begins to bloom in my chest, a small trickle of ease among the relentless pain. My final season at last. I will endure these three months and be free. I want to jerk free of Grey's hold so I can kiss her feet and weep with gratitude.

"What will happen," Lilith asks then, "when you fail with this girl and you are condemned to spend eternity as a monster?"

The question nearly stops my heart in my chest.

"I did not leave you with one man to command," she says, and her voice has turned into the sound of a thousand knives scraping together. "I did not plunge Emberfall into poverty and terror. I will not be the one to destroy all your people."

A sound chokes out of my throat. I want to weep for an entirely new reason. The burning pain has reached my head, and my eyes begin to cloud with stars.

"You are responsible," she says, her terrible voice fading away. "You, Rhen. You alone will destroy them all."

CHAPTER SIX

HARPER

I'm plotting an escape.

It's not going well.

This bedroom is stunning and as opulent as the rest of the castle, but it might as well be a steel cell. There's nothing here that I can use to pick a lock—as if I had any idea how. Still, I'm pretty sure "find pointy metal things" would be step one, and I've already failed at that. There aren't any hairpins in the dressing table, but if I want to do a makeover, there are plenty of cosmetics, ribbons, and jars full of scented lotions.

Maybe later.

The four-poster bed is massive, layered with heavy down blankets and satin sheets. Everything is pink and white, with tiny flowers stitched everywhere, small jewels forming petals along the edge of the coverlet. I've crawled along the baseboards, but no electrical outlets hide anywhere. Light shines through the windows, but oil lamp sconces line the walls, too. The washroom has running water—thank god—that requires a pulley. A full, steaming bathtub looks as if it were just drawn—though the steam has been rising for over an hour now, so it's either part of this "curse," or there's a heater somewhere.

For a different girl, the best part of this bedroom would be the closet. It's large enough to be a bedroom on its own, with hundreds of dresses stretching from wall to wall. Silk, taffeta, and lace crowd for space, fabrics in every color of the rainbow. At the back of the closet, beneath a small window, sits a dresser with five drawers. I hoped maybe I'd find hairpins or even a spare set of keys there, but no.

I find lots of jewelry.

Diamonds and sapphires and emeralds sparkle in the sunlight, each piece nestled on a little satin pillow that reminds me of a high-end jewelry store. Earrings. Bracelets. Necklaces. Rings. Every style, from large and gaudy to simple and delicate. This stuff looks real . . . and expensive.

I think of Mom pawning her engagement ring to keep Dad out of trouble and anger swells to fill my chest.

Rhen has nothing to do with her illness, with Dad's poor choices, with the "business partners," but this room feels like a smack in the face anyway.

I have to swallow the anger before it steals my ability to think.

Move on, Harper.

In the second drawer, I find three circlets, each adorned with more jewels. Tiaras. Because of course.

I sigh and open the third. Clothes, though these are more practical than the racks and racks of dresses. Doeskin-lined riding pants, heavy cable-knit sweaters, thin, light undershirts.

I consider my worn jeans and threadbare sweatshirt. If I want to get out of here on horseback, I'll need better clothes.

I pull a pair of riding pants from the drawer, then an undershirt and a light sweater in dark green. The sweater has leather laces along the sides and at the ends of the sleeves, and I pull them snug.

The fourth drawer has long, thick woolen socks. I pull them onto my feet, lace up the borrowed boots, and re-buckle the dagger around my waist.

The dagger. It's another puzzle piece that just won't fit. If they meant me harm, why would they let me hold on to a dagger?

If they *don't* mean me harm, why would they lock me in this room?

I don't understand. Either way, I need to get out of here.

Except the only way to really do that is through the window. There's a stunning view of the stables and the sunlit forest—and a clear view of the ground, two stories below. Unless I want to tie dresses together to make a rope, just so I can pretend my body could handle such a thing, I'm not going anywhere.

I've been avoiding the food all morning, but the scent of warm biscuits and honey has swelled to fill the room. I haven't eaten since last night, but fear of drugged food is stopping me. I lie on the bed, boots and all, and think.

All I can think about is food.

Eventually, I take a tentative bite.

The biscuit flakes in my mouth. The honey is warm and gentle on my tongue. The cheese all but melts. It's literally the best food I've ever tasted.

Nothing happens, so I eat my fill.

My earlier panic has faded, leaving cold determination in its wake. Once I can get out of this room, I can get away from these men.

I fish Jake's phone out of my pocket. I've checked the signal a dozen times, and it's been consistent: nothing works.

According to the screen, it's almost noon. Rhen said he'd return at midday.

My muscles are stiff and tight, so I won't be able to run fast, but I might be able to take him by surprise. I move a chair near the door and drop myself into it.

This solitude leaves me with nothing to do but worry. If Jake got out of the job safely, by now he'll definitely know something is wrong.

If he *didn't* get out safely . . .

"Oh, Jake," I whisper at the screen. "I wish I could see you."

The phone responds by doing absolutely nothing.

There's *one* way I can see him, I guess. I click on the photo app. He's not exactly a selfie guy—I don't even think he has a social media account—but he takes them with Mom when she asks.

I want you to remember me, she always says. There's no way to refuse that.

Sure enough, the most recent picture is of Jake and our mother. She doesn't get out of bed much anymore, so he's lying next to her, giving her a goofy kiss on the cheek. His dark curly hair is too long, twisting into his eyes, and she's got a frail hand on his chin. Her eyes are shifted to look up at the camera, her own dark hair limp and thin on the pillow.

I wish I knew. I wish I knew they were okay. I swallow hard past the lump in my throat and quickly swipe to the next one. Another picture with Mom. And another. Then a picture of me and Mom, my arms around her, snuggled against her shoulder. We're watching television, a pinkish glow splashed across our faces. I don't even remember Jake taking this picture.

Swipe. Me and Jake making faces at the camera. I was trying to cheer him up after a job.

Swipe. Jake giving the camera the finger. Classy, big brother.

Swipe. Jake snuggling his face into the neck of another guy, his eyes closed, his lips parted just enough for me to know this is more than a friendly peck.

My fingers freeze on the screen. The other guy is African American, with dark brown skin and close-cropped hair. His smile at the camera is lazy. Blissful. He has kind eyes. From the angle, I can tell he's the one taking the selfie.

I've never seen him before.

Slowly, I slide the screen to the next photo.

They're together again, in the same clothes. Jake has a baseball cap on backward, an arm around the guy's neck.

He looks happy. I can't remember the last time I saw my brother look happy.

I tap the photo so I can see the date it was taken.

Last week. Jake never mentioned anyone, so maybe it was a one-night thing. I can't begrudge my brother getting a little action. He probably needs the stress relief.

It feels weird that he wouldn't have said *anything* about it, though.

Swipe. Another photo of the two of them, another day. My brother is laughing, covering his eyes. The other guy is grinning.

I keep swiping. More pictures. Lots of them.

They go on for *months.*

My heart is pounding now. Jake never mentioned a relationship with anyone. Not once. Not at all.

I don't know what this means. I don't know if it even matters. I'm still locked in this room. Jake could be hurt. Jake could be—

My breath hitches. I can't think like this. I need to distract myself.

With shaking breath, I click on my brother's text messages. I've never snooped on him before, but I have nothing else to do.

Four message conversations sit on the screen.

Lawrence, Jake's "boss." I scowl.

Mom.

Me.

Noah.

Noah. I shouldn't click.

I click.

The last message exchange happened an hour before the job.

NOAH: My shift ends at 7. Are you OK?

JAKE: Yeah. I'll be done by then.

NOAH: Please tell me what you're doing.

JAKE: I will. Soon.

NOAH: Please be careful. Promise?

JAKE: I promise.

NOAH: I love you.

JAKE: I love you, too.

I love you. He loves someone? My brother is in love?

I wish I'd known. I wish I knew more. I wish I knew what this meant. We've always told each other everything. Or at least, I have. Friends have been an impossibility since Dad got tangled up with Lawrence, and Mom spends most of her life sleeping now. It's just been me and Jake for so long.

Keys rattle in the lock.

My breath catches. He's back.

The lock gives. The door creaks open.

I draw my dagger and throw myself forward. I don't have a plan more intricate than *stab and run,* but I don't even get that far. A hand brushes my arm aside, a foot catches my ankle, and before I can find my balance, I'm crashing into the hard wooden floor. The dagger clatters to the ground in one direction. Jake's phone skitters in another.

I'm not staring up at Rhen. I'm staring up at Grey.

I roll to seize the dagger and hold it up in front of me, but he's not coming after me now. He hasn't moved from the doorway. My heart is a wild rush in my ears, but he's barely even breathing quickly.

"Draw a weapon on me again," he says, "and I am certain you will not be pleased with the result."

I tighten my grip on the dagger. "I did okay with the crowbar."

"Ah, yes. The bar." He gestures around the room. "Tell me: Are you pleased with *that* result?"

"What do you want? Where is Rhen?"

"He is indisposed." His eyes flick left, past me, to Jake's phone, lying six feet away.

My heart stops. It's my only connection to Jake and to Mom. Sort of.

I make a dive for it, but Grey is closer than I am—and really, there's no contest. He's frowning at the screen before I've crossed half the distance.

I scramble to my feet in front of him, the dagger pointed up at him. "Give that back to me. Right now."

My voice is full of fury and fear—more than I'm ready for. His eyes shift up to meet mine. This close, I can see that the welts I left on his neck have turned an angry red, worse than they were earlier. Good. I hope they're infected.

He glances at the blade between us, and his eyebrows raise by a fraction. "You would fight me for it?"

Grey's tone is ice-cold and backed with steel. Rhen seems to be all about chivalry and thoughtful contemplation. This man is not. This is a man of violence.

I tighten my grip on the dagger. "Yeah. I will."

Without warning, his hand shoots out and he catches my wrist. I choke on my breath and throw myself back.

His grip is strong. "I know better than to underestimate you now."

I'm fighting like a fish on a line, but he's immovable. My breath echoes in my ears. I'm so *stupid*. I twist, bringing back a knee so I can drive it right into his crotch.

He steps into my motion, giving me no room to do anything at all, then lifts my arm to hold me in place. Just when I'm sure he's going to clock me in the face or cut my head off, he says, "Here now. There's no need for all that. Take it."

His voice is calm, completely at odds with our relative positions. My pulse rockets in my head and it takes me a second to realize he's holding out the phone.

I seize it with my free hand and shove it in my pocket. I want to whimper with relief.

I also want to whimper at the way he's pinning my arm overhead.

He lowers it slowly, but he doesn't loosen his grip. "Those devices do not work here."

"I don't care. Let me go."

He doesn't. Instead, he begins prying my fingers off the dagger.

"Stop." I try to grab his wrist, to wrestle him away. "You can't take it."

"I am not taking it." He pries it free, flips it in his hand, and presses it back into my palm, the point angled down. "This way."

I stare up at him. "What?" I say dumbly.

"Keep wielding a dagger like a sword and you're likely to lose your hand."

"I'm—*what*?"

Grey speaks as though we're in the midst of a casual conversation, not like I'm a deadweight against his grip. "You are quick to fight. I thought some technique may be useful."

He's not going to kill me. My heart begins to settle.

He turns my wrist and puts the hilt against the center of my chest, the point level with his own. "See? Now you have some defense when an opponent grabs you. If you were lucky, you could pull me right into your blade."

My mouth is working, but no sound is coming out. I can't decide whether to be impressed or angry. "Can I do that right now?"

He smiles, and his eyes light with genuine amusement. "Perhaps next time."

Then he steps back and releases me. I'm breathless and caught in this space between terror and exhilaration. It's a miracle I haven't dropped the dagger.

Grey nods at the window, where bright midday sunlight courses into the room. "Dinner will be served at full dark. His Highness will return for you then."

I force myself to nod. Swallow. Speak. "Okay. Sure."

Then he's gone, and the door is locked once again.

CHAPTER SEVEN

RHEN

I wake with a belly full of fire. My body feels torn apart.

I draw a hand across my abdomen. No bandages, no stinging tightness. Lilith didn't break the skin. Sometimes that's worse—when the pain is all magic. Magic takes longer to heal.

A crackling fire throws shadows on the wall. Music carries from the Great Hall, a slower flute melody that tells me we have an hour until dinner. I'm in my bedroom, an early autumn draft from the window fluttering across my face.

I am also alone.

I struggle to right myself, but pain ricochets through my body. I hiss a breath between my teeth and remember Lilith's admonition. She said this would be the final season—something that should be a relief, yet instead she's turned it into a darker form of torture.

I clutch an arm to my stomach and make it to sitting. "Grey." My voice sounds as though I've been eating ash from the fireplace.

He appears in the doorway. "Yes, my lord?"

I run a hand over my face. "What happened?"

He moves to a side table and uncorks a bottle. Red liquid glints in the light as he pours. "Lilith appeared in the arena."

"I remember that." I shift forward. The pain is easing a bit with my movement. The marks on his throat have darkened and scabbed over. "Did she harm you after I fell?"

"No." He holds out the glass, and I take it. The first sip burns my throat, and then my stomach, but I welcome this pain because it will dull the other.

Grey pours none for himself. He never does. At one time it was forbidden among the Royal Guard, but now there is no one here to care.

Still, he would refuse if I offered. I've been down this road before.

"Have you checked on the girl?"

He nods. "I have."

After I turned the lock this morning, I expected her to pound on the door in fury. Instead, I was met with a silence that seemed loaded with furious resignation. "Would she speak with you at all?"

"She drew a dagger and seemed willing to fight over one of those devices they all carry."

I sigh. Of course. "Anything else?"

"She is interesting."

My eyes flick up. That's not a word I've ever heard Grey use to describe one of the girls. "Interesting?"

"She's impulsive, but I believe she would fight to the death if cornered. If there was something she wanted."

That *is* interesting.

Considering that she wants nothing more than to go home, it's also disheartening.

She's afraid of me *now*. Such a turn of events. Just wait until she sees the monster.

These thoughts are not productive. I drain the glass. Grey moves to refill it, but I wave him off. I need to move.

He steps back to stand against the wall, his right hand gripping his left wrist. Something has changed about him, and it takes me a moment to discern what it is. He's fully armed, from his long dagger to his throwing knives to the steel-lined bracers guarding his forearms.

Grey hasn't been fully armed in ages. We so rarely leave the castle grounds, and there's certainly no one here to pose a threat. I smile as I pour. "Does this girl have you spooked, Commander?"

"No, my lord."

His voice is even, unaffected. He never lets me bait him.

Like his refusal to drink, this is part of Grey's unfailing commitment to duty. It's something I envy, but also something I hate. He is not a friend or a confidant. Maybe he could have been, once, if the curse had begun a different way. If I had not failed in my obligations—and if he had not failed in his.

I drain the second glass. I could order him to drink. He would obey then.

But what fun is a drinking partner if you have to *order* him to do it?

Grey was like this in the beginning, too, before the curse trapped us in this hell together. Then, he felt he had something to prove. He would have carried lit coals between his teeth if I'd ordered it. He's lucky I never thought of it or I might have.

The thought makes me wince. I don't like to think of *before*, because too many memories crowd my mind, until the weight of loss and sorrow makes me want to fling myself from the ramparts. But Grey weaves through so many of them.

Grey, fetch me fresh water.

No, I said fresh *water. Bring it from the waterfall, if you must.*

Grey, my meal is cold. Fetch me another from the kitchen.

Grey, my meal is too hot. Tell the cook I will have you bring me his hands if he cannot do better. Make him believe it.

Grey, the Duke of Aronson says his man-at-arms could ride a full day without food or water, then win a sword fight at sunset. Could you do that? Show me.

Grey could do that. He did do that. I watched him almost die trying.

I pour a third glass and take a sip. "Grey, I have orders for you."

"Yes, my lord."

"When I begin to change, I want you to kill me, while you still can."

I've ordered him to do this before. Sometimes it works. Sometimes it doesn't.

This time is different.

I've watched him long enough that I know he is weighing the words. "If Lady Lilith has declared this to be our final chance, killing you would be a true death, not a new beginning."

"I know."

"I swore an oath to protect you," he says. "You cannot order me to break it."

"I can," I snap, then wince as my body protests this motion. "And I will."

"You would leave your people with no one to rule them."

I want to slam the glass down. "There is no one to rule *now,*

Grey. If this is our last season, I will not risk destroying more of them. I refuse."

He says nothing.

"You will do this," I say.

"I can lead the monster through the forest. I can keep it away from the people. We have been successful for many seasons."

It. The monster. As if we both don't know what I become. What I can do.

"Silver hell, Grey. Are you prepared to lure me away from the people *forever*?" I gesture at the window, at the sunlit stables beyond. "Are you prepared to run a horse to ground *every night* for the rest of your life?"

He says nothing.

"Are you prepared to die, Grey?" I demand. "Because that is all that exists at the end of this path. I am sure of it. This was never a curse to be broken. This is a death sentence. The true curse has been the thought that we might find escape."

His eyes flash with something close to defiance. "We may yet escape."

"If I have not succeeded by the time signs of the change begin to appear, you will do this, Grey. It may happen quickly, so I am giving you this order now. I will release you from your oath."

"So you limit your final season to what . . . six weeks? Eight?"

"If I have not broken this curse by then, there is no hope once I am lost to the creature."

His voice is cold now, irritated. "And once it is done? Do you have further orders?"

"Find a new life. Forget Emberfall."

"An easy task, I am sure."

"Grey!" I slam the glass onto the bedside table so hard that the base chips and glass tinkles to the marble floor. "This is my last chance. I can offer you nothing here. I barely have a kingdom left to rule. I have no life left to live. *Nothing.* I can offer fear and pain or death, or I can offer you freedom. Do you understand?"

"I do." Grey is unmoved by my outburst. "But you owe me nothing. You are all that matters here. You alone can break this curse. You must find a woman to love you. *You,* not me. If Lady Lilith wants to break me again, I would ask you to let her."

"I will not watch her cause more damage, Grey."

"Time and again, she finds your weakest point."

I look away. Once, I would have punished him for voicing my vulnerability.

Now I feel nothing but shame.

Darkness is beginning to crawl across the sky. I meet his eyes. "You will obey, Commander."

"Yes, my lord." He does not hesitate. He's said his piece.

I sigh. I'm so tired of this.

One last season.

I throw the chipped glass into the fireplace. It shatters into a thousand sparks that flare and die.

"I will dress for dinner. Let us play this game one last time."

CHAPTER EIGHT

HARPER

I'm going out the window.

I'm also trying not to think about it too hard, because if I do, I'm going to panic and change my mind.

From outside the castle, the wooden trellises along the back wall didn't look too tall—but from up here, all I can see is my future in a body cast. Or a coffin.

Flowers and ivy climb each trellis frame, set at even intervals between the windows. Most of the windows are too widely spaced for this to matter—I'm not ten feet tall. But the windows in the bathroom and the closet are pretty close together, and the trellis sits almost near enough for me to reach it.

I shift on the windowsill and keep my eyes off the ground. This is the most reckless thing I've ever done.

Wait. No. The most reckless thing I've ever done was attack a guy on the street with a tire iron. So I guess this is fine.

I found a satchel in the closet, and I've filled it with an extra sweater and everything from the food tray, but none of that is going to be helpful if I can't get out of this room.

And if I don't get out of this room, it's going to be painfully obvious that I was planning to, and they might lock me somewhere else next time—somewhere I won't have a chance at escaping.

My breathing has gone thin and reedy. The trellis is six inches out of my reach. I can jump six inches.

My heart pounds and says I can *not* jump six inches. It says that falling thirty feet to the ground will hurt. It says I am an idiot for even considering this.

If Jake could see me, he would be losing his ever-loving mind.

But then I think of my mother, possibly dying alone in her bedroom.

Without warning, my eyes well. The day has been too long. My chances keep running too short.

Okay, I need to get it together. I swipe my sleeve across my face. Those six inches might be the only gap I need to cross to see my brother and my mother, and I'm just sitting here *crying*? Darkness is maybe fifteen minutes off, so I need to chop-chop.

I check the strap of my bag, steel my nerve, and leap.

My hands close on wood and tangled vines. The satchel swings wildly from my shoulder and my right foot struggles to find a ledge to grip.

There! Relief washes over me, sweet and pure. I press my face into the ivy and almost sob. *Thank you.*

The wood beneath my feet snaps.

I fall.

And scramble.

And scream.

But then my foot finds purchase. A decorative stone ledge that juts out an inch from the castle wall. I've come to a stop ten feet below the window, clutching at the trellis. My fingers burn like I lit them on fire, and my knees have crashed into the exposed rock, but pain means I'm alive.

Stars spin overhead and for a terrifying moment, I think I might faint.

No. I can't faint. I have like NO TIME HERE, so my body NEEDS TO WORK.

Wood cracks. The trellis gives way again.

I keep grabbing, fighting for a grip, but my muscles won't respond quickly. The wood keeps breaking. Raw knuckles. My biceps burn. Wood is splintering everywhere. Ivy scrapes my cheeks. I'm going to crash into the ground and die.

No. I crash into the ground and *hurt*. I can't breathe.

Oh, this was a spectacularly bad idea.

I lie in the grass for the longest time, debating what would be worse: death, or those guys finding me like this.

But after a while, breath floods back into my lungs, bringing with it a sense of clarity. I hurt, but nothing feels broken. The splintering trellis slowed my descent. This is like falling from a horse, and I've already done that once today.

I finally manage to roll onto my stomach and rise to all fours. It's almost fully dark. Time isn't on my side. I need to get to the stables before they discover I'm gone.

I find my way back. Will whickers to me when I put out a hand.

"Hey, buddy," I whisper, feeling better the instant his warm breath tickles my palm. "Feel like taking another ride?"

As I'm saddling him in the dimness of the stall, I notice something I missed earlier: a large map spanning the opposite wall, running almost entirely from the floor to the ceiling. *Emberfall* is written in huge cursive letters at the top. I hook the bridle over my shoulder and step across the aisle. I run my fingers over the surface of the map, dried paint slick where it notates cities. *Wildthorne Valley. Hutchins Forge. Blackrock Plains.* At the center of the map, near *Silvermoon Harbor*, is an elaborately painted castle.

The map doesn't look like the United States, that's for sure.

Behind me, Will stomps a hoof against the ground. He's right. We need to go.

It's easy enough to find my way to the woods, especially because the horse seems to know the way. Darkness cloaks the trail, but a cool breeze whispers between the trees. I keep darting cautious glances back at the castle, but I haven't seen any motion or heard any shouts behind me. A burst of adrenaline surges in my chest, and it takes everything I have to keep the horse at a sedate pace. We did it. *We got away.*

Without warning, it's snowing.

I gasp and draw back on the reins, pulling Will to a halt. Snowflakes tumble through the air around us as my breath blows out in a cloud of steam. My brain doesn't want to process this change, but I can't deny the sudden frigid chill on my cheeks or the snowflakes collecting in the horse's mane. Snow coats the trees around us, and the trail ahead is blanketed with white, snow crystals gleaming in the moonlight.

I look behind us, and the trail we just traveled is equally coated in snow. Large flakes filter down through the trees.

This can't be happening.

I turn Will around and urge him back toward the castle. At once the snow vanishes. Warmth soothes my chilled face. The snowflakes turn to water droplets in Will's mane.

The castle looms large in the distance, firelit windows winking at me through the trees.

Cursed.

My breathing grows quick and shallow. The musical instruments could have been an intricate trick, but I don't know of any way to make the weather suddenly change like this. Even a snow machine wouldn't drop the air temperature by forty degrees.

Will tosses his head, fighting my grip on the reins, begging me to make a decision.

Cursed or not, those men kidnapped me. Back into the snow we go.

The change steals my breath again, especially as I quickly realize I'm not dressed for this. Wind surges beneath my thin sweater, making me shiver. After Will has been trudging through snowdrifts for a minute, I rein him in and dig in the satchel for the heavier sweater. My fingers shake from the cold.

The trees thin gradually before giving way to open fields. The moon hangs huge and white, turning the wide, unbroken drifts into a winter wonderland. Snow stretches on for miles, with no sign of human-made light in any direction. No sign of civilization at all.

The snow is more packed here, indicating people have been through this way at some point. I urge Will into a trot, but my body is half-frozen already, and the gait jolts me out of the saddle. I squeeze him into a rocking canter.

The cold begins to make my muscles tighten, and as we canter on, I still haven't seen signs of . . . anyone. I escaped two armed men and a cursed castle, and I'm going to die of exposure.

Just as I begin to consider turning back, an orange glow blooms in the distance. My nose picks up the scent of smoke.

If nothing else, it's a sign of life after countless miles of moonlit snow. Hope provides a burst of warmth inside me. I urge Will forward, but Rhen's warnings about curses and there being no soldiers patrolling the King's Highway haunt me. As we canter on, my thoughts begin whispering fairy-tale warnings about will-o'-the-wisps, about people who followed fairy lights and were never heard from again.

The glow has turned into clear plumes of flame, however, pouring blackness into the sky. For one second, I think it must be a massive bonfire.

Then I hear the screams. A baby wails.

It's a house. A house on fire.

I shorten the reins and urge Will into a gallop.

Snow swirls from the sky, melting into raindrops from the heat of the flames. In front of the flaming structure, three crying children are trying to hide behind a woman who clutches a squalling infant. They're all dressed in loose nightclothes. The children are barefoot in the snow.

A middle-aged, red-haired man stands in front of them, his sword pointed at the woman.

I haul back on the reins, skidding to a stop while I'm still cloaked by darkness.

The man sneers at the woman. "You think you can deny us entry? This land will be property of the crown soon enough." His accent is different from Rhen's and Grey's, although I can barely hear him over the roar of the flames.

From somewhere near the blazing house, another man yells, "Kill the children, Dolff. Take the woman."

"No!" the woman screams, backing up, pulling the children with her.

The man follows her, until the point of the sword touches her chest, right above the wailing baby. She keeps backing up, saying, "You can't do this. You can't *do* this."

"I do what I'm told. Who knows? Maybe you'll like it."

Another man yells, "Keep the girl, too! I like them young."

The girl is maybe seven.

The woman spits at Dolff. "I hope the monster comes to hunt your family."

He shifts his blade, and the baby's wail turns into a high-pitched scream.

I dig my heels into the buckskin's sides. I have no idea what I'm going to do, but Will responds immediately. His hooves tear up the ground. The woman's eyes widen as we bear down on them, and I distantly register a small child crying, "Look! A horse!"

Then we slam into the man.

The impact almost throws me off, but I have the pleasure of seeing him go down. His sword flies in an arc of shining steel, clanging to the ground somewhere to my left. I sit down heavily in the saddle and wheel around for another run.

The man is already rising from the ground. Blood pours from a wound at his temple. He stumbles. *Good.*

I draw my dagger, the point down, intending to swipe at the man on this pass. All I can hear in my head is Grey's stupid voice saying, *Keep wielding a dagger like a sword and you're likely to lose your hand.*

I'm likely to lose a lot more than that. My heels brush Will's sides, but he's already galloping.

The man is better prepared. When I reach to swipe at him with the blade, he dives for my leg and pulls me off the horse. I'm grateful there's a foot of snow on the ground to break my fall—until the man leaps on top of me.

Somehow, the dagger is still clenched in my hand. I raise it, ready to shove it into his—

Wham. I'm seeing stars. It takes me a second to realize the back of his hand has slammed into my face.

It takes another second for the pain to register. Blood is in my mouth. His hand draws back to hit me again.

I jab my arm down against his back. He jerks a little and his hand falls.

I stabbed him. *I stabbed him.*

Part of me wants to burst into tears.

A darker part of me wants to celebrate. *I did it. I saved myself.*

The man's face goes slack, and he slides to the side, landing in the snow.

I look up. The woman stands over me, her blond hair coming free from her braid and her rapid breath clouding in the night air. She's claimed the man's sword, and she looks like she was ready to finish him off if I didn't. The girl clutches the baby. Blood stains the swaddling blanket.

Maybe it's the blood, or maybe it's the body in the snow. Maybe it's the terror on these kids' faces. But reality hits me like a bullet.

This is real.

"Is the baby okay?" I ask.

The woman nods. "The blankets are thick. Just a scratch."

Men are yelling, sounding like they're coming closer. "Dolff! Man, what's going on?"

"There are more," says the woman hurriedly. "They will see. We must run." She puts a hand out.

I grasp it and scramble to my feet.

Or I try to. It's freezing outside, and my left leg refuses to cooperate. I can barely get to my knees.

"Go," I gasp. "Run."

"Hey!" shouts a man. Smoke thickens the air, but he sounds very close.

The woman scoops up the toddler and gets in front of me, blocking me along with her children.

If this woman can be fierce with a kid on her hip, my body can stand up. I force my leg to *work,* then shift to stand beside her.

Four men face us, all with swords, all in clothing trimmed in green and black and silver. Two of the men are younger, probably not much older than Rhen and Grey. The other two are older.

One has hold of my horse, who keeps half rearing and jerking his head to get free.

Behind us, the children shiver and cry.

The oldest man looks at me and his eyes narrow. "Where did *you* come from?"

"Your worst nightmare," I snap.

He laughs like he's truly amused, then raises his sword. "I can fix that."

My heart roars in my head. This is it. I'm going to die right here.

The wind whistles, and I hear a *swip*. A fletched arrow appears in the man's chest.

Then another, directly below it.

He collapses on my feet. Blood flows over my boots and into the white snow. I give a short scream of surprise and jump back.

"You are to leave this property," calls a newly familiar voice. "By order of the Crown Prince of Emberfall."

Rhen and Grey. They're on horseback, just behind me. Rhen has a bow in his hands, another arrow already nocked.

The woman gasps and draws closer to me. Her hand suddenly grips mine and her fingers are shaking.

The men all shout and move like they're going to charge forward with their swords.

Rhen's arrow flies. The man in the middle takes it in the shoulder. Then another in the leg, so fast it's almost a blur. He cries out and falls.

The other men hesitate.

"I have enough arrows to kill you all twice," Rhen calls. Another sits ready on the string.

One man grits his teeth and takes a step forward, right toward the woman. She gives a short scream and stumbles back, pushing the children behind her.

Swip. Swip. The man takes two arrows to the chest and falls.

That does it. The last man scrambles and runs.

Silence falls like a guillotine, broken only by the ragged, terrified breathing of the children.

And my own.

I stare up at Rhen and Grey, their faces flickering with gold from the still-raging fire. They look furious.

There are dead bodies at my feet and children whimpering in the snow. Any minute, my brain is going to catch up and I'm going to collapse into sobs.

Instead, I say the only thing my addled mind can come up with. "Thanks."

CHAPTER NINE

RHEN

I wonder what path the curse would have taken if we had arrived a minute later and found Harper dead.

I'm so furious that I'm tempted to nock another arrow and find out.

Flames billow toward the sky, countering the wind and snow that whip around us all. I look at Grey. "Check the men. See who they are."

He swings down from his horse.

I hook the bow on my saddle, then climb down more gingerly than he did. My insides still ache, and hard riding to chase after Harper hasn't helped.

The pain is doing nothing to improve my mood, either.

That and the fact that Harper is glaring at me as if I single-handedly caused all this.

Grey stops beside one of the fallen men, kicking him onto his back. "This man wears a crest," he says to me. "But I do not recognize it." We so rarely leave Ironrose anymore that it's not a surprise. Well, Grey does—but only in an effort to lead the monster *away* from the people.

Grey moves to the next man and pushes the flap of his jacket to the side, pulling a knife from his belt. "Decent weaponry. Better than common thieves, I would think."

The infant fusses to my right, and the barefoot woman pales and tries to hush her when I look over. She seems to be clutching Harper's hand. Considering their clothes and the thinness of the woman, this family has little worth taking—and even less now.

When I approach, the woman gasps and falls to her knees in the snow.

"Children," she hisses, and they all mimic her immediately, though they draw closer to their mother. The toddler clings to her shoulder, huge dark eyes staring up at me.

The woman tugs at Harper's hand. "He is the crown prince," she whispers. "You must kneel."

Harper meets my eyes, and hers are full of wary defiance. "He's not my prince."

I stop in front of her. Snow is collecting in her dark curls, and she lacks appropriate clothing for this excursion. Her hands are streaked with dried blood.

There's blood on her lip, too, and her cheek is swelling. I give her a narrow look and reach out a hand to lift her chin. "Do you still claim to be uninjured, my lady?"

The woman gasps and lets go of Harper's hand. "My lady," she whispers. "Forgive me."

Harper brushes my hand away. "I'm fine."

Beside us, the smaller boy's breath is hitching as he shivers in the snow against his mother. I look at the woman. "Rise. I will not have children kneeling in the snow."

She hesitates, then rises from the ground, keeping her head down. Each time her eyes shift to the burning structure at my back, her breath shakes.

"We are in your debt," she says. "Take all we have."

"I will not take from those who have nothing," I tell her. "What is your name?"

"Freya." She swallows. Her eyes are as large as serving platters. "Your Highness."

"Freya. Who are these men? What do they want with you?"

"I do not know." Her voice trembles. "Rumor speaks of an invasion in the north, but—" Her voice breaks. "My sister and her husband are dead. This is all—this is all we had—"

Two of the children start crying, clinging to their mother's skirts.

Harper moves close to Freya. "It's okay," she says gently. "We'll figure something out."

Her censorious eyes shift to me.

Clearly I am to figure this out.

"There once was an inn just north of here," I say. "Do you know it?"

The woman chances a look up. "The Crooked Boar? Yes, of course, but . . ." She glances at the flames again. "I have nothing. I have no money—nothing to pay." She pulls the infant closer. A shaking hand swipes at her cheek.

The girl moves closer and speaks through her own tears. "But we're together. You always say all is well if we're together."

From the looks of it, they will all freeze to death together. Even if I can get them to the inn, they cannot stay there forever. I consider

Lilith's threats and wonder if it would be more merciful to kill them all now, before the monster can hunt them for eternity.

This woman and her children are so thin. My kingdom has fallen into poverty, and I am unable to do anything about it. A reminder that if I manage to break this curse, I will still be left with nothing.

Harper glares at me. "Staring at them isn't helping."

I imagine her criticizing my father this way.

I then imagine him backhanding her across the other side of her face.

If he were here right now, he would likely backhand *me* for not doing the same.

She has been here one day and I am already exhausted.

"My lady," I say tightly. "Perhaps I could have a word with you privately."

"Fine." She stomps away, her limp pronounced, leaving me to follow.

At ten paces, I catch her arm and turn her around. I glare down at her, incredulous. "Just who do you think you are?"

"Who do you think *you* are?" she says. "You've got a huge castle with a hundred rooms. You can't give them a few to use?"

My eyebrows go up. "Ah, so you run from the castle, but you'd submit another woman to your fate?"

"You'd rather leave them to freeze in the snow? Some prince you are."

She moves to turn away from me, but I catch the sleeve of her wool blouson and hold her there. "Do you know why those men were after her?" I point to the bodies in the snow. "Do you know they meant to *kill* you? Do you wish to invite more?"

She sets her jaw. "I know they would have slaughtered those kids if I hadn't shown up. I know they were trying to claim her land for the crown. What do you know about that?"

"They would have slaughtered those children if *Grey and I* hadn't—" I freeze, my irritated thoughts seizing on her second statement. "What did you just say?"

She jerks out of my grasp. "I said those men were trying to claim her land for the crown. That's *you*, right?"

"If that is what they said, they were *lying*."

One of the children laughs, full out, with pure glee. I snap my head around.

Grey has laid his cloak in the snow for the children to stand on. He looks to be making ridiculous faces at them. A little boy of about four has found the courage to step in front of his mother, and the toddler giggles between shivers and says, "Again, again."

When Grey sees me looking, he straightens and sobers immediately.

Harper has lost patience with me. "They're all freezing," she says. "Either help them or get out of here. But *I'm* going to help."

She returns to Freya's side and unwinds the satchel from around her shoulder. "There's food in here," Harper says, biting back a shiver. "It might be a little squished, but it's something."

The woman's eyes go from Harper's face to the bag and back. "My lady," she whispers. "I cannot—"

"You can." Harper gives the bag a little shake. "Take it."

The woman swallows and takes the bag like it contains something poisonous—though the children begin digging at it.

"Mama!" says the toddler. "Sweets!"

"The Crooked Boar is not far," I say. "We will ride ahead and arrange for a room for you and the children."

Harper looks startled. "You're going to leave us alone?"

I ignore her and unfasten my own cloak. "Grey, divide the children between the two horses." I stop in front of Freya and swing the cloak around her shoulders.

She stiffens in surprise and backs up, shaking her head. "Your Highness—I cannot—"

"You are freezing." I glance at Grey, who is settling the older boy on his horse. "My guard commander will keep you safe on the road."

Harper watches all of this, her expression nonplussed. "You just said you and Grey were going to ride ahead."

"No, my lady." I turn to look at her. "I meant you and me."

She opens her mouth. Closes it.

Checkmate.

But then her lips flatten into a line. "There aren't any horses left."

"There's one." I turn my head and whistle, three short chirps that cut through the night air. Hoofbeats hammer the ground and Ironwill appears out of the smoke. The buckskin slides to a stop in front of me and affectionately butts his face against my shoulder. I catch his bridle and rub the spot he likes, just under his mane.

Harper's eyes go wide and then her face breaks into a smile. "He didn't run away!" She rubs the bridge of his nose, then hugs his face. "That's a neat trick. Do all the horses come when you whistle?"

"Not all," I say easily. "Only my own."

She loses the smile. "Your . . . own . . ."

"You chose well." I straighten the reins, then grab the pommel and swing into the saddle. Then I put out a hand for her.

She stares up at me. The indecision is clear on her face.

I nod toward Freya and the children. "They grow no warmer,

my lady. We should not delay." I look back down at her. "Then again, I forget that you left Ironrose on a journey of your own. Would you prefer to go on your way?"

That catches Freya's attention, because she hesitates before lifting the toddler to sit in front of the girl. Her eyes worriedly dance from me to Harper.

Harper sees this, too. She sets her jaw. "No. I'm coming."

Then she reaches out and takes my hand.

In another time and place, I would be glad to be riding double in the snow, the weight of a girl against my back as we canter along a silent road. The air is crisp and cold, and I haven't felt snow on bare skin in ages.

But tonight, the magical wounds in my abdomen ache, pulling with every stride. Harper clings to my sword belt instead of wrapping her arms around me, a clear refusal to get any closer than she needs to. Cold silence envelops us, broken only by Ironwill's hooves striking the ground in a familiar cadence.

Eventually, the dull pain turns into a hot knife and sweat begins to collect under my clothes. I draw the horse to a walk.

"What's wrong?" says Harper. "There's nothing here."

A note of alarm hides in her voice, and I turn my head just enough to see the edge of her profile. "The horse is winded."

"You sound like *you're* winded."

Indeed. But she is, too, I realize. Her breath clouds on the air every bit as quickly as my own. I wonder if her stubbornness has kept her from calling me to stop earlier.

Much like my own stubbornness has done exactly the same thing.

"You seem to have a knack for finding trouble," I tell her.

She's silent for a bit, but I know she is thinking, so I wait.

Eventually, she says, "I was trying to find a way home. Or at least . . . someone to help me."

"There is no one in Emberfall who could help you get home." I lift a hand to point. "Though you should head south if you wish for different companionship. Westward travel from Ironrose leads through sparse farmland, as you see."

"All I see is snow, Rhen." She pauses. "*Prince* Rhen."

She says it like she means for the word to be an attack, but I do not rise to the bait. "The snow runs deep this season," I agree.

"Am I supposed to call you *Your Highness* now?"

"Only if you can do it without such contempt."

"I still don't understand why I can't go home."

"There is a veil between our worlds. I do not have the power to cross it."

"But Grey can."

"The curse grants him the ability for one hour, every season. No more, no less." I turn my head to glance back at her. "Magic was once banned from Emberfall. You will find no one else who can help you."

She goes quiet again. Wind whistles between us, lacing its way under my jacket. At my back, she shivers. Her fingers tremble on my sword belt.

Swiftly, I unbuckle the straps across my chest and pull my arms free of the sleeves, then hold the jacket back to her. "Please, my lady. You're freezing."

She's silent for a moment, but the cold must be quite convincing, because she snatches it from my hand. When she speaks, her voice is small. "Thanks." She pauses. "You'll be freezing, too."

With any luck, I'll freeze to death. "I have survived worse."

"You really didn't send those men to burn down that woman's house? So you could claim her land?"

"No." I can't even muster indignation. I remember a time when I would have done so without a thought. Honestly, I shouldn't be surprised that vandals are claiming such activity on my behalf.

"Why is it so cold here, when it's so warm at the castle?"

"Ironrose—the castle and its grounds—is cursed to repeat the same season, over and over, until I . . ." I search for the right words. I am rarely forthright about the curse. "Until I complete a task. Time outside the castle grounds passes more slowly, but it does pass."

Harper is quiet as a ghost behind me, except when a shiver makes her breath tremble. Snow dusts across my hands, collecting in the horse's mane.

"My lady," I say, "you are still shivering. You need not keep your distance."

Wind rushes between us, accenting her silent refusal.

"We do not have far to travel," I add. "It would not be—"

She shifts forward and slides her arms around my waist so suddenly that it makes me gasp. Her head falls against the center of my back. Tremors roll through her body and she pulls the jacket around both of us.

Her grip is tight enough to be painful, but I do not move.

This is more about the weather than about trust, surely. But as her body warms and she relaxes against me, I realize *some* measure of trust must be at work here. The thought feeds me hope, crumb by crumb.

She adjusts her grip, and I hiss a breath and grab her wrist. "A few inches higher, my lady. If you do not mind."

She moves her hands. "Why? Were you hurt?"

"No," I say. "An old injury."

She accepts the lie readily, but I do not like it. Earning this moment feels a thousand times more satisfying than plying women with pretty falsehoods and empty promises. In the darkness, together on the back of a horse, it's tempting to forget the curse and pretend my life doesn't exist outside this moment.

"What would you have done," I ask quietly, "if we had not arrived?"

"Did you see their swords?" she says against my back. "I'm pretty sure I would have died."

Her voice is so earnest that I laugh. "I'm beginning to wonder if you would have found a way to escape even that. How did you manage to leave Ironrose without Grey noticing?"

"I'm assuming you haven't seen your trellis."

"You climbed down the *trellis*?" She can barely mount a horse. She is crazy, surely. "It is not even beneath your windows!"

"Trust me, I realized that when I hit the ground."

No wonder I found her facing a cadre of swordsmen in front of a burning house. Next time, it will likely be an army. "Injured as you are, you chose to *leap*—"

"I am not *injured*!"

"Then what are you?" I demand. "There is a difference between pride and denial, my lady."

She says nothing, but her silence feels like resignation instead of anger. I half expect her to pull away from me, but she doesn't.

"I have cerebral palsy," she says quietly. "Do you know what that is?"

"No."

"Something went wrong when I was born. The cord was wrapped around my neck, and I got stuck in the birth canal. I didn't get enough air. It causes problems in the brain. Some muscles don't develop the right way."

She stops, but I sense there is more, so I wait.

"It affects everyone differently," she says. "Some people can't walk, or they can't speak, or they have to use a wheelchair. I was a lot worse off when I was younger, so I had to have surgery to correct my left leg. I still have trouble with balance, and I walk with a limp, but I'm really lucky."

I frown. "You have an unusual definition of *luck*."

She stiffens. "Spoken like someone who lives in a castle with an endless supply of food and wine, but calls himself *cursed*."

I bristle, my pride pricked. "You know nothing about me."

"And *you* know nothing about me."

A nettlesome silence falls between us now.

"Have you caught your breath?" I finally say.

"Yeah. You?"

"Yes." Without another word, I kick the horse into a canter.

It's not until later, when we reach the inn, that I realize she never let go of me, despite her sharp words.

CHAPTER TEN

HARPER

For some reason I thought an "inn" would be comprised of more than a two-story house with tightly shuttered windows and a thin plume of smoke rising from the chimney. If there's a sign, the dark and snow keep it hidden.

When Rhen pulls the horse to a stop, I straighten and let go of his waist. We've formed this little cocoon of warmth, and his jacket—fur-lined leather—smells like oranges and cloves. My body wants me to stay *right here.*

Which is exactly why I need to let go. He might be handsome and chivalrous and well-mannered, but underneath all that, he's a kidnapper. He turned the key in that lock this morning.

The air between us is suddenly awkward. "Are you sure this is the right place?"

It's the first thing I've said since we snapped at each other, and he looks over his shoulder at me. I can't read his expression, so I have no idea whether he's mad or we've formed a truce or I'm going to have to find a way to run again. "Yes, my lady."

"Would you stop calling me that?"

"It is meant as a mark of respect. When you travel with me, people will assume you are a lady, a servant, or a whore." His eyebrows go up. "Would you prefer one of the latter?"

Now I want to punch him. "Get off the horse, Rhen."

He swings a leg over Will's neck and drops to the ground, then turns to offer me his hand.

I don't take it. "Would you offer your hand to a servant or a whore?"

He doesn't move. "You asked a question. I answered it. I meant no insult."

"What about prisoner? What if I tell them you kidnapped me?"

His hand remains extended. "I am their prince. They will likely offer to bind you and lock you in the stables."

He's so *arrogant.* I ignore his hand and slide my leg over the buckskin's rump. I do it too fast, just to spite him.

I spite myself. My left knee buckles when I hit the ground.

He steps forward to catch me.

It puts us close, his hands light on my waist. In the dark, he looks younger than he seems, like life has injected age into his eyes, but the rest of his body hasn't kept up. His tan skin is pale in the moonlit shadows, the first hint of beard growth showing on his cheeks.

"Can you stand?" he says softly.

I nod. For a heartbeat of time, the world seems to shift, like I'm a breath away from figuring all this out. I want him to wait, to hold right there, to just give me one more second.

But he draws away, moving toward the door of the inn, giving it a forceful knock.

Nothing happens. I shiver. My body is missing his warmth, and

I need to keep convincing myself that this forced companionship is false, that he's the enemy here.

He raises a fist to pound on the door, and it swings open this time. A heavyset middle-aged man stands there with a lantern in one hand—and a short knife in the other. A thick mustache and beard frame his mouth, and a stained leather apron is tied around his waist.

"You move on!" he shouts, gesturing with the lantern with enough force that Rhen falls back a step. "This is a peaceful household!"

"I am glad to hear it," Rhen says. "We are seeking peaceful shelter."

The man raises the knife. "No one with good intentions seeks shelter after dark. You *move on*."

Movement flashes behind him. A woman peeks from around a corner, her white fingers gripping the molding.

Rhen takes a step forward, his voice sliding dangerously close to anger. "Are you running an inn or are you not?"

I move to his side. "Rhen," I say quietly. "They're afraid. Let's leave them alone."

"Rhen?" The man's face turns white. He draws the lantern forward to look Rhen up and down, then drops the knife. "Your Highness," he cries. "Forgive me. We have not seen—we have not—" His knee hits the floor so hard that I wince. "I did not recognize you. Forgive me."

"You're forgiven. Doubly so if you have rooms available."

"I do," the man sputters. "We do. My family can sleep in the stable, Your Highness." He scrambles to get out of the way, half bowing as he does. "Take our home. Take our—"

"I do not need your home," says Rhen. "A woman and her

children have been the victims of a fire. My guard commander should arrive with them shortly."

"Of course. Of course. Please come in." The man gestures, then looks over his shoulder to yell toward the staircase at the back of the room. "Bastian! Come, see to their horses!"

We step through the doorway, and the warmth is so inviting that I want to lie down right here on the rug. "Horse," I say to the man. "Just one."

He nods rapidly, as if this is the most common thing ever. "Yes. Yes, of course."

Rhen takes hold of my jacket gently and turns me to face him. "I will see to the arrangements. Warm yourself by the fire, *my lady*," he says, with just the slightest emphasis on the words.

I open my mouth to protest, but Rhen leans in close. He whispers low along my neck. "I would never travel alone with a female servant. The choice is yours."

Goose bumps spring up where his breath brushes my skin. "My lady" it is.

"Bastian!" the man hollers again. "Horses!" A quick abashed glance at me. "A horse!"

A boy who can't be more than nine comes stumbling down the staircase, rubbing his eyes, reddish-brown hair sticking up in all directions. "I was sleeping, Da. What horse? What?"

"Bastian." The man's voice is short, and he speaks through his teeth. "We have royal guests. You will see to their horse."

The boy is still rubbing his eyes. He glances at me and Rhen, his face barely alert. "But the royal family ran off years ago."

Beside me, Rhen stiffens.

"Bastian," the man hisses.

"What? You always say they're too good or too dead to bother with the likes of—"

"Enough!" The man puts up placating hands in front of Rhen. "Forgive him, please, Your Highness. He is young, he is not yet awake—"

"We are neither too good nor too dead." Rhen looks across at the boy, who blanches a little at the sternness in his tone. "But we *are* here now."

"Go!" the man snaps at his son.

Bastian scurries down the rest of the steps to fling his feet into boots. He scoots past us, grabbing a cloak from a hook by the door.

"I will put soup on the fire, Your Highness," says the woman hurriedly, as if to make up for her son's rudeness. "I have some fresh bread, too, if it suits your fancy." She doesn't even wait for an answer, just disappears around the corner.

I stay close to Rhen and keep my voice low. "Do people always do everything you want?

"Not always." He turns to look at me, his expression inscrutable. *"Clearly."*

My cheeks warm before I'm ready for it. I have to look away.

"Go," he says, and his tone is a fraction more gentle. "Sit."

Sitting sounds better than standing here blushing at him. I move across the room to perch on the edge of a chair near the hearth. The fire is so warm and the seat cushioned so plushly that I find myself sinking back almost against my will.

The woman reappears with two large, steaming mugs. She offers one to Rhen first, then brings the other to me. "Apple mead, my lady," she says with pride in her voice. "We had a good batch this season."

"Thank you." The warmth of the mug feels so good against my

battered fingers. I take a deep swallow. For some reason, I was expecting something like hot cider, but mead tastes like a bushel of apples drowned in a vat of beer and honey. "This is amazing."

The woman curtsies. "My boy took care of your horse," she says. "He is lighting the fires in the upstairs rooms. His Highness said you have had a long day of travel."

I run a hand down my face. "You could say that." I blink up at her. "I'm sorry—can I ask your name?"

"My name is Evalyn, my lady." She offers another curtsy. "My husband is Coale. And you have met our son, Bastian."

"My name is Harper."

"Ah, the Lady Harper. We are so honored." She pauses. "If I am being too forward, please tell me so. But we hear so little of royalty nowadays. I am not familiar with your name or your accent. Are you from a land outside Emberfall?"

I blink. "You could say that."

"Oh, how wonderful!" The woman claps her hands. "For years, the king has kept our borders closed and many believe our cities have suffered without the opportunity for trade. Travelers have been few these last couple years." Her face pales. "Not that I would ever question the king, my lady."

"Of course not," I agree. Her expression evens out in relief.

"But you are here with the prince, so this must mean changes are afoot. Tell me, what is the name of your land?"

I glance at Rhen and wish he would stop talking to Coale and come help me figure a way out of this conversation. "DC," I say weakly.

"The Lady Harper of Disi," says Evalyn, her voice hushed with awe. "Such happy news." Then she gasps. "Are you *Princess* Harper? Is there to be a wedding?"

Maybe the cold has frozen my brain cells. "I'm not—did you say a *wedding*?"

Evalyn shifts closer and flicks her eyebrows at me. "Yes, my lady. A wedding?"

It takes me a second.

"No!" I sit bolt upright and almost spill the mug. "No. No wedding."

"Ah. There are negotiations in play." Evalyn nods sagely. "I understand." She pauses. "People will be pleased. There has been so much worry. The rumors of invaders from the north are terrible indeed. We've had to bar the door at night."

What on earth is Rhen spending all this time *talking* about? I crane my neck around.

I don't even want to think about how quickly he's gone from captor to jailer to savior.

"My lady," Evalyn whispers, her voice low. "Did you take a fall during your ride? I can offer an herbal remedy to draw the bruise out of your cheek. If you need to keep his attentions, perhaps it would help—"

"Yes. Sure. Thank you." Anything, anything at all, to stop this woman's questions.

After she's gone, a hard knock sounds at the door. When Coale throws it open, bitter wind swirls through the house, making the fire flicker and drawing another shiver from my body. Grey stands in the doorway, one child on his shoulders, half-covered by the cloak. Another is in his arms, sound asleep and drooling against the front of his uniform. Snow dusts all three of them. Behind him, Freya is carrying the infant, followed by the older girl. She and the children all look worn and weary and exhausted.

I uncurl from the chair. "Here," I say. "I'll help you."

Evalyn is faster, coming around the corner. "Freya! Oh, Freya, you poor girl. When he mentioned children, I was so terrified it was you. Come, the rooms are prepared. I will help you get them upstairs. There is soup on the fire." With quick, businesslike efficiency, she takes the children from Grey and ushers them toward the staircase, with Freya close behind.

Grey shakes the snow from his cloak and offers it to Coale, who hangs it by the door.

"Please, warm yourselves by the fire," says Coale. "I will bring food. Bastian will see to the other horses."

The men sit across from me on the hearth, blocking most of the light from the fire. Grey's hair and clothes are damp with melted snow, and his cheeks are pink from the cold, but his dark eyes are bright and alert. For as worn and wounded as I feel, Grey looks almost energized.

Something heavy hits the front door, and I nearly jump out of my chair. Grey is on his feet, his sword already half-drawn. But the door swings open and the boy comes through, shaking snow out of his hair. "The horses are in the stables." He throws his cloak at one of the hooks by the door.

Grey lets the sword slide back into its sheath, then eases back onto the stones of the hearth.

If I didn't know any better, I'd say he was disappointed. "What's wrong?" I say. "You *want* to fight someone?"

His eyes meet mine. "Is that an offer?"

"Commander." Rhen's voice is sharp with warning.

But Grey's expression isn't hostile. If anything, there's a hint of dark humor in his eyes. I think of his level voice in the bedroom, when I was so ready to fight him for my cell phone. *Here now, there's no need for all that.*

I think of how he made faces at the children in the snow.

Or the way he carried them in here.

"It's okay," I say quietly. "He's okay."

This feels like the moment when I crossed a line in my head and wrapped my arms around Rhen's waist. A cautionary voice in the back of my mind says that this is dangerous—all of this. They kidnapped me. They imprisoned me.

But then I think about those men attacking Freya's children. How the one was ready to use his sword on an infant. How the other said, *Keep the girl, too! I like them young.* I think about how Rhen fired a volley of arrows to save my life.

How Rhen could have directed that horse to take us anywhere, and I wouldn't have known any better until it was too late—and he'd kept his word and come here.

Rhen is glaring at Grey. "You should not wish for violence."

How he'd make statements like *that.*

"Not violence," says Grey, his expression losing any humor. "I had almost forgotten what this was like."

Rhen doesn't answer that, so I say, "What *what* was like?"

"Being useful."

Coale reappears from the kitchen with a serving tray topped with three steaming bowls, another mug, and a basket of rolls. He serves me first, and I look down at some kind of brown stew, with large chunks of cheese beginning to melt.

Rhen and Grey take their bowls, but Grey waves off the mug Coale offers him.

"It's only hot tea," Coale says. "I know the Royal Guard forsakes spirits."

Grey nods and takes it. "You have my thanks."

Interesting. I look up at Coale. "You have my thanks, too."

"You are most welcome." Coale's eyes linger on my face for a moment, and something in his expression tightens. "My wife added some herbs to take the pain out of your cheek." He gives a cool glance at Rhen and Grey before moving away.

It takes me a minute to figure out why—and considering my life outside of this place, it shouldn't have taken me any time at all.

I tear off a hunk of bread and dip it in the soup. "Coale thinks you're knocking me around," I say quietly.

Rhen snaps his head up. "Who thinks *what*?"

"The man." I flick my eyes toward the kitchen, where Coale has disappeared. "He thinks you did this." I gesture vaguely at my face, then tear another piece of bread. "His wife thinks we're getting married as part of some negotiation between rival nations."

Rhen sets down the bowl of soup. "Exactly what did you tell these people?"

"Nothing!" Heat floods my cheeks. "You were talking to the guy and I didn't know what to say!"

"We are not alone," says Grey, his voice very quiet. He gives a significant look at the far corner of the room, where Bastian is sitting.

I lower my voice. "I don't know anything about all this!" I hiss. "How do you expect me to answer their questions?"

"Ah. So you determined that an engagement to ally divided kingdoms was the best path." Rhen picks up his soup again. "Perfectly reasonable."

I scowl. "Why are we even whispering? Can't you just tell them we're not?"

"Not *now*. Do you have no understanding of how gossip works?"

I can't tell if he's mad or not. "You mean if you try to tell them it's not true, they'll believe it even more?"

He nods, then tears a hunk of bread for himself.

I feel like I've screwed something up without even trying. "Well. You've hardly told me anything about yourself, so it's not like I have any idea what to say."

He dips the bread in the soup. "I might have told you more if you'd joined me for dinner instead of climbing down the trellis."

Grey stares at me. "That is how you escaped? You climbed down the *trellis*?"

"Fell," I say. "I fell down the trellis. I took most of it with me." I look at Rhen, then glance at Bastian in the corner. "He said royalty was either too good or too dead to leave the castle. What does that mean?"

"Let's ask him." Rhen sets down the soup bowl again. "Boy!" he calls. "Come here."

Bastian jumps and looks around, clearly seeking his parents. Coale appears in the kitchen doorway, then gives his son a look. The boy approaches slowly, but lingers at a distance, fidgeting with the hem of his shirt. He glances between Rhen and Grey but says nothing.

"Did you take good care of the horses?" says Rhen.

Bastian nods. "I rubbed their backs and their legs, like Da showed me."

"And water?"

Another nod. "I knocked the ice off the trough."

Rhen shifts to reach a hand into his pocket, pulling out a silver coin. "You have my thanks."

The boy's eyes grow wide, but the coin lures him closer, and now he stands between me and the men. He takes it and turns it between his fingers. "I've never held a silver before." He glances at his father in the kitchen doorway, then back at Rhen. "Can I keep it?"

Rhen nods. "Brush them and feed them in the morning and you'll get another."

"I will." Bastian grins.

"When we arrived, you spoke of the royal family. What do you know?"

The smile melts off the boy's face. Coale has moved out of the kitchen now, and hovers near the doorway, obviously torn between obedience and protecting his son. With one question, Rhen has tripled the tension in the room.

He must know it, because he puts up a hand. "You have nothing to fear from me if you speak honestly."

Bastian swallows and glances at his father again. "I—I do not know."

"What have you heard?"

"My da says—" He stops and licks his lips, as if realizing that's not the best way to start.

Coale comes across the room to stand behind his son. He puts his hands on the boy's shoulders and for the first time, his voice isn't deferential, but resigned. "His da says a lot of things. Many of which are spoken in jest."

"I do not want pretty words, innkeeper. I want truth."

"Then ask your questions of *me*, not my son."

Rhen's eyebrows go up. I'm frozen in the chair, trapped by this confrontation. This tension reminds me of how it felt when the loan sharks would come to hassle my father. I want to run so badly that I try to will myself invisible.

Coale falters as if realizing that he's made a demand. "If you please. Your Highness."

"Then speak your mind," said Rhen.

Silence hangs in the room for a moment, as both men struggle with truth and protocol.

"You're all hiding," says the boy, his voice hushed. "From the monster."

The monster? There's a *monster*?

Then I remember what Freya said. *I hope the monster comes to hunt your family.*

I clear my throat. "The monster?"

Rhen sits back and picks up his mug. "You see why I seek answers from children."

"Yes," says Coale, his voice sharp. "There are some who believe our rulers have abandoned Emberfall, living in safety elsewhere, leaving the people to suffer at the hands of that creature that inhabits the castle, whatever it is. It is no wonder we are vulnerable to attack from outsiders. For five years, we have begged for help, but our cries go unanswered, our people starve, and our kinsmen die. So you will forgive me for careless words, but it seems that the king has no sympathy for the people who make up this kingdom, and cares only for those in his own circle."

Silence falls over the room, the tension so thick it's like a blanket smothering us all.

Rhen sets down his mug and stands. Emotion clouds his eyes, but he gives Coale a nod. "I thank you for your honesty." He chucks the boy under the chin. "I meant it about the coin in the morning. We'll leave at daybreak."

He moves away, toward the stairs.

I shove myself out of the chair and go after him. "Rhen. Stop. Wait."

He stops, but he does not look at me. "Please do not run again, my lady. At the very least, allow me some sleep first."

"What just happened?"

"You wanted answers. You got them."

I feel like I know less than I did before. I drop my voice. "Is that true? Does your father really keep his family safe somewhere else, while some kind of wild monster is killing people?"

"Do not be ridiculous." He finally meets my eyes. "Of course not."

I hold my breath and study him, feeling like there's more he isn't saying.

Rhen puts his hands on my arms and leans in. When he speaks, his voice is very low, very quiet, just for me. "My father is dead, my lady. My whole family is dead." He pulls back, meeting my gaze, but his voice doesn't change. "That monster killed them all."

CHAPTER ELEVEN

HARPER

The tension in the house eventually gives way to exhaustion, leading to a dense silence broken only by the wind outside and the crackling fire in the living room. The back half of the inn is divided into three upstairs bedrooms, with the kitchen, dining area, and the innkeeper's family quarters on the main level. Freya and her children took two of the upstairs bedrooms.

Rhen offered me the third, but I have no desire to be locked in again, so I told him he and Grey could have it.

Coale and Evalyn tried to get me to accept *their* room for the night, but I'm not going to force them out of their bed—especially if it means they'd have to sleep in the stables, like Coale said when we first got here. Instead, I'm curled up in the cushioned armchair of the main room, with a heavy knit blanket I got from Evalyn.

When Evalyn and Coale retire to their room behind the kitchen, I catch the words *negotiation* and *royal wedding*, which makes me sigh. The day must have caught up with me, because I fall asleep and stay that way until a loud *sizzle* and *pop* jerk me awake.

Grey stands in front of the hearth, feeding wood to the fire.

My eyes feel like sandpaper. All the candles were extinguished when everyone went to bed, so the only light in the room comes from the fireplace. Grey's expression is in shadow, but I can tell that he's fully dressed. Fully armed.

"What's wrong?" I whisper.

His voice is equally low. "The fire had gone to embers, my lady."

"No—I mean, why aren't you sleeping?"

He glances at me. "Perhaps you are unfamiliar with what a guard does?"

I'm finding that Grey has a dark sense of humor hidden under the formality. It's subversive. I like it. "You think Coale and Evalyn are going to murder Rhen in his sleep?"

He shakes his head. "My worry lies more with the men who burned the farmhouse." He looks toward the door, where the wind whistles through the lock and around the frame. "The snow should cover our tracks, but we would have been easy to follow."

I sit up straighter. I hadn't even considered that. "And you think they'd attack the inn?"

"Men died." His voice is dispassionate, practical. "It is certainly possible."

"Okay. I'm done sleeping."

"Suit yourself." He retreats to the corner by the stairwell, his black clothing blending seamlessly into the darkness. If the firelight didn't glint on the edges of his weapons, I wouldn't know he was there.

"Have you been there all night?" I whisper.

"Yes."

I don't want to be reassured by this, but I am.

I dig the phone out of my pocket to check the time: 4:02 a.m.

I've been gone for almost twenty-four hours. Somehow it feels like a tremendous amount of time, yet also not like any time at all.

Jake must be flipping out.

Without warning, my face begins to crumple. I *hope* he's flipping out. I hope he's not dead, or in a jail cell, or watching a coroner zip a body bag around Mom.

I sniff hard and push the button to bring up his pictures. I want to see my mother, but the phone is still on the last image I looked at: Jake and Noah.

They look so happy. It's odd to think of this guy being somewhere in the world, possibly worrying about my brother every bit as much as I am.

"What are you doing?" Grey's voice speaks almost right on top of me.

I yip and scramble to push the button to turn off the screen. I clutch the phone to my chest. "Nothing."

He stands behind the chair, looking down at me. His eyes narrow.

I tighten my grip on the phone. "You can't have it."

"I did not try to take it." He pauses and a new note enters his voice. Not quite concern, but more surprise. "You're crying."

Great. I swipe at my cheeks quickly, then bury the phone under my blanket. "Don't worry about it." My voice comes out low and husky.

He moves away from the chair and at first I think he's going back to his corner. His footsteps are light and he moves like a shadow.

Instead, he comes around to sit on the hearth. A low table sits between the chairs, and he drags it between us. Then he unbuckles a small pouch on his belt and withdraws something wrapped in a fold of red fabric.

In spite of myself, I'm curious. "What are you doing?"

He unwraps the fabric, spreading it across the small table. His eyes flick up to meet mine. "You said you will not sleep. Do you care to play?"

In his hands sits a deck of cards.

I wet my lips. "You carry playing cards with you?"

A ghost of a smile. "A guardsman always has cards."

The deck is larger than what I'm used to, and the paper looks thicker. "Can I see?"

He nods and places them in my hands.

They're heavier than I expected, the paper thick with gilded edges. When I look closely, each card appears to be hand-painted, with no numbers, but obvious quantities of different images. No clubs and spades here, though.

"What are these suits?" I ask, holding up a card with six black circular shapes.

He nods at the card. "Stones." When I hold up the next, he says, "Crowns."

I find another. "Don't tell me. Swords?"

He nods again, then gestures to the next in the deck. "Hearts, my lady."

I spread them out on the table, studying the designs. The number cards are similar to a regular deck from home, though they only go to nine. The face cards are stunningly detailed, from a frowning king with a crown that seems inlaid with real, sparkling jewels to a queen whose dress feels like satin is affixed to the cards. The suits on these are identified by a marking on the king's breastplate and on the queen's skirts. No *K* or *Q*, but the faces are obvious.

Then my hand stops on what should be the jack. A blond man holding a shield, with a large red heart in the center.

"Rhen," I whisper.

Grey taps the edge of the card in my hands. "The prince of hearts." He reaches out to scoop up the other cards, loosely shuffling them between his hands.

"He's on his own playing cards," I mutter. No wonder people recognize him on sight. "Wild."

"Your own leaders are on your currency." Grey gestures for the card I hold, then deftly shuffles it into the deck. "Is this so different?"

I blink at him. "How do you know that?"

"I am not completely ignorant of your world. How could I be?"

"I have no idea. I still don't understand what you were doing there. Why you were kidnapping that girl. Rhen says he has to complete a *task*."

He begins to deal the cards between us. "There are many things I am forbidden to say."

I sigh. "Of course."

"Yet many I am not." He finishes dealing, leaving seven cards in front of me, and seven in front of himself. The rest of the deck he places between us, with one card faceup: the five of swords. "Ask your questions."

"My first question is, what are we playing?"

"King's Ransom. Match the suit or the face. Queens and princes are wild. First person to finish with only kings in their hand is the winner—but if you play a prince card, you can steal one of your opponent's kings."

I repeat that back to myself. Matching suits or numbers. My tired brain can manage that. I have a five of crowns in my hand, so I lay it down. "You know about our money. So that woman wasn't the first you've tried to kidnap."

"No." He places a seven of crowns on the pile.

I put down a seven of stones. "How many have there been?"

A three of stones. "Hundreds. I admit, I have lost track."

My hand freezes on a three of swords. I have no idea what number I was expecting, but that wasn't it. "*Hundreds?* You've kidnapped hundreds of women?" I narrow my eyes at him as I work through that in my head. "Exactly how old are you?"

"*Exactly?* That, I cannot say. The curse began on the first day of autumn in my twentieth year, and lasts one season. When it is not broken, the season begins anew."

"So you've been twenty for like . . . *ever*?"

"Longer than most, it would seem." He gives a brief shake of his head. "When the season begins again, it does not feel as though time has passed. I do not feel as though I have aged. It is more like a dream than a memory."

Interesting. "How old is Rhen?"

"You arrived on the eighteenth anniversary of his birth."

"The eighteenth—his birthday? Today was his birthday?" My voice rises as I remember the instruments, the tables loaded with cakes and pastries and delicacies. The party without people. "You kidnap him a *girl* for his *birthday*?"

The look Grey gives me is unyielding. "I choose a girl to break the curse. No more, no less."

I study him. "Okay, so what do I need to do?"

"Once I would have had an answer for you. But I have seen the curse go unbroken for so long that I'm not sure there is anything you can consciously do."

"Rhen said he must complete a task."

"In a way." His voice is careful, and I sense we're treading near questions he cannot answer.

"So I'm stuck here."

He nods.

"Forever?"

"If the curse goes unbroken, you will return home when the season ends. Not before."

Three months. I slide my cards between my hands and try not to let panic overtake me. Nothing has changed. Nothing is different. I can deal with this. "What happened to all those other women?"

"That depends on the season and the girl."

"Did they die?"

"Not all. But some did. Yes." He gestures to the pile between us. "Play your card, if you please."

I drop it on the pile. My breathing feels very shallow suddenly.

He drops a card on top of mine, and we play in silence for the longest time, the fire snapping behind him.

Eventually, he has to draw. "So few questions, my lady?"

"Why do you do it?"

He lays down a queen of stones. "I swore an oath to protect the royal family, for the good of Emberfall. Only I have been granted the ability to cross over to your side." He pulls at a strip of leather where armor encircles his forearm, and a silver band gleams beneath. "At the start of each season, this band allows me one hour to cross over to your world. If I fail to retrieve a girl, there is no chance to break the curse. We must wait out the season and begin again."

I roll that around in my head for a minute. "Does the season restart for everyone?"

"No. Only on the grounds of Ironrose Castle. Outside of Ironrose, time marches on."

So that's why the seasons changed when we passed through the forest. "What about the monster people keep talking about?"

"What do you want to know?"

"Coale says it lives in the castle."

He hesitates. "That is a rumor to protect the people from the curse. Nothing more."

"What kind of monster is it?"

His hands go still on his cards. "It is always different. But always horrible."

"Different how?"

"Sometimes the creature is a giant beast with horns and fangs. Sometimes it is reptilian, with claws like knives. Sometimes—the worst times—the monster is winged, and can take to the air."

I frown. "But it's all one creature? How do you know it's not a bunch of them?"

His eyes glance up to find mine, but he says nothing.

I chew at my lip and lay down another card. Everyone is asleep, but I lower my voice anyway. "Rhen said his family was killed by the monster. The king and queen?"

A slow nod. "And his sisters, my lady."

This knowledge shouldn't tug at something inside of me, but it does. I don't want to feel sympathy for Rhen—but thoughts of Jake and my mother are so consuming that I can't help it. "Coale and Evalyn think the king and queen have locked themselves away. They don't know they're dead?"

Grey hesitates. "If the people were to discover their rulers are dead, the problems could be far-reaching. Revolt. Civil war. The kingdom could be attacked, and we have no army with which to fight."

I study him. "So the king closed the borders. Sealed up the castle. That's why Evalyn said there's no trade. That's why they're worried about invaders."

"Prince Rhen closed the borders. Using his father's seal. He started the rumors of possible invasions, inspiring the people to turn away others. He denied trade attempts and claimed it was his father's order. At first it was wise, a protective maneuver. But as time has gone on, you can see that the people have suffered."

Yes. I can see. I saw it in Freya and her children. And now, though less so, I see it in Coale and Evalyn.

We play for a while in silence, until my cards run down to three, and I have to start drawing. I end up with a prince of swords.

I smile and turn it around. "Ha! Didn't you say I could kidnap your kings with this?"

"Just one." He tosses it down.

I slip the king between my other cards. "Now it's just a matter of time until I win."

"We shall see."

"Did you play cards with the other hundreds of girls?"

"No."

That surprises me. "Why not?"

He rubs at his jaw. "That is a complicated question, my lady. Likely for the same reason I never found need to face them with a weapon."

I study him. "Are you insulting me?"

"No." He sets down a four of hearts. "Quite the opposite, in fact."

I'm not sure what to do with that. Words spoken in the dark in the middle of the night always feel so much heavier than they would at any other time. "Do you play cards with Rhen?"

He nods. "Often."

"Can I ask you another question about the curse?"

"You may certainly try."

I put down a two of hearts, leaving only two cards in my hand. The king I kidnapped, and the nine of swords. Grey has four cards left in his hands. "Who was cursed? Is it just him? Or you too?"

He takes a long breath, and I don't think he's going to answer. But then he says, "My answer to that question has changed over time, my lady. Once I would have told you that His Highness alone suffered." He places a nine of hearts on the pile.

A nine! I begin to slide my last card free.

But then Grey turns around his other three cards. All kings.

I'm stunned. I've been watching him pick up and lay down cards since we started and I never would have guessed he had *any,* much less three. "You win."

He doesn't revel in the victory, but instead begins gathering the cards. "Another game?"

"Sure." Now I want to watch him do it again.

While he deals, I say, "You never finished saying who's cursed. If it's not Rhen, is it you?"

"No. Nothing so simple." He picks up his cards and meets my eyes. "Have you not figured it out yet? The curse torments us all."

CHAPTER TWELVE

RHEN

Like so many other things, sleep eludes me.

I listen to the wind as it whistles through the shutters. The fire has fallen to almost nothing, but I don't care to feed it. The cold suits my mood.

Morning can't be far off, but no light slips through the edges of the shutters, so it must still be early.

I've hardly slept. I would like to blame the lumps in this mattress, or the rough woolen weave of the blankets, but in truth, it's Coale's parting words that keep ringing through my thoughts.

For five years, we have begged for help, but our cries go unanswered, our people starve, and our kinsmen die.

I wish I could claim ignorance, but I can't. Regardless of how I chose to keep myself sequestered in the castle, I knew it was happening.

My fault. All of it.

I keep thinking about those men who burned the house. *This man wears a crest*, Grey said. But he did not recognize it. *Decent weaponry. Better than common thieves.*

Five men. Organized. Burning a house. I can't think of *why* they would do such a thing, unless Freya is lying. But—

I stop these thoughts in their tracks. This line of thinking is useless. Any soldiers under my command were sent to the border years ago, and I have no one to enforce laws that have clearly long since been forgotten or ignored. *Five years*, the innkeeper said. It is truly a miracle that my subjects will still kneel to me—especially since I have nothing to offer them.

A gust of wind knocks the shutters against the window, and I jump.

I will never find sleep this way. I need a distraction.

I pull on my boots and fasten my doublet, leaving my sword and belt on the chair. I don't want to wake our hosts and risk eavesdroppers, so I quietly ease across the floor to open the door to call for Grey.

But Grey is not there.

Surprised, I swing the door fully open. My guard commander sits on the hearth, playing cards with Harper.

He spots me immediately and stands. There is no guilt or chagrin in his expression, but then, there shouldn't be.

That said, I can't identify the feeling that swells inside me, hot and sudden. Not quite anger, and not quite bitterness. Those are familiar.

This is not.

"What are you doing?" I say.

"Playing cards," says Harper. "Keep your voice down."

"I was not talking to you."

"I don't care. People are sleeping."

Grey steps away from the fire and moves halfway across the room. "Forgive me, my lord. How may I serve?"

His voice is even, formal, and practiced. The way he speaks when he's unsure of my temper.

"Is the inn secure?" I say to him. "Or have you been too busy to check?"

His expression does not flicker. "The inn is secure."

"And the horses?"

"I did not want to leave while you slept."

"I'm awake. Go. Check."

He nods, turns on his heel, and heads for the door without question. He barely pauses to pull his cloak from the hook by the door, and then he's gone, disappearing into the darkness and swirling snow. Bitter wind whips through the doorway, making the fire flicker. The chill reaches me from across the room.

I ease down the remaining stairs and take Grey's seat on the hearth. His six cards are abandoned in a small pile on the table.

"We were in the middle of a game," Harper says.

"I see that." I survey the arrangement of the cards and pick up Grey's hand. "King's Ransom?"

"Grey taught me." She slides her cards together and tosses them on the discard pile, then sits back to draw the blanket up over her body.

I gather the cards and begin to shuffle. I feel like arguing, and I'm not entirely sure why. "You no longer care to play?"

"You sent my opponent out into the snowstorm."

"Grey has duties to attend to."

"Sure he does."

My hands go still on the cards. The room is thick with warmth from the fire, and the light plays across her features, making her eyes gleam when she looks at me. She has an uncanny talent of pricking every nerve ending I have.

I hold her gaze. "If you mean to say something to me, I insist that you say it."

"I don't think I need to."

We sit there silently glaring at each other until Grey returns, shaking snow from his cloak and brushing it from his hair.

If he notices the tension, he chooses to ignore it. "The horses fare well. I saw no tracks."

"Good." But I don't look over. I don't want to be the one to break this standoff.

As soon as I have the thought, I feel childish. Petty, the way I felt when I ordered Grey out into the snow.

Harper looks away anyway, but not like she's giving in. More like she doesn't care. "Are you done in the bedroom, Prince Rhen?"

As before, she makes my name sound like an insult, but now it makes me surly. "Why?"

"Because I'd like to get a few hours of sleep somewhere other than a chair." She folds the blanket over her arm and limps toward the staircase.

Her gait takes me by surprise every time. She's so strong-willed, so certain of herself, that I expect her to move with a grace and assurance that matches her temperament. I can understand why Evalyn would immediately think of an engagement to align distant nations. Harper speaks in a manner that leaves no room for disrespect. Like a ruler, not a subject.

She must be stiff and sore, because her limp is more pronounced now than it was earlier, and she moves slowly, grasping the railing to climb the stairs. Once she's closed herself into the bedroom, I become very aware of Grey standing to my left.

I look down at the cards and shuffle them between my hands. "Sit, Commander. Play."

He sits. I deal. We play in silence.

I like cards. I like games in general, especially games like this: simple on the surface, where the real strategy lies in figuring out the player. This was one of the few things I enjoyed doing with my father. When I was very young, he told me that playing games is less about the cards in my hand or the dice on a board, and more of an opportunity to understand an opponent and the way he thinks.

Grey always plays like he fights: direct, without hesitation. A man trained to make a judgment and act immediately. He plays well, but his moves are never calculated in advance, and are always in response to mine.

I wonder how Harper plays.

A part of me hates that Grey already knows.

"How did you get her to play with you?" I finally ask.

He lays a card on the pile. "I did nothing."

I scowl, thinking of the carefully weighed words that led to her shifting an inch closer to me on horseback. "This will never work. She does not trust me. Worse, she regards me with contempt."

Grey inhales like he wants to say something, but he must think better of it, because he does nothing more than toss another card on the pile.

"Say it," I tell him. "Whatever it is, Grey. Say it."

"With all due respect, my lord, I believe you regard *yourself* with contempt."

I make a disgusted noise. "We battle uphill with this girl. She will present a challenge at every turn. Can you not feel it? If we cannot make progress now, there is no hope in the future."

Grey says nothing at all and simply waits for me to play a card.

I sigh and place one on the stack. "I know you have thoughts, Commander."

"Yes. Many."

"Out with them."

He looks up at me then. "You are good at discovering my moves well in advance. I sometimes think you know what cards I will play before I myself do. Even without knowing my hand."

Silver hell. "Not *cards.*" I fling them down, done. "I want your thoughts on the girl."

"I'm giving them to you." He pauses. "You speak of progress. You speak of challenges in the future. Your thoughts, as always, are twenty moves ahead."

I stare at him.

Grey sighs and gathers up the cards. "You asked how I got her to play with me. As if there were some trick to it." He wraps up the stack. "My lord, I did nothing. *I sat down and asked.*"

CHAPTER THIRTEEN

HARPER

We return to Ironrose by mid-morning. A part of me wants to resist, but I can't stay at the inn with everyone thinking I'm part of a royal engagement—and the events of the past twenty-four hours have convinced me that I'm a long way from finding a telephone.

Once we're back in the castle, Rhen leads me past the spread of food and music in the entrance hall—slow and somber today—to the same bedroom.

I refuse to go in. "If you think I'm letting you lock me in there again, you've got another think coming."

His eyes are tired, but he pulls the key from the lock and holds it out. "The midday meal will be served in a few hours. Can I trust that you will not climb down the trellis in that time?"

My joints are already stiffening to a point where walking hurts. I won't be climbing down the trellis anytime soon. I take the key from his hand. "I won't need to."

His expression is *not amused*. "I *will* send Grey to guard this door."

"I think Grey needs a chance to sleep."

"Indeed. Should *I* guard your room?"

His eyes are dark and intense, lending weight to the words. I think of his breath on my neck at the inn, when he spoke a warning against my skin. He has this uncanny ability to make his words a veiled threat and a whispered promise at the same time.

I tuck a loose lock of hair behind my ear and glance away. "You don't need to guard my room." I turn to move through the door.

Then I stop short.

The bed is freshly made, with the pillows fluffed. A fire roars in the fireplace. The marks of dirt and dust I left on the bed coverings yesterday are gone without a trace. A new vase sits on the side table, spilling over with white flowers. The scents of jasmine and honeysuckle hang heavy in the air.

Rhen speaks behind me. "As with the music and the food, the castle follows a predetermined order of events. You will find your room set to order daily."

I turn and look at him. "What if I trash it?" My voice is dark with sarcasm—but I'm also genuinely curious.

He doesn't play. "Try it and see."

I approach the flowers, leaning in to inhale. Each petal is perfect. There's not even a dead leaf. "These are beautiful."

He nods. "Arabella loved flowers. You'll find a new arrangement often." His voice is even, without a hint of emotion.

"Arabella?"

"My elder sister."

I freeze. I don't want to feel sympathy—but standing in this room, surrounded by his dead sister's things, I can't ignore it. For the first time, I wonder what it must be like to live in a place that resets over and over again—minus his family.

Rhen hasn't moved. I don't know what to say. It's one thing to feel sympathy—quite another to extend it.

He spares me the uncomfortable silence. "I will leave you to your rest," he says.

"Thank you."

He hesitates before the door closes, and for a breath of time, I expect him to trick me and lock it somehow, or to wrestle the key away from me. But maybe this is his version of extending a measure of trust. The door clicks closed, unlocked. And then he's gone.

I'm relieved. I need a break. Prisoner or not, I don't need to be filthy. I get in the bathtub.

The water is the perfect temperature, soaking the pain out of my muscles and slicking the blood and dirt from my hands. Various jars and bottles sit on a mirrored tray near the window. I have no idea what's what, but it all smells good, so I pick one and dump it into the water. Once I have suds, I go under and scrub at my hair. Twice, because it just feels so gross. Then I lie there in the warmth and stare at the ceiling.

When I was young and I'd wake with nightmares, my mother always used to say, *All you have to do is think of me, and I'll appear in your dreams. I'll help you chase the nightmares away.*

That story always worked. Too well, really. I used to think I could summon my mother by thought until I was way too old to keep believing such things.

Right now, I would give anything to be able to summon her.

I get out of the tub before emotion chokes out of me.

I don't want to borrow more clothes from a dead girl, especially Rhen's sister, but practicality takes over. I can't walk around naked.

Today's doeskin breeches are black, and pair comfortably with a looser red top with leather laces up the sides. Without any product, my curly hair is wild, so I let it air-dry and weave it into a thick, loose braid that hangs over my shoulder. A dozen different pairs of boots line the floor under the dresses, and they fit better than the pair I swiped from the stable, so I choose a black pair that go all the way up to my knees. When I catch a glimpse of myself in the mirror, I look like a roughed-up warrior princess, right down to the faint mottled blue-and-yellow skin along the left side of my face. No swelling or pain, though. I owe Evalyn for that.

I flop down on the bed and stare at the ceiling. Thoughts of Jake and my mother flicker in my brain, spinning with worry until I can't take it.

I need to do something. I need *action.*

Rhen didn't say I *had* to stay in the room. I open the door, fully expecting him to have posted Grey outside, but I'm pleased to find the hallway empty. The violin melody from below makes it impossible to hear anything at all, and I ease into the hallway.

I peek into the open rooms as I pass. Each is more lavish than the last, with velvet wall hangings, fur rugs, silver trays with crystal glasses. Wine sits out in some of the rooms, along with small trays of food.

The end of the hallway offers a wide staircase—and a choice. I can travel down into darkness, or upward into light.

Up I go.

The rooms on the third floor are larger than the ones I just left, each more of an apartment than a room. Every door stands open, leading to a sitting room first, then a set of double doors, with lushly adorned beds and magnificent wall hangings. Along this hall, a wide opening is set into the wall opposite each doorway, though no furniture occupies these spaces. Weird.

Then I figure it out. It's a space for a guard. If there were guards to stand. If there were people who needed guarding.

By the fourth room, I'm beginning to tire of all the rich elegance. It's like exploring a museum without placards.

I look in the fifth door.

All I see is blood.

It takes my brain a second to catch up—and it's a second longer than it takes my nose to inhale the scent of copper. Blood streaks the walls everywhere, in every shade of red: dark slashes on the white walls, rust streaks on the bedclothes, large viscous pools of crimson on the marble floor.

Blood isn't all there is. There are thicker things lying in the pools. Darker things. Visceral things.

I stagger and grab the door frame. I can't breathe. My vision spins.

No one could lose that much blood and live. No one could lose that much . . . tissue.

I'm screaming. I don't know how long I've been doing it, but my throat suddenly feels raw.

The scent keeps hitting me, wet copper with an undercurrent of something more bitter. An old penny on my tongue. I gag. My vision swims again. I'm going to pitch forward and pass out in a pool of blood.

Arms close around me from behind, dragging me back. "Harper."

Rhen's voice. His arms, tight around mine. A solid chest at my back.

Blood still fills my vision. My screams have dissolved into a thin keening.

"Harper, look at me." Rhen jerks me around, the movement forceful. He gives me a little shake. *"Look at me."*

I look at him.

Rhen. Alone.

My chest feels like it wants to collapse. If he weren't holding me up, I don't think I'd be on my feet. "Grey?" My voice cracks. "Is that Grey?"

"No. Commander Grey is unharmed." His voice is urgent, yet not without compassion. "Calm yourself."

I inhale—and catch the scent of blood again. It's so thick in the air. My throat closes up and I nearly double over.

The world spins again. Everything turns upside down and then right-side up. I'm passing out.

But no—I'm not. I'm moving down the hallway, wrapped in warmth. The room of horror is shrinking, becoming nothing more than a doorway.

I force my head to swivel up to look at him. It puts my face against bare shoulder, which takes me by surprise. His jacket and shirt are gone, and he wears something snug and white and sleeveless, like a heavy undershirt. The neckline is damp, as is the lower half of his jaw. He's warm and smells like mint, and I spot a thin white line of cream.

He was shaving.

It's so normal, so disarming. I could close my eyes and pretend I'm a little girl again, before our lives turned to crap, swept up in my father's arms, inhaling his scent just like this.

But I'm not.

And this is Rhen.

I swipe a trembling hand across my face. A pleasant memory of my father is less welcome than the carnage in that room. "Put me down."

I expect him to refuse, but he stops and eases my legs to the ground. We're at the top of the stairwell, and he doesn't move away. His calmness is reassuring and terrifying at the same time.

"Better?" he says quietly.

I have no idea. "Is that blood real?"

"Quite real." His expression darkens. "Perhaps you recall saying a guard was unnecessary?"

"Trust me, I'm totally regretting it." I'm still worried I'm going to be sick all over the velvet carpeting. "You knew that was there?"

"Of course." A pause. "I usually have Grey bar the doors, but we've been somewhat preoccupied since you arrived."

That's a pointed comment, but my thoughts tumble along, trying to find a way to make sense of this. That blood was fresh and real and vivid. "Is someone hurt?"

"No, my lady. Not in the way you mean."

I stare at him. "What other way is there?"

There is no give to his expression. "This floor is no place for the weak of stomach. Can you walk?"

"I can walk." I take hold of the banister and step down. My fingers shake from leftover adrenaline, and I feel twitchy and unstable.

Rhen walks beside me, his manner completely unconcerned.

He's so relaxed that it's starting to mess with me, making me feel like I imagined it all.

We reach the landing and I turn, ready to head to my room, but

Rhen continues around the corner. "Come," he says, gesturing with a hand. "There is nothing frightening in the kitchens."

I don't have a shred of an appetite after seeing the carnage in that room, but I follow him anyway. He can eat. I want information. "Is it the monster?" I ask in a hushed voice. "Is the monster here?"

"No. The blood in that room is unfortunate to look at, but is ultimately of no real concern." He continues down into darkness, leaving me to follow.

I do my best to scurry after him. At the bottom of the staircase, light flickers along the shadowed hallway and warm scents of flour and yeast reach my nose. I should have chosen this path to begin with.

"Is the blood part of the curse?" I whisper.

He turns and gestures around, his expression incredulous. "All you see is part of the curse."

I hesitate, thinking of his dead family, though I can't make wet blood match up with people who've been dead for numerous seasons.

I shouldn't have worried, because his voice remains casual and unbothered. "Do you care for some wine? I can fetch a bottle from the cellar."

"No. Rhen—" I swallow, and my voice goes husky. Grey told me about the hundreds of girls—some who made it out alive, and some who didn't. "Who died in that room?"

"No one."

"That's not possible." I pause and wonder if I should try to run from here again. I edge toward the doorway. "Was it—was it from the last girl here? Did she die in there?"

"No. She returned home when the season reset. If not wine, do you prefer mead, or possibly—"

"I don't care what we have to drink!" I stop in front of him. My pulse is a roar in my ears and I'm sure my expression is fierce. "How can you talk about lunch when you've got a room full of blood upstairs?" I slap my hand against the stone wall. "Stop evading my questions."

He gives me a level look. Light from the oil lamps flickers across his eyes. "I have answered quite directly. If you feel otherwise, you are asking the wrong questions. What is it you want to know?"

"Whose blood is that?"

The first hint of anger slides into his voice—but it's backed by resignation. "The blood you saw was mine."

CHAPTER FOURTEEN

RHEN

I'm rethinking my decision to allow her freedom. If she found my former suites terrifying, it does not bode well for what's to come. In truth, I should probably be on my knees, grateful that she hasn't bolted from the castle again, and has instead willingly followed me into the warm depths of the palace kitchens.

I have fond memories of this part of the castle. I used to come down here often as a child, and the pastry girls would reward me with twists of dough and cups of sweet cream. My nurse was friends with the cook, and they would gossip and laugh while I traced pictures in the flour that seemed to coat everything.

My visits to the kitchen stopped—and my nurse disappeared—when I asked my father what it meant that no girl could hold his eye longer than a fortnight, or why that would make my mother a pitiable thing.

But the memories remain intact. After Lilith cursed me, after the echoing emptiness of the castle began to haunt me, I would seek refuge down here. The warmth and the heavy smell of sugar and yeast remind me of childhood.

When I was harmless.

Without a staff, the kitchen seems huge. Food sits everywhere, almost spilling out of the shadows. Loaves of bread by the dozen wait on shelves by the hearth, where a massive fire roars. Soup bubbles in a huge cauldron, a roasted corn chowder the cook would have served with the evening meal. Six pheasants roast on a slowly turning spit above a fire on the other side of the room. Vegetables have been sliced and roasted to line serving platters. Cheese. Nuts. Pastries. Everywhere.

The only available work space is a large table in the center of the room, dusted with sugar and cinnamon and lined with piles of dough.

Harper stops in the doorway and looks around. "Holy . . . wow."

I move to the table and shove the strips of dough to the side, then pull a stool over. "Sit, my lady. Wine?"

"I'm pretty sure I'm going to need some."

I fetch a bottle from the storeroom at the back of the kitchen, then pour. Harper watches.

The weight of her eyes makes me uneasy. I lost the ability to feel self-conscious long ago—or at least I thought I did. I'm used to the weight of prying eyes and critical glances.

Harper's judgment is different. She is my final chance. The stakes feel immeasurably high.

Once the glasses are full, I hand one to Harper, then down mine in one swallow. I pour more.

She takes a small sip, watching me. "So you *are* upset."

That makes me pause. "What makes you think so?"

"In my experience, men drink like that when they're upset."

I don't like that she seems to see right through me. "Indeed? And what is your experience?"

She flinches almost imperceptibly. She swirls the wine in her glass and keeps her voice light. "I don't want to talk about me."

I take a slower sip from my glass. "Do you wish to talk about me?"

As with any other time I challenge her, it sparks a light in her eyes. "Yes, I do. What really happened in that room?"

"I made a mistake." I take a longer sip of wine. I'm already feeling the effects of the first glass. "One of many, in fact."

She leans against the table and studies me. "What kind of mistake?"

I hesitate. Weigh my words. Take another, longer drink. "I enjoyed the company of the wrong woman."

"And what? She tore you apart?"

"Yes."

Her question was flippant and she clearly did not expect that answer. Her voice quiets. "Then how are you standing here? Where are your scars?"

"Not all scars can be seen, my lady." I drain the glass again. "I somehow think you have already learned that lesson yourself."

She goes still. I've shocked her. Or offended her. Or something else entirely.

"What made her the wrong woman?" she finally asks.

"To understand that, you must understand our history." I pause. "During my grandfather's rule, a small colony of magesmiths from the western colony of Verin took refuge in Emberfall, near our northern border. From what I remember of my lessons, they were the last remaining magesmiths, and the King of Verin had sought to destroy them all, so they fled east. They swore allegiance to my grandfather and caused few problems. They would sell their spells to the people, and my grandfather saw it as an indulgence to allow it. Their magic was small, harmless. He would tax them heavily for the privilege. There were surely tensions there, but he ignored it—or he did not care. When my father reached marrying age, a young woman visited the castle, presenting herself as a candidate for marriage. But she was a magesmith in disguise, and once she was here, she bewitched my father. She tried to trick him into marriage.

"She was not very powerful," I say. "The guards were able to imprison her and execute her once she confessed. But my grandfather took out his wrath on the magesmiths who remained. He sent an army, because it was said that as each one of the magesmiths was killed, the magic would be passed on to the others, making the magesmiths who remained increasingly powerful. To avoid that, they had to be slaughtered all at once—and so they were." I shudder, then continue, "The stories of their deaths would put that room to shame."

Harper's expression has lost any suspicion or disbelief. "So what happened?"

"One escaped," I say. "Or one was hidden." I pause. "And she appeared on the night of my eighteenth birthday. Dressed as a courtier, ready to seduce a prince."

"And she had the strongest magic—because she had absorbed all the magic of the rest, who were dead."

"Yes."

"Why did she curse *you*, if it was your grandfather who killed them all off?"

I look down into my glass. "She was not solely seeking revenge. She truly did want to align herself with the royal family. She is quite powerful—but her magic only extends so far. To me, to Grey, to the territory of Ironrose. She cannot cast her web over my entire kingdom. She seeks true power. For that she needed me."

"And you turned her away."

"I did."

I say nothing more, and after a moment, Harper's eyes light with understanding. "You turned her away after spending the night with her."

"Yes."

"Probably after promising her the world on a string."

"I promised nothing." I hesitate. "Though I allowed her to believe our night meant more than it did."

"Charming."

I pour another glass of wine and meet her gaze. "I have learned my lesson, my lady. I assure you of that."

She twists her glass in her hands and studies me. I wish I could read the emotion in her eyes. After countless seasons of hiding the truth behind pretty lies and extravagant stories, I have laid the truth at her feet, and I am no more sure that she will accept it.

Guilt pricks at me. I am lying to myself now. I have not laid the *entire* truth at her feet. Not about what I will become.

"I can offer you no proof," I say to her, "if that is what you are after."

"So she cursed you to perform a task." Her tone is musing. "Why won't you tell me what it is?"

"I have found that revealing the nature of the task is the quickest way to assure failure."

"Why? What am I supposed to do?" she says, her expression piercing. "Fall in love with you?"

I almost drop the glass.

"Don't look so surprised," she says. "I've been trying to think of what would require you to kidnap someone each season, and that's all that makes sense. Now I understand what Grey meant when he said it's not something I can consciously do."

I sigh.

She continues to watch me, and her eyes narrow. "Now I understand why you're shirtless."

"You screamed," I say. "Many times, and quite loudly. Would you rather I had waited to dress fully? It is lucky I did not find you facedown in a pile of entrails."

She makes a face. "Can we not use a word like *entrails*?"

"Does seeing me in a state of undress sway you so easily?"

That pink on her cheeks darkens and she looks away to pick at a twist of dough from the side of the table. "Grey said you've tried to break this curse with hundreds of women."

"I have."

"He also says it doesn't feel like you're aging. That it's more like a dream than a memory."

"He is not wrong." I refill her glass. "Five years have passed in Emberfall. I'm surprised it's not longer, but I have no way to keep track. And many seasons do not reach their close."

She studies me, her expression inscrutable. "Why would the season restart earlier?"

"The season begins again if I die."

She nearly chokes on a piece of dough. "If you *die*?"

"Yes."

"But . . . how?"

"At this point, I've tried everything. A fall from a great height. Impalement by whatever you can imagine. Drowning. I ordered Grey to behead me once, because I was curious, but he refused—"

"Okay, okay, I get it." She looks a bit queasy again. "So you just . . . come back to life?"

"Every season begins in the room where you first appeared, regardless of how the previous season ended."

"What happens to the girl when you kill yourself?"

"She is returned home. As far as I know."

Harper goes still with her hand on a new twist of dough. "So I could kill you and get to go home?"

"I have no way of knowing for sure. The seasons begin again. The girls are gone."

She's studying me. Imagining my death. Plotting it, probably. Wondering if it's worth the risk.

I shrug and take a sip of wine. "Any other season and I would hand you a weapon and invite you to try."

"What's different this time?"

"This is my final season," I say quietly. "My final chance. If you were to kill me, I would truly die." I lift my eyes to find hers. "I have no idea what would happen to you."

She goes very quiet at that. We both eat twists of dough.

When she eventually speaks, it's not a question I'm expecting. "Did you get naked with these hundreds of women, too?"

She's so direct that she'd be intimidating under other circumstances. "Such questions you ask."

She rolls her eyes. "Well, that's sure not a no."

"It is, in fact." I wonder how honest to be. "I lured them all into my life. I abhor the idea of luring them into my bed—and I certainly would not force them. In truth, there is no greater crime in Emberfall."

"Murder?"

"In death, the crime ends."

She evaluates me for a long moment. "I believe you."

"I have no reason to lie."

"Why are you telling me all of this?" she says. "I thought you couldn't."

"Why would you think such a thing?" I lean across the table and swipe another scrap of dough. Cinnamon and sugar melt on my tongue. The perfect foods from the Great Hall and my personal rooms have grown interminably boring, but eating bits of dough in the kitchen reminds me too much of childhood to hold much rancor.

As I lift the piece to my mouth, Harper's eyes drift down across my chest, following the motion of my arm.

Interesting. Especially after her censorious glare when she thought I was bedding every young woman Grey drags back to the castle.

She pulls a piece of dough for herself. Her eyes shy away from mine now. "Because Grey couldn't."

"He is ordered to keep his silence." Though now I'm curious how much he said.

"And you are not."

"I am the crown prince." I pull a larger scrap of dough from the pile and twist it in half, extending a piece to her. "I am ordered nothing."

"Do you always pull women from DC?"

"Not at first. But now, yes."

"Why?"

I reach for another piece of dough. "At first, I sought courtiers from among the noble women of Emberfall. I thought such a curse could be easily undone. Who does not love a prince?" My chest tightens as I remember. "As it turns out, many women do not."

"So you eventually ran out of noblewomen . . ."

"I sought a woman from the village," I say. I drain my glass again, and will likely need another. "Her name was Corra. A very kind, simple girl. I rode into town with much fanfare. Her mother wept when I announced my intention to marry her daughter. The entire village filled a trunk with offerings, providing a dowry. As if I needed their riches."

I hesitate.

"What happened to Corra?" Harper says quietly.

"The monster tore her limb from limb. Her mother sobbed on my steps and demanded to know why the king had not been able to offer her daughter protection."

Harper stops chewing. "And the king was dead."

"Yes. The king was dead. I turned her mother away."

"So then what?"

"I declared that I would no longer risk my own people. By that point I had lost so many. I refused to sacrifice any more."

"Oh, but people from my home were fair game?"

I slap my hand against the table. "You must know that my intent with each woman was to break the curse. Not to prolong it."

She glares at me. I glare at her. We fall into silence.

The fire crackles in the hearth, and the soup threatens to bubble over. It won't, I know. An invisible chef will stir it and lower the heat before it has a chance. The scent of cooked poultry is beginning to fill the room.

Then Harper looks up and meets my eyes. "Declared to who?"

"Pardon me?"

"You said you declared you would no longer risk your own people. Who did you declare this to?"

I'm frozen in place.

She narrows her eyes at me. "Who's the enchantress?"

I drain my glass. "Her name is Lilith."

"So *she* can send me home."

"No, my lady."

"Maybe I should ask her. How do I find her?"

My eyes flick at the corners, as if this conversation could summon the enchantress. "You do not want to find her."

"But—"

"Do you not understand that she was the cause of the damage you found on the third floor?" My voice is low and vicious and full of remembered pain.

Harper goes pale.

I take a breath. My head is so tangled up with memories of death and suffering. The hundreds of girls swirl through my mind, each one a reminder of how I failed them and failed my people.

Grey was wrong. The failed seasons are not like dreams. They're like nightmares.

I shift off the stool to stand. "Forgive me, my lady. I am keeping you from your rest. Shall I escort you back to your room?"

"Are there any other surprises in the castle?"

"Not today."

"Then I want to stay here." She grips the edge of the table as if worried I'm going to physically drag her out of the kitchen.

I give her a nod and turn for the door.

"Rhen," she calls after me.

I pause in the doorway and face her.

"I'm not going to fall in love with you," she says.

Her words are not a surprise. I sigh. "You won't be the first."

CHAPTER FIFTEEN

HARPER

I poke around the kitchen until I find a bowl and a spoon, then move to the cauldron hanging over the fire. A large ladle hangs from a hook set into the masonry. I scoop out a large serving, then pull a hunk of bread from the end of a loaf on the counter.

Images from the blood-soaked room threaten to replay in my mind, and I shove them away.

Instead, my brain is content to fix on what he said about asking Grey to behead him. How he was *curious*.

Yesterday, he talked about throwing musical instruments into the fire. This morning he mentioned impalement and drowning. And hundreds of women, all of whom failed to fall in love with him.

If he just had to find a woman to *lust* after him, he probably would have been free of this curse in a day. I can't deny that he's easy on the eyes. The high cheekbones, the dark blond hair that turns gold in the firelight, the brown eyes that reveal nothing. Muscle cords his arms from shoulder to wrist, and he carries himself with purpose. People are quick to kneel before him—but he's also quick to expect it.

When he opens his mouth, though, he's arrogant and calculated. There's no shred of vulnerability or weakness. In fact, if there's any weakness, it's the obvious frustration that he can't just wave a hand and order a woman to love him.

Something about it all makes me immeasurably sad. I've been trapped here, separated from my family, for two days. He and Grey have been trapped here for what must feel like forever. They're seeming less harmful, and more desperate.

That's almost worse.

But *love*. I've never fallen in love with anyone, much less someone who snatched me right off the street. Mom always says she's still in love with Dad, despite his mistakes, despite the fact that he *left*, and that makes me and Jake crazy. Their relationship sure isn't a standard of true love. I know about Stockholm Syndrome. Even if something like that kicks in—if this line of thinking isn't proof already—would that be real love? Anything else clearly isn't enough to break this curse. He didn't kidnap Corra, the poor girl from the village, but she couldn't have loved him, or the curse would have broken. Maybe she loved the idea of being a princess.

They've trapped me, but this Lilith trapped them. And now apparently his entire kingdom is suffering while he sits in this castle, just letting it happen.

I tear another hunk of bread from the loaf.

This time, I hesitate with it halfway to my mouth.

Freya and her children stood shivering in the snow, thin as rails. Evalyn and Coale and young Bastian clearly struggled to make do with what they had, despite the fact that it's the middle of winter.

I look around this kitchen with new eyes. At the shelves overflowing with food that no one is eating.

Then I shove the bowl away and go back to my room to fetch a satchel.

This time, it's easy to find the trail through the woods.

I considered taking a different horse, but Will pricked his ears at me and looked eager to go out again. The saddlebags are double loaded with bread, meats, and pastries on one side, and tightly wrapped bundles of vegetables and hard cheeses on the other. I'm wearing a cloak and two sweaters, and I found gloves and a quarter sheet for the buckskin in the stable.

No one stops me.

Then again, I don't ask for permission.

When warm sunshine gives way to snow-coated trees, I brace myself for frigid air, but this afternoon's winter weather seems more temperate. Wind does not weave through the trees, and instead the sun beats down, causing a constant *drip-drip-drip* around us.

Just when I begin to worry I might be heading off course, I come upon the remains of Freya's home. The building is burned to the ground, leaving a blackened stone chimney to stand sentry over a pile of charred lumber and ash. The bodies are gone; buried in the snow or burned in the fire. I'm not checking.

A hill looms ahead, and I remember that from there, it's a straight shot to the inn. I'll be able to see the entire road. I spur Will into a gallop and we sprint up the hill.

A horse-drawn wagon is coming up the other side.

"Whoa!" yells a man. "Whoa!" Two cream-colored draft horses shy and prance sideways. Slush and mud spray everywhere.

I wrench the reins to the side, trying to avoid a direct collision. The buckskin slips in the slush and nearly dumps me. The wagon gives a creak and a groan and nearly topples, but the man cracks a whip and the horses quickly yank it straight.

It doesn't help his cargo. Several crates spill out of the back, falling into the wet snow with a *splat*.

Will champs at the bit and tosses his head, but I keep a tight hold on the reins. "I'm sorry," I call. "I didn't see you."

"You're sorry?" the man growls. He loops the reins around a hook and jumps down from the wagon, his boots splashing in the mud. The hood of his cloak falls back, revealing him to be middle-aged with olive skin and dark hair. Shadows cling to his eyes and pool in his cheeks.

"Yes. I'm sorry." I grip the hilt of my dagger under my cloak in case this goes south, but he doesn't even look at me. Instead, he storms around to the back of the wagon to stare at the fallen crates.

He swears under his breath, then reaches out to grab one.

It must be weighted poorly, because when he tries to drag it into the back of the wagon, he can't get it over the rail. The crate clumsily slips out of his hand and crashes into the slush again. He swears again and this time it's not under his breath.

As soon as I start to wonder why he's not using both hands, his cloak spills back and I realize he's missing his left arm.

I slide off Will's back and go to the man's side. "Here. I'll help you."

He ignores me and struggles to maneuver it over the railing. Again, it crashes into the mud. The wood cracks and breaks open at the corner.

"Silver hell," he snaps.

I can appreciate that he wants to do it himself, but I'm kind of done with prideful men. I throw the cloak back over my shoulders and move forward to pick up the other one.

It's heavier than I'm ready for. I can't believe he's getting these off the ground one-handed. I stumble in the mud and almost drop it myself.

But the man catches the other side, and together, we heave it over the side of the wagon, then go back for the others.

When we're done, mud clings to our boots, and we're both winded. I fight to straighten the cloak.

The man swipes a forearm across his brow. "I suppose you think I owe you thanks, girl. You're not getting it. I'll lose a few coins for the damage—" He stops short as his eyes fall on the royal lion-and-rose insignia that's settling into place over my chest. He blinks and takes a step back. The irritation falls out of his voice, replaced with a bit of wonder. "You are—I did not—"

"I really *am* sorry," I say. "I don't expect thanks. But if you wouldn't mind me using the back of your wagon to get on my horse—"

"Of course." He scrambles ahead of me to catch Will's bridle. "Allow me, my lady."

I grab hold of the wagon and pull myself onto the ledge. It's not as precarious as clinging to the trellis, but it's still a feat of strength and balance, and I always doubt my body. It takes my contracted muscles a moment to ease back into the saddle, but if he notices, the man says nothing.

Rhen was so confident as he flipped a silver coin to the innkeeper's son, and I wish I could do the same thing now. I have no coins to offer.

But then I remember the saddlebags. "Are you hungry?" I say. "I have plenty of food."

He frowns and shakes his head quickly. "I cannot take food from a lady traveling alone."

"I'm not traveling far." I unbuckle a saddlebag and pull out some meat pies wrapped in a stretch of cheesecloth. They're still warm. "Here."

He looks dumbfounded, but he takes them, pulling them close to his body. "Thank you."

I pick up the reins. "You're welcome."

He takes a step closer. "Forgive me." He hesitates. "I should apologize. I did not expect a lady of the court to be traveling without protection."

"I don't need protection," I say.

A man's voice calls from behind me. "Are you certain, my lady?"

I whirl in the saddle—but I recognize his voice now. Rhen. And Grey. Their expressions give away nothing. No anger. No humor.

"Did you think we would not come after you?" Rhen says.

I force my expression to stay equally neutral. "You said I wasn't your prisoner."

The man with the wagon looks utterly astonished. He glances between me and the men. "Your Highness," he says, his voice reverential. He drops to a knee right there in the slush.

"Rise," says Rhen. His voice is low and controlled, which I'm beginning to learn is a better clue to his mood. He's more heavily armed than last night. A sword hangs at his hip, and a full quiver of arrows is strapped to the saddle near his knee. Under the cloak, his entire chest is covered in leather, with buckles at his waist, the lion-and-rose insignia embossed in gold over his heart.

He was handsome yesterday, but that was nothing on this. All he's missing is a crown.

Then again, that might make me forget that he's got an ulterior motive in coming after me. I hate that my heart flutters, just a little, sending warmth to my cheeks. "Do you have another one of those coins?" I say. "One of this man's crates broke when I ran into him."

Rhen's eyebrows go up, but he sighs and nudges his horse forward.

The man shoves himself to his feet and shakes his head fiercely. "No—no, my lady." He holds up the wrapped meat pies. "The food is more than enough."

Rhen pulls coins from a pouch on his belt anyway and extends his hand. His forearms are covered by metal-and-leather cuffs, laced all the way to his elbow. "Will two silvers cover the damage?"

The man swallows. He looks at the coins held between Rhen's fingers, but does not reach for them. "You have my thanks, but there was little damage."

"For your trouble, then," says Rhen.

"With all due respect . . . I cannot accept that." He glances between Rhen and Grey again, then to me. He looks like he wants to pinch himself. "I take half a year's time to earn that amount, Your Highness." He pauses. "I would be thought a liar or a thief."

"Why?" I say.

The guy looks like he wishes he could just climb back on his wagon and ride off. "No one has seen the royal family in years." He looks away and there's shame in his expression. "I can barely find work as a porter. No one would believe I came by such coins honestly."

Grey rides forward and pulls a small bag from a pouch at his waist. "Here. Twenty-five coppers. Can you spend that?"

The man blinks. "Yes—but—"

Grey tosses him the bag.

The man's hand is occupied with the food, and I'm worried the coins are going to sail right into the mud, but he's more agile than I expect. He snatches the pouch out of the air with the same hand that's holding the food.

He offers a clumsy bow. "You have my thanks. Your Highness. My lady." Then he backs away to climb into his wagon.

He's barely seated before he's clucking to his horses, driving them down the hill.

I wish I could follow right behind him. The weight of Rhen's gaze is almost painful. His expression is full of disapproval and his tone matches. "The longer I know you, the less I see your acts as those of bravery. Did you forget the attack from last night?"

"Did you forget your people are suffering?"

His jaw tightens. "You speak of things you do not know."

"I think I've seen enough."

His expression darkens like thunderclouds rolling over a summer sky. He says nothing.

Grey speaks into the silence. "You mentioned that you are not a prisoner. Does that mean this is not an attempt to escape?"

"Of course not." I pat a saddlebag. "I'm bringing food to Freya and her kids."

"You're bringing food," Rhen echoes. "To the inn."

"It seemed like they were already short and we dumped five more people on them."

He looks incredulous. "But why would you not ask?"

I draw back and stare at him. "*Ask?* Are you kidding me? When you've got a kitchen full of food that's going to be replaced every day—"

"You misunderstand." He puts a hand up. "Why would you not ask for *assistance*?"

Oh.

"I didn't think you'd do it," I say quietly.

He stares back at me. I wonder if he's going to ask why.

Looking at his expression, at the trace of resignation that flickers in his eyes, I don't think he needs to.

"Very well," he says finally. He turns his horse away.

"You're letting me go?" I might fall off this horse in shock.

"I'm escorting you to the inn," he says, as if I was too stupid to figure it out. "Unless you have changed your mind?"

I sigh and turn my horse to follow.

CHAPTER SIXTEEN

RHEN

I'm used to loneliness. Despair. Sorrow. Disappointment.

I'm not used to *fear*, at least not this kind. I have never met someone so reckless.

She is not the first girl to run, or to fear me, or to question my motives. She *is* the first girl to force me into situations requiring armor and weaponry.

We walk in silence, Grey riding behind, waiting at the crest of the hill as we descend into the valley. Her words keep piercing me. *Did you forget your people are suffering?*

"I did not forget," I say to her.

It's been a while since we've spoken, but she needs no clarification. "Well, you don't do much to fix the situation."

"One day in Emberfall, and you know so much about my failures. I suppose you believe you are doing a good thing, visiting a mercy on suffering people?"

Her eyes are icy, but I can tell that she does think this.

I shake my head. "Even if we empty the castle of food at every meal, every single day, it would not feed all of my subjects."

Her voice is quiet. "It would feed some of them, Rhen."

"Yes, but not all." I look over at her. "How would you choose?"

Frustration is painted all over her face. "Why would I *have* to choose?"

"Why would you not? The people of Emberfall fear Ironrose. They believe a monstrous creature sleeps on the ramparts, waiting for an opportunity to destroy them if they approach. My people will not willingly come to me. And even if I were to hire a wagon to take everything I have, how would you determine the most needful?"

"I—"

"And before you answer that," I press on, "what would you say to those for whom you could not provide? Imagine we arrive at the inn, and there are half a dozen more guests. What you've packed into your saddlebags will not feed them all. What will you say then?"

"I'll go back and get more."

Silver hell, she is so *stubborn*. "Say you were to visit every day with a bounty of food. Word would spread. People would line up. There would be small skirmishes among the people, gradually riots would form—"

"I think you've made your point."

"Fighting would ensue, and with no enforcers to quell the violence—"

"Okay, I get it!" Her cheeks are red, her breathing quick. "I don't care. I'm still bringing them something. It's better than nothing."

"Is it?" I say. "Are you certain, my lady?" I reach out to grab her reins and pull both our horses to a halt.

She whips her head around to glare at me, tussling for control of the reins. Her eyes are hot with anger. "Let me go."

I keep my voice even. "You know I do not mind honesty and civil discourse. I would hope I have made that clear. But I will not tolerate bald-faced disrespect."

"But it's acceptable to disrespect *me*?"

Her horse—*my* horse, in truth, though she seems to have no hesitation in claiming him for her own—tosses his head and stomps in the slush, but I keep a tight hold on the reins. Her skill at firing me up and beating me down is truly admirable.

"I have asked you to examine the ramifications of your actions," I say tightly. "If you see that as disrespect, you are mistaken."

"Fine." She looks away.

I draw a short breath. "There are reasons I have confined myself to the castle for so long. If you force me to interact with my people, you must be aware of what that means for—"

"No one is forcing you to do anything. Now *let me go*."

I take a moment to gather my mettle, then cast my gaze to the sky. Of course my final chance would be a girl determined to undermine me and create new obstacles at every turn. Every step forward seems destined to end in two steps back.

"Now, Rhen. I'm not one of your subjects. You're not *my* prince."

My voice is very low. "I may not be your prince, but you are in *my* kingdom. Not your own."

"And whose fault is that?"

"You have no comprehension of the tenuous control I have here. You have no consideration for what I have done to provide for the safety of my kingdom." My jaw is tight, lending ice to coat my words. There was a time when this tone in my voice meant people would scurry. The same tone in my father's voice meant people would die. Yet she stares at me defiantly, and it takes every ounce of self-control for me to keep my voice level. "You speak to me with contempt and disregard, as though I do not feel the weight of what my people endure. You speak as though *you* rule over *me.* I will remind you of our roles here."

"What, kidnapper and kidnappee?"

I raise my eyebrows. "You wish those to be our roles? Fine." I turn my head. "Commander!"

"What are you doing? Rhen, let me go." She tries to pry my hand off the reins. She must be digging her heels in, because Ironwill dances at the end of the reins and fights my grip. "Let me *go*—"

"My lord." Grey's horse skids to a stop beside Harper, spraying slush and blowing steam in the air.

"Return Lady Harper to the castle. Bind her if necessary. Lock her in—"

"No!" She pulls the dagger. Aims for my wrist.

Grey's sword appears at the bend of her elbow. He's got hold of her cloak, pulling her back and away from me.

She's frozen, her face pale, her eyes wide with fear and fury.

I should feel remorse, but instead I feel satisfaction. Finally *something* gets through to her. "He'll take your arm off if I order it." I glance at the dagger in her hand. "I drew no weapon on you, my lady."

"The reins." Her voice grows tight, almost choked, and I wonder what kind of pressure Grey is putting on her neck. "I was going to cut the reins."

"Ah." I glance at him. "Release her."

Grey obeys. She slides the dagger back into its sheath, then gives the cloak a jerk to right it. Her breath still shakes and tears glitter on her eyelashes.

Now I feel remorse.

She doesn't look at me. "I just want to go to the inn." Her cheeks are pink. She swallows and her voice is quiet. "I don't—I don't want to play games. I just wanted to help them." With that, she glances up and a spark of her usual fire reenters her tone. "Do you understand that?"

Her words lodge in my thoughts, tangling with Grey's near-admonition over the card game. I do nothing without careful thought regarding the impact. He was right: I do plan my moves out far in advance.

Maybe she's right, too.

I look at Grey. "Escort her to the inn. I will follow in a moment."

Grey's eyebrows go up. "My lord—"

"Go. Make sure she does not go astray again."

Harper jerks the reins out of my hand. Without a word, she gives the buckskin a solid kick, then canters down the hill. Grey follows without hesitation.

Once they're gone, I turn my horse in the opposite direction and drive my heels into the animal's sides.

CHAPTER SEVENTEEN

HARPER

This stings. I feel like I've been smacked on the wrist.

Grey sticks to my side, cantering easily along in the slush, and we cover ground quickly. I expected some tension between me and him, especially after the incident with the dagger, but there's none. He might be ten times more dangerous than Rhen, but he's a hundred times easier to get along with.

This is all so confusing. *Rhen* is so confusing. He doesn't act like a man who's trying to fall in love. He plays this whole thing like a game, where underneath his pretty words is a man full of cunning and guile. He acts like a tethered animal that's learned the limits of its chain—but knows how to lure prey to its death.

That is why I don't trust him.

After the showdown in the snow, I realize he doesn't trust me, either. Somehow, despite the fact that *he* trapped *me* in Emberfall, *his* distrust seems to run deeper.

When the inn comes into view, I slow the horse to a walk. A

glance over my shoulder reveals a blue sky sitting atop a slushy landscape. Rhen is nowhere to be seen.

Grey has slowed to match my pace.

"Would you really have cut off my arm?" I ask.

He gives me a glance. "I would have prevented you from causing harm," he says.

"So that's a yes."

"I follow orders," he says equably. "I bear you no ill will."

Somehow that's completely reassuring, yet not at all. "Where do you think he went?"

He sighs and a shadow of irritation slides into his voice. "You know as much as I."

As we dismount in the courtyard of the inn, the front door is flung open. Small sections of snow slide from the roof and land with a *plop*. The horses throw up their heads and snort.

Coale stands in the doorway. "My lady!" he booms in surprise. "You have returned?"

"Yes. I brought . . ." But I trail off as Rhen's warnings about riots and skirmishes echo in my ears. "Um . . ."

"Lady Harper has brought gifts of goodwill," offers Grey, moving forward to hand me the overloaded saddlebags.

"Oh. Yes. Here." I'm completely off balance. I thrust them at him awkwardly.

Coale looks dumbfounded.

Evalyn's voice calls from behind him. "Do we have guests? Why are you—oh, my goodness!" She appears beside her husband and gives a low curtsy. "Lady Harper. You have returned."

"With gifts," Coale says numbly.

"It's nothing." I feel a blush crawling up my cheek. "It's

just some food. I know we dumped Freya and her family here unexpectedly."

"But . . . His Highness paid handsomely for six months' worth of lodging. It is hardly an inconvenience."

I'm frozen in place. I didn't know he'd paid them anything.

Evalyn speaks quickly, misinterpreting my silence. "You must think us greedy. We tried to refuse." She wrings her hands.

"No! No. I—I misunderstood. I wanted to bring a little something for the kids."

"Oh!" Her face breaks into a smile. She claps her hands. "You must come in."

We're ushered into the front room. The fire is banked and low, embers glowing. I smell baked bread. Coale takes our cloaks and shouts to the back of the inn. "Children! The Lady Harper has returned to see you."

I move close to Grey. "Did you know he paid that much money?" I whisper under my breath.

He frowns. "You thought otherwise?"

"I didn't—I didn't—"

"Lady Harper!" Feet thunder down the steps and across the wooden floor. Three children come running, obvious glee in their faces. Freya descends the steps more slowly, the baby cradled in her arms, but even she is smiling.

I'm not sure I deserve it. Their home was destroyed.

The girl does not stop until she tackles my waist. The two boys tackle Grey's legs. Their joy is infectious. I'm glad there are frosted cookies in the saddlebags.

Even Bastian comes out of the kitchen, drawn by the commotion. Everyone presses in against the table, eager to see what I've brought.

The girl reaches out a hand and traces a fingertip over the yellow stitching, while the older boy pokes at the inlaid jewels on one of the saddlebags. Their brown eyes are wide.

Freya moves to pull them back. "Dahlia. Davin. Don't touch."

"No, it's okay," I say. "Dahlia can open it."

Her slender fingers fuss with the buckle, but it finally gives, and wrapped pastries and cheeses roll out onto the table. She laughs with delight. The other children gasp and press in more closely against the table.

"This is too much," Freya whispers.

It's barely enough for a meal to feed her family. But silence falls on the room as everyone stares. No one touches anything.

"Look," whispers the older boy, who must be Davin. "Sweet cakes."

I feel awkward, like I've made a misstep. I find myself wishing for Rhen to work out the politics here, and I want to kick myself because of it.

All of Rhen's warnings are echoing in my head. "Did I . . . offend you?" I whisper.

"My lady." Coale's voice is heavy. "We have never known royalty to bestow gifts on the people. We are—we are overwhelmed."

"And grateful," Evalyn says hurriedly. "So grateful, my lady."

"Perhaps I should get everyone a nice glass of mead," Coale booms.

A loud knock sounds at the door, and Evalyn hurries to answer it. When she swings the door open, Rhen stands there, his blond hair shining in the light. He looks none the worse for wear, his cloak and armor hanging perfectly.

"Your Highness," says Evalyn quickly. "We are doubly honored. Please, come in."

"You have my thanks." His voice is mild. He steps across the threshold.

I meet his eyes without meaning to. His eyebrows lift just a fraction, and in that one tiny motion I can tell that he knows I'm flailing, unsure how to proceed. Half an hour ago, I yelled at him, and now there's a tiny part of me that wants him to rescue me from this situation. I wonder if he planned on it. I wonder if he knows.

I force myself to hold his eyes and stand my ground.

"Coale," I say. "Mead would be great."

Rhen and I end up sitting by the fire again. I've reclaimed my armchair, and he sits on the stone hearth, sipping from his mug. Grey stands at the edge of the mantel, near the corner, firelight glinting off his weapons.

Rhen hasn't said one single word to me since entering the inn, aside from a nod and a brief "My lady."

The air feels prickly and uncertain. The fire crackles behind him, and the children eat and play in the main part of the room, but silence hangs like a woolen blanket strung between us.

The only child with the courage to draw near is little Davin—and he seems fascinated by Grey. He can't be more than four, with thick hair and large brown eyes, and he keeps sneaking over to peer up at the guardsman. Grey has been immobile, impassively ignoring him. He stands so still that he could be a part of the fireplace.

But when Davin sneaks close and dares to put a hand on Grey's sword hilt, the swordsman feints as if he'd chase him away.

The boy jumps and darts back a few feet—but then he laughs,

full out. Grey smiles and tousles his hair. "Go," he says, his voice kind but leaving no room for disobedience. "Play."

Davin scampers off, but a mischievous look over his shoulder says he'll be back.

I look at Grey, remembering how he made faces at the children in the snow. "You're good with kids," I say. "That's like the most . . . incongruous thing about you."

"Is it?" he says, his voice dry. "Truly, my lady?"

"Actually . . ." I hesitate. Rhen's eyes are on the room and the people in it, but I know he's listening to every word I say. I turn my attention back to Grey. "Yeah. It is." I make my voice careful, not wanting to wound. "Do you have children?" I pause. "Did you?"

"No. To enter the Royal Guard, you must forswear family for ten years. A spouse—and children—are a distraction from obligation and duty."

Evalyn overhears us, and steps toward the hearth. "Is it not the same in the Land of Disi, my lady?"

Oh, right. The Land of Disi.

Rhen is looking at me, his eyebrows raised again, clearly waiting for my answer, too.

"No," I say, spinning wheels in my head. "It's not the same. People in the Secret Service can get married and have kids."

"Ohh." Her voice is hushed. "The Secret Service. Such a mysterious name."

"Is it an honor to enter this Secret Service?" asks Coale.

Suddenly I'm the center of attention. "I . . . guess so?"

"Here, it is considered a great honor to even apply." Coale stops beside his son, who's taking a pastry from the platter on the table, and rests his large hands on the boy's shoulders. "And a boon for the family if the child is admitted to the Royal Guard. We never dared to hope that Bastian might one day be considered, but perhaps things are changing for the better."

"There are certainly roles to fill," says Grey.

Rhen cuts him a sharp look. "Commander."

"There *are*?" says Evalyn, with wonder in her voice. "Then indeed there *is* hope for change." She smiles at me.

I swallow. She thinks *I* will bring change. With some engagement to align Emberfall with a country that doesn't exist. If the only hope for these people is for me to fall in love with Rhen, then they ran out of hope the very minute I swung at Grey with that crowbar.

"I don't want to fight the monster," says Bastian. His father hushes him.

Freya looks up from her baby. "Perhaps the monster will be vanquished before you come of age," she offers hopefully. "If the Lady Harper's people can lend their forces to ours."

"Tell us, my lady," says Evalyn. "Does the creature terrorize your lands as well?"

I glance at Rhen, unsure how to move forward from here.

He looks back at me. "Yes. Do tell us."

"No monster in my lands," I say breezily. Then I look into my mug and take a long sip, just to avoid the need to say more. It burns my throat all the way down.

"Is your country a long journey away?" says Coale. "I admit, I have never heard of Disi, though it has been so long since we've housed travelers from outside Emberfall."

"I'm not really sure of the exact distance," I say. "It seems I got here in a flash."

A knock sounds at the door. "Innkeeper!" a man yells from outside.

"More guests?" says Evalyn. She smooths her skirts. "So unusual this early in the season." She gives me a smile. "You bring us luck, my lady."

Coale moves to the door and throws it open. "Gentlemen! Welcome—"

The joy in his voice dies. I can't see much around his form, but I can see booted feet. The ends of sheathed swords. Five men. At least.

I'm on my feet without realizing it. Rhen moves to stand beside me, and Grey moves in front of us both. A hand rests on his sword hilt, but he hasn't drawn a weapon yet.

"Welcome," Coale finishes uneasily. His form blocks most of the doorway. "Are you in need of rooms? We have one available, if you are willing to share—"

"We are here to seize this property for the crown."

"To seize this property?" Coale takes a step back. "We pay taxes every season to the Grand Marshal. We owe nothing—"

"You have one hour to vacate."

Coale gasps. "That's ludicrous! This is our home!"

The man steps forward menacingly. "You will leave, or your home will burn."

Evalyn moves closer to me and Rhen. "I assure you, Your Highness," she whispers quickly. "We pay every season. There surely is some mistake—"

"These men do not work for me," says Rhen, his voice low.

"They wear the same colors as those men yesterday," says Grey.

Rhen glances at him, then moves forward, toward Coale.

"Children," Freya whispers quickly. Fear is alive in her voice. "Children, go to our room." They scurry toward the staircase.

"Move aside, innkeeper," growls the man at the door. "If you will not leave willingly, we will leave you in a pile of ash."

Coale does not move. "You will not threaten my family—"

"I said, *move*." The man draws his sword and all but pushes his way inside. "Gather your things and *go*."

Beside Rhen, Grey moves to draw his weapon, but Rhen gives a brief shake of his head.

Four others follow the first man, and they crowd into the entranceway. They wear dark clothes trimmed in green and black and silver, like the men from last night. Their expressions are fierce and uncompromising. Hard-edged.

Their eyes search the room. They stop when they find Rhen and Grey, and I see two of the men exchange a glance.

I recognize one of them. It's the man who ran last night. He leans in to the leader of the group and whispers something low.

The lead man's eyes linger on Freya for a moment, but when he hears whatever his compatriot whispers, his eyes shift to me, then to Grey, but he finally stops on Rhen. "Who are you?"

Rhen takes a step forward. "Lord Vincent Aldrhen, Prince of Emberfall, son of Broderick, King of the Eastern Lands." His eyes narrow. "A better question is, who are *you*?"

The man spits on the floor. "The prince is dead." The men behind him chuckle.

Evalyn gasps and clasps a hand to her chest.

Rhen smiles, but there is nothing friendly about it. "I assure you, I am very much alive." He pauses and his voice sharpens. "And you will leave these good people in peace."

"If you're the prince, where is your guard? Your entourage?" The man glances around the room, stopping on me this time. "This land will be under the rule of Karis Luran soon enough. I'll take what I came for." He steps forward. "Burn it. Kill them all."

Rhen's hand falls on the hilt of his own sword.

"Wait." I lift my chin and put a hand on his forearm.

Loan sharks once came to the door, looking for my father. He was long gone. I was younger, but I wasn't stupid enough to miss the glint of light on steel under one of the men's jackets. My mother sweet-talked them and offered cookies and coffee. I still remember her fingers shaking as she lifted the coffeepot.

Apparently honey really does catch more flies than vinegar, because the men believed her when she said her husband was traveling on business, and she was just the silly wife, left home with the children, ignorant of her husband's bad debts.

I can't fight, but I know how to bluff.

I step forward. "You would *dare* threaten the first daughter to the King of Disi?" Without waiting for an answer, I turn to face Rhen, who's looking at me like I've grown a second head. "You never specified that your lands are under control of another monarch. This was to be an alliance. When I alert my father, his armies will waste no time in seizing this territory—"

"What armies?" says the man. He sounds suspicious, but he stops the others from moving farther into the inn. "Who are *you*?"

"I am Princess Harper of Disi," I announce. "You have not heard of me? My kingdom's soldiers number in the thousands."

"Per regiment," Rhen adds quickly. "We look forward to combining our forces with Disi's legendary army."

"Yes, per regiment. Obviously." I almost falter. "And my father has *hundreds* of regiments—"

"Dozens," says Rhen.

"Yes, *dozens* of regiments, and they stand ready to invade Emberfall on my order if this alliance fails—"

"What alliance?" says the man. He sounds exasperated. "Who—what is—where is *Disi*?"

"You are in no position to make demands." I fill my voice with steel and fire, remembering the way those men talked about Freya and little Dahlia. "I have already sent word to my father about the men who threatened me last night. You will identify yourselves, and then you will leave these people. I wish to know the names of the men my father will execute first. In fact, I believe I would enjoy watching."

The man hesitates.

Rhen seizes the moment. "Princess Harper," he says to me. "These men are clearly following orders. No harm has been done here today. Surely there must be a misunderstanding. Allow them time to return to their general before beginning an international incident."

The man's eyes narrow.

Rhen leans closer to me. "Have mercy, my lady. I know your soldiers are said to enjoy tearing men limb from limb, but—"

"Goodness," Evalyn gasps. "The Secret Service sounds positively *vicious*."

The man meets my eyes. He's not an idiot. "I don't believe you. We will burn this inn to the *ground*, girl."

I hold his gaze and refuse to look away. "Commander Grey. Prove how serious I am."

Grey's hand flicks out. The man shouts and drops to the ground. The hilt of a knife protrudes from his knee.

Whoa. I have no idea what I expected him to do, but that's even better.

The man is screaming hoarsely. Blood seeps around the dagger, slowly staining his pant leg. His men shuffle and look confused, glancing from their leader to me, and then to Grey. None have drawn a weapon.

There's a sword in Grey's hand now. "Shall I remove his leg for you, my lady?"

"Yes," I say. "A trophy for my father."

Grey steps forward without hesitation. I suck in a breath. I think he might actually do it.

"No!" the man yells. "No!" He glares back at his men. "Help me, curse you! Get me out of here!"

They hustle to drag him out. "The queen will hear of this!" he yells. "Mark my words, our queen will—"

Coale slams the door on him.

Then he turns to me. His normally ruddy face has gone pale. "My lady. Again, you have our thanks."

"Yes." Evalyn comes around the table and goes to her knees. She grasps my hand and kisses it. "Your kindness knows no bounds."

It's all I can do to keep from jerking away from her. "No. Please." Now that the men are gone, my adrenaline is catching up, and my heart beats a rapid pace in my chest. "It's nothing—"

"It's not nothing." When Evalyn looks up at me, tears have formed in her eyes. "The inn is all we have."

Freya joins her. She takes my other hand and kisses it. "Again, you protected the children. I would offer my service, my lady, as a lady-in-waiting, or a servant, or—"

"No! No. No, thank you." I don't know what to do with this. They're being genuine—after I made it all up—the kingdom, the armies. I have nothing to offer them in reality.

Desperate, I look to Rhen for help.

He's watching me with a kind of bemused wonder. "My lady.

He gives me a bow. "I, too, offer you my gratitude."

I am going to punch him. *Stop it*, I mouth. *Help me.*

He looks across to Coale. "Innkeeper," he says. "The princess has endured much travel over the last two days. I believe she may need a space to rest. Could I trouble you for a room for a short while?"

"Yes!" says Evalyn, leaping to her feet without even waiting for her husband's response. "Yes. My lady, allow me to prepare a room immediately."

"I will prepare a plate for your room," says Coale. He hesitates. "Your Highness . . . will you be joining the princess?"

I open my mouth to say no, but Rhen is quicker.

"Yes." He smiles. "Princess Harper and I have much to discuss."

CHAPTER EIGHTEEN

RHEN

Fate is surely playing a trick on me. Fury and fascination wage war in my thoughts.

Fury that armed men are terrorizing my people.

Fascination that this reckless, maddening girl stood up to them.

We're back in the room I used last night. A fire has been freshly laid in the hearth, and Coale left a platter of food beside a pitcher on the dresser.

Harper's face is a shade paler than usual, her eyes a little wide. "That—that was—" She lets out a long breath and drops onto the side of the bed. Her palms press together in front of her mouth. "I can't believe that worked."

Nor can I. Everything she does is so unexpected. Even now, after boldly facing those men, she surprises me by looking like a loud noise would send her bolting from this room.

"If I knew no better," I say, "I would have believed you myself." I give her a sideways glance. "*Are* you born of royalty? In your world?"

"No." She gives a short, humorless laugh. "Definitely not." Her eyes lift to settle on me, almost as if she's just realized I'm here. Her eyes narrow. "I'm still mad at you."

"Truly?" I fold my arms and lean back against the door. "Then let us resolve that."

She stands, her expression fierce. "You told Grey to cut off my arm—"

"I did not."

"—after telling me that bringing someone food was going to start an international incident—"

"My lady."

"—and *then* you rode off without telling us where you were going—"

I sigh. "Are you quite done?"

"No! And when you got here, you sat by the fire and wouldn't even speak to me until some armed men came barging in—"

"Which you stopped."

"Which I almost *screwed up* because I don't know what a stupid *regiment* is." Her cheeks are flushed, her breathing rapid. She pushes a stray lock of hair out of her face, but it falls right back. "Is a thousand soldiers not a lot?"

"In an army? No." I pause, fixated on the one part of her tirade that's taken root in my head.

You sat by the fire and wouldn't even speak to me.

For that to matter, she would have to care, at least a small amount.

She's still glaring up at me. "Is your name really Vincent Aldrhen or was that made up, too?"

"Such questions you ask." I would be insulted if she weren't so candid. "Why would *I* have need to invent a name? I truly am the Crown Prince of Emberfall."

"Then who are those men? What's a Karis Luran?"

"Karis Luran is not a *what.* She is the Queen of Syhl Shallow." My shoulders are tight. This day has been long and exhausting already and seems to have no end.

"Okay, what's Syhl Shallow?"

"It's a country far northwest of here. On the other side of a mountain range." The mountains should be impassable at this time of year. My father never had a quarrel with Karis Luran—but then, he was alive to prevent such a thing. Harper made a good show of presenting the King of Disi as a bloodthirsty tyrant, but Karis Luran truly has to be. Her country is landlocked, with brutal winters and dangerous game animals. It's no wonder her men destroyed Freya's house and threatened her children. They would have done the same here if Harper hadn't tricked them.

"What do they want here?" says Harper.

I frown. "I have no idea."

She gives me a cynical look. "You have *no idea* why some queen could be sending soldiers here?"

My jaw tightens. "Do you not understand that my entire staff, my entire armed force, consists solely of Commander Grey? I have no advisers. No couriers. I once had soldiers stationed at the border cities, but I have no way of knowing if they still stand. The mountains should provide a natural barrier to the west, and open sea to the east, but . . . given a strong enough force, there very well *could be* dozens of regiments behind those men who came here."

That seems to shock her into silence.

Frustration has built a camp in my chest. I've spent over three hundred seasons trying to save my people from a merciless creature, and it's left me with no way to save them from outsiders.

Perhaps this is the reason for Lilith declaring this season to be my final chance. Perhaps she knows. My country will fall to enemy forces.

Perhaps this is the true curse. She is not destroying me. She is destroying Emberfall.

"So what are you going to do about it?" Harper says.

I raise my eyebrows. "Unless you truly *are* the Princess of Disi and your father *does* have thousands of soldiers standing ready, I am unsure I can do anything at all."

"But you might have soldiers guarding your border cities? Is that the same as an army? Could you—"

"It is not the same as an army." There's hope in her voice, and that's almost as surprising as everything else. I hate to destroy it—but that's clearly all I have talent for. "There may be soldiers standing guard, but with no way to swiftly communicate with them, I have no way of knowing if those guard posts still stand."

"But—but can't you pay people to take messages—"

"Surely you must realize that I cannot simply put a person on a horse with a sensitive message about military movements. Especially not now."

She chews at the side of her lip. "What happens if Karis Luran takes over?"

"I do not know. My lands have not faced the threat of a hostile takeover since my great-grandfather's reign—and he defeated the invaders and expanded Emberfall's territory."

"Well, aren't you technically the king now? Can't you do *something*?"

I look away. All my love for strategy is proving fruitless now. "I have nothing, my lady. Nothing I can offer." I pause. "While we were able to chase those men off this time, that will not prevent them from coming back. I worry what will happen when they do."

She swallows. "I know. I thought about that." Her hands press to her cheeks again. "Oh, these poor people."

Her tone of voice cuts straight to the core of me. She knows nothing of my subjects. Nothing. By all rights, she should hate me and everything I represent.

Then she says, "Can we stay?"

The words shock me into stillness and I find myself picking them apart in my head. Can *we* stay. Can *we*.

We.

I shift away from the door and give her a narrow look. "You wish to stay here? In the inn?"

She nods. "Just for tonight?"

At this very moment, I would deny her nothing. "Of course."

Relief lights her eyes, but it's short-lived and she grimaces. "I know it's stupid. Like with the food. We can't stay here forever. Just because they're not burning *this* inn doesn't mean they're not burning an inn a mile down the road—"

"My lady."

She must hear the gravity in my tone, because she blinks in surprise. "What?"

I step closer, until I'm right in front of her. "For now, we can help some. Not all, but some."

She inhales sharply as I feed her words back to her. "Rhen . . ."

Her voice trails off, and I find myself wishing that she truly was a warrior princess from a distant land. I believe she would make a formidable ally. She faced those men without fear. She faces *me* without fear.

I reach to tuck that errant lock of hair behind her ear. "I did not intend to upset you earlier."

When my fingers brush her temple, her breath catches, just the tiniest bit, but she doesn't pull away. "Which time?"

That makes me smile. "When we did not speak. By the fire."

"Not the time you told Grey to kill me?"

"I told Grey no such thing." Her hair slips loose again, and this time, when I reach to push it back into place, I let my hand linger. Her lips part as my fingers brush the rounded shell of her ear.

But then her hand flies up to catch my wrist. She's suddenly breathless and angry. "I know what you're doing. You've had three hundred women to practice this on. Stop."

The words hit me like a dozen arrows, piercing flesh and hitting every nerve. I jerk free and turn away. My fists are tight at my sides and my voice is full of ice. "As you say, my lady."

"You're not going to trick me into falling for you."

I glare at her. "You have made that quite clear."

"I don't trust you, Rhen."

Each word brings another bolt of pain with a chaser of resignation. "You have made that quite clear, as well."

She throws the door open. "Well, you don't trust me, either, so I guess that makes us even. Don't do that again."

With that, she storms out.

I sigh and sit on the edge of the bed, then run my hands through my hair. I should have let Karis Luran's men run me through. That would have been less torturous.

I touched her without thinking. So very careless. She was

right—I have had over three hundred women to practice on. I should have known better.

But for one brief moment, I forgot the curse. I forgot that she is not some simple girl who sparks intrigue with every other word from her tongue.

And for one brief moment, I *remembered.* I remembered what it was like to *want* to touch a girl, not as part of a carefully planned seduction designed to lure her into breaking this curse.

Silver hell. This is terrible.

Grey appears in the doorway. "My lord?"

"What."

He's quiet for a brief moment. "May I be of service?"

Yes. He can end this torment.

The thought feels immeasurably selfish now. He can kill me, but that will do nothing to spare my subjects from an invading force. My death ends my suffering. It does nothing for him or for my people.

In truth, my survival does nothing either. The creature will destroy them all just as easily.

I look up. "Lady—*Princess* Harper has asked to stay here tonight. Will you inform the innkeeper?"

"I will." He doesn't move from the doorway.

I study him, wishing again that Harper did have a battalion of soldiers at her beck and call. At the very least, wishing I had a fully staffed castle guard, to give the impression of defense. Something. Anything.

I have nothing. I have Grey.

"Why do you stay?" I ask him.

"My lord?"

"Why did you not run with the others, the first time?"

He needs no further clarification than that. "I swore an oath. When I did so, I meant it."

I give him a wan smile. "I am certain the others meant it, too, Grey."

"I cannot speak for them." He pauses. "Perhaps I meant it more."

Perhaps they meant it less.

"Do you regret your oath?" I say.

"I do not."

His answer is quick, a practiced response. I won't let him out of it that easily. "Have you ever?"

"No."

"This is our final season, Commander. You must know you can speak freely without much consequence."

He hesitates, which is rare for him. When he speaks, I realize the pause is not for the reason I would expect. His voice is quiet. "I do speak freely, my lord."

His loyalty should inspire me. It does not. I have done nothing to earn it.

I find that *I* regret his oath.

"Leave me," I say.

The door whispers shut. Grey has always been good at following orders.

And for the first time, I wish he wasn't.

CHAPTER NINETEEN

HARPER

I hide in the stables.

At first, I tried to join Evalyn and Freya in the kitchen, hoping to lose myself in their chatter, but they were too busy fawning over me.

"Your father's power must be immeasurable, my lady. Tell us of life in your court."

"Your beauty knows no bounds. It is no surprise you caught the prince's eye. Are curls a trademark of your people?"

"My lady, are the women of your lands known to be warriors? You spoke with such fierceness."

I had to get out of there.

The stables are small, offering six stalls, a low overhang, and a narrow aisle down the middle. The innkeeper—or Bastian—keeps it orderly, the stalls clean. Hay and sweat fill the air, underscored by the cold, wet scent of melting snow. I'd give anything to saddle up and ride out of here, but armed men will now be watching for "Princess Harper of Disi."

The buckskin blows warm air on my hands, looking for food, then lifts his head to nose at my face.

"I'll bring you an apple next time," I whisper. "I promise."

I have no idea what just happened with Rhen.

Maybe I was overwhelmed from chasing the men out of the inn. Maybe it was the bickering. Maybe he read that wrong. Maybe I did.

I know how quickly a skilled con artist can talk their way into your head and convince you their path is the best path. I saw it happen to my father. Jake and I were paying the price.

Well, right now, Jake is paying the price.

I pull the phone out of my pocket. The clock says it's three thirty in the afternoon in Washington, DC.

The battery meter is glowing red and I have no way to charge it.

Emotion swells in my chest, tightening my throat. I've barely looked at the pictures, but I guess leaving it on drains the power.

Once it dies, I won't have any connection to them left.

I sniff the tears back, and the buckskin pushes at my fingers again, running his velvet nose over the corner of my phone.

"I have learned that when you go missing, I should check the stables first, my lady."

I turn my head to find Grey at the end of the aisle.

I look back at the buckskin and slide the phone into my pocket. It's hard to chase thoughts of Jake out of my head, but standing in this stables, listening to snow dripping off the roof outside, leaves me with the bizarre, disorienting feeling that *here* is real, and *there* is not.

"I'm not good at pretending," I say quietly.

"Pretending?"

"Acting like someone I'm not."

He steps into the aisle and stops beside me. "I did not see much *pretending*, Princess Harper of Disi."

I blush. The horse lips at my fingers, and I pull them out of the way before lips turn to teeth. "When I said for you to prove how serious I was, I wasn't entirely sure you'd do anything."

"You give orders well."

"I'm surprised you listened." He glances at me, so I add, "To me, I mean. Instead of Rhen."

He says nothing to that. Instead, he says, "You are the first girl I've claimed from the other side who has such familiarity with horses. Why?"

"I used to ride a lot. When I was young. Mom took me—" My voice wavers at the mention of my mother. "At first it was just therapy, after I had surgery to fix my leg. But as I got older, it became a passion." I pause and stroke my hand along the buckskin's cheek. "I hadn't realized how much I missed it until . . . until I came here."

"Yet no weaponry?"

That startles a laugh out of me. "Those don't really go hand in hand where I come from." I pause. "How did you learn to throw a knife like that?"

"Practice and repetition."

"Was your father a guard, too?"

"No. My father was a farmer." He hesitates. "My mother had been a lady's maid in the castle, and my uncle was a soldier with the King's Army. When I was a child, my uncle would show me what he knew. I was a quick study. It became a fun pastime."

"So you grew up wanting to be a soldier?"

He shakes his head. "I grew up intending to inherit farmland." A pause. "When I was young, my father was badly injured. He became caught in a thresher, then dragged by the horse. He could no longer work. He could no longer *walk*. I had nine brothers and sisters—"

"Nine!" No wonder he's good with children.

Grey nods. The horse butts at his hands and he gives the animal a soft word and strokes his muzzle. "I helped as best I could, but I was a boy trying to do a man's work. Over time, much of our land was sold. Much of our livestock. Our crops suffered. *We* suffered. Every year, the castle would accept ten new guards. As you heard, it is a significant mark of favor for the family. I would have to forswear any connection to them, but I knew it would end their misery. When I came of age, I applied."

I study him, charmed by his story. My eyes flick over his broad shoulders, the sheathed weapons, the armor he has not yet removed. I try to imagine him in denim and flannel, throwing hay bales into a wagon.

I completely and wholeheartedly fail.

I lean against the stall door. "So underneath Scary Grey there's a big softy who's good with kids and animals?"

His eyebrows lift just a hair. "Scary Grey?"

"Oh, please. You know you're scary." The buckskin presses his face against my chest, so I gently wrap my arms around his muzzle. "So you joined the castle guard and got stuck with Rhen."

That earns me a rueful look, and it takes me a second to figure out why.

I sigh. "Fine. You joined the castle guard and you earned the monumental privilege of guarding Rhen."

"The Royal Guard. And not at first. Guarding the royal family truly was an earned privilege. I spent many months in training." His voice turns dry. "And then many months guarding closed doors."

"Not much use for knife throwing then, huh?"

He gives the barest hint of a dark smile. "As I have mentioned, I would rather be useful."

"Can you show me? How to throw like that?"

His smile vanishes. A line appears between his eyebrows. "My lady?"

I glance at the inn. "I don't want to go inside. I don't want to talk to Rhen. I don't want to leave. I just—" I make a frustrated noise. "I would rather do something useful, too."

He says nothing. His eyes are dark and inscrutable.

I stare back at him and realization dawns. Something inside me shrivels a little bit. I think of how Jake would tell me to hide in the alley, always with a warning of how vulnerable I am. Grey has never treated me that way, and I don't like the idea of him starting. "Do you think I can't do it?"

"I have no doubt you can do it. I think His Highness will not like it."

"Oh! Well then, *posthaste* or whatever you'd say here."

He doesn't move.

If I have to stand in these stables worrying about my mother and brother—to say nothing of the people in this inn—I'm going to rattle myself apart.

"Please?" I clasp my hands in front of me, the way I used to do when I wanted Jake to walk me down the street for ice cream. "Pretty please, Scary Grey?" I tease.

He sighs and lifts his eyes skyward—which is what Jake used to do, too, and how I know I've won.

"As you wish," he says.

In my head, I expected to feel fierce and lethal.

In reality, I can barely get a knife to stick in the ground.

More than half my throws result in the knife bouncing away or skidding into the slush. The rest barely stick, and then tip over. I feel like an idiot.

I wish I could blame it on the frozen ground. But when Grey demonstrated, his blades drove right through the melting snow and into the softening turf below.

Sweat has set up camp between my shoulder blades, and I'm ready to lose the cloak despite the chill in the air. My right arm aches all the way to my shoulder. The blades are heavier than they looked. We've only been at this for twenty minutes, but I wasn't ready for the physical exertion.

I look over at Grey. "Are you sure I shouldn't be throwing at a plank of wood or something?"

He leans against the side of the stables, off to my left. "Would you prefer to watch the knives bounce from something else, my lady?"

Ha-ha. I scowl and flex my wrist, rubbing the muscles and tendons. "I had no idea this would be so hard."

"Once you can stick a knife in the ground, you can stick it in a target." He nods at the remaining knife in my hand. "Try again."

My fingers slide along the curved etching in the hilt, which is inlaid with silver, stamped with the same lion-and-rose crest that decorates everything else. For all their lethal power, the weapons are beautiful, with marks of true craftsmanship. So different from my life in DC, where everything seems disposable. Even the people.

"You know what really sucks about this curse? Whoever put it in place screwed a lot of people who did nothing wrong." I put my thumb against the blade and push just hard enough to feel the bite without the sting. "I didn't spend the night with the wrong woman."

"Nor did I."

That makes me stop and look at him. "How *did* you get caught up in this?"

I actually don't expect him to answer, but he says, "I did my best to defend him. I failed." A pause. "So perhaps you should not count me among those who did nothing wrong."

"Why do you defend him if he got you trapped by the curse?"

"I swore my life to defend the crown. To be a part of something bigger than myself."

I wait for him to say something else, but when he doesn't, I realize it really is that simple for him. "You have a lot more faith in him than I do."

"I have faith in you, too, my lady. Put the blade in the ground."

I grit my teeth and draw back my arm, thinking through everything he told me about grip and release and timing—and snap my arm forward to let the knife fly.

It skids in the mud and flips over.

I sigh.

I move forward to fetch the knives from the ground, but Grey beats me to it. He wipes them on a rag we claimed from Evalyn. "Loosen your grip. Just let the knife go, and it will finish the movement for you."

"Will you show me again?"

He nods. His knife drives straight into the ground. Effortless.

Then he turns and hands me the other two.

I take one. My fingers wrap around the hilt, and I draw back my arm.

Grey catches my wrist. "Relax. Your hand is the guide. The blade is the weapon. Do you understand?"

"Maybe?"

He moves behind me, putting his hand over mine, shifting my fingers to match his. His left hand closes on my shoulder, holding me in place. "Soften your grip," he says.

I swallow. He's not against my back, but he's close enough that a few deep breaths would brush me against him. The entire length of my arm rests against his, from the buckled leather encircling his forearm to the hard muscle of his bicep.

"Softer," he says.

I force my fingers to loosen until I'm worried I'm going to drop it.

"Yes," he says. "Now breathe."

I take a deep breath. My back brushes his armor.

He lets go. Steps back. "Throw."

I throw. My arm feels faster somehow. The blade goes *flying.*

Then it drives straight into the ground with an audible *thock.*

I throw my arms up in victory and ignore the fact that my knife landed at least ten feet closer than the knife Grey used to demonstrate. "I did it!"

He holds out the other blade. "Do it again." But he looks pleased.

I take the next one and try to re-create the same grip. "This is so weird. Yesterday I wanted to kill you."

"Indeed. That gives me hope."

"Why?"

"If you have come to trust me, that means you may come to trust him."

I think of Rhen's fingers brushing along my temple. Heat begins to crawl up my neck, against my will. "I don't think so."

"Would you not have said the same of me?"

Okay, so maybe he has a point.

I draw my hand back again. This throw bounces off the ground, and I sigh. "I hope I don't ever have to defend myself this way."

He reclaims the weapons and wipes them clean again. "If you need to defend *yourself*, do not throw your weapons away. Never arm your opponent."

"What would you have done if you'd missed that guy's leg?"

Grey gives me a look, then takes a knife, flips it in his hand, and throws hard. The other two follow in rapid succession. All three drive into the ground, each landing an inch apart. *Thock. Thock. Thock.*

Whoa. I turn wide eyes back to him. "Now I'm wondering why you didn't impale all of them, Scary Grey."

He grins, probably the first real smile I've seen from him. The expression steals any tension from his eyes. "Someone had to drag him out, my lady."

This reminds me of yesterday morning in Arabella's room, when he showed me how to hold the dagger properly. I wonder if this is what he was like before the curse. More lighthearted. Less burdened.

As soon as I have the thought, I wonder what Rhen was like before the curse.

Grey fetches the knives and wipes them clean.

"Is this how you won your spot?" I ask. "Knife throwing?"

"No one skill would win a man a spot in the Royal Guard. Weapons can be learned. Technique can be perfected. To serve the royal family, one must be willing to lay down his life—or her life—in favor of another. That is what must be proven."

"Do you think it's worth it?"

His eyebrows go up. "Worth it?"

"Guarding Rhen. I know you swore an oath. Do you think he's worth the sacrifice?"

He hesitates. The easy smile is gone. He holds out the knives to me. "Time will tell."

CHAPTER TWENTY

RHEN

I stand at the window, just inside the sheer curtain, and watch. My cloak and armor sit abandoned on the table by the door, and the cool breeze bites at my skin. I ignore it. I enjoy it, in fact. After so many seasons of temperate warmth, cold air remains a novelty.

The open window allows me to listen.

I cannot hear every word. But I can hear enough.

Guarding Rhen. Do you think he's worth the sacrifice?

Time will tell.

"Prince Rhen." Lilith's voice, light and almost mocking, speaks from beside me. "What is happening outside that holds you so rapt?"

I should not be surprised that she would follow me here, that she would choose this very moment, when my chance at success seems most bleak.

I have little patience for her. As I said to Grey, this is our final season, and that invites boldness.

Then again, speaking freely to Lilith will likely carry far more consequence than Grey speaking freely to me. I wish I had not removed my armor.

I do not move from the window. "See for yourself."

She shifts to stand beside me. She smells elegant, something exotic and alluring. A scent meant to draw attention. I fell for it once.

She presses her hands together. "A lesson in weaponry. How charming of Grey to patronize her."

My jaw is tight. She doesn't need to taunt me. My own thoughts are doing it quite thoroughly. I wonder if Grey offered to teach Harper how to throw—or if she asked.

My guard commander's words from early this morning haunt me now. *My lord, I did nothing. I sat down and asked.*

I want to slam the window closed.

"Oh, look!" Lilith claps her hands, delighted. "Your girl is getting better. Commander Grey must be an excellent teacher."

This has not escaped my notice. Harper seems to have discovered the *feel* for it, because now she lands more than she misses. Grey seems pleased. Harper seems pleased.

I am not pleased.

"Oh! I have had the most wonderful idea, Your Highness." Lilith feigns a gasp. "If you are unable to earn her love, perhaps you could find her a position in the Royal Guard. She lacks experience, but Commander Grey seems capable of educating her." Lilith puts a finger to her mouth. "But I have forgotten. By the end of this season, there may no longer *be* a Royal Guard. Ah. Troubling."

"Do you have some purpose here, Lady Lilith?"

"I am intrigued that you would waste your final season in this little inn, when you have an entire palace at your disposal."

I have an entire palace where I am forced to listen to the same music over and over again, to watch the same shadows crawl along the wall, to smell and taste the same foods.

The inn may be small and simple, but right now I much prefer it to Ironrose.

Lilith runs a finger along the windowsill. No dirt clings to her finger. "I must say the innkeeper does a marvelous job keeping the lodgings clean."

"I will pass on your comments, my lady."

"You are in such a sour mood." She gives a disappointed sigh. "It is no wonder she seeks companionship with your guardsman."

"It is no wonder," I agree.

Lilith says nothing to that, and we stand in silence for a while.

Harper truly has improved. She lands three in a row.

"Your Highness," Lilith says quietly, leaning toward me, her voice conspiratorial. "What do you intend to do about the terrible rumors of an invasion from the north?"

My shoulders tense. "You know how rumors can be. It's so difficult to separate them from fact."

"True, true." She sighs. "Though I do believe it to be a fact that your soldiers stationed at the mountain pass were eviscerated months ago. It was really quite brutal to watch, especially in the summertime. You know what heat does to a dead body—though I must say the soldiers from Syhl Shallow loathe wasting meat of any kind, and made quick work of—"

I round on her. "Are you behind this?"

"Me?" She laughs. "No. Why would I need to be? When soldiers fall, their king should send reinforcements. When their king does not, who can blame a rival force for exploiting such weakness?"

The true tragedy here is that she's right. I suppose I should count myself lucky that we are not under attack from all sides.

Then again, perhaps we are.

"Do you truly hate me so much?" I ask her. "That you find entertainment in the destruction of my kingdom?"

She looks up at me and any mockery slides off her face. "Prince Rhen. Is that what you think?" She reaches up and puts her hand against my face. "I wanted you to love *me*. We could have made a formidable pair."

My people once feared the actions my father would take against them. I cannot imagine submitting them to the frivolous violence Lilith seems to enjoy.

"Surely you would be happier with one of your own kind." I sigh wistfully. "A pity they're all dead."

She snatches her hand away. "You seek to wound me."

If only I could. My voice is flat. "Forgive me."

"Your words are worthless, anyway. I am not the only one of my kind left."

I swing my head around to look at her.

She laughs. "Do you think you could find them? That they would somehow free you from my curse?"

Before that thought can take root in my mind, she sighs. "I have failed to locate them, so you would have no chance." She flexes her hand in the air before her. "But I can feel the web of magic. It does not end with me."

Somewhere in Emberfall, another magesmith may lie in wait for his or her own chance at revenge on my family. They'll have to get in line—if there's anything left of me.

"You disappoint me," Lilith says. "I never thought you would let this curse drag on as long as you have."

I cannot argue. I disappoint myself.

"I cannot wait to see how your monster manifests this season," she says. "Perhaps I will keep you on a chain and put you on display for my enemies."

A sudden chill grips my spine. This is an outcome I have never considered.

"Would you like that?" she says, moving closer again. "Mine for all eternity, Prince Rhen?"

"No," I say. "I would not." I have very little sense of myself once the change overtakes me, but the thought of being at her mercy even then is nearly enough to crush me.

She sighs. "You were such fun once. Honestly, visiting you feels like quite the chore lately."

"I would not be offended if you stopped."

She laughs lightly. The sound is like glass shards being ground underfoot. "Until later, Your Highness." She gives me a low curtsy and disappears.

I scowl and turn back to the window. Harper is landing every throw now. Grey is a good teacher.

That gives me an idea.

My boots crunch through the slush as I cross the inn's courtyard toward the stable, Lilith's taunts echoing in my head.

Grey notices me first and straightens. His expression gives away nothing—but then it never does. "My lord."

I glance at him. "Commander."

Harper turns, two knives remaining in her hand. Her eyes cut right into me. "I think I'm ready for a target, Grey."

Clearly, she is still in a pique.

My temperament right now makes for a good match. "Do you believe I'd have cause to worry, my lady?"

Her expression darkens. "Hold still. Let's see." Then she draws back a hand.

Grey catches her wrist. He looks annoyed.

Her eyes are locked on mine. The anger there is unmistakable, but it's laced with hurt, which is much more telling.

"Let her go." I hold her gaze. "She will not throw a knife at me."

Grey does. Harper lowers her arm.

I know when to call a bluff.

She frowns and slides the knife hilts together in her hand. "Did you just come out here to insult me?"

"No," I say.

"Oh, so you're going to order Grey to do something inane so he stops talking to me. Got it."

Well, I am most certainly not going to do that *now*. I consider Grey's comments about the card game and wonder if I have been looking at this moment the wrong way. "No, my lady. May I join you?"

She falters, surprised. She recovers quickly, though, and extends the two knives in her hand. Some of the anger and hurt has leaked out of her demeanor. "Sure. Here."

Now I'm surprised. And pleased.

But then she says, "My arm feels like it's going to fall off. I'm going back inside. Is it okay if I take the room for a little bit?"

There's a part of me that wants to demand that she stay. That part of me feels small and jealous and I do not like it.

I have to make myself nod. "Certainly."

She turns to my guard commander and gives him a smile. "Thanks for the lesson, Scary Grey."

He says nothing. Grey's no fool.

Then, without a backward glance, she turns and walks to the inn, her left foot shuffling through the slush.

Every word I want to say feels petty.

The silence fills with expectant tension. I remember this tension from before, when my guardsmen anticipated a rebuke—or worse.

I consider the way my nurse once spoke about my father, and I wonder what my guards once said about me.

It would not have been good. I know that much.

"Commander," I say.

"My lord." His voice gives away nothing, but he expects an order to do something grueling or torturous. I can tell.

"Considering what we've seen, if you had to assemble a contingent of guards, how many would you need?" I hold out the throwing knives Harper handed to me.

He frowns as he slides them into the sheaths on his bracers, as if trying to map the direction of this question. "For what purpose?"

"For me to be able to walk among the people. To make my presence known." I pause. "Harper's presence as well."

He says nothing. He expects a trap.

"Do you have a number or not?" I say.

"I do. Forty-eight."

"Forty-eight!"

"Your personal guard was once half that, not including castle guards." His tone borders between frustrated and curious. "One must allow time for training, and drills, as well as alternating schedules to ensure vigilance—"

"Fine." I raise a hand. "Could you find and train forty-eight new guards before the change overtakes me?"

"Presuming . . . what? Six weeks? Seven? If we had an army and

I could choose from among skilled warriors—maybe. As things stand now? Unlikely." He pauses. "Why?"

"How many do you think you *could* find and train?"

"If you wish to order me to stay away from the Lady Harper, you need not create diversions—"

"That's not what I'm doing. How many?"

"I have no idea." His expression turns incredulous. "I have been confined to the castle with you. I have no sense of the state of the people aside from the few we've encountered." He raises a hand to point at the inn. "Do you wish me to enlist children? Perhaps the infant will display a talent for swordplay."

I level him with a look. "Watch your tone, Commander. I seek your counsel, not your contempt."

"If you seek my counsel, then I need to understand what you hope to accomplish."

"Those men assumed I was dead. The people think the royal family has abandoned them. I want to be able to walk among my people and show them I still live, that this is still my kingdom."

"But—for what purpose? Your obligation is to Harper—"

"No. My obligation is to the people of Emberfall." I take a step forward. "And your obligation is to *me*."

He does not back down. "As always."

The wind whistles between us, and I bite back a shiver. "Could you do it or not?"

"Even if I could find individuals willing to serve—which is doubtful, given what we've learned—and even if we cut that number by *half*, there is no way they could be effective at providing any kind of unified defense in a matter of weeks."

He's right. Of course he's right. "What if we do not concern ourselves with defense?"

He frowns. "Forgive me, but—"

"What if we fake it?"

Grey looks as though I've completely lost my mind. He might not be too far off the mark. "So—to be clear—you wish for me to recruit individuals to the Royal Guard, outfit them with weapons and uniforms, and . . . what? Allow them to accompany you into the masses with a bare modicum of training?"

"Yes! Exactly that."

His eyes narrow. "And this is not a diversion?"

"Do I have *need* to create a diversion, Commander?"

Grey does not look away. "No." He pauses. "You have a plan, then?"

I have the shadow of a plan. The barest glimmer of a plan. "Yes. Could you do it? Could you create the impression of a functioning guard?"

"I suppose." His words are cautious. "What happens if you are truly at risk?"

I imagine it, riding into the more populated cities, people crowding near. I haven't done such a thing in ages. The people of Emberfall are hungry and desperate. The very idea is akin to insanity. To suicide.

But what difference does it make? I have nothing left to lose.

"That's why I have you."

He looks taken aback.

I clap him on the shoulder before turning for the inn. "You did say you prefer to be useful, did you not?"

CHAPTER TWENTY-ONE

HARPER

Coale and Evalyn are bickering.

My hands and face are frozen after being out in the cold for most of the afternoon, but overhearing an argument about what to serve the royal guests convinces me to slip up the steps.

The room is freezing despite the snapping flames in the fireplace. When I move to check the window, it's closed, but down in the courtyard, Rhen and Grey are locked in tense conversation.

I think His Highness will not like it.

Well, that was patently obvious.

I sigh and draw the curtains closed, then move to drop on the side of the bed. I rub my hands against my thighs, trying to warm them. The bulky hand-stitching of the doeskin riding pants catches on my knuckles. I wonder how it's possible I've only been here a day and a half.

That moment in the stables, when *here* felt real and *home* felt like a dream, has grown stronger, like a bizarre kind of vertigo. Or maybe it's the reverse. Maybe all this still feels like a dream and I'm not panicking because I'm just waiting to wake up.

I pinch myself.

This isn't a dream.

I close my eyes and hug my arms to my body, thinking of my mother. When I was little, she would tell me that we all have a spark inside of us, and our sparks can find each other no matter where we are. It gave me a lot of comfort when I was young.

It's giving me a lot of comfort now. I never asked her what would happen to her spark if she dies.

When she dies.

I have to press a hand to my chest and hold my breath.

No, I need to breathe. I gulp for oxygen and try to sob without making any noise.

But then it passes. I can breathe. I can survive.

I don't know how long Mom can. A season is three months.

I pull the phone out of my pocket. The battery tells me there's six percent left. I go to the photo album again. Mom. Jake. Noah. Me. Repeat.

The phone flashes a warning: *5% power remaining*. It's meaningless, really. What does that mean? Five minutes? Ten? One?

My face itches and I swipe at my cheeks, surprised when my fingertips come away wet. I remember once reading an article about the psychology of crosswalks, how adding a countdown makes it less stressful for drivers because they know how long they have to wait at a light. There was something about *knowing* how long you have to suffer that was better than just *waiting*.

The article was right.

It makes me think of Rhen, too, the indeterminate length of this curse. It's some kind of miracle it hasn't broken him.

I keep swiping through pictures.

Four percent.

I swap over to Jake's text messages. Nothing has changed. They're all there. I read as far as the chat history will load for his messages with Noah and with Mom—but it's not far. The screen scrolls back about twelve hours, and then I get the spinning wheel. With Mom, I can imagine her voice. With Noah, I'm just curious, but the messages don't give much context. He mentions working a night shift, but that could be anything.

For the first time, I click on the messages from Lawrence.

LN: If he doesn't have it, take care of it

JAKE: I will

LN: No excuses

JAKE: I know

LN: You will, or we'll take it up with your sister

JAKE: I'll do it

My heart turns to ice. *I'll do it.*

I don't want to guess. I don't *need* to guess. I know what they've tried to get him to do.

"No, Jake," I whisper. My gentle brother.

The timer counted down. He wasn't out.

We'll take it up with your sister.

If he made it out, I wouldn't have been there. He would have been frantic trying to find me.

If he didn't make it out . . .

I press an arm against my abdomen, using my other hand to cover my face. I can't stop the tears now. My shoulders shake fiercely. I'm sobbing openly.

The phone vibrates. *Powering down.*

"No!" I scream. I jam my finger on the button. The screen dies anyway.

The bedroom door swings open. Grey stands in the doorway, his eyes seeking a threat. "My lady?"

I gasp and press the phone to my chest. My heart is beating so fast I almost can't breathe. My hands are shaking to where I can barely keep a grip on the phone.

I don't even know why. It's nothing now. A brick of glass and plastic and circuitry.

"My lady." Grey's voice is very quiet and right in front of me. He's dropped to one knee. "What has happened?"

"It died."

"Your device?" I can hear the confusion in his voice. "But they do not work—"

"I know." I sniff hard. "I know. But there were pictures. My mother—my brother—it's all I had."

I don't know if he understands. But he says, "Should I call for—"

"No." I almost choke on my tears. I can't stand the thought of facing Rhen's arrogant composure when I'm dissolving into despair. "Please."

He's quiet for a moment, during which my tears sound very loud. "You have a way to see your world?" he finally says.

"No. Maybe. Sort of." I drag a sleeve across my eyes. "Not

anymore. Just—just pictures. But it died. I don't know if they're okay. They don't know if I'm okay."

"Your brother. Your mother."

"My brother was in trouble. Before—before you took me. I was his lookout. And my mom is sick—she could be dead—"

Rhen appears in the doorway. I watch as he registers our relative positions.

Great. Like I need this right now. I glare up at him. "Go away. You're the cause of all of this."

Grey stands. Turns. "My lord. A word?"

"I would hope more than one."

Grey steps through the doorway, closing the door behind him.

I sit on the edge of the bed and listen to myself breathe. I set down the useless phone.

I count to ten. To twenty. By fifty, my brain starts working again.

By one hundred, I'm angry.

I glance at the strip of window visible between the curtains. The sky has gone from piercing blue to red-streaked clouds. Sunset.

I stand and walk to the door. I throw it wide.

Rhen and Grey stand in the hallway.

This time, Rhen's eyes are full of empathy. Manufactured, I'm sure. He straightens and comes to stand in front of me. "My lady—I did not—"

I draw back my hand and slap him as hard as I can.

He doesn't see it coming. It throws his head to the side.

I don't wait for a reaction. I duck back into the room and slam the door in his face.

And then I turn the lock.

CHAPTER TWENTY-TWO

RHEN

No woman has ever dared slap me across the face. My jaw stings like a burn that needs a salve.

I want to break down this door and challenge her, but I keep seeing her tear-streaked cheeks, the ragged emotion in her eyes.

Even now, if I listen closely, I can hear her crying on the other side of the door.

Her mother is dying. Her brother is in trouble.

I feel like such a fool.

The innkeeper appears at the base of the staircase. "Your Highness?" he says hesitantly. "Is all well?"

"Yes," I say, my words clipped. "Leave us." I do not look away from the door. They will gossip about whatever they heard, but I will not feed that mill with a reddened cheek.

The man offers a bow and moves away.

To my right, Grey stands motionless. I cannot look at him either. I have never felt so powerless.

I reach out and try the door handle, but she has locked it.

She must hear me try, because she shouts, "Go away!"

I have no idea how to solve this.

Grey unbuckles a pouch on his belt and withdraws his deck of cards. Without a word, he holds them out.

His intention is clear. "I'm more likely to get this door to play with me, Grey."

"You could ask."

I sigh, then reach out and take the deck. "Go." I nod toward the staircase. "Join them for dinner. See if you can learn anything new about Karis Luran."

He obeys, leaving me with the pressing quiet of the hallway.

Silence will solve nothing. I raise a hand and knock softly.

She does not respond.

I flatten my hand against the wood and move closer. Grey's presence downstairs will prevent eavesdroppers, but I keep my voice low anyway. "My lady."

Nothing.

"There is no trellis outside your window," I say. "Please tell me you are not climbing the chimney."

"Go away, Rhen."

She speaks from right on the other side of the door. My heart kicks to find her so close.

"I wish to speak with you," I say.

"You don't get something just because you want it. Most people learn that by the time they're six."

"Not most princes, clearly." I keep my voice light, hoping she will open the door.

She does not.

I sigh. Turn the cards over in my fingers. "I don't suppose you would like to play a game of King's Ransom?"

She's quiet for quite some time. When she finally speaks, her voice is low and sorrowful against the door. "Do you have any idea what you've done to me?" She sniffs, which makes me think she is crying again. "To my family?"

"No," I say. "I don't."

Silence again, but this has a weighted quality.

"My mother has cancer," she finally says. "She's dying. The doctors gave her six months to live, nine months ago. Her lungs are full of tumors. She says every day is a gift—but really, every day is torture. She can barely breathe. My brother and I are the only ones to take care of her."

Harper feels this torture. I can hear it in every syllable.

She sniffs again. "When we were younger, we did all right, but then she got sick, and we ran out of money. My dad got involved with some bad people who loaned him money, and I don't know how he ever thought we'd pay it back, but then he ran off, and my brother is—he's doing terrible things to try to repay—" Her voice breaks. "If I were there, I could help them. I could be with my mother. I could be with my brother. They need me. Can you understand that? That they need me? *Can you?*"

I press my forehead against the door. Her pain reaches me through the wood, tightening my own chest and dredging memories of my family. "Yes. I can."

"No!" Her voice is fierce, her rage pure. "You can't!"

"I can," I say softly.

"How?"

"Because *I* need you."

Silence again. It seems to stretch on forever. Until I think she has given up on me and moved away from the door.

I speak anyway. "When the curse began," I say, "I thought undoing it would be simple." I hesitate. A familiar shame has curled around my throat and gripped tight. "But then . . . the creature destroyed my family." I swallow. It's so much easier to think of my monster as something separate. Something I have a chance at stopping. "I'd been so cavalier—and it ripped them apart without thought. I had no chance—I can't—I can't bring them back. I can't undo any of it."

My breathing has gone shallow. I have no memory of their deaths—only the memory of their bodies, dismembered and scattered about the Great Hall. The way I found them when I returned to myself, an hour before the season reset. The way I found myself, covered in their blood.

And then the season began again, and it was gone. All of it. The castle returns to that first day, but aside from me and Grey, the dead stay dead.

I have long since locked away any emotion over my own destruction, but warmth collects in my throat, thickening my words. "By the end of the second season, the creature turned on my people. By the third . . . My lady, please—please know I meant you no harm. I meant your family no harm. I have tried everything I can think of to break this curse. I have tried to destroy myself. I would undo it if I could. I promise you."

Silence. Again.

I have nothing left to offer her. Nothing more than this truth.

The lock turns. The door swings open. We're face-to-face. Her cheeks are reddened and her eyes damp.

My own tears don't feel far off.

She studies me. "I never know when to trust you. Everything always sounds so calculated."

I jerk back, stung.

"Until you said all that."

And then, because fate seems content to surprise me this season, she steps forward, presses her face against my chest, and wraps her arms around my waist.

I'm so startled that I can't move. She could draw my weapons and stab me and I would be less shocked.

"I'm so sorry about your family," she says.

"I am sorry about yours, my lady." My voice sounds hollow, even to me. I stand frozen, unsure what to do with my arms.

She looks up at me. I'm not sure what she finds in my face, but she takes a step back.

Her expression is some mixture of amused and perplexed. "What's wrong with you? Hasn't anyone ever given you a hug?"

I feel so off balance. "Not—not in recent memory."

"I believe that, too." She glances down at my hand. "You really do have cards."

"I do."

She pushes loose hair behind her ear. "We can play. Come on."

We take seats by the fire. The cards flip between my fingers as I shuffle. I am glad for a task to occupy my hands. I have no idea how to move forward.

I deal quickly, then lay the remaining cards on the table, turning one faceup. I have two princes, which means I can steal her kings, but I never waste them early. Normally, I would watch her movements, trying to determine what cards she holds, but my mind is trapped in the moment when her arms were wrapped around my waist.

Silently, she lays a card on the pile. Beside us, the fire snaps.

I play a five of stones. She plays a five of swords.

We play in silence, drawing cards when necessary.

I fall into the rhythm of the game. Lilith made a comment about how this inn was lacking, but I like the intimacy of this room, the warmth of this fire. The familiarity of a game, the newness of my opponent. The castle was cold. Empty. This inn, this moment, is not.

Eventually, Harper draws and her eyebrows go up, just a little. She moves the card to the leftmost part of her hand and draws another, adding to the right side of her hand until she finds one to add to the pile.

I play a prince card.

Her eyes shoot to mine, but she pulls the leftmost card free and hands me her king of swords. "I literally just got that."

"I know."

She considers that, then lays down a ten of stones. Her tone is contemplative and quiet. "I don't think I can keep hating you."

"Such sweet words of affection, my lady." I play a ten of hearts. "You honor me."

Her expression turns ruefully amused—but she quickly sobers. "I kept thinking about all those women you kidnapped, how it made you seem like this arrogant, entitled jerk. I didn't realize you were only doing what you had to do."

I add a card to the pile. "My father once said we are all dealt a hand at birth. A good hand can ultimately lose—just as a poor hand can win—but we must all play the cards fate deals. The choices we face may not be the choices we want, but they are choices nonetheless."

She says nothing, simply adding another card to the pile herself.

"Grey has grown skilled at finding girls who have no family, no one to miss them." I pause and look at her. "Often there is no trickery to it—they come willingly, with little more than the promise of a safe place to sleep. You, I suspect, would not have been lured so easily."

Her eyes are hard. "No."

"Why *did* you attack him?"

"He had a girl. I thought he was some psycho murderer. I tried to stop him."

Of course she did. "So your choice led you here."

"Don't try to pin this on me."

"I am not. I am saying that no matter how much I try to plan a means to end this curse, fate keeps dealing new cards."

Her expression goes still. Again, we play in silence for the longest time.

I watch her draw another king. She's more savvy this time, but she's slower to add it to her hand.

I play my other prince.

"Stop it," she says.

I take the card she offers. "Stop being obvious."

She draws until she has a card to play. "I have a question for you, about all those other girls. Did you ever come close?"

I sigh. "Sometimes victory seemed very close—other times, miles away."

"May I make an observation?"

My hand goes still on my next card. "For certain."

She looks across at me. "You just said 'victory.' You didn't say 'love.' "

I'm not sure I have a response to that. My initial reaction is to ask why that matters.

My second reaction is to wonder why I ever thought it wouldn't.

Harper is not done. "Have *you* ever felt anything for any of these girls?"

I lay down a two of swords and try not to think about how badly I want to push the hair back from her face again. "I do not feel *nothing*." I pause. "But failure seems such a certainty that I have learned to guard myself from disappointment."

"Hmm." She plays another card and lapses into silence again. From the kitchen below us, I hear ringing laughter from the innkeeper.

It makes me wistful. I cannot remember the last time I sat at a crowded table, sharing stories and laughter.

Then Harper says, "Do you really have no way to contact this enchantress who cursed you?"

"No." I play a card. "And I would not even if I could."

"Not even to help me get home?"

I go still. I look at Harper. She does not know what she asks. "The Lady Lilith does nothing without cost. I have nothing to offer. Do you?"

Her mouth opens, and I add, "You have seen my chambers on the third floor. Regardless of what you think of me, I would ask you to consider carefully what you're asking."

She pales a little, but her voice is strong. "I will do whatever it takes to get home. If I have to face some sorceress, I'll do it."

That makes me smile, but it's grim. "Spoken like the Princess of Disi."

She blushes and looks back at the cards in her hand. But then she looks up at me. "I'm not kidding, Rhen. Do you have *any* way to contact her?"

"No." I pause, weighing how much to say. I imagine brazen Harper facing the capricious Lilith. Even if Lilith would return her to her home, any scenario I can fathom seems fraught with peril. "She shows herself from time to time, but her appearances are unpredictable."

"Would you ask her?" When I say nothing, Harper adds, "Or would you keep me prisoner?"

My jaw is tight. "You do not know what you are asking. She is vicious. Cruel."

"But she *will* show up."

"She will." I have no doubt.

"You could tell her I want to go home. You could tell her I want something from her."

"She has sworn not to interfere with my attempts to break the curse. She may refuse."

Harper swallows. "But . . . but those are your attempts." When she speaks, her voice isn't fully certain. "If you promise to get me a meeting with Lady Lilith, I can promise to try to break the curse for you."

I sigh. She bargains like she plays cards—her emotions are fully on display. "I do not hesitate because I desire something from you. I hesitate because I am loath to sacrifice another person to her power."

"I have nothing to offer, either, Rhen. But that also means I have nothing to lose."

"Nothing to lose? Your brother? Your mother?"

She looks away again. "There must be something you want."

Yes. There is much I want. But nothing so much that I would bargain for an audience with Lilith to get it. She is bad enough when she shows herself of her own accord.

I open my mouth to refuse but then I consider the Queen of Syhl Shallow. I consider my plan. I consider my conversation with Grey.

I look at Harper and play my next card. "As a matter of fact, there is."

CHAPTER TWENTY-THREE

HARPER

We've formed a truce. Sort of.

Even this conversation about the sorceress who cursed him doesn't feel like bargaining. There are no stakes, no veiled risk, not like when Dad tried to negotiate for more money or time. It's leaving me off balance because I was ready to fight with Rhen for what I want, and there's no fight in the man sitting across the table from me.

Then again, he just said there *is* something he wants.

I hold my cards close to my lap. "I told you I'd try to break the curse if you can make a meeting happen."

"An empty promise if your intent is to bargain for passage home." He shrugs and lays down a queen of swords. "And unnecessary. That's not what I want."

I raise an eyebrow. "Come on."

"Do not misunderstand. I would give anything to break the curse. But I do know that bargaining for love will end in disappointment."

"Fine." I add a queen of stones to the slowly growing stack. "Then what do you want?"

"I would like for you to be Princess Harper, first daughter to the King of Disi. I would like to spread word of Emberfall's alliance with your people, especially your father's promise to send an army to drive Karis Luran out of my lands."

Each word hits me like a bullet. I expect him to crack a smile and say, "Just kidding." But he delivers all that with the same gravity as everything else he says.

I stare at him. "You . . . what?"

"Do you truly need me to repeat it?"

"No—but—" Maybe I do. "What?"

"If I can convince my people—and Karis Luran—that Emberfall is not defenseless, that future conflicts may arise, I may be able to convince her army to leave." He gives a slight shrug. "We may have to negotiate for trade, or possibly yield access to our harbor, but from what I have seen, our closed borders have led to suffering, so that may not be a poor outcome."

I might need to remind him I'm not actually a princess. I barely understand what he's talking about. "But—"

"It is not a perfect plan, admittedly." He plays another card casually, like we're discussing the weather. "But if we were to visit the biggest cities and make a declaration of our engagement—"

"Whoa! Wait."

He offers a rueful smile. "Forgive me. A declaration of our *alliance*."

Like that one word is what tripped me up. "So you're saying you want to keep this going? I just—I made that up! To get those guys to leave the inn! I can't stop a whole army."

His eyes narrow, just a fraction. "Are you certain, my lady? You have surprised me before."

That makes me blush. "But there's no army on our side. What if they don't believe us?"

"Then we have lost nothing."

I feel like we've fallen into the Twilight Zone—and considering the last couple of days, that's saying something. "You want *me* to pretend to be a princess? I don't know anything about Emberfall—or royalty—or—"

"Such is your charm," he says. He must see my expression, because he adds, "Truly. My people have never heard of Disi. That means your customs, your mannerisms, your version of royalty—none of it is subject to question."

"They haven't heard of Disi because it *doesn't exist*," I hiss.

"My father always warned that it does not take an army to defeat an army. He spoke of insurrection within Emberfall—but the same can apply to the army of Syhl Shallow. If they believe they are outmanned, they may retreat to await further orders, rather than walk into a trap."

I can't stop staring at him. "Do you have any idea what you're saying right now?"

He hesitates, then sits back. "You are right." His tone is resigned. "This is foolhardy. I have gotten ahead of myself. And you have your own troubles. There is no reason to risk yourself for mine."

"No—I'm not—" I stop and rub my free hand over my face. This conversation has turned around too quickly. Piled on top of my worry about Jake, all this is a bit much to process.

"My lady," he says quietly.

Slowly, I lower my hand and look at him.

"This is not a bargain," he says. "You ask me for a meeting with an enchantress; I ask you to risk your life for my people. Neither option guarantees your safety—or even a path home. As always, I have nothing to offer you. I can promise to intercede with Lilith on your behalf, but that is not worth what I am asking of *you*."

His voice is so earnest. Like when he spoke in the hallway, these words feel like truth. Like we've moved past pretense, and I'm finally seeing the real Rhen. Maybe it's because he's stopped talking about being cursed by something—and he's started talking about *doing* something.

"This was my father's kingdom," he says. "This is now *my* kingdom. I may not be able to save myself—but I may be able to save my people."

I think about what he said earlier, how the choices we get may not be the choices we want—but they're still choices.

I have a choice here. I can say no to this. Climbing down the trellis was risky—but this is insane. There's no way it'll work. Pretending to be a princess for three minutes doesn't mean I can do it again.

But what are my options? To say no? What will that mean for the people downstairs? What will that mean for me?

My mother never backed down from the men who came to our door. She never left my father's side—not even when she should have. She did it for me. And for Jake. And for our father, too, in a way.

I swallow. "Okay." I pause. "I'll do it."

"My lady." He looks as shocked as he did when I hugged him. It's almost comical.

"I'll help you save your country and you'll help me get home. Deal?" I put out a hand.

He extends a hand, and I clasp it with mine. His palm is warm, his grip stronger than I'd expect.

"Deal." His hand holds mine like he doesn't want to go. If he keeps looking at me like this, I'm going to start blushing.

"It's time to let go," I say. My stupid voice is breathy.

He lets go and sits back. "Play your next card."

Yes. Good. The game. Right.

I have seven cards. He has six—two of which I know are kings. I have a king in my hand from when he originally dealt, but if I don't find another, he'll win.

I lay down a four of stones on the discard pile. "What do we do now?"

He plays a four of swords. "I think you should accept Freya's offer."

"Freya's—what?"

"She offered to serve as lady-in-waiting, did she not? I believe you should accept. I will have Commander Grey seal off the problematic rooms in the castle. I have spoken with him about re-creating the Royal Guard so we may travel among the people and make our presence known."

I was stuck on wondering what a lady-in-waiting even *does*, but his last comment throws me. "You've already talked to Grey about this?"

His eyes meet mine. "Of course."

Of course.

I play a ten of swords. "How did you know I'd say yes?"

"I did not." He tosses a ten of stones onto the pile.

I can't decide if he's infuriating or amazing. "But you just started making plans anyway?"

He looks at me like I'm deliberately being obtuse. "My lady, I began joining my father on matters of state when I was ten years old. I had my own advisers by the time I was sixteen. I may not be able to find a path out of this curse, but I *was* raised to rule this kingdom."

Something about that is fascinating—but also a little sad. When I was ten, Mom was throwing my blankets on the floor to wake me up for school.

Mom. My throat thickens and I have to clear it. I add a six of stones to the pile. "When I was ten, I could barely organize a bowl of cereal."

He adds a card to the pile. "Surely your courage and tenacity more than made up for it."

I frown at that. "I already said yes. You can save all the pretty words."

He draws back. "You believe me insincere? Do you think I would have asked this of just anyone?"

I study him, thrown. "I don't know."

"I assure you, I would not." He glances meaningfully at my cards.

He's so matter-of-fact that his voice leaves no room for argument. I quickly put a card down, then fidget with the ones I have remaining. "Do you . . . do you think the cerebral palsy will be an issue?"

"Do you believe it will be an issue, my lady?"

"Don't do that. Don't turn it back on me."

He plays another card. "While your weakness may be a disadvantage in some ways, it is an advantage in others. One I think you could use to your benefit."

That's a pretty frank assessment. I'm not sure I mind. "How?"

"It is easy to underestimate you." He pauses, his gaze never leaving mine. "I know I did. I believe Grey did, too."

I'm blushing again. I sift through my remaining cards and draw. "Why do you want Freya to be my lady-in-waiting?"

"Because I believe she will be loyal, and we will need people we can trust." He waits for me to lay down a card, then matches it with one of his own. He only has three cards left. "Silvermoon Harbor is the closest major city. They once had a winter marketplace that drew merchants from all over Emberfall. We will ask the innkeeper if the market still stands. If so, that should be our first outing."

"What does Grey think of all this?"

"He believes it is a plan fraught with unnecessary risk, but I have no better ideas." He gives a humorless laugh. "If Silvermoon Harbor is as densely populated as it once was, he will certainly have his work cut out for him."

Well, that's super reassuring. I stop deliberating and lay down a four of hearts. I have no idea what suit he's got in his hand, but no matter what I play, I figure I've got a seventy-five percent chance of forcing him to draw. "So what's our next move?"

"We go downstairs. We join them for dinner. We discuss Karis Luran and share a bit of our intent."

I wet my lips. "And what if Lady Lilith shows up tomorrow and agrees to take me home?"

"Then you return home, my lady." He pauses. "And I will say you were called back to Disi to make arrangements to lead your father's army."

He really does think of everything. "Do you seriously believe this will work?"

"In matters of the heart, I am clearly hopeless." He puts down his final card—a prince. A wild card.

I stare at him, stunned. It didn't matter what I played. He would have won anyway.

"In matters of strategy," he finishes, "I am not."

CHAPTER TWENTY-FOUR

RHEN

Darkness has fallen, and along with it, a hushed quiet has overtaken the inn. Freya has put her children to bed, and Evalyn is tidying the kitchen. Harper has curled into the chair by the hearth, a stein of tea balanced in her hands. Her eyes are tired, but there is a certain beauty to her expression. Maybe it's the way the firelight paints silver in her hair or makes her eyes gleam. Or maybe it's the fact that some of her exhaustion was earned on behalf of defending my people.

She finally trusts me—and just as clearly wants nothing to do with me.

"Grey's outside," she says quietly. "Did you order him out there?"

"No," I say. "He worries they may attempt to take the inn during the night. I trust his judgment."

She glances at the door and hunches down in the chair.

I study her. "Are you frightened?"

"A little."

"You should be more worried about Lady Lilith. Grey can do nothing to stop *her*."

"I haven't done anything to her. I don't have a part in this curse. I just want to go home."

I want to beg her to reconsider. She knows not what she asks, but she is too suspicious of my motives. I worry that warnings will sound like a trap to keep her here, and I much prefer this path of trust we've found.

"You must be worried, too," Harper says. "You brought your arrows down here."

My bow sits at my feet. "Not worried. Prepared. They will not be able to take Grey by surprise. He knows how to keep himself hidden."

She does not look reassured. "He's one man."

"Do not underestimate *him*, my lady."

"You didn't mention something in all your plotting."

My eyes narrow. "What is that?"

"The . . . the monster."

My eyes shy from hers. "My people have nothing to fear from the creature now. It will not reappear until later in the season."

Coale approaches from the kitchen. His voice is low. "Your Highness. Will you need anything else this evening?"

I begin to decline, then change my mind. "Innkeeper, I was wondering if the princess and I could bring you into our confidence."

Harper's eyes do not leave the fire, but I know she is listening. She's so perfect for this role.

The man looks stunned. "Yes, Your Highness. Anything."

"Your discretion would be required."

He puts a hand to his chest and he lowers his voice. "Of course."

I lean in a bit. "What you have heard is correct. The royal family has fled Emberfall."

The innkeeper's eyes grow round, and I continue, "Years ago, after the monster attacked the castle and destroyed most of the guardsmen, the King of Disi offered sanctuary, which we gratefully accepted. We are currently in the midst of negotiations so we can finally rid Emberfall of this terrible creature." I pause and glance around conspiratorially. "We believe the monster is under the control of Karis Luran. Rumor says she has the ability to wield a dark magic, something that prevented our guardsmen from defeating the creature."

Harper takes a sip from her mug. I watch her absorb every word.

"Goodness," says Coale. "We had no idea."

"In truth," I say, "I was unaware the Queen of Syhl Shallow had begun to advance her forces into Emberfall. When we learned that the monster had abandoned Ironrose to return to its home with Karis Luran, the princess and I came to assess whether the castle could support a neighboring force. We have decided to remain until Disi's army is ready to move. I am certain you see many travelers. Would you be willing to spread word that the castle will need to be restaffed? I have silver to pay."

Beneath his beard, the innkeeper has paled. "Yes, Your Highness." He pauses. "Please—I feel I should beg your pardon for my harsh words last night—"

"No need," I say. "I prefer honest discourse. I would ask that you always speak true."

"Yes. Yes, of course."

Wind whistles through the shutters. I wonder if it has begun to snow again. "Before you retire, another two mugs of tea, if you please."

He gives a short bow and moves away.

Harper is staring at me. "You're too good at this."

"We shall see. It is good for people to have a common enemy. It breeds unity—and we will need plenty of that."

"You might be scarier than Grey."

I nearly smile—but then consider that a time will come, and soon, when I truly will be more frightening than my guard commander. "You should rest. The room is yours if you want it. There will be much to accomplish tomorrow."

I expect her to refuse, but she grimaces and uncurls from the chair. "All this riding is beginning to catch up with me."

I stand. "Would you like assistance?"

She gives me a look. "I've got it." For a brief moment, she hesitates, and something like sadness flickers across her face. Before I can parcel it out, she says, "Good night, Rhen."

There are so many things I want to say to her. Earlier this evening, when I asked Freya to serve as her lady-in-waiting, the young woman nearly got to her knees to kiss Harper's hands again.

After what Harper has promised to do, I have the same urge.

I do not. I give her a nod. "Good night, my lady."

I sink back onto the warm stones of the hearth. Another whip of wind cracks against the shutters and I nearly jump.

When Coale returns with tea, he is surprised to find Harper gone. "Shall I take one up to the princess?" he says.

"No need," I say. "The second is for Commander Grey."

The night air slices into me when I step outside. Any temperate warmth from the afternoon has bled from the sky, leaving frozen snow underfoot and bitter wind to sneak under my cloak. I do not want to make a target of Grey or myself, so I carry no lantern. The darkness is absolute.

When I told Harper that Grey knows how to keep himself hidden, I meant it—and he is proving it now. I look out at the dark stretch of snow and I'm glad of the bow strapped to my back.

A shadow shifts at the corner of the inn. "My lord." He sounds surprised—or maybe concerned.

"All is well," I say. Grey stops in front of me, barely more than a shadow.

I hold out a stein. "Hot tea."

He hesitates, then reaches for the handle. Steam curls into the air between us. His eyes are dark and inscrutable and his expression is impossible to read.

"Drink it," I say. "You must be half-frozen. You've been out here for hours."

He takes a sip—and there's a part of me that wonders if he's doing it only because I ordered him to. "The cold is no hardship," he says, taking another, longer sip while looking out at the night.

I wrap my hands around my own stein. I had intended to discuss the night's events with him, but I find the cold, silent darkness somewhat intoxicating. Peaceful.

We stand quietly for the longest time, until he says, "May I be of service, my lord?"

"No." Overhead, the stars stretch on forever. When I was a child, my nurse told a story of how the dead become the stars in the sky. At the time, I found it frightening—I remember worrying that they would fall to earth one day, that we'd be surrounded by dead bodies.

Now I find it shameful to think that my father and mother could be looking down, watching my failure season after season.

"Was it always like this?" I ask.

"Like this?"

I glance at him. "Standing guard?"

He seems surprised by the question, but he takes no time to consider. "No. I was never alone. The nights were never this silent."

There's a note in his voice that it takes me a moment to identify. "You still miss them."

"I counted many as friends. I mourned their loss." He glances at me. "As you mourn your family."

Yes. As I mourn my family.

Grey and I never discuss the time before. It's laden with too many wrongs on both our parts. But maybe the knowledge that this is our final season has loosened something in him, the way it has changed something in me.

"Who would have stood guard with you?" I ask.

"Anyone," he says. "We changed frequently." A pause. "As you know."

In truth, I never really paid attention to the operations of the Royal Guard. They were good at being hidden in more than one way. Or maybe I was good at not noticing what was right in front of me. "Who would been the best?"

"Marko."

He says it without hesitation, which must mean Grey knew him well. I barely remember Marko. My brain conjures an image of a sandy-haired guardsman. He was one of the few who survived the first attack by the creature—but not the second. The only guardsman to survive the second attack is standing in front of me. "Why?"

Grey looks at the sky as if searching for an answer. "You could find no one better to fight at your back. Terrible at cards, but he always had a good story. Never fell asleep on duty—"

"Fell asleep on duty?" I stare at him, surprised. "Did that happen?"

He hesitates, and I can read in his silence that he's worried he's said too much, but he must realize it makes no difference. "Sometimes. That is why the cold is no hardship. Nothing calls for sleep like a warm night and a full stomach."

Fascinating. "Did *you* ever fall asleep on duty?"

Even if he did, I don't expect him to admit it, but I should know better. Grey is nothing if not honest. "Once," he says. "My first summer."

"Commander." My voice fills with mock admonishment. "I should have you flogged."

"The king would have," he says, and he's not teasing. "If I'd been caught." He pauses, then glances over at me. "But not you, I do not think."

With that one comment, my good nature sours. He is right on both counts. I frown at my mug and say nothing.

"I've angered you," he says. "Forgive me."

"No," I say. "You haven't." Or perhaps he has. I'm not sure. "I was cruel in other ways, Grey."

He says nothing, which makes me think he agrees. When he speaks again, his voice is contemplative. "You were never cruel."

"I made you ride a full day without food or water, then forced you to fight." Wind whips between us, beating at my cloak, as if the weather itself seeks to chastise me. "For sport. For my own pride. You could have died. For *entertainment.* That is cruelty."

He is quiet for a long moment, then frowns and looks at me. "Are you speaking of the Duke of Aronson's man-at-arms? When we fought at Liberty Falls?"

"Yes."

"You did not *force* me." He sounds puzzled, almost incredulous.

"I *ordered* you." I make a disgusted sound. "That is no different."

"You asked if I could defeat him. I said yes." He pauses. "There was no order."

My anger rises. "Do not split hairs with me, Commander. I ordered you to prove it."

"You think I would make such a claim without being ready to *prove* it?"

"Regardless of the outcome, I know what my intent was."

"To prove the superiority of your Royal Guard? To prove your pride was not without merit?" The first edge of anger sharpens his tone, too. "Do you not think my intent would be the same?"

I take a step closer to him, but he does not back down. "I challenged you in front of a crowded room. In front of your opponent."

"Yes," he snaps, his words pointed, "the crown prince challenged *me,* out of the entire Royal Guard, and I succeeded, before the king and queen and most of the nobility. Your cruelty surely lacks for boundaries, my lord."

"Enough."

He goes still, but it's not so dark that I can't see the anger in his eyes.

Twenty minutes ago I told Coale that I prefer honest discourse, and now I long to order Grey to shut his mouth and return to his duties.

At the same time, it is oddly satisfying to argue. After season upon season of cajoling women and listening to Grey's quiet deference, it feels good to push—and have someone push back.

"I was not referring solely to that one incident." My voice is tight.

"If you wish to analyze every perceived slight," he says, "by all means, proceed. But if you intend to convince the Queen of Syhl Shallow that we have her forces outnumbered, now seems a poor time to become mired in uncertainty."

I have nothing to say to that. The weight of my failures is too heavy.

"Allow me to remind you of another moment," he says. "When I believe your memories may differ from mine."

I do not look at him. "Go ahead."

"I am referring to the first season," he says. "When your creature first terrorized the castle."

"When I slaughtered my family." My voice turns rough. "I remember it well."

"There were few of us left," he says. "So many lives lost—especially the royal family—"

"Silver hell, Grey, I *remember*. What is your point?"

He is quiet for a moment. "We thought it would break you." He pauses. "It did not. You took action to protect the kingdom. Your first order was to seal the borders. You sent word to each city to govern from within."

I do not understand how he can speak of my failures as if they are victories. "It was all I *could* do."

"You asked why I keep my oath. In that moment, I never meant it more."

"I do not deserve your loyalty, Grey."

"Deserved or not, you have it."

I have nothing to say to that. The night air seems to wait for my response, but nothing I come up with is sufficient.

Grey takes a step back. He sets his empty stein in the snow. "We have been here for some time. I should walk the property."

I nod. "As you say."

When he moves away, I think of one of the first things he said. *I was never alone. The nights were never this silent.*

"Commander," I say.

He stops and turns, waiting for an order.

I have none to give. "Wait." I set my own mug in the snow. "I'll walk with you."

CHAPTER TWENTY-FIVE

HARPER

We survive the night without incident, but Rhen calls for me early. Now that he has a plan in mind, he's a man on a mission. With a promise to send a wagon back to the inn for Freya and her children, Rhen and Grey have the horses saddled and waiting before I've even finished lacing my boots.

By the time we're on horseback, the sky stretches blue and cold overhead, with just enough wind to nip at my cheeks as we canter through the snow. We fly across the open ground, Grey galloping from hill to hill to act as lookout. By the time we reach the final crest, I'm relieved that Grey calls for us to stop—until I see that he's concerned.

"A man waits at the tree line, my lord. He appears to be alone."

I look past him. There's a man with a large wagon and two draft horses, but they're too far to see much detail.

"Good," says Rhen. "I asked him to wait for us here. He is a porter and we'll have need of his wagon."

Grey frowns. "You know this man?"

"You do as well. You gave him your bag of coins." He glances at me. "If I recall correctly, you damaged his cargo?"

The one-armed man with all the crates. "When did you ask him to wait for us?"

"After your lecture on whether I know how to do something nice."

When Rhen rode off and left Grey to escort me to the inn. "But . . . why?"

Rhen's expression is piercing. "I asked him to wait so he can distribute the castle's endless food among the people. I'm sure he'll assist with fetching Freya as well, if I request it."

I open my mouth. Close it.

Rhen doesn't wait for a response. He wheels his horse and canters down the hill.

We learn the man's name is Jamison. His shocked bewilderment from yesterday is gone and he seems pleased to have a service to offer. His horses look better fed than he does, and I like that he threw a blanket over their backs while he was waiting. Rhen gives him the same story he gave Coale, how the enchanted castle was cursed by the wicked queen of Syhl Shallow, then asks the man to keep his confidence.

When we finally ride through the woods, Rhen and I lead, followed by Jamison's wagon and Grey behind.

We're walking now, so I look over at Rhen and keep my voice low. "You keep asking people to keep this a secret. I think Coale and Evalyn really will, but you just met this guy. How do you know he won't tell everyone about this?"

"My lady." He glances over, looking genuinely startled. "I am counting on them telling everyone."

I feel like I've missed something important. "So . . . wait."

"Again, I must ask. Have you no sense of how gossip works?"

"You're making it seem like a big secret so they *will* tell people?"

"Of course." He looks at me like this shouldn't be a surprise. "Do you truly think I would reveal genuine secrets in such a cavalier way?"

I clamp my mouth shut. No. I don't. Everything he does is calculated. I should have figured this was no different.

"Are you *ever* reckless?" I ask.

"I was," he says. "Once."

Then we step out of the snow, into cursed warmth and dappled sunlight.

Jamison works hard. We've been carrying food out of the castle's front hall for the past hour, and even one-handed, he makes quick work of loading everything into trunks and stacking his wagon. He was a little awestruck by the warmth in the air and the copious food—to say nothing of the music ringing through the castle. It's sad that I've only been here for a few days and I'm already over it.

Jamison seems more shocked that Rhen and Grey work alongside him, bringing food up from the kitchens once the hall tables have been emptied.

I'm a little shocked that Rhen is helping, too. I'm not sure why—because I can't see him lounging on a silk chaise, either. He just doesn't strike me as the roll-up-your-sleeves type, but he did exactly that. He's long since ditched the weapons and armor and his buckled jacket, and once packing turned to loading, he turned back the sleeves of his shirt. Seeing him in the sun with bare forearms and sweat on his brow makes my eyes want to linger.

I lock my eyes on the trunk in my hands and tell my brain to knock it off. There's probably something calculated about all this, too. He probably hopes Jamison will spread word about what a swell guy he is.

Rhen sees me approaching and he turns to take the trunk.

"I've got it," I say, but my voice is too quick. I might be blushing.

He steps back and extends a hand, giving way. "My lady."

I heave the crate onto the back of the wagon, where Jamison waits to drag it into place. Rhen watches me the whole time. My blush goes nowhere.

Jamison grabs hold of the trunk. "Your Highness, if I may ask . . ."

Rhen finally looks away. "You may."

"Do you fear providing enchanted food to your people?"

"I fear not feeding them more."

My heart flutters, just the tiniest bit, and I have to remind myself that he does nothing without intention, that all of this is part of a plan. A means to an end. A good end, that will help his people, but a calculated effect nonetheless. He's playing a role. Just like I am.

Jamison nods. "Yes, Your Highness." He drags the trunk onto the wagon and deftly stacks it atop the others.

Grey emerges from the castle with another trunk and tosses it onto the back of the wagon as well, springing up to stack it himself. The only weapon he's set aside is his sword. "I believe this is the last of it. For now."

Jamison straightens and gives him a nod. "Commander. You have my thanks."

"Don't worry," says Rhen. "Commander Grey likes to feel necessary."

Grey pushes sweat-dampened hair off his forehead and says, "Commander Grey is going to regret saying that."

Maybe it's the shared purpose, but they seem different today. Less . . . something. I can't quite put my finger on it.

The men jump off the back of the wagon, and Jamison latches it closed. "I will return with the Lady Freya by sundown, Your Highness."

"Good," says Rhen.

"Thank you," I add.

Jamison gives me a short bow. "Yes, my lady. Of course." He turns to Grey and offers a sharp salute. "Commander." Then he turns away to head for the front of his wagon.

"Wait," says Grey.

Jamison turns. "Yes?"

"You saluted me." Grey frowns, seeming disquieted. "You were not in the Royal Guard."

"The King's Army. Until I lost my arm defending Willminton last year." Jamison looks abashed. "Forgive me. Old habits die hard."

"What was your rank?"

"Lieutenant."

"Can you still hold a sword?"

"I can do more than hold one."

Grey nods. "When you return at sundown, come find me."

"Yes, sir." Jamison hesitates, then says, "Why?"

"Because I have need for a lieutenant."

The man starts to laugh, but Grey's expression hasn't changed, and he quickly sobers. "Yes, sir." He offers another salute, then climbs onto his wagon and urges his horses forward.

Once he's out of earshot, Rhen says, "Commander, that man is missing an arm."

"Duly noted." Grey picks up his sword belt from the marble steps and buckles it into place.

"What's Willminton?" I say.

"One of the northern border cities." Grey glances at Rhen. "If he lost an arm defending the city, he may have information on Karis Luran's army."

"I considered that." Rhen is staring at him. "I am not sure that qualifies him to act as your lieutenant."

"I did not offer him the position. I simply made it known. You asked me to assemble a passable contingent of guards—"

"Yes. Passable. If a missing arm would keep him out of the army, it would *certainly* keep him out of the Royal Guard."

"He is experienced." Grey pauses. "That carries weight with me. I would like to offer him the opportunity to try."

"It is essential that we appear united and strong—"

"Hire him," I say.

Rhen snaps his head around. "What did you say?"

"I said, hire him." I swallow, but refuse to look away from him. "Or give him a fair trial at least. I don't care if he has one arm. I trust Grey's judgment. Just like you said you do."

He sighs and turns to look at me. "My lady, please. You do not know—"

"Don't patronize me," I say. "Is this an alliance or not?"

That draws him up short. He studies me, then inhales to speak.

I take a step closer. "Am I a princess or not?"

His eyes narrow. I can practically see the wheels turning in that strategic little head of his.

I turn to look at Grey before my nerves can get the best of me. "If you think Jamison is suitable, test him. If he passes, hire him. That is *my* order, Commander."

I wait for his eyes to flick to Rhen, for him to wait for an order from his prince.

He doesn't. His eyes never leave mine. "Yes, my lady."

I turn and stalk up the marble steps into the castle.

Adrenaline chases through my veins at a rapid clip, and I'm worried I'm going to collapse into giggles or hysterics or have a full-on nervous breakdown. I hurry along as quickly as I can, heading for the staircase that will lead me to my room. Arabella's room. Whatever.

A hand catches my arm and turns me around.

Rhen. His touch is gentle, but firm. He all but pins me against the banister, and his expression is a combination of irritation and amusement. "What are you doing?"

I feel a little breathless again. "Going to my room. I need to change out of these clothes."

His eyes search mine. "Are you playing with me?"

"I'm not sure how sweaty, day-old clothes could be a game." I move to slip away from him.

He puts a hand on the railing, trapping me there. "Do you think me inflexible, my lady?"

It's not a question I was expecting, and his closeness combined with all this adrenaline has my heart pounding. "Why?"

"Because I sense that you feel every move you make must be an act of aggression. If you truly had an army at your disposal, I would be worried." His voice is light, almost soft, but the words carry weight.

I study him. "I don't know what you mean."

"You act as if you must take before I can give." Rhen shakes his head slightly. "You need not countermand me with Grey." He looks almost disappointed. "As with yesterday, when you secreted the food. You need not hide your motives if there is something you want."

"I still don't understand."

"My lady. Harper. *Princess*," he says pointedly. "How is it you are not understanding?"

"Understanding *what?*"

Rhen puts his hands on my arms, and even through my sweater, I feel his strength. Goose bumps spring up along my skin.

He leans in a bit. "Whether the curse breaks or not, you are willing to help my people. I am the Crown Prince of Emberfall. If there is something within my power to give you, all you must do is ask."

I stare up at him. My lips part, but no sound comes out.

He lets me go. "Forgive me. I am denying you your rest."

I still don't know what to say.

While I'm standing there trying to figure it out, he moves away, strides across the grand foyer, and heads out into the sunlight.

CHAPTER TWENTY-SIX

RHEN

There are children in the castle.

They are loud.

And seemingly everywhere at once. They're delighted by the music that fills the halls, awed by the candies and pastries that appeared with the late-afternoon tea. Freya seemed frightened at first, but eventually became charmed as well, her eyes wide as she tried to keep the children in order.

I didn't think I would mind, but their ringing laughter proved to be too much of a reminder of my life before, and I sought the relative silence of the training arena, where Grey spars with Jamison. The only thing ringing here is steel on steel.

Sweat slicks Jamison's hair and his breathing is heavy, but he has been holding his own. I expected his missing arm to affect his balance, but he seems to have learned to compensate. He fights like a soldier, aggressive and lethal on offense. Soldiers in the King's Army are trained to kill expediently. The Royal Guard is—*was*—trained to disarm and disable first. It's making for an interesting match.

Grey went easy at the start, but there's no restraint now. When Jamison falls back, Grey takes advantage, driving forward to hook the soldier's sword with the hilt of his own. The weapon jerks out of Jamison's hand. I expect that to be the end of it, but the soldier is quick. He snatches his dagger to block Grey's next attack.

Grey raises a hand to call a stop. He nods at the blade on the ground. "Again."

They've been at this for over an hour. Jamison's labored breathing fills the empty arena, but he nods and fetches his sword.

Lilith's voice speaks from the shadows behind me. "Prince Rhen. I see you have found a new toy for Commander Grey. He must be so pleased."

I'm never truly surprised when she chooses to show herself—especially not now, when I've dared to allow myself the smallest bit of hope.

I need to play this very carefully.

"And there are children in the castle." Lilith claps her hands lightly. "Such fun."

I turn. She stands in the darkness, barely visible aside from the spark of light on her eyes.

"You said you would not interfere," I say to her.

"I am not interfering. I am observing."

"You are interfering with *me*."

Her eyebrows go up, but then she smiles mockingly. "Your Highness, you do not seem yourself today. Have you not yet found true love with that tatterdemalion?"

"You know I have not. If this is my last season, I will not see Emberfall burned to the ground before there is nothing I can do about it."

"And what of your dear, sweet, broken girl?" Lilith presses a finger to her lips and her voice drops to a whisper. "Oh, Your Highness, has she already fallen for Commander Grey? Tell me, do you find it an odd bit of irony, your seasoned fighter matched with a girl who can barely walk with grace?"

"No." My voice grows bored. "She has asked me to secure a meeting with you so that she may make her case for an early return home."

"A meeting with *me*?"

Lilith's voice is hushed, and I cannot tell whether this impresses her—or angers her. If it's anger, I need to draw her ire. Better to have it directed at me than at Harper. "Yes." I lift a shoulder in a half-hearted shrug. "I could see no reason to keep you a secret." Swords clash behind me. "If you do not mind, my lady, I have interest in watching this match."

Without waiting for a response, I return to the arena railing.

My chest is tight. I promised to do this for Harper, but I feel as though I've sworn to arrange a meeting between a mouse and a lion.

Lilith steps up to the rail beside me, but she says nothing. Grey and Jamison fight in the center of the arena, though there's no elegance to it now. The soldier's swordplay has taken on an air of desperation—but he still fights.

Eventually, Lilith says, "You should have mercy on this man, Prince Rhen. Grey will run him into the ground."

She is right, but I will not interfere. I am waging my own battle here on the sidelines. "You wish to speak of mercy, Lady Lilith? I find *that* to be an odd bit of irony." I glance at her. "If you have no interest in meeting with Harper, leave this place. I have no time for you."

"You will not dictate to me, Rhen. Must I remind you of our roles here?"

The words hit me hard. I said something similar to Harper. Hearing them from Lilith makes me wish I could take them back.

"I need no reminder," I snap, turning to face her. "You've cursed me. You've cursed my kingdom. If you've grown bored with your game, end it. If you're unwilling to return Harper to her home, take your leave."

"Such fire! Prince Rhen, it has been quite some time since I have seen your temper. I must say, I have missed your spirit." She lifts a hand and steps forward, reaching as if to touch my chest.

A sword point appears against hers. "You will keep your distance," says Grey. His breath is barely quick, and though sweat dampens his hair, his sword does not waver.

Lilith scarcely spares him a glance. "This does not concern you, Commander," she says. "You will keep *your* distance."

Grey doesn't move. His sword point does not either.

Now she looks at him. "Haven't you learned your little sword cannot truly kill me?"

"I have learned it can hurt you."

Yes. He has. It never ends well for him.

Lilith moves her hand as if to touch his blade. I have no idea what she plans, whether she'll turn his sword to molten steel or drive it back into him—or maybe send it spinning to slice into both of us.

But Jamison's sword appears at her throat, forcing her to lift her chin.

She freezes. Her eyes shift to the soldier. "You have no part in this. You want no quarrel with me."

He stands strong. He's tired, but his sword does not waver either. "I know an enemy when I see one."

Her eyes, full of fury, lock on mine. "I will destroy them both," she hisses.

"Stand down," I say to them at once. I don't take my eyes off her. "You will not harm my people."

Their swords lower. Jamison takes a step back, but Grey remains at my side.

Lilith steps closer to me. "Tell your other man to give us privacy, or I *will* destroy him."

"Jamison," I say. "Go. Wait in the armory."

He hesitates—then says, "Yes, Your Highness," and withdraws.

"I have the power here," Lilith says. "You are to remember that, Prince Rhen."

"I have not forgotten."

"Why do you ask me to return the girl? It does you no good for me to take her away."

"She does not love me. Her mother is dying. You have cursed me, not her. It seems cruel to deny her the final days with her mother." I keep my voice bored. Disinterested. Anything more, and Lilith will use it against me.

She considers this for a long moment.

Finally, her eyes flick to Grey. "Fetch the girl, Commander."

Grey does not move.

Lilith steps forward and walks her fingers up his chest. "I do not like being ignored," she whispers as her fingers reach the skin of his throat. "I could carve the bones out of your neck while he watches."

"Harper has come to trust him," I say to her. "She will not react well to his loss. You yourself swore not to interfere."

"Who says he needs to die?" Her fingernail presses into his skin and a pearl of red wells up.

"Commander," I say. "Go."

"Yes, my lord." He doesn't like it, but he'll obey. Grey heads for the passage into the palace proper.

Lilith moves to stand in front of me. Irritation fills her eyes. "I do not like this," she says. "You seek to trick me somehow."

"This is not my request. As you said when Harper arrived, she is an unusual choice. If home calls to her so strongly, I will not trap her here. She will never love me if I keep her prisoner."

Lilith moves close enough that I feel the weight of her skirts against my legs. "Ah, so you're altruistic now? I have heard men become so when the end is near. An attempt to right their wrongs, I believe."

I say nothing.

She folds her arms and gazes up at me. In anyone else, it would be a girlish gesture. "There is a part of me that will miss this."

"There is no part of me that will," I say.

Her hand lifts lazily and she traces a finger down the center of my chest. "Are you sure, Prince Rhen?"

With those words, the pain begins.

CHAPTER TWENTY-SEVEN

HARPER

I'm hiding from my lady-in-waiting. Freya and her children share the suite next to mine, and she has knocked at the door at least three times over the past hour.

"Shall I lay out a dress for this evening, my lady?"

"Do you need assistance in the bath, my lady?"

"My lady, tea has appeared in the drawing room. Would you like me to serve?"

The last offer was delivered with a mixture of awe and fear.

I've declined all of it. I'm not used to people waiting on me—and playing princess to stop the destruction of the inn feels a whole lot different from letting someone brush my hair.

A knock sounds at the door when I'm in the middle of re-braiding my curls.

"I'm fine!" I call. "I don't need anything!"

"My lady." Grey's voice, low and serious, muffled by the heavy wood of the door. "His Highness requests your presence."

I tie off the braid and go for the door. He's tall and foreboding pretty much always, but right now his face is a mask of tension.

"Something's wrong," I say.

"Lady Lilith has agreed to speak with you."

Surprise kicks my heart into double-time. "Now?"

"Yes." His voice indicates he is not happy about this. That makes me more nervous than any of Rhen's warnings.

I swallow. "Let me get my boots."

Grey leads me down the staircase where I followed Rhen yesterday. I have to scurry to keep up with him, but I don't want to tell him to slow down. "They're in the kitchen?"

He glances at me. "The training arena."

Fear and excitement battle for space in my chest. In ten minutes, I could be thrown back to Washington, DC. I could be there for my mother. I could be there for Jake. This could all be over.

In the back of my head, a twinge of guilt pricks at me. I'm leaving these people. I'm leaving Emberfall to its fate—and I'll never know what happened. Princess Harper of Disi would vanish. The people here would be left to the curse and the monster.

But this curse is not my fault. I have nothing to do with this place. I have no obligation to any of them.

The guilt doesn't go away. In fact, it seems to cling harder.

"Grey." I catch his arm, my fingers digging into the leather buckled around his forearm. He's replaced the knife he lost to the man in the inn. The steel of the hilt is cold under my palm. "Did Rhen tell her what I want?"

He stops and looks down at me. The hallway is so quiet around us, shadowed with flickering candlelight. "She knows what you have asked. She has agreed to hear your request."

"Do you think she'll send me home?"

"I think she will do whatever causes the greatest harm."

An arrow of fear pierces right through any hope I had. "To me? Or to Rhen?"

"To him." He pauses, and his voice is resigned. "Which may work in your favor."

The warning in his tone is chilling, and nothing about those words is a relief.

An ornate steel door sits at the end of the hallway, flanked by large oil lamps. Grey reaches for the handle and swings it wide.

The floor turns to dirt, and we're in a huge open space. The walls to my left are lined with weapons, from swords and axes to lances and spears. The ceiling stretches two stories overhead, crossed with wooden beams and painted white. Late-afternoon sunlight streams across the space from above.

In the center of the arena stands the most beautiful woman I've ever seen. She's almost too stunning to look at, from the shine of her black hair to the jeweled satin of her skirts.

At her feet, on his knees, one hand braced in the dirt, is Rhen.

He's spitting blood at the ground.

The room full of gore flashes in front of my eyes. Every time he tried to warn me about Lilith, and I didn't understand.

"Stop!" I scream. "What are you doing to him? Stop it!"

I don't realize I'm running until Grey catches me. His arms wrap around my waist, pinning me against him. His voice is low and quiet against my ear. "She can kill you without thought, my lady."

I struggle against him. My voice breaks out with a sob. "She's killing *him*."

"Killing him?" The woman laughs, and even that is beautiful, in a grating, shimmering way, like discordant wind chimes. "I would never kill him." She glances down at Rhen. I don't see her move, but he jerks and makes a low keening sound, then coughs more blood into the dirt.

I had no idea she would be like this.

Rhen grips his abdomen now. His labored breathing echoes through the arena.

"Stop," I gasp. "Please stop."

"Remember this, girl. Remember how easily he falls."

There is no danger of me forgetting. I strain against Grey's hold.

Lilith watches me. Her face is so young, her eyes clear and vibrant. She takes a step toward Rhen and he tries to recoil. "No matter how much power the crown prince would have you believe he holds, it is truly meaningless."

I redouble my struggles. I have no idea what I can do, but I know I can't just watch. "Grey," I cry. "We have to help him."

He's too big. Too strong. His arms encircle my rib cage, and my feet barely touch the ground.

"We cannot," he says.

"You believe our prince cannot take the pain?" says Lilith. "Do you hear that, Rhen? She thinks you're weak."

I shake my head fiercely. I think of whatever Jake has had to do to keep us safe. I think of the men who used to deliver "reminders" to my father. I didn't think I would ever see anything more terrible. I was wrong. "Please," I say. "He's not weak. Please stop."

"I assure you, I've had time to find his limits. This is nothing."

I don't want to see his limits.

Rhen coughs again, wetly, and presses his forehead to the

ground. He's coughed up enough blood that a dark pool sits beneath his jaw.

Lilith reaches down and grabs a fistful of his hair, wrenching him somewhat upright. I expect him to look furious. Desperate. Terrified, maybe.

Instead, he looks resigned. His eyes center on nothing. Not on Grey. And certainly not on me.

"Am I to understand you have a request for me?" says Lilith.

I can barely process her words. I can't look away from Rhen. "Please stop." My voice breaks. "Please stop hurting him."

"That is your request?"

I freeze. That's not my request, but right now, I'll do anything to stop this.

Lilith jerks his head higher and he winces. "She *begs* for you, Rhen. And you asked me to send her home. You're such a fool."

No. I was the fool.

"Make your request," says Lilith. "I grow bored, girl. Rhen knows what happens when I grow bored." She jerks his head back and he makes a sound I never want to hear again.

I don't know what's happening to my mother or my brother, but the unknown can't compete with what she's doing right in front of me. I pry at Grey's arm, trying to use the buckles for leverage. He holds fast.

Rhen coughs again. Lilith reaches down with her free hand. A spot of blood appears where her fingers touch his neck. He jerks away but she holds him in place.

My hand slides across the hilt of one of Grey's throwing knives. I jerk the blade free. I hold it just like Grey showed me.

Softer.

I throw it straight at Lilith.

The blade flies true, but only skims her skirts before driving into the dirt beyond.

Lilith snaps her head around to look at me. I expect fury in her eyes, but there is only surprise.

She lets Rhen go and he all but collapses into the dirt, his breathing rapid. His forehead isn't pressed to the ground now.

He's turned his head to look at me.

Lilith steps away from him and picks up the knife I threw. It hangs between her fingers, the steel swinging gently, catching the light.

"You tore my dress," she says.

"I was aiming higher," I say. "But I'm still learning."

"Perhaps you need a demonstration."

"Lilith." Rhen speaks, his voice harsh and broken. "You cannot harm her. You swore to never interfere with the girls."

Lilith keeps moving toward me. She's so graceful that she could be floating over the dirt floor of the arena. "She threw a knife at me, Your Highness. I did not interfere. She did."

Rhen is lying in the dirt, crouching over a pool of his own blood. It makes Lilith's approach all the more terrifying. I think of my mother facing my father's harassers—and later, cancer treatments. I know pain. So does my mother. I've lived it. I've watched my mother live it. I can get through this.

I grit my teeth. "Grey. Release me."

He lets go but does not leave my side.

Lilith's eyebrows go up. "Impressive. Commander Grey will not even listen to *me*. I see you have brought him to heel."

Her voice makes me want to flinch. I refuse to give her the satisfaction. "He's not a dog."

"If one is not the dog, one is the master, and Grey is certainly not that." She pauses. "Which role do you play, girl?"

"Beats me, but I know which one you are." I glare at her. "I have another word for it, though."

Lilith goes still. Any amusement melts off her face.

Rhen has made it to his feet. "You cannot harm her," he says. "You swore."

"I swore not to kill them," Lilith says. "I swore not to interfere with your attempts at courtship." She steps closer to me. "That," she says, "is all I *swore.*"

Beside me, Grey draws his sword.

She does not glance at him, and she makes no move toward me. Her eyes are fixed on mine. "You wished to ask me for passage home? That is all?"

I swallow. "Yes." But now I don't want to ask her for anything.

"And that is all you want?"

"Yes." My voice is soft.

"Do you not see my power?" She takes a step closer. "What if I could end the torment of your broken body?"

"No," says Rhen. He staggers forward. "Harper, what she offers will come at a cost."

"My body is not broken," I say.

"You amuse me, girl. What about your mother's body? Would you consider *hers* broken?"

I go very still. My eyes fill against my will. "You know about my mother?"

"I've been to see her." A heavy, vicious pause. "She thinks I am an *angel*. She believes I can ease her pain. Perhaps I can."

"No," says Rhen. "Harper, the cost will be greater than her loss—"

"What about my brother?" A tear spills down my cheek. "Is my brother okay?"

"Ah, your brother. The great enforcer. He is a man of violence. I find I admire his talents."

"He's alive." My voice breaks.

"Oh, he is alive," she says. "But he is far from well."

"Please," I whisper. "Please let me help them."

She steps closer to me. Her free hand reaches out to touch my cheek. I flinch and expect to feel a flare of pain, but her palm is cool. Almost motherly. "You poor girl. You know nothing of this side. It is unfair that Prince Rhen has trapped you in this curse."

My breathing hitches. "So you'll help me?"

"No." Her expression tightens. "If you wish to ask me for favors, you would do well to learn respect."

Then she brings up the knife and swipes it across the opposite side of my face.

The motion is so sudden and unexpected that I don't realize she's done anything until she's already gone. Vanished.

Then I feel the sting. The burn as my tears find their way into broken skin. I slap my hand to my cheek.

There's dampness. Stickiness. I can feel the edges of my skin where she cut me.

I whimper. I can't breathe. A wet trickle snakes down my neck.

Rhen has made his way to me. "We need to get you into the palace." His voice is hoarse and worn.

"She cut me," I say. The pain is setting in now, a fire that lights up the entire side of my cheek.

Rhen catches my arm. There's blood streaked on his face, on his jacket. Dirt clings to some of it. He looks as pale as I feel. "Please, my lady. There is a lot of blood."

I'm shaking. Trembling so hard I can barely stand. My entire palm is slick and crimson.

"There are supplies in the armory," says Grey.

"Supplies?" My own voice seems to be coming from a distance.

"It needs stitching." Rhen's voice sounds like it's underwater. Slow and lethargic. "My lady, please allow me to—"

I can't give permission. I can't do anything.

My vision goes black.

CHAPTER TWENTY-EIGHT

RHEN

I have never kept a bedside vigil.

When I was young, I would have considered such a thing tedious and boring—if I ever considered it at all. I never needed to—and I likely do not need to now. Harper's wound could have been far worse: The knife could have caught her neck, or sliced into the muscle of her arm. She could have lost her eye.

Harper will wake. She will survive. She has a lady-in-waiting who could sit at her bedside. I do not need to be here.

But I find I cannot leave.

Ironrose has never felt so quiet, the silence pressing in around us, broken only by the soft crackle of the fire, and Harper's slow, even breaths. The music from the Great Hall is silent tonight, and I am grateful. I study the slightly arced line that bisects her cheek, the twenty stitches holding the skin closed. An angry wound that seems out of place on the soft curve of her face.

Her words from the arena keep repeating in my head, complete with the broken emotion in her voice.

Please stop. Please stop hurting him.

And Lilith's response.

She begs *for you, Rhen.*

Instead of running from what she saw, Harper drew Grey's weapon.

This feels like the cruelest season of all, to present me with a girl with the fierceness to stand at my side—yet with a home and family she needs to return to so badly.

A log on the fire snaps, collapsing in a short burst of ash. Harper stirs, then takes a long breath, and her eyes flutter open. She blinks a few times before focusing on me.

"Rhen." Her voice is rough and worn. "What—where—" She winces and lifts a hand to her face.

I catch her wrist, but gently. Freya added an ointment for the pain, but she warned of infection. "Be still. You do not want to pull at the stitches."

"So that really happened." Her voice is so small.

"Yes." She has not pulled away and her wrist rests in my grip, her pulse a soft beat against my fingers.

She stares at me, and all I can do is stare back at her. My meetings with Lilith have been a source of private shame for . . . ever. An eternal hell shared only with Grey.

And yet Harper has still not seen me at my worst.

I break the eye contact and look at the fire. Now that she is awake, waiting here feels like a mistake. I feel too raw, too exposed. "Shall I call for Freya?"

"No." She shifts and tries to roll toward me. "I need—I need to sit up."

"Go slowly. You have been asleep for hours."

She slides her wrist out of my grasp and struggles to push

herself upright. One arm presses against her abdomen and her eyes close.

Eventually, her breathing slows. “My head is pounding.”

“A dose of sleeping ether,” I say, though it could also be the loss of blood. Her skin seems more pale than usual. “We worried you would wake during the stitching.”

She swallows and her eyes widen further, flicking past me to the hearth, the windows, the tapestries lining the walls. “This isn’t Arabella’s room.”

“No. This is mine.” I pause. “I worried the children being so near would not let you sleep.”

She looks down at herself. A sudden tension seems to grip her body. “And this—I wasn’t wearing this.”

“Freya,” I offer. “She brought a new chemise. Yours was—quite soiled.”

“Oh.”

For a moment, my emotions are unsure where to settle. I want to sit beside her and offer my gratitude, to tell her how no girl has ever risked herself for me. I want to hide from the knowledge of what she saw. I want to fight—to prove that I am not vulnerable.

She’s seen the truth.

Harper’s eyes rise to meet mine. “I want to see it. Do you have a mirror?”

“I do.” I rise slowly, and then, out of habit, extend a hand. I fully expect her to refuse.

She does not. She takes my hand, her fingers wrapping around mine, then pulls herself to her feet.

Once there, she does not let go.

She stands a foot away from me. I want so badly to touch her face, to whisper my thoughts against her skin. This torture is nearly as bad as what I endured in the arena.

"Steady?" I say softly.

"Enough." Her steps hitch behind me, and I lead her to my dressing room, where a mirror stands in the corner.

When we stop in front of it, she stands in silence, her expression flat. Her hair is unbound, the curls cascading wildly over her shoulder. She stares, her eyes fixed on the wound. The incision is an angry red, but clean. The medicine Freya applied has forestalled any swelling.

Harper lets go of my hand and moves closer, until her breath faintly fogs the glass. She swallows and touches her fingertips to the mirror. "The stitches are smaller than I expected."

"Your lady-in-waiting has a steady hand."

She turns to look at me. "Freya did it?"

"She did." I pause. "She was quite forceful, in fact. Yelled at Commander Grey."

"She yelled at *Grey*?" Harper's eyes widen.

"Yanked the needle right from his hand."

"What did she say?"

I raise my voice into a lilting imitation of Freya's. " 'You will not put field sutures in my lady's *face*! She is not a common *soldier*!' "

A ghost of a smile finds Harper's lips. "That's amazing."

"She is quite protective." I pause. "I thought she might drag him away by his ear."

That makes her laugh—but then she gasps and raises a hand to her cheek. *Now* her eyes fill. She draws a long, quavering breath, then steadies herself.

"Come." I take her hand again—and I am equally shocked when she lets me. "You should sit."

I lead her to an armchair by the fire. "Wine?"

She shakes her head. "Water?"

"Of course." A pitcher sits on a low table by the bed. I pour a glass for her, then a goblet of wine for myself.

My movements are slow, and she watches me. "Are you . . . okay?"

The question is touching and humiliating at the same time. I ease into the chair beside her. "Lilith is quite good at discovering ways to cause the most pain without causing lasting damage."

Harper looks down into her glass. "I thought—I thought she was going to kill you."

"Killing me would end her fun." I take a sip from my glass and feel the burn all the way down. I welcome the numbness that will trail behind it. "She prefers to make me beg for death."

Harper swallows that information. "I've seen—I've seen bad things before. But not—" She falters, then shudders. "I couldn't let her—I couldn't—" Her voice chokes to a stop. "I couldn't watch."

"My lady." The emotion in her voice turns my own rough. "What you did for me . . ." I find I have no words myself and I flinch away from her eyes. "I regret that you have been injured so . . . permanently."

That seems to steady her, but at the same time, she sinks into herself a bit. "Why didn't Grey do something? Why did he just stand there?"

"In the beginning, Grey would try to stop her. But she finds creative ways make him watch. Severed tendons, broken limbs . . . a favorite was to pin him to the wall of the arena on his sword—"

"Stop. Please." Harper holds up a hand.

"Ah. Forgive me." I look away. "I have learned to draw and hold her attention. What she does to me is bad enough. I can endure it. I will not watch her visit pain on my people."

We fall into silence again, staring at the fire. I keep expecting her to ask me to leave, but she does not.

After a while, motion flickers to my left, and I look over to find her dabbing at her cheeks. Tears have snaked their way down her face, collecting along the stitches to make them gleam in the firelight.

"My lady." I shift forward to the edge of my chair.

Despite the tears, her voice is steady. "I'm so stupid. You warned me, but I didn't realize what you meant."

"That is not stupidity," I say.

"It's something close." Her voice is flat and bleak. "I ruined my chance."

For me. She ruined her chance by trying to help me. "You may get another. Lilith will return. She is never gone for long."

"What then? I can watch her do it again?" She glares at me, her expression made more fierce by the injury to her face. "I don't know what I can do to her, but I won't just stand by and watch it. I can't."

"What will you offer to stop it? What will you offer for passage home?"

"Anything." She draws a hitching breath. "God, Rhen. *Any—*"

"No!" My voice is sharp, and she jumps. I put a finger over her lips. "*Never* offer blindly, my lady. Not for your family. Not even for yourself. Certainly not for me."

She stares at me over my hand, until I feel foolish and pull away.

"Do not misunderstand," I say, and my voice is rough. "When

you bargain, you must know what you are willing to lose. If you offer all you have, be prepared for her to take it."

"Is that what you did?" she asks quietly.

I stare down into my glass and remember the first night, when I thought Lilith was just another courtier. The first morning, when Lilith tore me apart. When she tore Grey apart.

While I lay broken and bleeding on the floor, she threatened to tear my family apart. She threatened to start with my sisters, limb by limb.

In retrospect, I should have just let her. Now the guilt is mine alone to carry.

Harper watches me, waiting for an answer. I drain the wine in one swallow. "Yes."

She thinks about that for a long time. When she speaks, her voice is quiet and level. "So I've got a question."

Right now, in this moment, I would grant her my kingdom if she asked. "Go ahead."

"Do you still think your plan will work?"

"I do. I have sent Grey and Jamison to the inn to see whether any soldiers from Syhl Shallow have returned."

Her eyebrows rise. "So Grey hired him?"

"Not yet. But Jamison seems willing. And loyal. He believes Lilith is working with Karis Luran. He offered to stand guard at the inn overnight, though I do not anticipate more trouble from those soldiers."

"Why not?"

"Because they did not attack last night. They could easily have returned with reinforcements. I suspect, however, that they have retreated to send word to their queen, and to await further orders. That will take several days. Likely weeks. It is the dead of winter in Emberfall, and Syhl Shallow is on the other side of a mountain range."

Harper considers this. "Could Lilith get in the way?"

"Absolutely. She already suspects that I am trying to trick her somehow."

Harper points at her cheek. "How is this going to affect my part?"

"Do you still wish to proceed as the Princess of Disi?"

"I'm certainly not going to sit here feeling sorry for myself." She pauses and some of the fire drains out of her eyes. "Every time I go still, I think of my mother."

"I would undo it if I could," I say softly. I want so badly to reach out and touch her, but she has made her feelings quite clear. "I swear to you."

"I believe you." Her voice is equally soft, but she straightens. "Enough. Seriously. What are we going to do about this?"

I frown. I cannot decide if she is being self-deprecating or practical.

Her eyes narrow. "I'm sure you've thought of something."

"That we can tell the people of how the princess faced the evil sorceress from Syhl Shallow and drove her away with minimal injury? Yes, my lady. I have thought of something." I pause. "If you are still willing."

"I am."

"Then when Grey returns, I will have him send word to Silvermoon Harbor, announcing our intent to visit. I would like to go the day after tomorrow, if that suits you."

"It does."

I study her, weighing my thoughts. She seems to think that her wound will make her less convincing as a princess. In truth, watching her now, she has never looked more like one.

"I have underestimated you again," I finally say.

"How?"

"I have been waiting for you to wake for hours," I tell her. "I was certain this would . . . break you."

She frowns and looks at the fire. "It's not my first scar, Rhen. I wasn't perfect before. I'll get over it." Then her eyes shift back to mine. "Did you say you've been sitting here for hours?"

"Yes." I pause. "You are not angry about what Lilith has done?"

"Oh, I'm furious. But not about my face."

"Then what?"

Her voice fills with steel. "I'm mad I *missed*."

CHAPTER TWENTY-NINE

HARPER

The morning we're due to leave for Silvermoon, I finally let Freya do my hair. She comes in with tea, and I don't have the heart to refuse her offer. I keep thinking about Rhen's comment, how she was very protective. In my efforts to be self-sufficient, I've been pushing her away. Until I heard how she stood up to Grey, I didn't realize it was possible to be strong and yielding at the same time.

So I sit at the dressing table in Arabella's room, and Freya stands behind me, silently running the brush through my curls. The baby is swaddled and sleeping in the room next door, but I haven't seen her other children. Freya's skin looks clean-scrubbed, and her eyes are bright. The near-panic that's been in her expression since I met her is gone. Yesterday, she was still wearing her clothes from the inn, but today, she's in a lavender dress with a white-laced bodice, and her hair is in twin plaits, which she's pinned up into a twist.

"You look really pretty," I say.

Her hands go still and she blushes. "My lady. Thank you." She offers a curtsy. "I was borrowing clothes from Evalyn while I stayed at the Crooked Boar, but those are not appropriate in the palace. I asked the guardsman where the queen's ladies stored their garments."

We fall into silence again and she resumes brushing. I thought it was going to make a frizzy mess, but she used something from one of the dozen bottles scattered across the table and the curls relax. The motion of the brush is soothing. A reminder of childhood.

When my mother would do the same thing.

Without warning, my eyes fill. I press my fingers to my face.

"Oh!" Freya stops brushing immediately. "Did I hurt you?"

"No." I barely recognize my own voice. "No. I'm fine."

But I'm not. I can't stop crying. My shoulders are shaking before I'm ready for it.

Freya takes my hand. Hers is warm, her grip strong. "Shall I send for His Highness?"

"No! No—I'm fine." My voice breaks and it's obvious that I'm not.

She puts a hand on my shoulder and rubs gently, moving close. My hand is still gripped in hers. She says nothing, but her closeness is more reassuring than anything I've felt in days.

I think of home, and realize it's more reassuring than anything I've felt in *months.*

"My mother is dying," I say. I'm sure this isn't part of Rhen's plan, but I can't keep melting into a puddle or I'm going to completely unravel. "My mother is dying, and I can't be there. And I just keep thinking—I keep thinking she's going to die before I can say goodbye."

"Oh . . . oh, my lady." Freya wraps me up in her arms, and then I'm sobbing into her skirts like a child.

This isn't like with Rhen or Grey. I can wrangle my emotions into compliance in front of them. But Freya is all kindness and warmth, and it feels so good to be held that I allow myself to sink into it. She keeps smoothing my hair, whispering nonsense.

Eventually, reality catches up with me. I can't be Harper today. I have to be the Princess of Disi.

I draw back. I've left a huge damp spot on her dress. "I'm so sorry," I say.

She uses a thumb to brush the tears from my cheeks. "Here," she says quietly—though her voice is firm. She straightens my shoulders. "Sit. Allow me to finish."

I obey. The brush finds my hair again, her hands slow and sure.

"When my sister died," Freya says quietly, "it was very sudden. I had no time to say goodbye. But she knew I loved her. I knew she loved me. It is not the moment of passing that is most important. It is all the moments that come before."

I meet her eyes in the mirror. "Your sister died?"

She nods. "I took in her children. The thought of having four mouths to feed was overwhelming, but we have survived."

Surprise knocks some of the sorrow out of my chest. "Those are your sister's children?"

"Baby Olivia is mine. She had just been born when my sister was killed. I lived with Dara and her husband, Petor, in the farmhouse to help care for Dahlia and Davin and little Edgar." A pause. "But then the monster attacked Woven Hollow when Dara and Petor were there to trade goods, and suddenly the children were all mine."

"The monster." Every time someone mentions it, the fear in their voice is undeniable.

"Yes, my lady." Freya hesitates. "When the men came to raid the farmhouse, I thought fate had finally found us all. But then you came to our aid, and now we are here, in this enchanted place." She pauses. "I do not presume to know what you face, my lady. I know nothing of your land, your customs. But I do know your bravery and kindness seem to have no bounds. I have no doubt your mother knows that, too."

My throat tightens. "You're going to make me cry again."

"Well, at the very least, hold still so I can do your plait."

That makes me smile. "I'm glad you're here, Freya."

"As am I, my lady." She begins to braid, her fingers quick and sure. "I am always surprised to discover that when the world seems darkest, there exists the greatest opportunity for light."

The dress Freya selects for me is navy blue, but every inch of stitching is shot with silver, with tiny diamond-like stones affixed along the bodice. A blue overskirt spills from the waist, split at the hip to reveal a cascade of white petticoats. Beneath the dress I'm wearing calfskin leggings and heeled boots that lace to my knees. She arranges my curls into a loose, loopy braid that falls over my shoulder, with jeweled hairpins arranged at regular intervals. Then she dusts dark charcoal across my eyelids.

When I stand in front of the mirror, a stranger stares back at me. This is the kind of dress little girls dream of, but my eyes center on the stitched line across my cheek. It's healed to the point of being sore and itchy, but there's no swelling left. Now it's just ugly. My reminder that actions have consequences.

I put a hand over my cheek, hiding the imperfection.

Freya takes my wrist gently and lowers it. "Proof of your bravery," she says. "Nothing less." She holds a tiny stretch of twisted wire adorned with a few jewels. I think it's a necklace until she reaches to slide it into my hair.

"Freya," I whisper. "This is . . . this is all too much."

She gathers a length of leather and fur from the chest at the end of the bed and holds it up. "Are you too warm? You can wait to add the coat once you've crossed through the woods."

That wasn't what I meant at all. I swallow. Until this moment, Princess Harper was something to consider in theory.

Right now, Princess Harper is looking back at me from the mirror.

A hard knock sounds at the door. "My lady, the horses have been brought to the courtyard."

Grey. He's been running errands for Rhen, so I haven't seen him since we confronted Lilith in the arena.

Freya moves to the door and pulls it open. "The princess is ready."

He steps into the room, and I feel the instant his gaze stops on me. His eyes give away nothing.

Some dynamic has shifted between us. I'm not sure if it has to do with the way he held me back while Lilith was torturing Rhen—or the way I stole his knife to stop her myself. Either way, it feels prickly and I don't like it.

I smooth my hands along the bodice. "Is it good enough?"

"Good enough?" His expression doesn't change. "You have me wishing I had more guardsmen." He glances at Freya. "The princess needs a weapon. Fetch a belt with a dagger. There are several in the chest."

"Yes, Commander." She scurries into the closet.

I frown. "A dagger?"

"We should give people a reason to think twice before approaching you."

That's both awesome and terrifying.

Freya returns with a stretch of dark leather, along with a simple dagger. A few jeweled flowers decorate the hilt, matched by a stitched vine of blue flowers on the sheath. Just as she hands it to me, the baby begins crying from the next room.

She looks apologetically at me. "My lady—"

"Go," I say. "It's fine."

I begin wrapping the straps around my waist, but there's just too much length, and no buckle.

I stop and look at Grey. "You know I have no idea what I'm doing with this. Would you help me?"

He nods and puts out a hand for the belt, then moves close to slide the leather around my waist, wrapping it double. His deft fingers thread the leather into a knot that lies flat at my hip, putting the light weight of the dagger along my upper thigh.

The effort puts him close enough for us to share breath, but his movements are quick and efficient. He doesn't quite meet my eyes.

"Thanks," I say softly.

"Yes, my lady." He pauses. "I have been ordered to stay at your side today. Jamison will accompany His Highness."

Grey doesn't sound like he approves of that arrangement, but I can't tell which half bothers him more: guarding me, or not guarding Rhen. Either way, I don't like this hum of tension between us.

"Are you mad I stole your knife?" I say quietly.

"You are welcome to every weapon I carry." His voice is level. "I showed you how to throw knives because you asked. Not because I expected you to use them."

"I'm *glad* you showed me," I say. "I got her to stop."

His eyes flick to my cheek. "At what cost?"

Warmth heats my face. "Grey—what she was doing to him . . . it was awful. No one deserves that." My voice tightens, some mixture of anger and fear and regret. "Rhen told me he ordered you not to stop her, but I don't know how you can do that. I'd do it again, and I will if I have to. I can take a scar."

"And if she cuts your throat?"

I set my jaw. "I'm not apologizing for what I did."

"I seek no apology. I understand your motives."

"Then what do you seek?"

"Your trust."

I don't have an answer for that.

He speaks into my silence and his voice is just as hard as mine is. "His Highness would like to arrive at Silvermoon by mid-morning, my lady."

My mood has soured, and I feel completely off balance. I grab the jacket and wish I could storm out of the room with an even step, though the boots Freya found in the closet are better than what I wore before. The dress sways as I walk down the empty hallway, my booted heels clicking on the marble unevenly.

Grey follows beside me, but slightly behind. He moves like a ghost.

Before we reach the staircase, I can't take it anymore. I round on him.

"Look. I do trust you. I trusted you before I trusted Rhen. You *know* that."

His eyes give nothing away. "You trust me not to harm you."

"Yes." Obviously.

"Do you trust me to keep you safe?"

I suck in a breath—then hesitate.

"That is the trust I mean," Grey says, and finally there is anger in his tone. "You are the Princess of Disi," he says, "and as you are to ally with His Highness, I will obey your order."

"But that's different," I say. "It's not *real*."

"It is real enough here in Emberfall," he says. "My obligation—indeed the very oath I swore—is to lay down my life in favor of his. And now, in favor of *yours*, my lady."

"But not with Lilith! How could you stand there and *watch* that, Grey? How could you?"

"Do you truly think it costs me nothing?" His voice is sharp, but torment sparks in his eyes. "I have seen her actions countless times. And to a much greater extent."

"I would try to stop her every time." To my surprise, emotion builds in my chest. "Every time, Grey. I wouldn't care what he ordered me to do. I wouldn't care what she did to me. He told me what she's done to you—I'm not even sure that would be enough to stop me."

"If His Highness allowed it, I would take her provocation by tenfold. I would fight her until I had no breath left to breathe." His voice turns almost lethal, and in the dim light of the hallway, Grey's eyes seem to darken. "*My* duty is to bleed so he does not. And now," he says, "my duty is to bleed so *you* do not."

Those words are chilling. I swallow.

"What you have agreed to do is larger than you think. Your life is no longer yours to sacrifice."

"I know," I whisper.

"You do *not* know." He's genuinely angry now. "Or you would not have risked your life so carelessly, as if your death carries no consequences. You would not—"

"Commander." Rhen's voice, by the stairs. I jump.

His tone isn't sharp, but Grey snaps to attention. His expression evens out so quickly that you'd never know we were having a heated discussion.

I don't know how much Rhen heard, but as he approaches, I'm guessing it was a lot. Or at least *enough*.

Shame has formed a lump in my chest—especially because I know he's going to lay into Grey, or order him to apologize to me, or something I won't be able to take.

"Wait," I say to Rhen. My voice is half-broken, and I'm a breath away from crying. I look up at Grey. "I'm sorry," I say. "I didn't understand. I'm sorry."

He lets out a breath and glances away. His voice is regretful. "A princess should not apologize to a guardsman."

"I'm Harper," I say to him. "And I'm apologizing to you."

He hesitates, then nods. "As you say."

Tension still wavers in this space between us. I wish we'd had five more minutes to play this out to the end.

"Is all well?" says Rhen.

"Yes." I inhale and turn back to face him—and all that breath leaves me in a rush.

A moment ago, I was embroiled in the argument with Grey. Now I'm really looking at Rhen, and it's like he's stepped out of a fairy tale. He wears no armor, but instead a jacket of blue-and-black brocade with a high collar. From what I can glimpse at his neck, it seems to be lined with the same fur as the jacket hanging over my arm. Slender stretches of silver are twisted in an intricate design along his collar, matched by similar metalwork on his black leather gauntlets and the hilt of his sword. Subtle, but there's no question he's the prince.

Or maybe that's just Rhen himself. He could stand there in a potato sack and he'd probably look like royalty.

"All is well," I finish, but then I realize he's staring at me, too.

A blush crawls up my cheeks and I smooth down my skirts. "Do I look like a princess?"

He steps forward and takes my hand. I think he's going to lead me toward the stairs, but instead, he bows low and kisses my hand. "You look like a queen."

My face feels like it's on fire. The rest of me, too. I have to clear my throat twice to speak, and even then, my voice is rough. "I understand you wish to reach Silvermoon by mid-morning?"

"I do." He glances past me, and I can see him weighing whether to pry. "I have asked Commander Grey to stay by your side today, but I can ask Jamison, if you prefer."

"No." I swallow and glance back at the guardsman. "I trust Grey to keep me safe."

We head south, the sun to our left. Snow and slush have been trampled down to reveal a rutted gravel that's clearly seen a lot of traffic already. Trees line the road on either side, the remnants of the forest that encircles Ironrose, but ahead the trees give way to a long sloping valley. Snow glitters on homes and farms that seem small in the distance. Well beyond that, the sun gleams on what must be water.

Rhen has been quiet for most of the ride, but I'm having trouble figuring out his mood. I keep my voice low and shift my horse closer to him.

"You think people will be happy that you're making an alliance with a country they've never heard of?"

"I think my people will be happy I am trying to save them from invasion." He pauses and his voice turns grave. "Jamison said the battle at Willminton was brutal and most lost their lives. Their regiment was destroyed, their encampment burned to the ground. It seems the soldiers of Syhl Shallow do not intend to simply overtake my kingdom, but to raze it."

I swallow. "You said there were a thousand soldiers in a regiment."

Rhen looks at me and the expression in his eyes reminds me of the anguish in Grey's voice in the hallway. "Yes, my lady."

"They accepted no surrender," says Jamison. "Men who tried were slaughtered before they could raise their arms."

Rhen looks over at me, and for the first time, I begin to understand the weight of what he's hoping to accomplish. "We are lucky to have secured the alliance of Disi," he says.

"Our soldiers stand ready," I say. These are practiced words, suggestions from Rhen, but my voice sounds hollow when confronted with the deaths of real men. "My father awaits my order."

"We will fight alongside," says Jamison. Contrary to the regret over the loss of fellow soldiers, his voice is full of anticipation. He loops his arm through his reins and hits his chest with his fist. "For the good of Emberfall!"

To my right, Grey does the same. Passion rings in their voices, strong enough that I feel it right to my core.

Rhen hits his chest, too. "For the good of all."

His voice carries an echo of the same passion—but something else. Something closer to sadness.

Before I can puzzle this through, Grey frowns and points ahead, ever vigilant. "A covered wagon on the road. Three horses." He glances at Jamison. "Check it out."

"Yes, sir." Jamison's horse springs forward, hooves spraying slush.

Grey stares after him. "I had almost forgotten what this was like."

"Having someone to order around?" I say.

"No." Rhen looks past me at his guard commander. "Being part of something bigger."

Grey nods. "Yes. That exactly."

Rhen shakes his head. "I'm not sure I ever realized." He draws up his reins. "I do not wish to treat my people as a threat." He nods ahead, toward the wagon. "Come. Let us greet them."

CHAPTER THIRTY

RHEN

We smell the harbor long before we reach Silvermoon. The scent of fish throws a faint metallic tang into the air. It's ten times worse in the summer; I remember. I would ride with my father to inspect our naval fleet, or to receive dignitaries from other ports, and the stench of fish and sweat and dirt is ingrained in my brain. The harbor sits at the northernmost point of Rushing Bay, bordered by land that stretches south on either side for over a hundred miles, which makes the bay—and Silvermoon Harbor—easily defensible from the south. When the creature made itself known and I closed our borders, I sent the naval fleet south to stand guard at Cobalt Point, where the bay opens into the ocean.

I have no idea whether my ships continue to stand guard at Cobalt, but after bringing word of our visit, Grey reported that Silvermoon Harbor stands in better shape than he anticipated. Their proximity to the sea would have kept them well fed—and provided ample resources for trading with towns farther off. Even still, I offer silver coins and good tidings to everyone we meet along the road. For those who look in need of food, I tell them to come to where the South Road meets the King's Highway, in two days, and I will have a wagon of food and supplies waiting.

For those who look well fed and able, I tell them we are seeking to rebuild Emberfall's army.

At my side, Harper has been quiet and aloof, reciting the lines I've given her to perfection—while adding her own flair. The King of Disi longs for another victory. The people of Disi are eager for trade with those of Emberfall. The children of Disi have so much to learn from Emberfall's rich and civilized culture. The mark on her cheek, the dagger at her waist, the cool edge to her words . . . she makes the perfect warrior princess from a different land. What I know is restless uncertainty comes across as distant composure.

Before long, the city wall looms ahead, the gates closed and guarded. A shadow flickers in the guard tower at the top of the wall, and after a moment, bells peal out, ringing loudly, a repeated *bong-bong-bong*. We've been spotted. The gates draw open.

"What does that mean?" says Harper. "The bells."

"Royalty approaches," I say. "They ring differently for different things. You will hear them at every city we visit."

Her jaw is tense. She says nothing.

"Are you nervous, my lady?" My voice is light, the question almost teasing, but the words are genuine. Tension has begun a slow, lazy crawl up my spine as well. We have one guard and one untested soldier. I have a bow strapped to the saddle and a sword at my hip. I can already see at least a hundred people lining the street leading through Silvermoon, drawn by the bells. In my former life, they would have been no cause for concern. I would have been traveling with a dozen guards at least—if not more while in my father's company.

Now if this crowd were to turn against me, to turn against my family's abandonment of them, it would not take many to have us outnumbered and dead on the cobblestones.

"Not nervous." Harper draws the words out. "But meeting people on the road feels different from . . . from *that.*" She nods ahead to the still-gathering crowd.

I lean closer and drop my voice. "I would be surprised if anyone dares to approach. It was once said that approaching the royal family without invitation was a good way to lose your head in the street."

Her head snaps around. "What? Really?"

"The Royal Guard has quite the reputation." I look across at Grey. "Isn't that true, Commander?"

"We take few chances." His voice is almost bored—or maybe distracted. His eyes are watching the crowd.

When we draw near, three armed men and a woman on horseback separate from the crowd and ride through the archway, blocking the road and therefore the entrance. One man and the woman wear armor, and carry as many weapons as Grey and Jamison. The other two men ride in front. At first glance, their attire fits well, sporting threads of silver and gold, but as we draw closer, the men's faces are drawn and wary. They may not be armored, but they are armed.

I don't recognize either of them. Many of the local lords ran—or died—when the creature first unleashed its terror on the lands neighboring Ironrose.

"The Grand Marshal, my lord," says Grey, his voice low. "And his Seneschal."

For a moment, I regret sending word of our visit. This man could carry nothing but resentment for the crown, for a royal family who has seemingly abandoned them for years. Tension builds in the air between our party and theirs. I'm tempted to draw to a halt, or to demand an expression of their intent. I'm tempted to send Grey across the remaining forty feet of road to inquire as to our reception here. The people behind their representatives are quiet, peering out of the opening.

Clearly Harper is not the only one harboring uncertainty.

To my left, Jamison's breathing is steady. A soldier used to following his commanding officer into war. It's reassuring. I have two men to fight at my side—and that's a one hundred percent improvement over yesterday. We ride forward.

At twenty feet, the two leading men dismount from their horses, followed by their two guards. They stride forward. They draw their swords.

Grey's hand finds the hilt of his own. Harper sucks in a breath.

But then the men and their guards fall to one knee. Their swords are laid on the stone road in front of them.

"Your Highness," says one. "Welcome. The people of Silvermoon have long awaited your return."

"We greet you with great relief," says the other. "You and your lady."

Beside me, Harper lets out a slow breath.

I do the same.

"Rise, Marshal," I say. "We thank you and your Seneschal for the kind welcome." I have to pause to make sure my voice gives away nothing. "We are eager to visit with the people of Silvermoon."

They rise and mount their horses, leading us toward the city. The Grand Marshal is a large man my father's age, with thick, graying hair and a stern yet kind demeanor. He compliments Harper, then begins listing the achievements of Silvermoon over the past few years, the ways they've bolstered the city's defense—including defense against the creature, which tightens something in my gut. But he seems anxious to please. His welcome feels genuine.

Like with the moment on the road, I remember what this feels like. To be a part of something.

As we pass through the gates, the people yield the road. They kneel. They call out, "All hail the crown prince!"

It is not the first time I have been welcomed this way.

It is the first time it has ever meant so much.

We leave the horses at the livery so we can walk through the harbor's marketplace on foot. The Grand Marshal offers to escort us with his guards, but he would undoubtedly have questions about the alliance, about the fate of the royal family, and I am not ready to feed a larger meal to the town gossip quite yet.

Once we step into the fray, however, I nearly regret the decision. The aisles are thick with people, voices raised to bicker and barter and trade. Bodies press in closer than I am ready for. A stray dagger could be anywhere. Harper suddenly grips my hand.

Grey knows his job, however. He steps forward and says, "Make way for the crown prince and his lady!"

A path opens before us. Men bow. Ladies curtsy.

But not all. Some stare. The stares are not friendly.

Harper leans close. "I'm sorry I'm so nervous."

Sharing my own tension will do nothing to calm hers. I glance over. "You seem resilient as ever."

"I'm not used to so many people staring at me."

"How regrettable. You surely deserve the attention." I gently move her hand from mine to the crook of my arm. I lean in close to speak softly along her cheek. "I need my sword hand free. You are not the only one who is nervous, my lady."

Surprise registers in her eyes, and she gives a small gasp. I half expect her to let go, but she doesn't. Her hand holds tight at the bend of my elbow.

The cobblestone walkway between rows of vendors and tradesmen has been swept free of snow, and large steel barrels of burning coals sit every dozen feet to warm the air. Every stall boasts something different: silk scarves, hammered silver pendants, beaded hair combs. Swords in one booth, knives in another. Frayed pennants advertising each artisan's trade wave in the cool breeze. I am glad for the open air of the marketplace, because the press of people is actually quite claustrophobic. People continue to yield a path, but many do so only grudgingly. Men meet my eyes and hold them.

It pricks at my pride. My father never would have tolerated it. He would have made an example of one, and no others would have dared such insolence.

My father also would have had twenty-four guards at his back. I have two.

I lean toward Harper again, and keep my voice easy. "What do you think of Silvermoon, my lady?"

"I'm trying not to stare too much."

"Stare all you like. Does anything catch your fancy?"

"All of it does."

"Name anything you like and it is yours." I say this more loudly, and every merchant's head swivels in our direction.

"You don't need to buy me off," Harper says under her breath. "I've already come this far."

"I'm not buying you off. I'm buying *them.* I want to spend silver. Give my people confidence." I pause and raise my voice again. "Silk, you say? Come, let us look."

We spend a small fortune. Vendors have been ordered to deliver bolts of fabric, dozens of dresses, endless trinkets in silver and gold and blown glass, and a pile of painted wooden toys Harper chose for the children. Everything she touches, I buy. When we pass a stall offering beer and spirits, we buy a round for everyone nearby. The men who scowled at me earlier have disappeared, and any uncertainty has vanished from the air.

Even Harper has relaxed into the role. Vendors fawn over her. Women whisper behind their hands, but their eyes are curious, not mean-spirited. Children offer baskets of sugared nuts and warm biscuits, and no one dares to crowd our path now. Grey and Jamison seem more at ease, giving us more space instead of hovering quite so close.

Underneath it all, uncertainty plagues me. I look at each face and imagine soldiers from Syhl Shallow slicing through them with a broadsword. Worse, I look at each face and imagine my creature slashing through them with claws.

By late afternoon, we're nearing the back part of the marketplace, where the stalls and aisleway are larger, and many vendors offer games of chance and entertainment. The scents of salted meats and roasted vegetables carry from the next aisle over, where the marketplace will spill out into a large open area for eating and gathering. Larger weapons are sold back here, too: swords, shields, longbows, and the like.

My eyes linger on the bowyer's stall, the long arcs of wood

ranging in color from bright polished amber to a dark, rich ebony. The stall is larger, with a long channel set up alongside, where shoppers can test a bow before purchase.

Harper follows my gaze. "You haven't bought anything for yourself."

"There is nothing I need." Except *time*, and I haven't yet seen that for sale.

"Well, technically I don't need anything you just bought, either."

The bowyer notices our attention, then turns to pull a long slim bow from the wall. Reddish-brown wood gleams from end to end, the grip wrapped in braided leather. He offers it on outstretched hands. "Do you care to shoot, Your Highness? Or perhaps your lady would? This is the finest bow I have. Wood from the Vuduum Forest."

I inhale to decline—but Harper looks up at me. "Can I do it? Will you show me?"

"Yes, of course."

We draw a crowd almost immediately. Two dozen people form a circle. Grey stands beside us, his back to the stand, and tells Jamison to make sure the people keep their distance.

"Are all these people going to watch?" Harper whispers.

The bowyer offers a slim wrist guard, and I take her hand to buckle it around her forearm. "Nothing generates interest like the opportunity to watch a royal fail at something."

Arrows lie along the ledge at the front of the narrow range, with a wooden target at the end, maybe thirty feet away.

I take an arrow, nock it on the string, and rest the end on the shelf of the bow. "Watch," I tell her. "Straight arm, draw back to the corner of your mouth, and shoot." I do as I say. The string *snaps* hard, and the arrow flies straight into the center of the target.

That earns me a smattering of applause. Harper's eyes are wide. "Way to keep the pressure down."

I smile. "A child could hit the target at this distance." I hold out the bow and another arrow. "Give it a try."

She takes the bow and arrow, then a long, slow breath. Her eyes center on the bull's-eye. She finds focus so easily. The nock of the arrow lands on the string like she's been shooting all her life, and she raises her arm to put it along the bow.

She's so confident about it that I nearly miss the fact that she's resting the arrow on her fingers instead of the bow shelf. I step behind her and close my fingers over her drawing arm before she can let go.

"Was I doing it wrong?" she says.

"If you want to shear the fingers off your hand, you were doing it exactly right." I adjust the placement of the arrow, matching my stance to hers. My arm rests below her forearm, my fingers closing around hers to hold the bow. "Here. Touch your mouth with the string."

When her fingers brush her lip, mine do as well. Her body is warm and close in the circle of my arms. The crowd behind us has melted away, and the moment centers on this one task. "Whenever you're ready," I say softly, "release the string."

Her fingers release. The string snaps, and the arrow goes flying.

It buries itself in the upper-left quadrant of the target. The crowd applauds again.

She turns to me and smiles. "I did it! I like this better than knives. Will you show me again?"

I find it amusing that she keeps asking, as if I would not do this a thousand more times. She seizes another arrow and lines it up on the bow, more sure this time. I lift her elbow to straighten her aim.

She hits closer to the bull's-eye this time. Her eyes are bright, and she's a little breathless. "Again?"

"Of course." I would give anything to touch her face again. Her chin, the soft curve of her lip. I settle for gently straightening her aim.

She hits the target again and smiles up at me. "I love this. Again?"

"As many as you like, my lady."

When she turns to shoot, she shifts closer to me. Whether by accident or intent, I am not sure, but I can feel her warmth. When I place my hand on her arm, I leave it there.

She does not pull away. Maybe fate has finally found me worthy of mercy.

Just as I have the thought, a weight slams into my midsection, and I'm thrown against the side of the bowyer's stall.

And then I hear Harper scream.

CHAPTER THIRTY-ONE

HARPER

An arm encircles my waist and I can't move. I'm so stupid—at first I thought it was Rhen grabbing me, to adjust my stance somehow, and I probably lost a moment to fight. But from the corner of my eye, I see Rhen being slammed into the side of the stall.

Hot breath singes my ear, and the heavy weight of a man is at my back. The arm around my waist pulls tight, lifting me just off the ground—and blocking the dagger that Grey belted onto me. I struggle, but his grip turns painful. An arm wraps around my rib cage from behind, a fist pressing into my neck.

"Be still, Princess," a vaguely mocking voice says in my ear.

Dozens of faces surround us, but I can't see Rhen now. I can't see Grey.

"Kill their guards," a man yells somewhere to my left. "Take the prince alive. Do what you want with the princess."

The bow is still clutched in my hand, and I whip it back over my shoulder. The man grunts in surprise, but redoubles his grip. His wrist presses into my throat. Hard. I can't breathe. Spots flare in my vision.

A *thwick* snaps right beside my head, and the hand at my neck drops away. I collapse into a pool of blue-and-white silk and lace. My knees crack into the cobblestones.

There's a man on the ground beside me. A knife sticks out of his eye. The other is open and staring and dead.

I give a short scream, but the sound is lost in the mayhem of the crowd surrounding us. My eyes find another dead man. A knife juts out of his neck. Another lies five feet to my right, blood staining the front of his clothing from chest to thigh. I scramble backward on the stones.

I finally find Rhen. He's on his feet, his sword in his hand. His eyes are wary, trained behind me. Jamison is beside him. Blood runs from a sharp cut over his eye.

No Grey. Where is Grey?

"Harper," says Rhen. "Are you all right?"

Before I can answer, another man rushes from the crowd, a dagger clutched in each fist. He leaps at me, one blade outstretched. I duck and throw up an arm to protect myself, but that's not going to stop a dagger.

Grey steps from behind me. His sword is an arc of silver in the sunlight.

The man loses his hand.

A quick blow from Grey's sword hilt sends him to the ground.

Blood is suddenly everywhere. I can't quite process it. I'm going to hyperventilate.

The man can't seem to process it either. He's almost instantly ashen. He stares at the stump of his arm and starts screaming. Blood collects between the cobblestones.

What did Grey say this morning? *We take few chances.*

Chaos surrounds us, and I can't tell if people are trying to swarm closer—or trying to escape. Maybe both. My breath roars in my ears, adrenaline coursing hard with every beat of my heart. I can't look away from the splattered blood in front of me.

Rhen steps forward to offer a hand and I take it. He pulls me to my feet and draws me against him.

I want to bury my face in his chest. That might not be what a princess would do, but there's blood in the air and gore on the cobblestones, and my brain wants to curl up and hide. But we're surrounded. I have no idea whether this crowd is hostile or friendly or if we have any way to get free.

Grey puts one booted foot on the man's severed forearm and levels the point of his sword at the man's throat. He must apply pressure, because the man's high-pitched screams change to choked whimpers.

Grey looks to Rhen, clearly waiting for an order.

"Not yet," Rhen says. He looks around at the crowd of people. "Anyone else?" he calls.

His voice isn't arrogant—it's full of fury. A voice that says anyone else will be swiftly dealt with.

The crowd seems to feel it, too. People move back, away from the carnage on the ground.

Grey's expression has no give to it now. This isn't the man who charmed smiles out of children in the snow. This isn't even the man who spoke passionately of honor and duty in the hallway. This is the lethal swordsman who kidnapped me. This is the scariest Grey of all.

"He's going to bleed to death," I say to Rhen, my voice broken and small.

"He has time." Rhen glares down at the man. "He was going to kill you, my lady. Let him think on his fate."

The man's face is white now, but he spits at Rhen. "You left us. Your family left us to that monster."

The metallic tang of his blood mixes with the scent of snow and fish in the air, turning my stomach. I was so cavalier in the inn, ordering Grey to show those soldiers I meant business. Every time something happens here, the stakes seem to grow larger.

Your family left us to that monster.

While I'm standing there staring at him with a dry mouth and trembling hands, the man is bleeding to death on the cobblestones.

"Kill him," Rhen says. "Let him be an example."

"No!" screams a woman from the crowd.

Grey lifts his sword. I stumble away from Rhen and put a hand on his arm. "Wait." My voice almost breaks again. "Wait."

Grey waits.

"Don't kill him." My voice shakes with adrenaline, and I have to fight to get the words out. "Do you have a doctor here? A—a healer? He needs—he needs a tourniquet."

An older woman pushes through the people, but stops at the edge. Her face is red and tear-streaked. She must be the one who screamed. She gives a rough curtsy. "Your Highness. I can bind his arm."

"Do it," I say. Rhen's hand is still locked on mine, but his fingers are like steel. I can't look at him. I'm worried that his face will show that I'm making the wrong decisions here, but I can't watch another man die in front of me.

The woman takes a hesitant step forward, then glances at Grey.

"Commander." I have to clear my throat. My eyes feel damp. "Let her work."

He takes a step back. He does not sheathe his sword.

The woman crouches beside the fallen man and pulls lengths of muslin from a satchel. She speaks to the man on the ground, and her voice shakes as much as mine. "Allin, Allin, why would you do such a thing?"

His voice is rough and broken. "They will bring war . . . war to Silvermoon. For their own . . . for their own selfishness."

A loud murmur runs through the crowd.

I flinch. The Queen of Syhl Shallow will bring war—a war I'm promising to fight with an invisible army.

Rhen looks at the people again. "Silence!"

Silence drops like a rock. Fear hangs in the air, more potent than even before. I can feel the uncertainty in the crowd. The man's whimpers mix with the woman's panicked breath.

"I will not have more blood spilled in Silvermoon," Rhen says. "You are my people and I have sworn to protect you." He glances at me. "The Princess of Disi has sworn to protect you, and even today, shows mercy to a man who deserves none."

A low murmur passes through the crowd.

"Silence!" Rhen calls again.

They obey.

He looks out at them. "You once swore fealty to my father. To me. I know you are afraid. I know the Queen of Syhl Shallow has begun an attack on Emberfall. I know you worry. I know you have been left to fend for yourselves for far too long."

Passion rings in every word. They're listening.

He takes a step forward. "I am here now. And I will fight for you. I will fight *with* you. I will give my life for you. My question for you is: Will you do the same for Silvermoon? For Emberfall?"

Silence hangs for the longest moment.

Rhen hits his chest and steps forward. "Will you do the same for me?"

His people seemed frozen.

But the woman crouched over Allin ties a last knot in her bandage, then straightens to kneel. "I will, Your Highness."

"No." Allin groans. "Marna. No."

Marna puts a hand over her chest. Her voice shook before, but now her tone is clear and solid. "For the good of Emberfall."

A large older man with a full beard and a belly that hangs over his belt steps away from the crowd. He falls to a knee. "I will, Your Highness."

Another man, younger, his face pale and fixed on the carnage left in the circle. But his voice, too, is clear. "I will, Your Highness."

Slowly at first, and then with more speed, the remaining people in the marketplace fall to a knee. Their calls of "I will" turn deafening.

Rhen raises his sword. "For the good of Emberfall!"

"For the good of all!" they call.

I stare at him. He's turned the energy of the crowd from tension and doubt to loyalty. They would form an army and stand against this invading queen right now if he asked it. I can feel it.

"Rise," he says. "Claim the dead. Have your bailiff take this man into custody."

Then he sheathes his sword and turns to Marna. "The princess has decreed that this man should live. If you make a list of what you need to treat his injury, I will have it provided."

The woman looks a bit stunned. "Yes, Your Highness."

"Who is he to you?" Rhen asks.

"My brother." Marna drags a shaking hand across one cheek. "The—the creature killed his daughter. Two years ago."

Beside me, Rhen goes still. "You have my sympathy." He pauses. "You were the first to swear. Why is that?"

The woman pushes a strand of gray hair behind her ear. "I remember the king's visits to Silvermoon, Your Highness. He would not have let this man live."

Rhen glances at me. "The Princess of Disi allowed him to live."

"But—you allowed the choice." Marna hesitates again, but then seems to steel her nerve. "We have long thought the royal family had abandoned Emberfall. If rumor is true, they fled to save themselves, leaving us all at the mercy of the creature. And now, at the mercy of Karis Luran."

Rhen frowns. "Yet still you swore to me."

"Yes, Your Highness." The woman bows her head. "You alone came back."

I want to go home.

Or at least back to the castle.

I'm screwed on either count. Rhen says we can't leave. He doesn't want to give the impression that we're easily cowed.

I am, though. I'm cowed.

Every time I blink, I see Allin's blood spilling across the cobblestones.

But the worst was hearing Rhen say, "Kill him."

And watching Grey lift his arm.

We've moved to the Commons now, an open area at the back of the market where food is cooked and sold. It's busy, but without the press of bodies that crowded the aisles of the marketplace. The scents of beer and cooked meat fill the air, undercut with the warm sweetness of baked bread.

Dusk has fallen, painting the sky with streaks of pink and yellow, bringing a chill back to the air. More barrels of fire have been placed near the tables. Strange faces flicker in the firelight. Everyone looks at me. It was mildly unsettling before. Now that I know people want us dead, it's terrifying.

The Grand Marshal and his Seneschal came to find us after the attack. They couldn't stop apologizing, and insisted on adding a contingent of guards to back Grey and Jamison.

Rhen declined. A further show of trust, he explained to me—though honestly I'd kind of stopped listening to him by that point. It's all I can do to keep this mildly bored look plastered to my face.

"My lady."

I blink and look up. Rhen's been talking to me again. "I'm sorry, what?"

His eyes are concerned. "Here. Sit. I will have some food brought."

"I don't think I can eat anything."

"You have eaten nothing since this morning."

I keep my voice low. "If you think I can eat after what happened, you're insane."

"Sit, then. The guardsmen need to eat, too."

That startles me into sitting. I hadn't thought about Grey and Jamison.

"I will return in a moment," says Rhen. A hand brushes over my shoulder before he strides away, Jamison close by his side. I'm alone at a large stone table, sitting on a wide wooden bench. Grey stands close by, the firelight flickering off the polished buckles of his uniform.

"Do you want to sit down?" I ask him.

He glances at me, but only for the briefest moment. I expect his voice to be short, sharp, the way his mood feels, but his tone is low, quiet. "I should not."

I follow his gaze to where Rhen is speaking with a woman tending a spit. The woman laughs and curtsies, and a coin sparks in the light as Rhen hands it over.

Grey's quiet voice gives me the courage to ask him a question I'm not sure I want the answer to. "Do you think there will be another attack?"

"We are sorely outnumbered. They very nearly got the best of us earlier. One more attacker and we might have had a different outcome."

I consider the *thwick* of his throwing knives, the way our attackers dropped on the stones. "You seemed to do okay."

"I am glad it seemed so. It should not have happened at all." He nods toward where Rhen is turning away from the hearth, Jamison at his heels. "It is dangerous for us to be divided, even momentarily. Jamison is a soldier, not a guardsman. I forgot earlier. I will not forget again."

I turn those words over in my mind until I figure it out. Grey is mad at *himself*.

Rhen has moved to another vendor. I watch more coins change hands.

"Did I do the wrong thing?" I say, and my voice is rough and quiet. "When Rhen told you to kill that man. Should I have let you do it?"

He looks out at the people milling around the Commons, and for a long moment, I wonder if he won't answer this either. Our relationship seems to tick forward like the hands of a clock, always changing in relation to each other.

Eventually, Grey says, "You are merciful and kind. But kindness and mercy always find their limit, beyond which they turn to weakness and fear."

"Where's the limit?" I say softly.

His eyes find mine. "That answer is different for each of us."

Rhen returns, carrying two earthenware mugs. He sets one on the table in front of me. "If you will not eat," he says, "please drink."

I hesitate, then wrap my hands around the mug. "Thanks."

He seems encouraged by this, then drops onto the bench across from me. "Food will be delivered soon." He glances up at the soldier. "Jamison. Grey. Join us."

Behind him, Jamison moves forward and places the two handled steins he carries in one hand on the table as well, then swings a leg over the bench. He pushes one stein across the table, his expression easy. "Commander?"

Grey remains next to me. From the corner of my eye, I see him give Jamison a look.

The soldier falters, then begins to rise.

"No," says Rhen. "Sit." He looks up at Grey. "That is an order."

Grey sits. He doesn't touch the mug.

"I believe we are winning over the people," Rhen says. "I want them to know we are confident despite the attack. That they have our trust." He looks at Grey. "Do you disagree, Commander?"

Grey may be sitting at the table, but his eyes are still on the people surrounding us. "Allow me to answer once I make it out of Silvermoon without an arrow in my back."

"Look around. The Grand Marshal has dispatched his own guards anyway. Anyone would be foolish to make a move now."

He did? I look around, and then I see them, the uniformed men and women lurking in the shadows. It makes me feel better. A little.

Rhen looks at me, and his voice is quiet. "Our visit has been a success, my lady."

I'm not sure I agree. I take a small sip from the mug he brought.

A woman approaches with a tray loaded with platters of roasted meat. She unloads everything onto the table between us.

"Eat." Rhen pushes a platter in my direction. "Please."

It's the *please* that gets me. There isn't much Rhen says that isn't a command. I gingerly pick at the food, which reminds me of a chicken stew, though slightly different. Instead of savory, there's a bit of sweetness on my tongue.

A young woman approaches the table, and Grey is on his feet in one quick, fluid motion. The girl stops short. She wears braids down to her waist and a red dress that looks striking against her warm brown skin.

Her dark, worried eyes glance from Grey to Rhen, and she offers a low curtsy. "Forgive me, Your Highness. I am Zo, apprentice to the Master of Song for Silvermoon. I wished to request an audience with you."

Rhen nods. "It's all right, Commander."

Zo says, "The king always opened an evening's dancing. I would ask if you and the princess might care to do the same."

Rhen looks at me. "Would you care to dance, my lady?"

He must be kidding.

"No," I say tightly. "Thank you."

Rhen gives me a long look, then turns back to the girl. "Another time, perhaps."

She hesitates before turning away. "Is it true that the Royal Guard is once again accepting applicants?"

"Yes," says Rhen. "If you know of someone—"

"I am asking for myself."

Rhen inhales to speak. I have no idea what he's going to say, but I remember how he reacted to Jamison, much less a girl my size. I'm already irritated, so I say, "Yes. Come to the castle to apply."

Her face lights with a smile, and she offers a curtsy before dashing away.

I take another bite of the stew and keep my eyes on my plate. My shoulders are rigid for an entirely new reason. We eat in silence for the longest time. Men and women begin moving toward the back part of the Commons, gathering in the open space that must be reserved for dancing.

Eventually, Rhen looks to Jamison and Grey. "Leave us."

They do, moving away to stand at a short distance.

I still don't look at Rhen.

"You seem displeased," he says, and his voice carries enough edge that I think he's the one who's displeased.

"Why would you ask me to dance?" I demand. "We just killed people. It's inappropriate."

"People attacked *us* and lost their lives. We did not randomly slaughter people in the streets. We cannot afford to appear weak, my lady."

I wonder if that's a dig about the man I allowed to live—or a dig about the girl I just invited to apply for the Royal Guard. Grey was right about limits. I have no idea where mine are. I have no idea where Rhen's are, for that matter.

"Fine," I say. "Even if it *were* appropriate, I can barely walk without limping. You think I can glide around a dance floor? I've got the mark of one failure on my cheek. I don't need to give anyone more evidence."

Rhen's eyes narrow slightly. "You believe I asked you as some form of . . . humiliation?"

"I have no idea. But are you even thinking about what you're asking? You think the people are going to see me as a fierce warrior queen when I fall on my face?"

"Enough." His tone is sharp. "You can ride a horse. You faced down a swordsman to save Freya's family. You faced down *another* at the inn. Still yet another attack this very morning." He leans in against the table. His eyes have turned dark and angry. "You asked Grey to teach you how to throw knives, and you asked me to show you how to handle a bow. You have convinced my people that you rule a neighboring nation, and I don't think you understand the magnitude of how very impressive that is."

"Fine. What's your point?"

He looks as irritated as I feel. "All of that, and you somehow believe I seek to humiliate you by dancing?" He slams down his beer stein. "My lady, I must ask—are *you* even thinking about what *you* are asking?"

Before I can respond, he rises from the bench and storms away.

CHAPTER THIRTY-TWO

RHEN

I storm to the edge of the Commons, where the ground drops away in a nearly sheer cliff, revealing the harbor below, docks and ships glistening in the rising moonlight. Smaller fishing wherries and larger crabbing boats are docked for the winter season, and ice clings to the posts in the water. Candlelight flickers in a few windows, but most buildings stand dark and quiet. Lanterns swing jauntily as sailors and dockworkers head home.

Along a deserted, icy dock, I spot a couple wrapped in a loving embrace.

So easy. So unfair.

Music carries across the clearing, and couples have joined to dance at the far side of the Commons. Torches blaze along tall posts surrounding the band. Despite the merriment, I can feel the weight of eyes on my back. I've provided enough gossip to occupy the people of Silvermoon for days. I seized control by stopping an attack and demanding allegiance—and now I'm about to undo it all because of one moment of irritation.

I never should have stalked off the way I did. I imagine my father's voice.

People can create scandal from a word. From a look. You, son, give them no shortage of either.

Harper draws up beside me. I don't look at her. I'm not sure what I want to say.

She must sense my quarrelsome mettle, because she says nothing herself.

I feel as though I owe her an apology—but possibly that she owes me one as well. We stand together, staring out at the water, at the night sky sprinkled with stars. Wind whips off the harbor to whistle between us, ruffling my hair and lifting her skirts. Silence stretches on for ages, until my irritation begins to dissipate, turning the quiet into something warmer. Easier.

"In the castle," I say eventually, "the music never changes. Every season, the songs begin again, no matter what I do."

She is quiet, and music swells from the opposite side of the clearing, muffled because we're so near the water, and the creaking of the boats and the gently slapping waves provide an undercurrent of sound.

"I used to love music," I say. "My family did, too. That is part of why the instruments play every day—my father once ordered it so. Music at every party, every event, every morning at daybreak. I once loved it."

She still says nothing, but I can see the edge of her profile. She's turned to look at me slightly.

I keep my eyes on the harbor. "Now I hate it."

She lets out a breath. A sound of acquiescence—or defeat. "But the music here is new." A pause. "Different."

"Yes."

"Asking me to dance wasn't part of a calculated effort to win over your people. This was about distracting yourself from the curse."

She's right, but put that way, my motives seem childish, especially considering our goals here. I frown.

"Okay," she says. "Show me."

I look at her. Raise an eyebrow.

She wets her lips. "I'm not going to be good at it. When I was younger, my physical therapist recommended ballet to help stretch my muscles and improve balance—but I hated it. I was terrible. Mom had to use horseback riding as a bribe to get me to go."

A bribe. To *dance*, of all things. So very Harper.

I extend a hand. "May I?"

She looks at my hand and hesitates.

I wait.

Her hand finally drops into mine, her fingers soft, light against my own. I turn her to face me, then place her hand on my shoulder.

Her breath catches. She is so still that I do not think she's breathing.

I step closer, until her skirts brush my legs, and I rest a hand on her waist. "I am inviting you to dance, not dragging you behind a horse." I sigh dramatically. "Must you look so *tortured*?"

That makes her smile. The expression must pull at the stitches along her cheek, because the smile flickers and vanishes. Her free hand hovers, pausing over my own as if she's debating whether to shove me away.

She is so tense. The girl who climbed down the castle trellis and threw a knife at Lilith is afraid to *dance*.

"Is everyone staring at us?" she whispers.

Very likely, but I do not turn my head to see. "Doubtful," I tell her. "The night grows dark." A bit of warmth heats my voice. "My own eyes see only you."

She blushes, then shakes her head a little and looks out at the harbor. "You're too good at this. How many other girls did you dance with?"

"What number would ease your worries? A dozen? A hundred?" I pause. "None? All?"

"You're dodging the question."

"I have no answer. Who would keep count of such a thing? Besides, you must be aware I danced with other women even before the curse." I pause and move closer. "I can say with certainty that I never taught any to dance at the edge of a cliff at Silvermoon."

"I'm standing. Not dancing."

"All part of your lesson. Close your eyes."

She scowls, but her eyes fall closed. I move even closer, until we're barely separated by breath. Not moving, simply standing, trapped between the quiet noises of the harbor and the louder melody carrying across the Commons.

The moment strikes me with a memory and I do not move.

"Before the curse," I say slowly, "I would sometimes dance with my sister—"

"Arabella?"

I'm startled that she remembers. "No. Never Arabella. She had no shortage of suitors—and no shortage of temper to keep them in line. My youngest sister. Isadore." My voice thickens with emotion, which takes me by surprise. I need to clear my throat. "She was barely fourteen, but the Grand Marshal of Boone River had expressed an interest in marriage. The man was three times her age. When he would come to court, Isa would make excuses about family obligations, then seek me out and attach herself to my side." My voice trails off. I'm not entirely sure why I began this line of conversation.

Harper opens her eyes. Her fingers have relaxed on my shoulder, and now her forearm rests along my bicep, her waist soft under my hand. "You and Isa were close."

"No." I shake my head. "I was the crown prince. I was raised apart from my sisters. In truth, I rarely saw her."

I blink, though, and I see Isa in my mind, the way I found her after my first transformation. Her body was nowhere near those of the rest of the family.

To this day, I still wonder if Isa was coming to find me. As if I weren't the cause of the very destruction she sought to escape.

Harper's eyes are dark with empathy. "I'm sorry, Rhen."

"It was quite a long time ago. I do not know what made me speak of it." My thoughts tangle with remorse, and I feel as though I have lost my way. I blink and shake my head, wishing the memories could be shaken off so easily. "Where were we?"

"Dancing lessons."

"Ah. Yes." I lean close again. "Close your eyes."

She does. We have not yet moved, but conversation—or pity—has distracted her. I step forward, giving a soft push with my hand, and she yields, stepping back too quickly.

"Easy," I say softly, keeping ahold of her waist. "Do not run from me."

"Sorry." Her eyes slide open. "I told you I was terrible at this."

I shake my head. "Eyes closed."

She obeys, which must be something of a miracle.

"Another step," I say, "and then three to the side, then three back."

While her motions are slow and halting, she stays within the circle of my arms and allows me to lead. Gradually, bit by bit, muscle by muscle, she relaxes into the movement. Our steps begin to match the music from across the clearing. For an instant, I allow myself to forget the curse. We dance in the moonlight at the edge of the cliff, surrounded by night air.

The song ends, quickly replaced by something fast and lively.

I stop, and Harper does, too. Her eyes open, and she looks up at me. "This one's too fast," she says quietly.

"We can wait for another."

I expect her to pull away, but she does not. "I think the standing-still part is my favorite."

I smile. "You do it quite masterfully."

Her eyes narrow a fraction, catching sparks in the moonlight. "You're not as arrogant as you pretend to be."

I go still.

"You're really good at laying on the charm," she says. "But I like this Rhen better."

" 'This Rhen'?"

"When you're not scheming, and you're just *doing*." She pauses. "Like your story about Isadore. You made it sound like she was an annoying little sister, but I think you liked it. Or the way you won't let Grey go after Lilith. At first I thought it was a pride thing—but it's not. You're protecting him."

Her assessment reminds me of Grey's when we stood outside the inn in the snow. When I teased him about punishment for falling asleep on guard. When he said, *The king would have . . . But not you, I do not think.*

At the time, his comment made me feel weak.

Harper's comment does not.

"And you're unexpectedly patient," she says. "For someone who expects everything to be done on his command."

She is wrong. My shoulders tense—but at the same time, I do not want her to stop. As always, her words speak right to the core of me, but these do not feel like censure and instead light me with warmth. "No one would ever call me patient."

"You are. In a different way."

"In what way?"

"In the fact that you're standing here, not making me feel like an idiot because I can't dance." She pauses. "The way you didn't make me feel like an idiot for asking you to show me how to shoot an arrow."

"You did that quite well," I say, and mean it.

Her voice goes quiet. "The way you don't treat me like I can't do something."

"Truly?" I release her hand to brush that errant lock of hair from her face. "You have convinced me you can do anything."

She blushes. "Don't start with the compliments."

"It is not a compliment." My fingers linger along her jaw, tracing the softness of her skin.

"Even now," she says, "you're out here risking our lives, trusting me to help you save your people, when you don't really know anything about me. When you're probably supposed to be back at the castle feeding me grapes and trying to get me to fall in love with you."

"Grapes?" I say. "Is that what it would take?"

"The red ones are secretly the way to my heart."

My thumb strokes over the curve of her lip. Her breath shudders.

Her free hand flies up to catch my wrist.

I freeze. She will shove me away again, the way she did in the inn.

"Wait," she whispers. "Just wait." Then her lip quirks and she repeats my line from earlier. "Do not run from me."

"I will not run."

To my surprise, tears form in her eyes, a glint of diamonds on her lashes. "I want to trust you," she says, so quietly that her voice could get lost on the wind. "I want—I want to know it's real. Not that you're trying to trick me to break the curse."

I do not understand how she can fill me with such hope and fear simultaneously. I pull her hand to my chest and lean in to her, until we share breath. My lips brush across hers.

It is barely a kiss, but she is somehow closer to me, her body a pool of warmth against mine.

I want so desperately to turn it into more, to see where this blossoming attraction will lead.

But I have come close before. I have found this moment before.

The only difference is that I have never wanted it so badly.

I draw back, then press my lips to her forehead.

"I want to know it's real, too," I say.

Her body goes still against mine, and then she nods. Her head falls against my shoulder, her face close enough to breathe warmth against my neck. It puts my hand at the small of her back, the other on her shoulder.

I speak low, against her temple. "Shall I have the guards call for the horses?"

"Not yet," she says. "Is that okay?"

"Always."

I stand and hold her until the music fades and the night grows too cold.

But inside I'm warm, and my heart wants to sing.

We arrive at Ironrose late. Stars light up the sky and torches burn along the front of the castle, lighting the spaces where guards once stood.

Grey and Jamison take the horses, and I walk Harper through the Great Hall and up the sweeping staircase. The air is thick with tired silence, and neither of us breaks it, but for the first time, no wall of tension stands between us.

We stop in front of her door, and she looks up at me. "Are we doing this all again tomorrow?"

I cannot tell from the tone of her voice whether she's eager or apprehensive—or simply exhausted. "No. I will have Grey send word to the Grand Marshal of Sillery Hill that we will visit in three days' time. I want to give news time to spread."

"So we'll stay here."

"If you find that acceptable."

"Maybe we could finish our lesson, since I didn't get to learn much."

"In dancing?" I say, surprised.

She swats my arm. "In shooting arrows." A faint blush finds her cheeks, and she adds, "But dancing would be okay, too."

"Anything you wish."

"I should probably go to bed," she says.

But she lingers and makes no move to open her door.

So *I* linger, wondering if this is an invitation to finish what we began at the edge of the cliff at Silvermoon. I'm not sure precisely what has changed between us, whether it's trust or respect or simply the ability to see each other in a different light. I'm not sure it matters. All I know is that I long to take her hand and lead her into her chambers, to sit at her side and share secrets. To run my fingers through her hair and discover the taste of her skin.

I cannot remember the last time I've felt this longing.

In truth, I'm not sure I ever have.

The door to Freya's room eases open. Harper jumps and takes a step back.

Freya's eyes flash wide. "Oh!" She bobs a curtsy and speaks softly. "Your Highness. My lady. Forgive me. I was going to stoke the fire in the bedroom."

What a coincidence, I think. *I was considering the very same thing.*

I turn to Harper before my thoughts can get ahead of me. "I should leave you to your rest." I bow, then take her hand to brush a kiss across her knuckles. "Until tomorrow, my lady."

It takes every ounce of self-restraint I possess to walk away.

My chambers are a well of darkness, the fire burning low in the hearth. The first season, I was asleep by now, well fed and worn out after a long day of hunting with the king and other nobles—men who had no idea what was in store for them. Exhaustion rides my back today as well, but it is no match for the tiny thrill of anticipation skipping through my veins.

I leave my candles dark, enjoying the quiet after the noise of the day. I shed my weapons, my bracers and greaves, then begin to unbuckle my jacket.

A long sigh escapes my chest. Hope is a luxury I cannot afford. An emotion I cannot dare to feel.

Hope blooms in my chest anyway, a tiny bud giving way to the first light of spring, petals daring to open to reveal the color inside.

I want to know it's real.

That must mean it's real for her.

The last buckle gives and I toss the jacket on the chair. When my fingers find the lacings of my shirt, hands settle on my shoulders. I freeze.

"Prince Rhen," says Lilith. "I'd forgotten what a fine form you have."

I jerk away and turn to face her. I want to snatch the jacket back from the chair. "What are you doing here?"

She moves closer to me, her eyes dark in the firelit room. "You once enjoyed my company in your chambers," she says. "Has so much changed?"

"You know what's changed."

She steps closer, until a breath would bring my chest against hers. "Did you have a nice visit in Silvermoon? I'm amused at your attempts to convince the people you have secured this mysterious alliance. Tell me, what will you do when they discover your family is not in exile, but is actually dead?" She feigns a gasp. "Will you disclose that it happened by your own hand?"

"If I can save Emberfall from Karis Luran's army, I will worry about that day when it comes." I point at the door. "Leave my room, Lady Lilith. You are not welcome here."

She lifts her hand to stroke down my chest, her fingers trailing a line of squirming discomfort along my skin that makes me gasp and jerk away before I can stop it.

This will lead nowhere good. I seize her wrist. "What do you want?"

She steps into me, pressing our hands together between our

bodies. It's like clutching a coal against my rib cage, and it pulls a low sound from my throat. I attempt another step back, but now she holds fast.

"I can stop this so easily," she breathes. "Have you never considered wooing *me* to break this curse?"

"Get off me." I want the words to be a threat, but they're more of a plea.

She rises on her tiptoes to brush her lips over mine, a cruel perversion of the moment I shared with Harper. I turn my face away, pain stealing my breath. "You—you are not to interfere."

"I interfere with nothing," she whispers against my cheek. "Your broken girl is nowhere to be found." A pause. "Do you wish to call for her? Perhaps she would like to beg for more—"

"No!"

Lilith laughs, her breath a rush of heat along my neck. "You are so easy, Rhen. This is why you will not reclaim Emberfall. This is why your kingdom would have fallen, even without my interference. Do you know I tried to seduce your father first, but he turned me away?" She leans down close again. "The King of Emberfall knew, even then, that succumbing to the wrong temptation could undo a man."

My father, the great philanderer, who would bed any courtesan in eyesight, had the wherewithal to say no to Lilith.

Ever the fool, I walked right into her trap.

Another bolt of failure to join the others lodged in my heart. I clench my eyes closed. "You will leave Harper alone. You will leave Grey alone."

Her tongue traces the length of my jaw and I shudder. "Of course, Your Highness. You know I would much rather play with you."

Her hand catches my chin. Turns my head. Her lips press against mine.

My jaw is locked, but it does not matter. This is the worst kind of torture. Something more than pain.

I think of Harper standing in the clearing, her hand on my shoulder, gentle fingers wound through mine. *I want to know it's real.*

I think of Harper throwing a knife at Lilith. *Please stop hurting him.*

Humiliation burns my eyes, my throat. When she breaks the kiss, relief nearly breaks *me*. I want to shove her away, but I am pinned to the wall. My breathing is rough and ragged.

I cannot look at her. I can barely move. My hands are still in fists, my muscles so tense I am trembling. Any hope that bloomed in my chest has now withered and died.

"You do not wish for my attentions?" she says.

I have to swallow to form a word. "No. Never."

"Such a waste." She lays a palm against my cheek, and I flinch. She smiles. "How do you propose to rally your people when you are so easily cowed?"

"I will do what I can to save them." A chilling thought wraps around my chest. "Are you going to ruin this, Lilith? Are you working with Karis Luran?"

"I have told you already that I have no hand in this. I can even swear that I will allow your charade to play out."

I blink at her. It's rare to obtain such a direct oath from her. "You will not interfere with my people."

"I will not interfere with your people."

I'm nearly breathless. "And Karis Luran. You will not reveal our plans—"

"I will not reveal your plans." Her palm is still pressed to my cheek and she leans in. "I truly wish to see her take Emberfall from you, Rhen. I shall enjoy watching."

This promise gives me strength. I straighten. "You shall be disappointed."

"Your Highness. Consider the state of your people."

"I have—"

A white light steals my vision. I'm suddenly in the middle of a village. Rain pours down. Bodies are strewn everywhere. Men. Women. Children. Some have been dismembered. Arrows jut from others. Blood mixes with rain to form glistening puddles along the road. In the distance, homes are burning, smoke a thick plume pouring into the sky.

My knees threaten to collapse, but I blink and I'm staring at Lilith again.

"You show me the future?" I choke out.

"No. I show you what the soldiers of Syhl Shallow did to your border city."

My mouth opens, but my room vanishes again. A city, this time, larger. Wildthorne Valley. A brawl has broken out. Men who are too thin to fight are battling over the remains of a roasted deer. A punch is thrown and a woman ends up in the mud. Men step on her trying to get to the dead animal. A child screams from somewhere beyond.

I cry out, but I'm back in my chambers.

"I show you the present," Lilith says, her voice low and vicious.

"Stop," I whisper. "Stop this."

My room disappears again. We're in the middle of a sunlit village. The scent of fish fills the air, but it is not Silvermoon. Another water-dependent town, though, and the people seem better fed. A young boy carries a plank laden with fish across his shoulders. He's whistling, and a woman from a nearby hut calls out, "Jared! Hurry with those to the fishmonger! The day's half-gone!"

"I'm going, Ma! I'm going!"

I can breathe. This scene isn't too terrible.

A low growl fills the air. The boy's whistle is cut short. He turns, a look of sudden panic on his face.

"Jared!" screams the woman. "No!"

A black shape rushes from the edge of my vision and tackles the boy. The creature is three times his size. Part wildcat, part bear, all claws and teeth and snarling rage. It tears him apart in less time than it takes me to blink. One moment, boy. The next, nothing but so much blood and flesh and viscera.

The woman screams so long and loud that I do not realize I have reappeared in my chambers. I'm on my knees, my arms gripped across my abdomen. I've bitten my lip and blood burns on my tongue.

I know what my creature does. I have heard stories from Grey. From my people themselves.

I have never *seen* it. Never with human eyes.

"Please," I whimper. "Please stop."

"Oh, but Your Highness, I believe you deserve to know the true state of your people." Lilith's eyes flash. "Before you lead them into war, you should know them all. Before you tear Harper limb from limb, you should know what you're capable of."

"No." A tear slides down my cheek. "Please."

She has no mercy. My rooms disappear. Lilith continues her onslaught.

No matter how much I beg, she does not stop.

CHAPTER THIRTY-THREE

HARPER

I wake up, still swooning. Sunlight beams through my open windows, the warm autumn air carrying the scents of honeysuckle and cut grass. I half expect cartoon butterflies to start flitting around.

I would have kissed him. I *wanted* to kiss him. I can see why he's failed at this curse so many times—he keeps so much of himself hidden. Even now, I feel as though I've barely scratched the surface. This arrogant front makes me wonder what was expected of him before the curse destroyed his life. People here seem afraid of royalty. They seem afraid of *him*. Based on my first days here, I understand it. But now I've seen the truth. Underneath the arrogant distance, he's caring. Deeply loyal. Gentle, in fact. So unexpectedly patient. He seems afraid to show that side of himself, as if his people will abandon him if they see it.

But he so genuinely cares about protecting them. That weighs on him more than the curse, I think.

The thought of finding him this morning leaves me a little giddy. Even Freya comments on it when she arrives to plait my hair.

"You had a nice evening with the prince?" she says coyly, then bumps my shoulder with her hip.

I blush so hard my cheek aches.

Freya ties off the braid. "I believe he is in the arena with Commander Grey." A teasing pause. "If you were curious, my lady."

I'm curious.

I expect to find more than just Rhen and Grey in the dusty circle, but they're alone, weapons swinging with near blinding speed. They're striking fast, each clash of steel making me flinch. Sweat dampens their hair, telling me they've been at this for a while.

I slow as I approach. The air feels different. Wrong, somehow. The blush fades from my cheeks as I try to figure it out.

Rhen ducks and rushes Grey, hooking his sword to disarm him. Grey slams into the ground, and Rhen follows him down, sword aimed for the other man's neck.

Grey snatches a dagger to stop the blade in time—and his other hand braces against Rhen's forearm, holding him back. Their ragged breathing echoes through the arena.

Something about this feels very personal. Like I've walked in on an argument. I want to back away and ease out of the arena.

But then I hear Grey's voice, low and edged with strain. "Your fight is not with me, my lord."

Rhen swears and shoves himself back, turning away to sheathe his sword. His expression is tight, his eyes hard and set. When he finds me standing by the railing, he seems startled.

The tension on his face does not ease when he sees me. He's as cold and distant as he was the day I arrived. The butterflies that had been frolicking in my abdomen seize up and die.

He offers a curt "My lady," then turns and walks to the side of the arena, where a small table stands with a pitcher of water. He pours, his movements tight and forced.

Something happened.

"What's wrong?" I say.

"Nothing at all." He drains the glass and ducks back under the railing. He still hasn't looked at me. "There could be another attack like in Silvermoon. We should be prepared."

I glance at Grey, but he is watching Rhen, too. He's reclaimed his sword, but he hasn't sheathed his weapon.

He watches Rhen like he anticipates another attack.

Probably a good thing, because Rhen draws his sword.

I duck under the railing and step in front of him before he swings.

He sets his jaw. "Move."

"No. Tell me what happened."

He steps closer to me, each movement full of barely contained rage. Finally his eyes meet mine. "You will move. Or I will—"

"My lord." Grey's voice is quiet behind me.

For a moment, I'm not sure Rhen's going to stop at all—but then he does. He looks away. "Please, my lady. Leave us."

"If something happened," I say slowly, "I need to know. If we're in an alliance, I need—"

"We're not," he says.

His voice is so soft that I think I must have misheard him. "What?"

"There is no alliance, Harper. It was foolish to think I had an avenue to success here. My people have been run into the ground. Your army is a charade. If we have to fight for Emberfall, who will stand against Karis Luran's army? There is no one."

I'm so confused. None of that is different from where we were two days ago.

The door to the arena slams open. Freya stands in the doorway, a little breathless. "Your Highness. My lady."

Rhen does not look away from me. "What."

"Jamison and I took the food to the crossroads as you directed, but the people who arrived were too numerous to feed—"

"As I suspected," Rhen says. His expression turns weary and he sighs. "Have Jamison tell them we will send more tomorrow."

"We did. But they followed the wagon back to the castle. We told them we would bring their message back to you, but there were far too many to refuse, and—"

"How many?"

"Hundreds, Your Highness."

"They followed you here?" Rhen glances at Grey and starts for the door. He flashes me an angry look, which says *I told you so* better than his voice could.

I wince. He did tell me so.

Rhen strides through the doorway. Each word he says is tight and clipped. "I will speak with them." He glances at Freya. "Where is Jamison?"

"Standing guard at the castle door."

"Against *hundreds*?" says Rhen. "They could tear him apart."

He jogs up the steps to the Great Hall, and I do my best to follow. Mournful music plays this morning, low strings plucked on a harp. Hopefully not an omen.

Freya lags behind to walk with me. "Word must have spread quickly," she says, her voice a quiet rush. "These people are not all from Silvermoon. At least a hundred people were in line when we arrived at the crossroads. More quickly joined."

"Are they fighting?" I say as we reach the top of the steps and hurry after Rhen and Grey. A sick feeling churns in my stomach.

Rhen wanted nothing more than to protect his people—and now my idea might be causing more harm than good.

"Fighting?" She's surprised.

"Yes," I say. "Isn't this some kind of protest that we didn't send enough food?"

Rhen reaches the door and swings it wide. Sunlight pours into the hall. After his worry about hundreds of people tearing Jamison apart, Rhen storms through, Grey right beside him.

A roar goes up from the crowd outside, and I run for the doorway, sure they're about to swarm him, to attack us all.

People have crowded onto the lawns and the cobblestone walkway. Freya was right—there are hundreds. Mostly men and boys, but many women and girls, too. Some are armed and wearing cruder versions of the armor I've seen Rhen and Grey wear. Others are in simple clothes, most too heavy for the temperate weather surrounding the castle.

They're not yelling.

They're cheering.

"For the good of Emberfall! Long live the crown prince!" Their voices ring out in the courtyard, echoing against the stones of the castle walls.

Rhen is staring.

Jamison moves forward. "Your Highness, they are here to fight. We could not stop them from following."

"To fight," Rhen echoes.

"To fight the soldiers from Syhl Shallow," Jamison says. "To join the King's Army."

I step up to Rhen. His eyes are still locked on the crowd in front of him. His expression is unreadable.

I think of his anger in the arena. At least when Grey is Scary

Grey, I know who his targets are. With Rhen, I have no idea what's going on inside his head.

"You wonder who's going to stand against Karis Luran's army," I say quietly. "I think you're getting your answer."

The crowd is still chanting. "For the good of Emberfall! Long live the crown prince!"

And because he is nothing if not enigmatic and calculating, Rhen seems to swallow his anger, then moves to the edge of the steps and raises a fist. "For the good of Emberfall!" he says. "For the good of all!"

CHAPTER THIRTY-FOUR

RHEN

I focus my thoughts on what I can control. Strategy. Tactics. Planning.

I block what I cannot.

Lilith.

She left before daybreak, but I did not sleep. I soaked in the bath for hours, sinking beneath the surface, holding my breath until my lungs screamed for release. I've drowned myself before, but I've never wanted it as badly as I did this morning. Every vision she showed me is locked in my thoughts, so vivid I could have lived through each tragedy.

I knew my people were suffering. I did not know how much, all at once. I wished for oblivion.

I came out of the bath ready to kill something. I am lucky Grey is so skilled.

Or maybe he's the one with luck.

"Rhen."

I blink. "What."

Harper opens her mouth, then closes it, her lips forming a frown. I haven't been able to meet her eyes all morning and now is no different. We're in the General's Library, my father's strategy room, and I stand at the window, watching the people in the courtyard below.

"I asked if you were pleased," says Harper. "People are showing up to volunteer. You can start building your own army."

"Do you remember our discussion of regiments?" My voice sounds hollow and I am unsure how to fix that. I speak through it. "One regiment of Syhl Shallow's army could eviscerate the people in the courtyard."

"You just got them all fired up!" she says. "If you didn't want them to form an army, why did you say all the 'good of Emberfall' stuff?"

"They were already 'fired up,' as you say." I keep my eyes on the people shuffling into a line below. "I have no desire to incite a mob. I merely gave them a rallying cry."

"It's a start," she says.

I have nothing to say to that.

I wish I were back under the water, holding my breath, waiting for oblivion.

I wish I were back in the arena, swinging a sword.

Instead, I stand here, every muscle tight as a bowstring.

Eventually, Harper says, "Grey, what do you think?"

"I think it is good that the people are willing to fight. That their loyalty has not waned. They seem to believe the royal family is in exile. Most have put aside their fear of the creature—of the castle itself—to come here. To fight for themselves and for Emberfall." He pauses, and his voice gains the very barest edge. "They will need someone to lead them."

Those words are a warning, of sorts. A reminder that I have a role to play here.

I've told Grey nothing of what happened with Lilith, but I am certain he's guessed at *some* of it. I was not subtle in the arena this morning.

"Can you lead them?" Harper says, and I think she's talking to me.

No, I think. *I can only lead people to their death. Do you not see?*

"I am not a general," says Grey. "I am not even a soldier. The King's Army and the Royal Guard did not train together."

"Jamison was a soldier. A lieutenant, right?"

"He was."

"I know he messed up at Silvermoon, but a lieutenant would be some kind of officer, right? Could you go talk to him and figure out a plan for what to do with all of these people once they're divided up by skill?"

"Yes, my lady." He leaves, the door softly falling closed behind him. He didn't even wait for me to issue an order.

Or maybe he knew I needed her to give one.

Harper appears by my side at the window, leaving a good two feet of space between us.

"It was Lilith, wasn't it?" she says quietly.

I jerk at the mention of her name, and Harper looks over at me with alarm.

"I wasn't sure if she was what had you so upset," she says, "but I haven't heard you talk about anyone else who has the power to throw you off your game like this."

"She is quite skilled at finding any weakness," I say.

"So she came back. Last night."

"Yes." I brace myself for her to ask what was done, or to ask why I did not invite her to my chambers for another session of bargaining. The very thought turns my stomach.

But Harper says nothing. She stands beside me and breathes, much the same way we stood together at the cliff at Silvermoon. So much changed overnight. On so many levels.

"Do you want to talk about it?" she says.

"No."

We watch the people in the courtyard for a while. I'm surprised at the variety of volunteers. A boy who can't be more than six stands in line. He stares at the castle in wonder, then pokes an older boy beside him—a brother, possibly. I think of young Jared being eviscerated in front of me and snap my eyes away. An older woman leans against a cane farther down, reminding me of a village elder who lay impaled by a Syhl Shallow spear in another vision. Emerging from the woods, more people stream toward the courtyard.

One young woman seems familiar, and it takes me a moment to place her.

Zo. The musician's apprentice. She is small in stature, but instead of a gown, today she wears breeches and boots, a bow strapped to her back and a dagger at her hip. A huntress, perhaps.

Interesting. I wonder if Grey will turn her away.

He should turn them all away.

I turn from the window and move back to the strategy table, dropping into the second chair—not the first, where my father would always sit. Maps are spread across the surface from whatever meeting my father would have had with his advisers during the first season. I no longer remember. This is not a room I visit often.

Harper drifts from the window as well. "This is like a big game of Risk," she says, coming to survey the largest map, pinned down in the center of the table. The northern lands, showing the mountain range bordering Syhl Shallow.

"Risk?" I echo.

"It's a war strategy game." Harper picks up a small iron figurine. "You even have the little men."

I give a short laugh, though I feel no humor. "To live in a world where war strategy is a game."

"Hey." Her eyes pierce me. "You know my life isn't sunshine and roses either."

I nod, conceding. "As you say."

"Show me how it works."

I hesitate, not wanting to think about the impending doom of my people to such an extent that I would map it out, but Harper is watching me expectantly.

I sigh and rise from the chair, gathering a dozen of the iron pieces into my hands. "Syhl Shallow is here," I say, placing six horse-and-rider figurines along the mountain range. "Jamison said there was a battle at Willminton, and his regiment was destroyed, which means I can assume Karis Luran's soldiers control access through the mountain pass."

"How wide is the mountain pass?" she says. "Could we set up an ambush or something?"

I glance up, impressed. "We could—but they likely control enough of the area surrounding the entrance to the path to prevent that very thing." I shake my head. "Our best bet will be to give the illusion of strength. To not engage in battle at all. To form the impression of an army of size, not necessarily of might." I place more figurines around Ironrose. "If we can form a battalion around the castle—"

"You know I don't know these military words."

"If we can place groups of soldiers around the castle, and then find a way to send messengers to the border cities instructing them to have their soldiers gather strategically *here* and *here*"—I place more figurines—"it will give the illusion of a well-prepared militia."

Harper comes around the table to stand beside me and she surveys the table as well. "So why don't you sound happier?"

I flash on an image of a home burning while soldiers bar the door, stabbing swords through the slats while people try to escape.

I shudder and move away. "Because I have no idea whether I still have soldiers posted at the borders. I have no one I trust to deliver a secure message."

"Grey?"

"We need him here if we are to continue visiting the closer cities. I will not send him away for weeks at a time."

Something in her expression flickers. "Right."

I frown. "What is it?"

"You said 'weeks at a time.' I just . . . I hadn't thought about this dragging on so long."

Ah. Her mother. This mission—this curse—promises nothing but misery in every direction. "You still hope to bargain for passage home. You would not have wanted to meet with the Lady Lilith last night, my lady. I assure you."

Harper studies me, and the weight of her eyes presses down upon me. "I've seen what Lilith can do," she says. "I don't understand what's different."

I cannot explain without telling her everything. I drop into my chair and study the array of figurines on the table. One remains trapped between my hands and I turn it end over end.

Harper steps toward me and that figurine goes still. My muscles are tense and I have to force myself to remain in the chair.

She must notice, because she doesn't come closer. She eases into the chair three seats away.

But then she says softly, "Do not run from me."

Our words from last night. So much has changed between then and now. One night changed so much, in so many ways. I can offer nothing but failure. This curse has proved that much. In truth, all Lilith provided was a reminder.

I look at Harper and take a breath to make sure my voice is as steady as ever. "I will not run." I pause, then rise. "But for now, my lady, perhaps you could avoid pursuit."

CHAPTER THIRTY-FIVE

HARPER

As days pass, preparations for war—or for the *impression* of war—hit a fever pitch. A messenger arrives from the North Loc Hills, a town south of the mountain pass, informing Rhen that more soldiers from Syhl Shallow have built a camp there. Suddenly there are people in and around the castle all the time: training in the courtyard and the arena, exercising the horses, and repairing weapons.

Rhen is always occupied. Everyone and everything demands his attention. The only time we spend together is on our rides to neighboring cities, but even then, he's walled off. He plays the role of doting prince quite well—but the moment the eyes of his people leave us, he becomes distant and distracted.

Grey is always busy, too. He selected ten guardsmen from those who applied, and now his days are filled with drills and training and practice—when he's not guarding Rhen himself.

To my surprise, Zo was one Grey chose—and the only female. Grey must trust her, because I regularly find her guarding my door when I wake in the morning.

"Did you hire Zo because I made a big deal of it at Silvermoon?" I ask Grey one evening, a rare moment when we're alone. We're in the stable, where he's been taking stock of what horses will be best suited for the guards he's chosen.

"I hired her because she can fight," he says. "She is quick with a bow, and surefooted. Her swordplay is weak, but she is not easily distracted. I believe she will do well."

I watched her spar with one of the other applicants, but I don't know what I'm looking at, so that didn't mean much. "But—wasn't she a musician's apprentice?"

"Yes, my lady." He cinches a saddle on a large chestnut gelding. "Just as I was once a farm boy."

Well, I guess there's that. He slips a bridle onto the horse's head.

In the days since people started showing up at the castle, Grey has been more reserved—probably the way he's supposed to be, out of deference to the Princess of Disi. He's one of two people who know the truth about me, though, and the only one I can ask about Rhen. In a minute, he's going to be through the doorway, and I'm going to lose another chance to talk to him.

"Grey," I say quietly. "Wait. Please."

He waits, of course, and looks at me, though his expression gives away nothing. I realize he expects an order, or some kind of request.

I don't want to give him an order. I need him to be my friend.

Maybe I've already closed the door on that.

"Forget it," I say. I suddenly feel more alone than ever. "Go ahead. You're busy."

"My lady," he says quietly.

When I turn back, he's taken a step closer to me. His eyes search mine. "You are troubled."

"Rhen's still not speaking to me," I say softly.

Grey glances away. He knows.

"Is he speaking to you?"

He hesitates. "No. He is not."

"Do you think Lilith is secretly torturing him at night?"

Grey glances at the opposite end of the aisle, where a stablehand is sweeping spilled grain. Even when we're alone, we're never truly alone anymore.

"We're riding to Hutchins Forge this evening," he says.

"I remember." Some dinner with a Grand Marshal who has his own private army. Rhen said I wasn't needed.

Grey says, "I do not believe Prince Rhen will be displeased if the journey lasts well into the night."

Meaning Lilith won't be able to bother him.

I swallow. "I can't help him if he won't talk to me, Grey. He's not trying to break the curse, he's not stopping her—" I break off, frustrated. "I've been trying to give him space, but . . . I don't know what to do."

Grey moves closer, until his words are for me alone. "He will deny you nothing, my lady. Not even that which he does not want to give."

Oh. I stare up at him.

Grey draws back. He glances at the doorway and the slowly darkening sky. "Forgive me. The light fades." He clucks to the horse and heads out of the stables.

Zo waits outside the stables, ready to escort me back to my chambers. When we get to my door, I stop before closing myself inside. "Zo, could you please send word to the prince that I would like to join him on his trip to Hutchins Forge?"

"Yes, my lady." She gives me a nod and moves away.

While she's gone, I change out of the rank riding clothes and rinse quickly in the ever-present warmth of the bathtub, then find fresh clothes suitable for visiting with nobility.

A knock sounds at the door.

"Enter," I say. "Please."

Zo opens the door and comes in, but her expression says she's not returning with good news. "His Highness says your presence is not warranted nor required."

My mouth forms a line. So much for denying me nothing. "Great."

"I am sorry," Zo says softly.

Rhen asked me not to pursue him. I've been trying. But this isn't an alliance anymore. It's . . . I don't know *what* this has turned into.

What did Grey say? *Not even that which he does not want to give.*

I look up at Zo and wonder if she'll take my order over Rhen's. "Call for horses," I say. "We're going after them."

Surprise lights her eyes. I expect her to refuse.

She doesn't. "Yes, my lady. Right away."

Hutchins Forge is smaller than Silvermoon, less fortified, and the tired guard waves us through the gate with barely a glance. In many of these cities, we've learned, security is only about the monster—not about people.

We've been traveling slowly, because I don't want Rhen to see me following and send me home. My only option here is to join him in front of his subjects, where he won't risk an incident.

It's late enough that the streets aren't crowded, and the horses' hooves clop on the slush-coated cobblestones. "The Grand Marshal's residence is there," says Zo quietly, nodding at a large home that towers over the rest of the city. A bow is strapped to her back, along with a quiver of arrows. "Should we circle around to come from the opposite direction?" She hesitates. "If your goal is to not be detected?"

I give her a surprised glance.

She smiles, but it's hesitant, as if she's unsure how I'll respond. "Was I not to have noticed?"

After Rhen's aloofness and Grey's austerity, it's nice to have a companion who knows how to smile—and who isn't telling me what to do. I can't help smiling back. "I'm glad you did."

We loop through the city streets. Few people are out, but rumor has spread this far. People notice the crest on my cloak or on Zo's armor, and they bow or curtsy as we pass. We navigate around to the far side of the Grand Marshal's home, then tie the horses at the post there. A low wall surrounds the building, forming a small empty courtyard out front. The guests have all moved inside.

I study the building. It's so quiet out here in the lightly falling snow. Candles flicker in every window, but there are no sounds to indicate danger. I have no idea where Rhen and Grey are—or whether this silence is meaningful or menacing.

The courtyard isn't huge, though, and it's clear we're alone.

"The Grand Marshal should have guards," says Zo quietly. "I was here with the Master of Song at summer's end. He had four guards in the courtyard."

Now there are none. I've been to enough cities to know this is unusual.

I've been so worried about Lilith torturing Rhen that I didn't really consider what would happen if a threat emerged in one of the cities. Most of our guards are young or untested—as proven by the girl who so eagerly accompanied me out of the castle.

"We should go in," I finally say.

The snow silences our footsteps. When we move into the courtyard, I realize Zo has drawn her bow.

She freezes and her voice drops to barely more than a breath. "My lady. Just there."

A body in the snow, hidden in the shadowed corner of the courtyard. Throat cut, a crimson stripe in the snow.

He's wearing the Royal Guard uniform. It takes me a moment, but then I recognize the shock of red hair. His name is Mave. A knife sticks out of his neck. Snow has collected in the hollows of his face, covering his eyes.

My breathing shakes. We were almost killed in Silvermoon Harbor, and then we had Grey and Jamison. Tonight I have a dagger and I have Zo. It's so cold and we're so alone.

I look at her—but she's looking at me. I'm the princess, and I'm in charge.

I've never been in charge of anything. At home, Jake told me what to do. In Emberfall, it's always Rhen, or, in his own way, it's Grey.

I feel a flicker of the responsibility Rhen must feel for his people. Zo will do as I say. She's risking her life.

All I can think about is Grey saying *My duty is to bleed so* you *do not.*

"Let's go," I say. Zo nods and follows, a shadow at my side. Her arrow sits ready on the string.

The door gives when I push, and for a long, ominous moment, I hear nothing. The home is eerily silent. The front room is empty, so we slip down the central hallway. A man laughs loudly from somewhere at the back of the house, a long booming sound. Others join in.

Then Rhen's voice. "Grand Marshal, I've missed your humor. My father would often speak of what a joy your support meant to him."

He's alive. He's laughing. For a second, I wonder if we're wrong. I wonder if I'm going to screw something up.

But Mave's body lies in the courtyard. That's not normal—and Rhen wouldn't be laughing if he knew about it.

To our left, a door opens and Zo swings around, her bow raised.

A serving girl shrieks and drops the platter she was carrying. Silverware rings to the stone floor. Dishes of soup shatter upon impact.

Suddenly, we're surrounded by guards—ours, including Grey, and some who must belong to the Grand Marshal. All have weapons drawn. Beyond them, three men have appeared at the far end of the hallway.

Rhen is one of them. His expression is tight. "My lady." He pauses. "I thought you were otherwise occupied this evening."

The servant girl is crouched on the floor, whimpering, her hands over her head.

"My plans changed." I count quickly in my head. Seven guards block the hallway, but only three are ours. Two men stand with Rhen. It seems like there are more people in the room behind him. We're outnumbered two-to-one—and I still have no idea who killed Mave. Nothing about this meeting feels right.

Rhen's eyes bore into mine—then flick past me to take in Zo, who still has an arrow nocked. I clear my throat before he can say anything. "Forgive my tardiness. I apologize for giving the serving girl such a fright."

I stride forward as if I expect the guardsmen to fall back and yield the hallway—and they do.

The hall gives way to a large dining room, with a marble floor and painted ceramic tiles lining the walls in gold and red, the colors of Emberfall. The guards shift to filter back into the room, taking positions along the wall. In the hallway, I hear the serving girl hurriedly trying to gather the dishes. Zo stays right at my side, her bow still in her hands, the arrow trained on the ground.

Rhen is glaring at me, but he says, "Allow me to introduce the Grand Marshal of Hutchins Forge, and his Seneschal."

"Gentlemen." I give them a tense nod. The Grand Marshal is a thin man with a lean, wiry build and a narrow beard. His expression is thoughtful and calculating. His Seneschal is his opposite in every way: large, with a belly that all but sits in his lap, a thick beard that seems greased, and small beady eyes. He's the smug one.

I wish Rhen and I weren't completely at odds. At least on my first day in Emberfall, I knew his motives. Now *nothing* makes sense.

"I would like to speak with you privately," I say to Rhen.

The Seneschal gives me a once-over and chuckles. It shakes his whole body. It's not a good sound. "Your Highness, I have heard talk of your scarred warrior princess, but I did not realize she would be so"—his eyes flick over my form—"small." He elbows the Grand Marshal.

They share a good laugh—but Rhen says, "Do not underestimate the princess." His voice could cut steel.

The Grand Marshal's laughter goes quiet, but he does not apologize. "We are all friends here. Surely you can speak openly, my lady."

I look to Rhen, hoping he'll disagree, but his gaze is still unyielding, and he's more concerned with the fact that I'm crashing his party.

This all feels so precarious. I stand behind a chair and fix my hands on the back of it to keep from fidgeting. "Where are your guards, Grand Marshal? I expected to be greeted when I arrived."

"You seemed to make your way in here all right." He narrows his eyes as if I'm still funny. "I don't control my men's every move. I have a private army. No one would dare attack my home."

"One of *our* guards is dead in the courtyard," I say. "Forgive me if I do not find much reassurance in the strength of your army."

Tension falls like an ax.

"Explain this," Rhen says.

Grey moves from the wall to stand behind him. He gives a low order to one of our guards by the wall, a sandy-haired man named Dustan. Dustan nods, then moves to leave the room.

"You must be mistaken," says the Seneschal. He laughs again, but now it's more of a choked sound. "Nim, go with their guardsman. Check it out."

A man who must be Nim shifts away from the wall to follow our guard.

As Nim passes me, he begins to draw his weapon.

I don't know why, but that makes my thoughts stall.

The Grand Marshal is glaring at me. "Why do I feel like you're accusing me of something, girl?"

"This *girl* is the Princess of Disi," Rhen says carefully. He must sense danger, too. "Perhaps you were unaware."

The Grand Marshal's eyes don't leave mine. "I'm aware."

"You invited Prince Rhen to your home for some type of negotiation," I say. "But to me it seems more like a trap."

"Why does Emberfall need my army if Disi is willing to provide its forces?"

I wish I could order Grey to throw a knife at him. This is so much more complicated than when we faced the soldiers in the inn. I raise an eyebrow. "Why would you kill our guard if your interest in negotiation were genuine?"

"Who says I killed your guard?"

When Rhen speaks, his voice is low and lethal. "I would like an answer to the princess's question."

The Seneschal leans forward. "If your man was a true member of the Royal Guard, he would not have fallen so easily." He coughs and his body shakes. "I suspect you are not being wholly honest, Your Highness."

"I suspect *you* are not," says Rhen.

"Your father would not have needed my men," says the Grand Marshal.

"Did you have my guardsman killed?"

"What difference does it make?" The Seneschal laughs. "What will you do?"

"Execute you both for treason," says Rhen.

"You and what army?" He slaps the table.

His hand has barely struck the wood surface before Grey's sword is level with his throat. The man's laughter cuts short. He strains back in his chair. A spot of red appears on his neck.

"I need no army to deal with you," says Rhen.

One of the guards begins to draw his sword. Zo's arrow is flying before I can even issue an order. The shaft drives right through the man's wrist. He screams.

Another guard draws his sword. Zo has another arrow nocked, but Rhen snaps, "Hold."

She holds. Her breathing is a loud rush beside me.

The other guards go still, too. Tension rides a knife's edge in this room. Everyone has weapons drawn now, but no one else has engaged.

Noise echoes in the hallway behind me, and Zo all but pushes me to the side. Her arrow is pointed, but it's our guard Dustan—and he's dragging a bound Nim back down the hallway. "Mave is dead," he says breathlessly. "This one did it. He nearly got me."

Rhen steps back. "This was an ambush. Kill them both."

"No!" cries the Grand Marshal. He slides out of his chair and falls to his knees. "We didn't ambush you. I swear it. I admit suspicion—but I have always been loyal to the crown."

"You killed a guard," I snap. "What else would you call it?"

"I swear it!" His voice has grown in pitch. "I swear!"

The Seneschal coughs again. "Have some pride, man." Then he spits at Rhen.

"Commander." Rhen's eyes shift to Grey.

"No," says the Grand Marshal. His forehead touches the ground. "Please. I swear. This was not treason."

"Wait," I say. I look at the guard Dustan has pinned against the wall in the hallway. "Nim, who gave the order to kill our guard?"

He says nothing.

Dustan punches him between the shoulder blades. The man coughs and drops to a knee. "I serve the Seneschal."

"I had him killed," the Seneschal says.

"Why?" demands Rhen.

"To show your weakness." He winces and gasps as Grey's sword finds his skin again. "To bargain a higher price for skilled soldiers."

Rhen steps forward and grabs the collar of the Grand Marshal's jacket. He jerks the man to his knees and his voice is tight and unyielding. "So you sought to trick the crown out of silver?"

"No, Your Highness. He acted alone." His voice is almost stammering. "I swear—I swear my loyalty to the crown. I would offer all I have."

Rhen looks at the Seneschal. "Is this true? You acted alone?"

"I didn't need help to outwit you, if that's what you're asking."

Rhen's jaw tightens. He looks down at the bearded man whose collar is still clutched in his grip. "Grand Marshal, I will pay your men a fair price for their services. I would like a full accounting of the taxes your people have been ordered to pay—and if I see that they've been charged one penny more than necessary, they will be reimbursed from your own coffers."

"Yes—yes, Your Highness." He winces. "Please—have mercy on my Seneschal—he has a family. You have been gone so long—forgive him—"

Rhen looks at Grey. "Fall back."

Grey lowers his weapon. The Seneschal puts a hand to his neck. His breathing still shakes, but then he chokes out a rusty laugh. "You'll never stand against Karis Luran. You could barely stand against this room." He coughs. "I hope the creature returns to the castle and slaughters you all."

"You took a man's life for your own selfishness and greed. You sought to undermine me and my personal guard. All by your own admission." He leans forward. "That, sir, is treason."

"I won't be the last."

"Surely not, but you'll be an example for those who seek the same." Rhen steps back. "Kill him, Commander. Leave the body."

I inhale—whether to scream or protest or something else entirely—but it's too late. The man's throat is cut. He slumps in his chair. Blood flows.

Beside me, Zo's breath is every bit as quick as my own. My hands are over my mouth.

Then Rhen is in front of me. His eyes are hard and his voice is steel edged. He glances at Zo. "Nice shot."

She swallows. "Thank you—thank you, Your Highness."

His eyes shift back to me. "My lady."

I'm staring at him over my hands. I don't know what to say. I don't know what to do.

An emotion flickers in his eyes, almost too quick for me to catch it—but I do. It's not the harsh censure I expect. It's resignation. Defeat. Sorrow.

Fear.

He must see the responding pity in my eyes, because he glances away. His expression is walled off. He sighs. "Come, Princess. I'll see you to your horse."

We ride back to Ironrose in silence, Rhen by my side, with Zo, Dustan, and Grey trailing behind. The remaining guards have been left to ensure the Grand Marshal follows orders. Tension makes the falling snow feel like daggers, and cold air snakes between us, reminding me of the night on the cliff at Silvermoon. The night we nearly kissed.

The night everything fell apart.

"Would you say something?" I say quietly. "Please?"

"You do not wish my conversation now, my lady, I assure you."

His voice is tight with fury, and his horse tosses its head, fighting his grip on the reins.

"I'll take anything over days of silence."

"You should not have come tonight."

"Maybe something is lost in translation, because that sure doesn't sound like *thank you*."

"You expect my *thanks*?" His head snaps around. "You did not know of his plot. What if assassins had waited in the halls? What if your guard were a lesser shot? What if they were working together? We were badly outnumbered. They could have slaughtered every one of us."

I don't know what to say, so I say nothing. He's right on all counts.

"What you did was reckless and foolish," Rhen says.

I turn my head and glare at him. "I *saved* you."

"The man's plot would have come to light. Grey could have stopped him." He takes a breath. "Now a man is dead by my order. Once again, I bring nothing to my people but death and suffering."

For an instant, I sense that resignation I caught a glimpse of earlier. I reach out to touch his hand.

He snatches it away, tense now, his eyes fixed ahead. "You are lucky it was not your body I found in the courtyard."

"I brought Zo."

"You are so very reckless. Just like in the arena. You act without thought."

"I acted in the arena to *protect* you."

His jaw is tight. I've never seen him so angry. It's triggering my own anger. I meant what I said—I'll take anger over endless silence.

I think of his flash of emotion in the hallway at the Grand Marshal's home. I force myself to take a breath.

"Please tell me what's happening." My words are so quiet, pressed into this tiny bit of space we occupy, as if even the night wants to keep this moment private. "I know it's Lilith. It has to be Lilith. You made an alliance with me. Keep it. Tell me what's going on."

He inhales. I watch his broad chest expand. His eyes flash with anger, a sure prelude to more fury. But then his breath hitches and he kind of . . . *deflates.*

We ride in silence. It's like all the fight has gone out of him.

"Rhen," I whisper.

"I will release you from our bargain," he says softly. "I no longer have anything to offer."

I turn and look over my shoulder at the guards. "Fall back," I say. "Please."

Grey meets my eyes, then gives me a nod. They drop back a dozen yards.

"I don't want you to release me," I say. "I want to know what's going on."

He doesn't answer. He says nothing. We ride for miles.

Finally, he says, "I feel trapped, my lady." His voice is so quiet. "I swore a bargain with you, but I find I cannot invite you into her presence again."

I inhale to speak, but then he looks over at me.

His eyes flick to the scar on my cheek.

Then I understand. "You think she'd hurt me again."

A nod.

"But she's hurting *you*, Rhen."

"I have endured it for hundreds of seasons. What is another?"

His voice is so bleak. "Does she torture you every night?" I whisper.

"She does nothing to me. She shows me what I have done."

"I don't understand."

He swallows. "Every night, she comes to me. She shows me my people. Those who have died. Those who are starving. Those in pain." He presses a hand to his abdomen. "She shows me the creature. She shows me their deaths. Their pain. Their suffering. I cannot endure it."

I want to kill her. "Rhen—you're trying to save them—"

"I am failing, Harper. Even tonight, I had nothing to offer but death and pain and fear." He presses the heel of one hand against his eyes. "I have never wished so badly for a season to end." His voice breaks and he takes a shuddering breath.

"You're not killing them," I say fiercely. "You're trying to save them."

"I am killing them, my lady. I'm doing it one by one."

"You are *not*," I snap. "Even tonight, when that guy was trying to trick you out of money for his soldiers, your first thought wasn't of yourself. You worried that they'd been stealing from their people, too."

"You cannot paint me in a better light," he says. "I know what I have done. I see it night after night."

"You're doing the best you can," I say to him. For some reason, my father pops into my head. The bad men he led to our family. He abandoned us—but maybe he thought he was doing the best he could, too.

Rhen drags his hand away from his face. "I do not know how to lead my people when all I see are my failures."

"You're leading them," I say softly. "The Grand Marshal swore to you tonight. You have a castle full of people who have sworn to you. You once told me you were raised to rule a country, and you're *doing* it."

"Please," he says to me. "Please. I beg of you. You do not understand."

I beg of you. The words break my heart, because they're not words he would ever say.

"Okay," I whisper. "Okay. Just ride."

We travel the rest of the way to the castle in silence. He's regained his composure by the time he hands his horse to a boy in the stable, then turns to lead me back into the castle.

He stops in front of my door. The last time he stood here, we'd just returned from Silvermoon. I'd been a breath away from kissing him.

Tonight his eyes are full of resignation. "I bid you good night, my lady."

Much like in the courtyard in Hutchins Forge, I don't know what to do, but I do know I need to help him. "Why don't you come in?"

That startles him. Maybe it's the tired eyes or the slumped shoulders, but he's never looked so young. "What?"

"Stay in my room tonight. Lilith isn't allowed to interfere in your courtship, right?"

A line forms between his brows.

"Let me court you." I falter, realizing how that sounds. A blush heats my cheeks. "I mean, not really. I mean—I'm just—"

"My lady." He straightens. "I will not put you at risk."

"You once said you would give me anything in your power."

He sighs. “Now you will trap me with my words.”

“I’m not trapping you.” I step closer. “I’m not chasing you. I’m not tricking you.”

He says nothing.

“I’m inviting you,” I say quietly.

He hesitates, then offers me a nod.

CHAPTER THIRTY-SIX

RHEN

Harper's room is warm from the roaring fire. A platter of hot tea, biscuits, and honey sits on the side table, and this season has gone so differently from the others that I no longer know whether those always appear on this day, or if Freya provided them.

The door closes with a soft *click* behind me. We're alone here. Together.

That should be encouraging, but in the face of all Lilith has shown me, it is not. I have failed to break this curse. No matter what I do this season, I have harmed my people. Likely irreparably.

Harper stops in the middle of the room and looks at me. "Please come in. You don't have to stand in the doorway."

We're not in my chambers, but the windows are full of darkness, and after days of facing Lilith at night, I feel tense and twitchy. I've seen men die by my father's order—but until tonight, no one has died by mine. "I ordered a man's death, Harper."

"Grey said that mercy and kindness can become a weakness if pushed too far. If that guy was willing to trick you tonight, who knows what his next move might have been." She pauses. "He killed a guard. Mave swore an oath to you two days ago. The Seneschal killed him. Over *silver coins.*"

I flinch. She is right, but even if the choice to kill this man was the right one, it does not negate all my other failures.

I think of my family, torn to shreds along the castle halls.

I think of the children the monster ripped to pieces in front of their parents.

I think of the people starving throughout Emberfall, those without access to a city, to walls and protection and work.

"What Lilith is doing to you is *wrong*," Harper says. "We all make mistakes. You slept with her without any intention of a relationship. Who cares? You're not the first man to do it. And she's not innocent! She sought you out because of who *you* are." Her jaw is clenched. "I hope she *does* come here. I hope she comes to this room. Because I don't care what I have to do. I'm going to *end* her."

I go still, my back against the door, unable to breathe. I'm terrified those words will summon Lilith right this very instant.

But the air does not change. Lilith does not appear.

Harper steps up to me. "I'm sorry. I didn't invite you in here to start yelling at you. Especially not right now."

I grimace. "On the contrary. Your passion on my behalf is quite inspiring."

A blush lights her cheeks and she takes a step back. "Well, your passion on behalf of everyone else is quite inspiring."

I move to her window and look out at the darkness. Soldiers stand at the entrance to the stables, stationed there by Grey or Jamison, I am sure. In the distance, torches light figures standing sentry on the guard towers at the edge of the forest. These men and women have sworn to defend me—while I cower in the castle.

"Some passion." I glance at Harper. "I am hiding in your room."

She joins me by the window. "You agreed to come inside. For a minute there, I wasn't sure you'd even do that."

I was not sure, either. My eyes fall on the scar on Harper's cheek—I was so sure Lilith's action would break her. Instead, after so many seasons, it seems Lilith broke me.

"Do you want to sleep?" Harper's voice is so earnest. "You can have the bed." She pauses. "You look like you haven't slept since we returned from Silvermoon Harbor."

"Indeed." I shake my head. "I cannot sleep. Not yet."

"I can light more candles. Do you want to play cards?" Her voice is almost teasing—but I can tell the offer is genuine, too. "Shoot arrows out the window? Dance?"

I raise my eyebrows. "You must truly pity me if you offer to *dance*."

Her expression loses any hint of humor. "I don't pity you, Rhen." She pauses. "Do you pity me?"

"Never. You are the strongest person I know."

"That's not true. You know Grey, for goodness' sake. You know Lilith."

I shake my head a bit. "It is true."

That blush finds her cheeks again. "Well. Same. About you."

For the first time, I want to tell her about the creature. I long to be honest with her so badly that my chest aches.

I do deserve this pain, Harper. You don't know what I've done.

"We can dance," she says. "If that's what you want to do."

If she touches me with any kind of gentleness I will collapse against her.

I turn back to the window and rest my fingers along the ledge. My voice is rough. "There is no music tonight."

That throws her for a moment, but then her face lights up. "Wait. I have an idea."

"My lady?" But she's already flown to the door, and she leans out, speaking quietly.

After a moment, she closes the door again. "Music is coming right up."

"I beg your—"

"Just wait. You'll see." She returns to my side, a little breathless. Her voice softens. "Do you want to lose the armor?"

I hesitate. I'm loath to remove any of it. This evening's events have left me shaken. Lilith's visions have left me gutted.

Harper's fingers close on my bracer, and I pull away.

"Do you trust me?" she says softly.

"Yes." When I blink, I see my creature eviscerating one of the first girls. I imagine doing the same to Harper and draw a shuddering breath. I force my eyes to open. "I do not trust myself."

"Well, I trust you." She takes hold of my hand. Her fingers are warm against my palm and I challenge myself to allow it.

After a moment, she turns my wrist over and goes to work on the buckles. "Is this okay?"

"Yes." My voice is barely more than a rough whisper. Her gentle touch is breaking me in an entirely different way.

Each strap of leather slowly gives. Our breathing is loud in the quiet space between us, and I find myself wishing there were more buckles than three. That bracer yields and she tosses it on a chair, then moves to the other.

The silence is almost too much to bear. Her closeness, her

kindness, the soft warmth of her touch. I long to rip the other bracer free and take her face in my hands.

I cannot. This trust is such a tenuous thing. On both sides.

"You are quite talented at this," I say softly. "You should be a squire."

"I don't really know what a squire is." The second bracer gives, and her hands shift to the buckle of my sword belt where it loops through my breastplate—and her fingers hesitate.

Her cheeks have turned pink. We're both fully clothed—more than, considering my armor—but this suddenly feels more like undressing than disarming. I can all but taste her breath.

Then she says, "I wish you'd told me about Lilith."

I've spent the last few days trying to protect her, not realizing that Harper could have protected *me*. I am unused to this feeling: some combination of gratitude and vulnerability and relief. "I wish that, too."

Harper seems to steel herself, and her fingers loop through the buckle. "I know I'm not a real princess. But when I said I would help you, I meant it."

I nod. The buckle gives. The sword belt comes free.

Her eyes meet mine, and she tosses it onto a chair. "No more secrets," she says.

I have one secret. The biggest one. The one I cannot share.

The one I want to share with her so badly.

Her fingers land on the leather strap of my breastplate and I nod, because there is nothing else I can do. "No more secrets," I agree.

"Good." She tugs the buckle free at the base of my rib cage.

I'm more than capable of doing this myself. I should stop her.

I do not. Instead, I reach to brush that one lock of hair from her eyes. My hand lingers on her face. Desire wars with fear as my thumb traces over the line of her scar. I imagine her blood in the snow. Her lying dead in the courtyard. Like the visions Lilith shared, it is too real. Too terrible. Harper is so foolish. So brave.

She has not pulled away.

My thumb strokes across her mouth, and her breath catches.

I hesitate, uncertain again.

A violin begins to play, a slow, mournful tune, and I startle. This is not a song I've ever heard in the castle.

Harper smiles at my reaction. "It's Zo. I asked if she would play." She blushes. "I remember what you said at Silvermoon. About the music."

Something pulls in my chest. That she remembered, that she thought of this—it's all too much. My voice is low and husky. "This is quite a gift, my lady."

At my side, Harper puts out a hand. "Do you care to dance?"

I unbuckle the other side of my breastplate and toss it onto the chair with my bracers. Her hand slips into mine, and suddenly we are face-to-face, with bare inches of space between us.

Her other hand lifts, but I hesitate.

"We don't have to," she says. "I really just brought you here to protect you."

My pride flinches. "It is *I* who should be protecting you."

"You've been doing that for a while. Maybe it's my turn."

I take her hand and move it to my shoulder, then step into her space until my hand falls at her waist.

As hiding goes, I do not mind it as much as I thought I would.

She is as tense as she was on the cliff at Silvermoon. I smile, bemused. "Is dancing truly so different in Disi?"

"Most people don't really dance. We more . . . sway."

"Show me."

She moves closer, letting go of my hand. Her arms settle on my shoulders. "You put both your hands on my waist."

I do, and she begins to move. We sway, I suppose, our feet shuffling from side to side.

"Amazing," I say. "What wonders we have yet to learn from your people."

She swats me on the arm. "Don't mock it. I told you I'm a terrible dancer."

"I am not mocking," I say. "This is indeed . . . something."

"It's not always this stiff," she says. "If a girl likes a boy she'll rest her head on his shoulder."

"Does this girl like this boy?" My voice is light, teasing like hers was, but my question is genuine.

Her blush deepens and her eyes sparkle in the light from the fire. She says nothing, but then she moves closer, until her body is against mine, and her head falls on my shoulder.

Lilith's torture has nothing on this.

When Harper speaks, her breath is warm against my collarbone. "There has to be a way to defeat her, Rhen."

"If there is, I have not yet found it."

"You can stay with me from now on," she says. "Or I can stay with you. Whatever. But you don't have to keep facing her alone."

"I'll stay tonight."

"Every night."

I do not wish to argue. There will come a night when she will not want me to stay with her. There will come a night when I will put her in more danger than Lilith herself would.

I brush my lips against Harper's forehead. "I will stay as long as you wish."

One night becomes two.

Two become seven.

Each night, I lie awake in Harper's bed, three feet of space between us, her quiet breathing taunting me with sleep that refuses to overtake me. I lie in tense silence, every *snap* of the fire or *creak* of the floor assuring a visit from Lilith.

Since I have joined Harper in her room, the enchantress has not reappeared.

By the eighth night, my body's needs take over and a deep sleep finds me. I awake to find Harper has shifted against me in the night, soft and warm at my side, her hair a wild spill of curls against the pillow. I am tempted to touch her, to stroke my fingers along her skin, but I felt her hesitation when my fingers traced her face.

She trusts me. I trust *her*. This feels more monumental than love. More precious. More earned. I keep my hands to myself.

Harper has fallen into the role of princess better than I could have anticipated. She is compassionate and kind to everyone she meets, a direct contrast to the royal family of Ironrose in the past. My sisters would have closed themselves away in the castle, but Harper is always with my people, always listening, always learning. Determined to be independent, she insists on training with the soldiers, throwing herself into their routines without hesitation. They believe her limp is the result of a war injury, but Harper is quick to correct them. "I was born this way," she'll snap, "and I'm going to die this way, so teach me to work around it."

They love her for it.

At night, when the soldiers retire, she seeks out Grey—or more often now, Zo. They throw knives until she has mastered her aim. They spar with daggers or fists or both at once. When her guards are not available, she brings me a quiver and bow and says, "Come on. Show me how to shoot." Muscle has begun to form on her frame, a warrior replacing the skinny girl who appeared in my drawing room so many weeks ago. Some nights we lie in her bed together and she tells me about her life in Disi. I hear how much she cares for her brother, how deep his worry runs for her—likely an equal depth to that of my feelings of guilt about trapping her here. I learn of Jake's secret romance with a boy named Noah, of Harper's uncertainty over this secret her brother kept from her. She tells me about her mother, and the illness ravaging her body.

She tells me about her father, and the mistakes he made.

In turn, she asks about my family, and at first, I'm reluctant to get lost in the memories. I tell her secrets about my sisters, about how my father was never faithful to my mother, how the castle staff would gossip about us. I whisper my fears of how I will never live up to the man my father was, how tenuous this control feels, as though it may slip out of my grasp at any moment.

I reveal far more than I ever have, to any girl.

A feeling has begun to grow in my chest, blossoming so slowly I almost do not notice it. It is not love, not yet, because that seems too far outside my grasp. It is more than lust and attraction, though. Something deeper. Something more real.

Retired officers and private soldiers have joined our forces, lending me desperately needed support and building loyalty. The castle churns out food for my people—the more we take out of the kitchens, the more that appears there. Two messengers arrive home, bringing news that regiments *do* stand at the southern borders, and that they will send half their forces to Ironrose. *True* soldiers, not new recruits.

All to save a country that may not have a ruler in a few weeks.

The change grows nearer by the day. An undercurrent of worry has built a camp in the castle, as my gathered subjects wait for the monster to rematerialize.

Time marches on, and so does the curse.

I've been expecting failure for weeks now, for this plan to collapse around me, for my people to turn on me and Harper and overrun the castle. When I am not worrying about Lilith, I worry about a military coup or Karis Luran's soldiers slaughtering my people.

The only time I forget is at night, when the bedroom is dark and the fire snaps and the world seems to melt away.

When Zo plays music outside Harper's door, and we sway.

CHAPTER THIRTY-SEVEN

HARPER

Rhen always wakes before I do—and he's usually gone before sunlight creeps through my window. By the time I'm dressed and fed each morning, he's been up for hours, meeting with his new generals or taking stock of the growing army. As weeks pass, he introduces me to nobles who have ridden to the castle, but I can barely keep track of the people living *here*.

Rhen, of course, knows them all. Some are clearly allies to his family, while others must smell blood in the water, because they dig at him for information about his father, the king, and try to interrogate me about Disi. After what happened in Hutchins Forge, Rhen is more cautious, but still as smooth with his people as he is with me over cards: all precision and strategy. When I flounder with the people, he says the right things to build them up or knock them down.

If I weren't lying right beside him at night, I'd say he never sleeps. I can't believe I once thought him lazy and arrogant.

Tonight, Rhen is having dinner with Micah Rennells, an older man who was a trade adviser to Rhen's father. I was prepared to join him, but Rhen told me it would be a boring meal full of false flattery and he felt certain I could entertain myself more effectively.

So I am. Zo and I are swinging swords while Grey offers instruction.

Well, Zo is swinging a sword. I'm sweating through my clothes and learning that swordplay might not be my thing. I just can't move quickly enough. My balance is lacking. Much like with ballet, this is more of a struggle than it should be.

After an hour, I put up a hand to stop, because otherwise I'm going to vomit in the dirt of the arena.

"You can tell me," I say to Zo. "This isn't my thing, is it?"

She smiles. "We can try again tomorrow." She puts out a fist.

I grin and hit it with my own.

"Take the training blades to the armory," Grey tells her. "Then relieve Dustan in the hall. I will escort the princess to her chambers."

"Yes, Commander." She offers a salute, then gathers the weapons to do as ordered.

Grey wordlessly pours me a glass of water at the table by the railing. I drain the whole glass in one swallow.

He gives me a look and holds out a fist.

I blush and hit it with my own. "It's a custom in Disi."

"I see." He refills the glass. "You and Zo have become friends."

"We have," I agree. Freya has become a kind of surrogate mother, but Zo is becoming the friend I've always wanted. Sometimes late at night, when Rhen is asleep and she's stationed outside my door, I'll sneak out into the hallway and we'll gossip about the silly posturing of the guardsmen or whatever frivolous request a noblewoman might make of Rhen. She'll tell me how her mother forced her into an apprenticeship with the Master of Song in Silvermoon to settle a debt, and she does an impressive imitation of the man's blustering.

She does an even better impression of Grey, one that made me laugh so hard we woke Freya's children. We have to giggle in whispers because I don't want Rhen to find out and put someone more boring outside my door, but I suspect he might know and doesn't care.

Grey has been pouring me water like a servant, so I pick up the pitcher and fill a glass for him. "Are you happy with how everything is going?" I say. "I don't think Rhen expected this kind of response."

"I am pleased that you have found comfort and friendship. I am pleased our people seem united." He hesitates. "I am not pleased that our time grows short."

Because Rhen hasn't broken the curse.

"I'm sorry, Grey," I whisper.

He sighs and looks away. "You owe no one an apology. You were brought here against your will. You have done more for us than anyone could rightly expect."

"Ah, yes," says a woman's voice from the shadows. "*Princess Harper* and her alliance have been quite a boon for the people of Emberfall."

Tension grips my spine, but I force myself to turn and face Lilith. She steps out of the shadowed corner. Tonight's gown is red, a deep crimson bodice that falls into a hundred sheer layers of silk spilling to the floor, where they fade to white at the hem. Rubies glisten everywhere, like drops of blood scattered across her skirts.

"What do you want?" I say.

"I wondered if you were still so intent on returning home," she says. "For I bring a message."

"Like I would trust a bargain with you after what you've done to Rhen."

"What I've *done*?" She laughs, a beautiful, childlike sound that hurts like a steel poker through my eardrum. "My dear girl, I merely showed him the state of his people."

"You're awful," I spit at her. "You are *despicable*."

Lilith is unaffected. She stands before me, her lips twisted into a bemused smile. "Do you know what I find despicable?" she says. "A prince who had the perfect opportunity to break this curse, time and time again, yet chose wrongly every single time. He could have ended this curse on the very first day, if he'd only seen what was right in front of him."

My breathing has gone shallow. "Rhen would never love you."

"Maybe not *now*." Lilith reaches out a hand to touch the scar on my cheek. "But perhaps once. Did you know that I bribed Grey to gain access to the prince's chambers?"

I knock her hand away. I don't believe a word she says. "Don't you touch me."

She draws back a hand to slap me. I see the swing coming and barely have time to brace myself for the impact.

But Grey steps in front of me and catches her wrist. His dagger sits against her stomach. "I am under no orders here," he says. "And you will not strike the princess."

She glares at him. "If that blade breaks my skin, I will make you pay."

"Is that your greatest threat?" he says. "Because there is truly nothing more you can take from me."

Then he slams the dagger home.

She half crumples, but he grasps hold of her arm, keeping her upright. Blood spills around the blade to mingle with the rubies.

"Kill her," I say.

"I have tried," Grey says. "I cannot."

"What if you cut her head off?"

His voice is grim. "It will rejoin her body."

Lilith smiles, and there is blood on her teeth. She pulls the dagger out of her abdomen, and blood spills freely down the front of her dress as she staggers, still held upright by Grey's grip. "I cannot be killed by simple steel." She flings the bloodied blade to the ground. "Not on this side, silly girl. Magic seeks a balance. Do you not know this yet?"

I can't decide if her morbid invulnerability is more disturbing than the blood pouring down the front of her gown. "I'll find a way to kill you," I say. "I don't care what it takes."

She laughs. A hand presses to her abdomen as she coughs blood. The scent is on the air, copper mixed with something bitter. "You? You stupid, broken girl. You did not even listen to me. You did not ask for my *message*."

"What *message*?"

"Your mother. Your brother. So sad."

Your mother. Your brother.

So sad.

I feel like I'm the one who just took the blade to the gut. "What happened?"

She lifts her bloodied hand and presses it against the cheek she cut.

The arena disappears. I'm in my family room with Jake. He's on his knees, his hands clasped behind his head. An unfamiliar scar bisects his eyebrow, and he looks slightly bigger somehow, as if he's been working out or gaining weight.

I can't pay attention to any of that because a man stands over him, holding a gun to his head.

"You've had enough time." The man cocks the hammer.

"My mother might not last the night." Jake's words fill me with relief and terror simultaneously. "I've been telling you for months, I don't know where my father is."

"Then you'd better find him."

"Please," says Jake. "My mother is in the bedroom. You can't be here. Can't we have—"

"Do you hear me, kid? You know how this works. We've been waiting long enough. We've got our orders."

Then a faint voice, from somewhere else. "Jake? Jake, what's going . . . what's going on?"

"It's okay, Mom!" Jake's voice breaks. His face twists. "Please. One night. My mother. Please. You owe me that, Barry. You know you do."

Barry inhales, then sighs. "You have until nine a.m. That's all I can give you." He pauses and his voice is bizarrely amiable. "If you don't get the money by then, I've got to do it."

"Nothing is even open!" Jake rages. "I don't know where my dad is! What are we going to do before—"

"What, you think you're gonna get a bank loan?" Barry sighs. "That's it, kid. That's all I can give you. Say your goodbyes. I'll be back."

Lilith lets go of my cheek. The vision disappears.

"Family tragedy," Lilith says. "Such the pity."

Rage builds in my chest. "Grey. Stab her again."

I don't expect Grey to obey, but he does. His blade flashes in the light and buries itself in her shoulder. She doesn't cry out, but a small sound escapes her lips.

The expression on her face isn't pain, though. It's closer to euphoria. "I would so enjoy visiting you tonight, Grey. But I believe I have a better idea."

She is so messed up. My thoughts won't work in any direction.

"What do you want?" My voice cracks. "What do you want to send me home?"

"From you? Nothing." Another cough. "Do you know why I granted Grey the ability to cross over to your side?"

I can barely think straight. "What? I don't—no. I have no idea."

"He is not trapped by the curse. He can leave at any time, but he will not. Not even when I gave him reason."

"I still don't understand."

"Commander Grey will not yield," she says. "Not even when I described how his family would die."

His expression is frozen, his eyes stony. He says nothing.

"I did not kill them *all*," Lilith says. "You had so *many* brothers and sisters. I likely did your wanton mother a mercy."

Every time I think Lilith cannot grow more terrible, I discover I am wrong. "Grey," I whisper. "I'm so sorry."

"I forswore family," he says. His voice is tight and dark.

He told me that once before. I never really thought about what it might mean.

"It is by virtue of Grey's loyalty alone that Rhen does not need to prey on his own people," says Lilith. She smiles up at him. "I truly underestimated you, Commander."

"Your mistake."

"But it wasn't a mistake. I believe your loyalty will work in my favor."

I don't understand. I'm so shaken by the image of my mother and brother that I can barely focus on what she's saying right now.

Then she says, "I will grant Grey the ability to cross the veil between worlds at his whim. He can return you home at any time, *Princess.*"

"You—what?"

"He can return you home. You need not bargain anything from me. The person you must bargain with is Grey."

With that, she disappears.

I can't stop shaking. My mother has been dying for months—her death was at the end of this tunnel before I even arrived in Emberfall. But this is more than my mother. This is Jake.

I stare up at Grey. His eyes are closed off.

"Please," I say.

"If I return you home, the curse has no chance to be broken."

I put my hands against his chest. "Please, Grey. My brother has no one."

"This is our final season. Our final chance."

He's right. I know he's right. There are people depending on us. On *me.* But I can't erase the sound of my brother begging from my ears. "Please, Grey. Please."

He looks away. A clear refusal.

"You broke your oath before," I say desperately. "She said you took a bribe—"

He whips his head around, fury in his eyes. "It was a coin pressed into my palm, from a woman I'd seen share his affections in the Great Hall. It was silly. Frivolous. A hundred other guardsman had done it before me. I was young and tired and bored. So *yes.* I took her coin and I allowed her to wait in his chambers. Instead of spending the night alone, he spent the night with her. If you think I have not regretted that moment for every minute of every single one of these seasons, you are wrong indeed."

"Please," I whisper.

"No."

The door at the end of the arena slams open. Rhen bursts through, slightly breathless. "Harper! I have good news! A messenger has arrived with word from—" He stops short, and everything positive drains out of his face. "Something has happened. Tell me."

I open my mouth to tell him.

Instead, I burst into tears.

Rhen moves before me. "My lady. Please—"

I jerk away from him. Blinded by tears, I run from the arena.

CHAPTER THIRTY-EIGHT

RHEN

I find Harper in her chambers, crying into her hands while Freya strokes her hair back from her face.

"Please, my lady," Freya is whispering. "Please tell me what has happened."

I stop in the doorway and put up a hand before Grey can announce me. The sorrow in her posture is so potent. Fear and grief have swept over her so quickly.

"Freya," I say. "Leave us, please."

Freya gets to her feet and gives a short curtsy. "Your Highness."

"No," says Harper. Her voice shakes and fresh tears fall. "Rhen. You go. I can't—I can't do this right now."

Freya hesitates, clearly torn between following my order and hers.

"The princess has received distressing news about her family in Disi," I tell her.

Harper laughs, but there's no joy in the sound. "Distressing. Yeah."

"Leave us," I say again, and this time my voice is final.

Freya bobs another curtsy and quickly ducks from the room. The door closes with a heavy *click* behind her.

"My lady," I say quietly.

Harper looks at me through her tears. "So Grey told you?"

"He did." I cross the room and stop by the bench where she's curled up. Her cheeks are flushed and damp, and there's blood on her chemise. "May I join you?"

She ignores the question and says, "I started to forget."

"To forget?"

"I started to forget them." She gazes up at me, torment in her eyes. "They started to feel like a dream. Another life. I was happy here. And now—now I know exactly how bad their lives are. They're going to die, Rhen."

"I know." I ease onto the bench beside her.

"It was ten seconds and it was awful. The sound, the smell—I could feel Jake's fear. I don't know how you put up with that for days on end."

I stroke her hair back from her face. "My lady."

"I begged Grey to take me back. He won't do it." She sniffs and presses a hand to her stomach. "The worst thing is that I understand why."

"Do you?"

"Of course. I don't even know if *I'd* do it. It's your last chance. I'm the only one who can break the curse. You've got all this going on with Karis Luran. I just—I just—I—"

"You do not love me."

"It's not about not loving you. It's about loving *them*."

The room is so warm and dim and we've spent countless hours

right here, yet this conversation feels more intimate than any we've shared. "You want to protect your family."

"Yes." Her voice breaks. "I'm probably being selfish. There are *thousands* of people here at risk. They're *two*. And my mother is living on borrowed time. But there's no one to help Jake. No one, Rhen."

"As I said, we are not always presented with the choices we want, but choices exist nonetheless."

"I know. And I know why Grey made the choice he did." She presses her hands to her face. "Even though I hate him a little bit right now." She draws a shaky breath. "Lilith is so awful, Rhen. The way home is *right there*, and I have no way to get it."

"Yes." My voice is grave. "She also knows that if we trap you here, you will never love me, and she will win. Yet if you return home, the curse will go unbroken, and she will win."

"She wins either way."

"Indeed." I run a finger along her jaw and tilt her face up. "Which is why I've ordered Grey to take you home."

She grabs my wrist. "What?"

"I have ordered Grey to take you home." I pause. "You mentioned some kind of issue with debtors, but that, at least, is something I can assist with, so I will have a satchel of silver, or jewels, if you prefer—"

Harper launches herself off the bench and throws herself against me. Her arms are tight against my back, her face pressed into my shoulder. "Thank you," she gasps. "Thank you."

Unlike our moment in the hallway in the inn, I am no longer at odds with how to respond to this. My arms fall against her back. I drop my head to speak along her temple. My throat is tight, but

I speak through it. "You act with such surprise each time. I told you I would give you anything within my power to give."

She jerks back to stare up at me. "But—Karis Luran—"

"It will be fine," I say. "You received word about your mother's declining health, and so you had to return to Disi. We knew this could happen. We planned for it."

"You plan for everything."

Untrue. I had not planned on how it would feel to let her go.

She is right. Lilith is awful. No matter what I do, she finds the cruelest way to torture me at every turn.

"I'm sorry," Harper whispers. "I'm sorry I didn't break the curse."

I lift a hand to brush the tears off her cheeks. *Oh, Harper.*

I wish she had. Not because of the curse, or because of Karis Luran, or because of Emberfall.

Because I have fallen in love with *her.*

"You're being so kind." She falls against me again. "I didn't—I didn't know this would be so hard—"

"Shh," I whisper. "You've done more for me than I could have asked."

She takes a breath and looks up, her dark eyes boring into mine. "I'll miss you so much."

She is breaking my heart. "And I you."

"I'll think of you all the—"

I lean in and kiss her.

I'm slow, and gentle, and it's barely more than a brush of lips at first. A question, not a command. I wait for her to hesitate, to pull away, but tonight her lips part and her hands find my face, and then she's kissing me back.

I pull her against me, tangling a hand in her hair, losing

myself in the sweetness of her mouth and the heady warmth of her scent.

This, I keep thinking. *There is no need to be sure. This is sure. This is real.*

I never want this moment to end.

I'm terrible. I'm selfish. My hands find her waist. Stroke the length of her side. My fingers resent the lacing of her vest, the way her chemise is so securely buckled under her dagger belt.

Her hands slip under my jacket. Pull my shirt free. Her fingers brush my side. This moment is worth an eternity of suffering. I gasp into her mouth.

Then she makes a squeal of pain and jerks back.

She's staring at her fingers. Blood decorates the tips. She's blinking in confusion. "What—what—Rhen?"

She's breathing heavily. So am I. We stare at those streaks of blood.

Then I jerk my jacket to the side, pulling the rest of my shirt free.

Scales of blue and green, luminescent and shimmering in the firelight, have grown over my skin in patches.

I stop breathing.

Scales. I cannot remember a time with scales. Fur, for certain, in every color imaginable. Reptilian skin in greens and browns. Exposed bone. Quills. Never scales.

I touch a hand to my side, where the largest patch has grown. The scales are deceptively sharp, with knifelike edges that slice at my fingertips. I jerk my hand away and gasp. Small stripes of blood well up on my skin.

Silver hell. Of course Lilith would offer her an escape this day. *Of course.*

Harper draws away. “What is it?” she whispers.

I cannot breathe.

“The change,” I say. My voice is rough with too many emotions to name.

“The change?”

I draw a shuddering breath. “The creature.”

She swallows. “The monster.” A pause for her own shuddering breath. “The monster that comes every season.”

I cannot meet her eyes, but I must. Hers are hot with betrayal.

And fear.

The fear allows me to hold her gaze. They all show fear eventually. I don’t know why I thought Harper would be any different.

“Yes, my lady. The monster.”

She says nothing. The silence between us could expand to fill the entire castle.

I remember our whispered promise. *No more secrets.*

“So you see,” I say, “if you have not fallen in love with me yet, I cannot see how your heart would change once my form does.”

“You’re the monster? You’ve killed all those people?”

My voice breaks as I say, “Please. You must understand.” I reach toward her.

She draws back before catching herself. We sit there breathing at each other, my betrayal heavy in the space between us.

“You’re going to kill them all again,” she whispers. “The castle is full of people.”

“I have planned for everything, my lady. My people will be safe.” I take a breath. “*You* will be safe.”

She wets her lips. “Rhen.”

There is only so much I can take.

I stand and turn away. “You must go.”

I wait for her to disagree. To call me back. To stop me before I reach the door.

She doesn't.

Commander Grey is not pleased with my orders.

He stands at attention in the hallway as we wait for Harper to say her goodbyes to the people she's grown close to, but I can read the frustration in his eyes. If the castle were as empty as it's been for the last three hundred twenty-seven seasons, he would challenge me. But we're not alone now. The door to Freya's room is open, and Harper is hugging Zo and Freya and the children. A page waits nearby, toward the staircase to the Great Hall. Guardsmen stand at the entrance to this hallway.

Even from there, they can probably sense his displeasure.

Our presence here, my rule over these people in my father's absence, is based on a precarious hierarchy. Insubordination could unravel it all, and swiftly.

With a start, I consider my father's short temper, his intolerance, and wonder if this was the reason for it. When my father was in power, I never thought about where that power came from. I wonder if his rule, his position in power, was equally precarious.

"You are to return at once, Commander," I tell Grey. "See the princess safely home but do not linger."

"Yes, my lord."

His voice is temperate, even, but he looks like he wants to draw his sword and run me through.

I cannot blame him. This curse traps him as effectively as it traps me. Sending Harper home removes all hope.

Grey will have his chance to run me through soon enough.

I pull a folded slip of paper from my belt and hold it out. "Your urgency is no small matter. This message was delivered when you and Harper were in the arena."

He unfolds the paper briskly. His expression goes still as he reads, frustration replaced with surprise.

His eyes flick back to mine, and he keeps his voice low. "Karis Luran wants to meet at sunrise." A pause, followed by a glance at Freya's doorway. Then he makes a guess: "You have not shared this information."

"The princess cannot afford to delay her return home," I say, conscious of the ears in this hallway. My voice drops. "Even if she could, I cannot assure Harper's safety if she were to remain long enough to join us. We may be victorious in convincing Karis Luran to withdraw from Emberfall—or the meeting may lead to all-out war. I do not need Harper physically here to speak of Emberfall's alliance with Disi. Enough people believe in it for the alliance to seem real." I pause. "But I need you, Grey."

He folds the note and holds it out. Any displeasure is gone from his expression. "I will return as swiftly as possible."

Harper appears in the doorway to Freya's room. Her eyes are red-rimmed and damp, but her voice is steady. She avoids my eyes. "I'm ready."

For an instant, the air seems to hesitate.

Grey wants to refuse my order.

I want to beg her to stay.

Harper finally looks at me. "I wish you'd told me."

"Look at where we stand, my lady. You know now. If you'd known earlier, would your choice now be different?"

That seems to steady her. We are all trapped by circumstance, seeking a path to freedom. A path that does not exist.

"No. It wouldn't." Harper draws a deep breath. "I don't . . . I don't want it to end like this. On a lie. On a betrayal."

I step close to her. Her breath catches but she doesn't pull away this time. I lean close to feel her breath on my cheek one last time. "Do not remember this moment, my lady. The important ones are all that came before."

"Rhen," she whispers. "Please."

I step back. "Commander Grey. Return her home. That is an order."

As always, he obeys.

CHAPTER THIRTY-NINE

HARPER

The smell of the city hits me first. The air is sharp and cold, full of exhaust fumes and cooking oil and an undercurrent of urine and a bonus of overfull dumpster. Grey and I have arrived in an alley, sandwiched between restaurants and a drugstore. The night sky hangs above, full of the same stars I saw in Emberfall, but they seem more distant here, blocked by the neon lights that shine everywhere.

The sound hits me next. I never realized how *loud* DC was, even in the middle of the night. Air compressors and buzzing neon and distant traffic. Even the wind is louder, whipping through the alley to lift my curls and slide between the threads of my sweatshirt.

Familiarity is slower, though I recognize this alley, the drugstore we stand behind. After six weeks in Emberfall, in breeches and vests or skirts and corsets, now my threadbare sweatshirt and jeans feel foreign. The only things I kept from the castle are my boots—and the simple leather satchel that hangs over my shoulder, which Rhen packed with a pouch of silver coins, half of Arabella's jewelry, and five bars of gold. I have no idea how much it's all worth here, but if nothing else, it'll buy my family time.

Grey stands beside me, completely anachronistic in his weapons and armor with a flickering sign for Chinese food behind him. His expression is closed off, unreadable.

He's said very little since Rhen gave the order for him to bring me home.

I feel immeasurably guilty. And betrayed. I don't know what I am.

I swallow. "I'm here." My eyes fill against my will, and I hastily swipe at my face. "You can go back."

"I am to see you safely home."

"You—you're going to walk down the street like that?" I suck in a shiver through my teeth. I've spent so long in woolen cloaks and fur-lined jackets that I've forgotten the life I left behind.

"I will keep out of sight." He unfastens his cloak and sweeps it around my shoulders. His fingers swiftly work the buckle at my shoulder. "You are not dressed for this weather, my lady."

"I'm not 'my lady' here," I say. "I'm just Harper."

"You are far more than just Harper, regardless of location."

"Grey . . ." But my voice trails off. Nothing I can say seems sufficient.

I am dooming him. I am dooming Rhen.

I am possibly dooming all of Emberfall.

I clench my eyes closed. "Grey . . . I'm so—so—"

"Time grows short and I must return."

"Right." I press my hands to my cheeks and take a deep breath. My fingers slide over the smooth scar on my face, and I drop my hands. "Sorry. Let's go."

He clings to the darkness so effectively that I barely know he's there. It's as if I walk the streets of DC alone, my boots making a small scuffling sound as my uneven steps scrape along the pavement. Grey's cloak hangs heavy from my shoulders.

Every step is a reminder of Rhen's words about choice.

I feel so certain I'm making the wrong one, but I cannot abandon Jake to whatever Barry is going to do to him.

At the corner of D Street and Sixth Avenue, I stop. My building stands across the street. Only one apartment has a lit window.

My family's. Mine, though it doesn't feel like it anymore.

I step into the shadow of a store awning, and Grey comes to my side. We're sandwiched between two glass display windows, close enough for me to feel his warmth.

I point across the street at the lit window. "That's my family's apartment."

He nods. "As you say."

I stare up at him. His eyes are cool and dark.

"Scary Grey," I whisper. "I'm so sorry."

His stoic countenance cracks a little. He sighs and touches a finger to my chin, then gives me a sad smile. "A princess should not apologize to a—"

I launch myself forward and hug him. In a way, it's like hugging a brick wall, but his arms come around my back and he sighs, his breath brushing over my hair.

I suddenly want him to take me back to Rhen and Emberfall and the people who have so quickly lodged themselves into my heart.

That lone lighted window across the streets taunts me.

If I stay, I'll never see Grey again. I'll never see Rhen.

He pulls away before I'm ready, but his thumb brushes the tears off my cheek. "If the choice were up to me," Grey says, "I would have trapped you in Emberfall."

"I know that. You think I don't know that?"

"Your family would have suffered," he says evenly. "You likely would have watched it happen, if Lilith had her way." A pause. "And you would never have forgiven me."

There's something stabilizing in that statement. To know this was no easy choice on anyone's side.

"I would see you truly home," he says, "if you wish." He glances across the street, his expression as vigilant as it is when he guards Rhen.

I imagine him striding through the hallway of my apartment building, sword hanging at his side. The elderly woman at the end of the hall who lives on social security would probably take one look at him and have a heart attack.

"I'm not in danger now," I say. "At least I don't think so. My family has a reprieve until morning."

Grey gives me a level look. Then he unbuckles the knife-lined bracer from one of his forearms.

"What are you doing?" I say.

He reaches out to take my hand, then pushes back the sleeve of my sweatshirt. "I have no coins or jewels to leave you with." The barest hint of a smile. "But I do have weapons."

"Grey." I swallow. "These are yours."

"I have more." He buckles the leather onto my arm, pulling the straps as tight as possible to make them fit—though they're still a bit loose. Then he unbuckles his other bracer and does the same with my other arm. When he's done, he pulls my sleeves down to cover them. The weight of the knives and leather hangs heavy against the edge of my hands, but it's a good weight. Reassuring.

"Far more effective than an iron bar," he says.

I blush. "I did all right."

"Indeed you did."

Another tear slips down my cheek. "Grey."

He steps back, allowing some space between us. "My lady."

My pulse kicks. "Wait."

"I have been ordered to return quickly," Grey says.

"Okay." I swallow my tears, but then I throw up a hand. "Wait! Wait."

Now he sighs.

"Come back," I say quickly. "Can you come back?"

I've never seen Grey look so startled. "My lady?"

"I need—I need to see my mother. I need to save my brother. But you—you can come back now, can't you?"

He's staring at me as if I'm trying to trick him somehow.

"Twenty-four hours," I say. "Can you come back in twenty-four hours? Right here?"

"For what purpose?"

My voice falters. I'm not entirely sure. Too much is up in the air, and I don't know if I'll be able to save my family at all. I don't know if I'll be able to break Rhen's curse. But I know I can't end this all right here, right now. "To bring me back to Emberfall." I swallow. "Lilith said you can go back and forth now, right? Please, Grey. I just—I need time to help my family. Please."

His expression doesn't change, but I can see him weighing the different outcomes of this.

"You know the truth," he says. "Of what he will become. And still you ask to return?"

"I don't know the truth," I whisper. "But I want to try."

"Midnight," he says. "One day hence. I will wait here. Fifteen minutes. No longer." He pauses. "I will not give him false hope."

With a start, I realize he expects that I won't show. "I'll be here. I'll be waiting."

He nods, then his eyes flick to the window across the street. "Your time grows short, my lady."

"I know." I draw a ragged breath. "I'll see you tomorrow night."

My voice lilts up at the end, almost a question.

"Yes," he says. "I will return."

"For the good of Emberfall," I say hopefully.

That makes him smile, a shadow of Grey's true nature peeking through. "For the good of all."

He takes a step back, and with barely a shimmer in the air, he's gone.

I stop in front of my door. I've been gone for weeks, but everything about this hallway feels so familiar, I could have left just yesterday. The number hangs a bit crooked under the tarnished knocker, just like I remember.

I knock gently, so I won't wake anyone else on this hall.

Silence answers me, a pulsing lack of sound that beats along with my heart. My palms are damp. I have no explanation for where I've been. No explanation for where I've gotten the coins and jewels I carry.

There's a part of me that wishes I'd just left the satchel on the front step, then asked Grey to take me back.

Or that I'd begged him to take my entire family back with us.

Back to what? I think. *Back to a war with Syhl Shallow? Is that really better?*

And what would you do with Mom, away from any doctors? Away from her morphine pump?

I don't know.

I don't know.

I do know I'm going to rattle myself apart if someone doesn't open the door. I knock again, a bit harder this time.

More silence.

Then from the other side, a muffled swear, and the locks are thrown.

Suddenly, Jake stands in front of me.

He looks both older and younger than I remember. I didn't notice that in Lilith's vision. His face is thinner, but he's definitely been working out, because his shoulders are broader, his chest stretching the T-shirt. A day's worth of beard growth clings to his chin, and his eyes are dark and tired and shocked.

He jerks me into his arms and crushes me in a hug. "Oh my god. Harper. Oh my god."

He's crying.

I've *never* seen Jake cry.

I'm not really seeing it now, because my face is pressed to his shoulder, but I can feel him shaking against me.

"I was so worried," he's saying. "I thought they had you. I thought you were dead. I thought—I thought—"

"It's okay." My voice breaks, and I'm crying, too. "It's okay. I'm home. I'm fine."

When I say that, he shoves me away from him. "You're not okay. Your face—who did this to you? Where have you been?" Before I can say anything, panic floods his eyes. "You need to get out of here. Did they see you come in? They're coming back in a few hours. Harp—it's bad. I don't—I don't—" He breaks off and runs a hand back through his hair. "Where *were* you?"

I don't even have a chance to answer, because he's shaking his head quickly. "You need to get out of here. You need to hide. I'm trying to figure out how to move Mom—"

"I'm not hiding," I say.

My voice is firm, and he blinks in surprise. "They don't even care that Mom is dying." Jake's voice is harsh. "Please, Harper. We can find a way—"

"I'm not hiding."

His voice changes. "Did they have you? Are you a warning? Is this—did they do *this*?" His eyes are on my cheek again.

I knew I was walking into a mess. I knew my homecoming would be bittersweet.

I didn't expect . . . *this*.

Grey's bracers are heavy on my arms. "Jake," I say gently.

He runs tense hands through his hair again. "We have until nine a.m. I don't know—"

"Stop!" I slide the bag off my shoulder. "Stop spinning, Jake. Take this. Let's come up with a plan."

He snorts disgustedly. "Harper, unless you have a hundred thousand dollars in there—or maybe a bulletproof vest—you need to get yourself somewhere safe. I don't know why you came back right *now*, but it's the worst possible time."

I'd forgotten this. How I could never solve anything before. How I was something to be shoved into back rooms or left playing lookout in the alley, because I never had anything to offer.

I shove the bag into his chest. The weight slams into him, and the coins inside clink together. “Take it,” I snap. “I’ve brought money.”

“What?” he whispers.

“I brought money. I want to see Mom.” My voice almost cracks. “I’ll tell you everything. And then we’re going to come up with a plan.”

CHAPTER FORTY

RHEN

Despite my orders, I half expect Commander Grey to return with Harper. My imagination conjures the thought of her kicking and screaming as he impassively drags her into the castle and right back up to my door.

These thoughts are fruitless. I should be planning my discussion with Karis Luran. I have spoken to my generals, and soldiers have been moved into position around the castle.

There is still a chance to save the people of Emberfall.

Perhaps there is time to find another woman to break the curse.

The thought would be hilarious if there weren't so much desperation behind it. I pull the crystal stopper from a bottle and pour, watching as deep red liquid fills the glass. I take a sip, then remove my shirt to prepare for bed, moving across the room to toss it over the back of a chair.

There, I catch a glimpse of myself in the mirror.

The scales have spread, even in the short amount of time Harper has been gone.

A sharp knock raps at my door.

Silver hell. I grab my shirt and yank it over my head. A glittering shadow is visible through the lacing at my neck, and I pull on my jacket as well, fumbling with the leather straps to hurriedly buckle them into place.

"Enter," I call.

The door swings open to reveal Grey. He is windblown and red-cheeked from his time outside the castle territory, and his bracers are gone, but he has returned unscathed.

And alone.

"So it is done," I say. "She is gone."

He nods.

I seize the glass and down it in one swallow. "Come in. Close the door."

He hesitates for the barest moment, then says, "I saw you have doubled the soldiers standing at the edge of the castle grounds. In preparation for Karis Luran's arrival, I would advise that we station guards at—"

"Grey."

My guard commander falls silent.

"I don't want to talk about Karis Luran." I pull the crystal stopper from the bottle and pour again. Deep red swirls to fill the glass.

He waits.

Without hesitation, I fill a second, then extend it to Commander Grey.

He looks back at me yet makes no move to take it.

"Do not make me order you," I say.

He takes the glass from my hand.

I raise my own as if to make a toast. A line forms between his eyebrows, but he does the same.

"Forgive me," I say quietly. "I failed."

He goes very still, lets out a breath, and to my surprise, drains the glass. It makes him cough.

I raise my eyebrows and smile. "Am I going to find you on the floor in a moment?"

"Possibly." He shakes his head and takes a breath as if it burned going down. His voice has gone husky. "That is not wine."

"No. Sugared spirits. From the Valkins Valley. My father always kept some on hand."

"I remember."

"I imagine you do." I wonder if he remembers that my father never let anyone touch it—not even me. The rule was so ingrained in me that it took many seasons before I dared to try it, even after he died.

I drain my own glass, then lift the decanter again. "More?"

He hesitates, then lifts his glass. "Please." Though he doesn't look entirely sure about that.

I give a wan smile and pour. "Had I known you would be a willing drinking companion, I would have offered ages ago."

"Ages ago, I would not have been willing." He lifts his glass the same way I did a moment ago, then waits for me to mirror his movement. The alcohol hasn't hit him yet; his eyes are clear and direct. "You owe me no apology."

He downs this glass with the same speed as the first.

My smile widens. "You truly will be on the floor, Commander." I nod at the chairs by the fire. "Disarm yourself. Sit."

When I claim the chair closest to the dressing room, he

unbuckles his sword belt and eases into the chair before the fire, laying the weapon on the floor at his side. He's definitely not drunk yet if he's keeping his weapons in easy reach.

"Another?" I say.

"Sunrise is not far off, my lord. I should not . . ."

His voice trails off as I fill his glass for a third time.

Grey sighs—but he takes the glass when I offer it.

I do not wait for a toast this time. I simply drain my own. "Do you remember the night Lilith attacked me and you brought me here, to my rooms?"

"Which time?"

Indeed. "The day Harper arrived."

"I do."

The alcohol is beginning to burn its way through my veins, turning my thoughts loose inside my head. "I said I would release you from your oath if I failed to break the curse."

His expression goes still. "You did."

I know he is remembering what I asked next: that he kill me if I had not yet broken the curse, and if a sign of the impending change presented itself.

The fire snaps in the quiet darkness.

"I release you from your oath, Grey," I say. "Once we have met with Karis Luran, I want you to—"

"No."

"What?"

He tips back the glass and drains this one, then slams it onto the table between the chairs with a bit too much force. He coughs. "I said no."

"Grey—"

He stands and draws his dagger so quickly that I jerk back, suddenly certain he's going to plunge it into my chest right here and now.

Instead he flips the blade in his hand and holds it out to me, hilt first. "Use my dagger if you wish. But I will not end a near eternity of service by destroying the very man I swore . . ." His words begin to slur together. "I swore to protect."

I snort with laughter, but cover it with a cough. "Put your weapon away before you hurt yourself."

His eyes narrow and he slams the dagger onto the side table. All the slamming—the glass, the blade—is curious, until he moves to sit and nearly misses the chair.

This time I laugh out loud. "Grey, hardly ten minutes have passed."

"Blame your father." His voice is still husky, but now that he's seated, he looks more stable. "It was his order that the guardsmen abstain."

"Regardless of the results of my meeting with Karis Luran—and regardless of whether you will grant my final request—I believe you should leave here once the meeting is complete, Grey."

"And where would I go?"

"You're a talented swordsman. You would have no trouble finding work. Shall I write you a letter of recommendation?"

"You joke about this."

"I have failed, Grey. I can drink myself into a stupor and stomp my feet in fury, but that will not change things. Harper is gone. She did not love me." I pause. "I had thought that perhaps she could . . ." I let my voice trail off and shake my head. Then I lift my eyes to meet his. "You should go back for her. Once all is said and done. I detected a spark between you . . ."

He looks away.

"Was I wrong?" I say. "Or did you leave your knives and bracers with another?"

"You are not wrong." He hesitates, then speaks quickly, tripping over his words in a way that is almost comical. "That is to say—I have never acted to dive—to divert her attentions from you—"

"I know."

He shakes his head, then does it again more forcefully. "I speak too freely. This cursed drink has bewitched my thoughts."

"Most people like it." I pause. "So you will go back for Harper?" The thought tugs at me in an ugly way. I want the best for her. I want the best for Grey. It seems fitting that they might find each other as part of my downfall.

But my failure burns from inside, so much more painful than what Lilith can do.

"I will," he says.

He doesn't need the dagger. This conversation is piercing my heart quite well. I pour another glass. "Good."

"Because she has asked for me to return."

I snap my head up. "What?"

"Her final order before I left her at her door. For me to return once she has had a chance to settle things with her family. For me to bring her back to Emberfall."

Now I am wishing I had not imbibed the sugared spirits. My thoughts trip and stumble in an attempt to keep up. "When? Grey—when?"

"Once day hence. Midnight."

One day. *One day.*

"Too late," I say.

His gaze sharpens—or it tries to. "Why?"

Any hope that flared in my chest has burned out quickly and turned to ash. I unbuckle the jacket across my chest, then pull the shirt wide, so he can see the scales.

He does not gasp, which I expect, but instead sighs, then picks up his glass again. "I have changed my mind. Another, if you please."

I pour. We drink.

We sit in silence for the longest time, until the alcohol begins to send my thoughts drifting toward sleep. The room is warm, the fire crackling invitingly. My eyelids flicker. A part of me wishes I could drift into death right now, as if it would be as easy a slide as sleep.

Not yet. I owe my people this much.

"I do not recall scales before," Grey says eventually.

My eyes open. "I thought they were new as well."

"They're really quite lovely—" He cuts himself short and swears. "Silver hell. My lord—I mean to say—"

I laugh again, but this time it's slow. Lazy. "You're amusing when you're drunk. I truly feel I have missed an opportunity."

His expression sobers. "You think Harper will be too late?" A pause. "I could return for her sooner."

"No. Grey. If you return at all, do it for yourself." I touch a hand to the scales again, gingerly so they do not cut me. "We may not have one day, let alone two." I pause. "If not love, Harper saw . . . promise in me. I would not—I would not have her see the monster I become."

"It is not—" He cuts himself off and swears again. "I should not speak freely—"

"You should. I have released you from your oath. You have served me far longer than any man should. Speak your mind, Grey."

He looks at me. "Your time is not up. You have rallied your people. You conceived a plan that I found ludicrous when I first heard it, but you have brought it to pass."

"Thanks in no small part to you."

He waves me off. "We have guards. An army. A meeting with the Queen of Syhl Shallow. A country full of people to protect."

I pick up my glass and fill it again. "Indeed."

He snatches the glass out of my hand and throws it into the fireplace. It explodes with a crash and a sizzle, and I stare up at him.

"You accomplished these things because you dared to act like you could." He picks up his dagger and re-sheathes it with a vengeance. "Lilith has not won. Not yet. *You* have not yet lost. Stop acting as if you have."

He's so commanding. So sure. It is no wonder he has gained the respect of his guardsmen so quickly. I smile. Incline my head. "Yes, my lord."

For a moment, anger flashes across his features, but he must decide it's not worth it. He drops back into his chair. "You are incorrigible. I have no idea how I put up with you for so long."

I raise an eyebrow, more amused than anything else. "Is that the drink talking?"

The shadow of a wicked smile finds his lips. "You told me to speak my mind."

I sit back in the chair. Sudden emotion sweeps over me, thickening my throat and biting through the haze of the drink. "I tried, Grey." My voice almost catches, but I stop it. "I truly tried."

"I know."

"There is no way out. You once said I plan my actions twenty moves in advance. There are no moves left to make."

"Then perhaps it is time to play like a guardsman, and not like a king."

I blink at him.

"Stop planning," he says. "Wait for them—Lilith, Karis Luran—to make their move. You've had season after season to dwell and plan and strategize." He fishes his deck of cards out of the pouch on his belt, then flips them between his fingers to shuffle.

His eyes meet mine. "Perhaps now it is time for you to think on your feet."

CHAPTER FORTY-ONE

HARPER

Mom has been sleeping for hours.

It's close to five a.m. now, and I've been curled up in bed beside her, listening to the *whoosh* of her oxygen tank. She smells like sickness. I'd forgotten that.

The longer I lie here listening to her quiet breathing, the more I worry that I'm too late, that she's going to pass away with me right here, never having a chance to say anything to her.

"Harp." Jake speaks quietly from the doorway.

I barely lift my face from the pillow to look at him. "What?"

"You've been in here for hours."

"I'm waiting for her to wake up."

"Sometimes she—she doesn't really." A pause. "You need—we need . . ." His voice trails off.

I know what he needs. What he wants. An explanation. I rub at my tired eyes. The knife-lined bracers are still bound around my forearms under my sweatshirt, and I'm aware of them every time I move.

"I'll wait," I say to Jake. "I want her to know I'm here."

He comes into the room and drops into the armchair beside her bed. His cheeks are flushed, his eyes red. He looks like life has thrown him against the wall a few dozen times—and it has no intention of stopping. He's changed so much in the weeks I've been gone. His eyes are harder than I remember. More wary. I want to throw my arms around his neck and beg him to be the sweet brother I remember.

"She's asked about you a lot." He sniffs, like he's sucking back tears. "I didn't—I didn't tell her you were missing. I read about how losing a child can accelerate death in a terminal patient, and I didn't—I couldn't—" His voice breaks and he pinches the bridge of his nose. "Harper, where were you? Where did you get everything in that bag?"

The question isn't emotional like the rest of his words. His voice is edged. Almost suspicious.

"I don't know how to explain." I'd prepared an explanation about being kidnapped and escaping with the bag of riches, but I don't want to lie to him. Not like this, sitting on my mother's deathbed.

"Harper, I need to ask you something."

Mom shifts and takes a deeper breath. I freeze, waiting, hoping she'll wake up.

She doesn't.

I look back at Jake. "Go ahead."

"Is this—are you working with them?" His eyes, dark and narrow just like mine, fix on my face. He's never been wary of me. "Is this some kind of trap?"

"What?" I exclaim. "No!" I want to hit him. "I came back to *help* you."

"Yeah, well, you've been gone for weeks and weeks, and you've shown up on the last day we can do anything to survive. It's all a little . . ." He takes a breath, but his eyes are still hard. "Convenient."

"Fine," I snap. "I was kidnapped by a fairy-tale prince. He made me a princess. He was cursed by an evil enchantress. I had a chance to help him break the curse or come back here—"

"Mom is dying and you're going to crack jokes? What the hell is wrong with you?" He stands up, looming over me. "Where have you *been*, Harper?"

"You aren't going to believe me."

He leans closer. To my surprise, his hands have formed fists. The tendons on his forearms stand out. "Try me."

He would be intimidating, but he's my big brother, and he's always been my protector. Besides, I've scuffled with Scary Grey and half the soldiers in Rhen's new army, and Jake's got nothing on that. "What are you going to do?" I say. "Rough me up like everyone else you've been shaking down for Lawrence?"

He jerks back, eyes wide. "What? How did you—?"

"Jake?" Mom's eyelids flutter. Her voice is whisper-soft. "Jake, what's wrong?"

His throat jerks as he swallows all his rage. "Mom." His voice is rough and hushed. "Sorry."

Her head slowly turns. "Oh! Harper. You're . . . here."

Her voice is so weak. I can barely hear her.

I'm crying again before I even realize it. "I'm here, Mom."

Her eyes fall closed. "I've been . . . thinking of you . . . so much. Did you . . . feel it?"

"I did." I choke. "I did."

"I'm so proud of you. You've been . . . working so hard."

I stop breathing. "Mom?"

"She doesn't always make sense," Jake whispers, so softly it's almost under his breath.

"It's so good . . . to see you two . . . together," she says. "Always . . . always take care of each other."

"We will." I lift her slender hand and kiss her wrist.

Her eyes flutter and she looks at me. "I'm glad you're here. I've been waiting so long." A long pause. So long I think she's fallen asleep. "I love you both so much."

"I love you, too, Mom."

I've been waiting so long to be with her, and now I'm here, and time is running out. It was awful watching her suffer—but now that I'm here, I want more time.

"I love you, too," says Jake. He's not looming anymore. His face is drawn and pale.

Mom takes another breath.

And then she doesn't take any more.

CHAPTER FORTY-TWO

RHEN

Karis Luran travels with few guards and servants. Her entourage is nearly nonexistent.

Grey and I stand in a high window and watch her carriage rattle into the courtyard. Four guards, two at the front, two at the back. Her guardsmen wear black armor trimmed with green and black, with a steel shield obscuring the lower half of their faces. They carry rapiers, lighter swords favored in the north. They're quick and vicious and deadly. Her guardsmen look that way, too.

The vehicle is covered with green silk, the horses adorned with silver bells that jingle along the harness. The carriage windows are blocked with gauzy white material that flutters in the breeze. We cannot see in—but Karis Luran can surely see out. My own soldiers line the courtyard, but many are new. Untested. So much of today's success lies in the actions of others.

Though . . . I suppose it was always so. Even for my father. I never truly realized.

"Only four guards," Grey says to me, his voice low. "Revealing weakness?"

"No." I nod down at the carriage stopping before the castle. "She believes she has nothing to fear." My original plan was to have her and her entourage welcomed into the Great Hall to wait there for me. A small show of superiority—something my father would have done.

But if she has arrived with such a small traveling party, she has already thrown down the gauntlet of superiority.

Think on my feet, indeed.

"Come," I say to Grey. "We must meet her."

I cannot control what music plays in the Great Hall, what food will be arranged on the tables, but today, the melody is light and lively, harp and flute played low, background music for an early-morning gathering. The ladies of the castle have gone to work to make things more festive. For the first time, cascades of autumn colors hang from the rafters and adorn the tables, dark greens and rusted browns and muted gold. The long carpet that leads all the way to the staircase has been exchanged for a newer one trimmed in vibrant gold and red. As I stride across the floor, the guards we have stationed at the base of the staircase move to follow. Grey signals for them to stay in place.

If she can enter my castle with four guards, I can face her with one.

My heart beats against my rib cage like a chained beast that wants to escape. I have nothing left to live for, but my people—they do. This is my final chance to protect them.

The guards at the door move to swing it open when I approach. As the wood shifts and creaks, I want to call for them to wait.

As always, I want to beg for more time.

Oh, Harper. Midnight. I don't think it will be soon enough.

I know it won't. The scales under my clothing catch and pull at the fabric.

The doors open. Cool autumn air streams into the Great Hall.

Karis Luran stands on the marble just outside the door, dressed in robes of green and ivory silk that trail behind her along the ground. A band of silver sits against the creamy skin of her forehead, gleaming in the early-morning light, disappearing under a spill of bloodred hair. She is not beautiful, but she is striking. Her eyes are darkly gold, which would imply some kind of warmth, but there is no kindness in her gaze. She commands the attention of everyone in the room immediately. This is a woman who can order her army to slaughter people by the hundreds—and *has*.

Her four guards form a square around her. They're all matched for height, though none are very tall. They're more leanly built, too, though thick with armor. The tight band of steel covering the lower halves of their faces turns them all androgynous—which is somehow intimidating.

Mind games. I know this. I'm *better* than this.

I bow. "Karis Luran," I begin warmly. "Welcome to Emberfall."

She meets my eyes, then glances away dismissively. When she speaks, her voice is sharply accented, but the words are perfectly clear.

"Fetch your father, boy."

Every word is an insult in a different way.

Fetch.

Your father.

Boy.

Emberfall has effectively been under my rule since the change began and I slaughtered my family—for all the tragedy that has unfolded, some good has transpired, too. Those changes are right here in the Great Hall with me, standing at my back, ready to fight, if necessary. I have arranged meetings with nobles. City leaders. When I fall—and I *will* fall, whether at Grey's hand or my own—Emberfall will not be lost. My army is small, but they are willing to fight. For the first time in my life, I feel a spark of pride in who I am and what I have created.

Karis Luran nearly douses that spark with one sentence.

I fight to keep my composure. The change simmers, not far off, and it is harder to keep my anger in check than it should be. I allow time for one slow breath. "I summoned you. You will meet with me."

"No one summons me."

She does not say this in anger. A simple declaration.

Behind me, the quiet harp music strums along. Commander Grey is a shadow at my shoulder. "I issued a summons," I say, my tone just as evenly declarative. "And here you are."

Her expression tightens by the barest fraction. "I will speak with the king. No one else."

"You will meet with me, or you will return to Syhl Shallow. My army will be happy to escort your forces to the border."

Her gaze is impassive. "Where is your father?"

"He sends his regards."

"Where is he?"

I want to declare that she has no right to demand answers from me, but I need this meeting to end in something other than all-out war. "He is visiting with the King of Disi. They are negotiating our alliance." Every word is even and measured, but this conversation feels more violent than swinging swords. "Your soldiers nearly killed Princess Harper several weeks ago. Her father is eager to send his forces to Emberfall."

"I am unfamiliar with this country of Disi."

"Much to your regret, I am sure." I pause, and a vivid tension falls between us, swirling with the breeze that winds through the open doorway. "Do you care to discuss what this alliance will mean for my country?" Another pause. "And yours?"

"In Syhl Shallow, if a man lies to me, I remove his tongue and force him to eat it."

Behind her, one of her guards draws a blade and lays it across both palms. A threat. A clear one.

To my right, Grey does not move, but his attention sharpens. He will not draw a weapon until absolutely necessary. I hope his guardsmen are equally patient.

"Fascinating. Tell me, Karis, do you have your chef prepare it first—"

"You will not address me in such a common manner." Her eyes darken. "And you will not mock me."

"You addressed me as 'boy.' I thought you wished to be familiar."

"I am the Queen of Syhl Shallow. You will remember your place."

"I am the Crown Prince of Emberfall." I refuse to allow a bite of anger to find my tone. "You will remember yours."

"Oh, I do." Her lips curve into what might have been called a smile if there were any kindness behind it. "My spies have warned me of this Disi. Of your alliance. I have heard of Princess Harper and the soldiers she promises to bring. The invasion this crippled princess hopes to subvert."

"You will not speak ill of the princess."

Karis Luran continues as if I have not spoken. "I have heard reports of your growing army, the way your return to Emberfall has rallied the people."

"I am glad to have returned from Disi with such good news for my subjects."

Her voice lowers. "My spies have seen no soldiers from Disi. No emissaries. No servants for your alleged 'princess.'" A pause, then she glances around. "Not even a princess to stand at your side. I will ask you again, boy. Where is your father?"

I am losing this conversation. I am failing. Again. "I have answered your question."

"I suspect you are being less than truthful. I will not ask a third time."

"I invited you here to discuss a way to prevent your soldiers from being driven out of my country by force. I bear the king's seal. My word is good. Are you telling me you would rather allow your people to die than speak with me?"

"You believe you will be able to drive my soldiers out of your lands? I invite you to try."

"You truly are so arrogant as to risk your subjects?"

"No. You are." She pauses. "Have your people flee to Disi if they believe its king will welcome them with open arms. I suspect they will find you have fed them an empty promise." Her eyes do not leave mine. "I suspect they will discover their king is dead, and their prince is hanging on to his throne by little more than hope and trickery."

Behind me, one of the guardsmen gasps. Maybe more than one. I don't know if it's a gasp of defense or betrayal, but it's a clear break from rank, and it does not go unnoticed.

Karis Luran smiles. “You have done quite the job creating an illusion. I must admit, you have impressed me, boy.”

I glare at her. She’s guessed too accurately on too much of it. “What will it take for you to withdraw your forces from my country?”

“There is nothing you can offer me that I cannot take on my own.” A pause. “I am not a heartless monarch. I will allow you to give your people one week’s notice to flee your lands.” That cruel smile again. “That should give them plenty of time to reach the mythical Disi.”

I take a step forward before I can stop myself. I don’t know if it’s the impending change or my own fury driving my steps, but her guards draw their weapons. Eerily, they do it in unison.

Grey draws his sword.

Karis Luran raises a hand. They all stop.

Nothing drives home her “boy” comment quite like this moment.

“I will stop you,” I snap.

“You are welcome to try.” Her expression does not change. “I was surprised when your father stopped paying the tithe, you know. That is how I know this is a farce.”

I go still.

I know of no tithe. Especially not one paid to a country such as Syhl Shallow.

Karis Luran continues, “At first, I was confused. Was this an act of aggression? A precursor to war? Your father knew the penalties of nonpayment. When the borders were closed, I was more certain. But when my spies began to report that no one was being admitted at court, I grew suspicious. Then rumors of a monstrous creature rampaging Emberfall began to surface. Months passed, then years. No one had seen the king in ages. No one had seen the royal family. It was said that the king had fled the lands and was ruling from afar. So I sent in a regiment of soldiers to take over a small city. To see what the response would be. Do you know what they discovered?"

They discovered that my cities had been left without defense.

I was lost before I began.

"Why was my father paying you a tithe?" I ask her.

"You will have to ask him." Her eyes flash with danger. "If you can."

"If he is no longer paying it, what harm could come from admitting the reason?"

"I no longer need to speak with you, boy."

"If you are so certain my father is dead," I snap, "you will address me with the proper respect due the King of Emberfall."

She laughs and turns away. "How certain you are that you are the true heir to the throne of Emberfall. Of all people, you should know your father's proclivities. How fickle his taste in women. When your grandfather would not allow him to marry that sorceress, do you truly believe he allowed her to be led to slaughter?"

"She was killed," I say. "There are records—"

"Indeed there are. There are records of his first marriage as well." Her eyes narrow. "Where do you think he wed? Where do you think the marriage was consummated?" A pause. "There was a male heir. Your grandfather ordered him killed as well—but your father tried to send him to me. I refused. A halfling child? In Syhl Shallow? Never. I saw the torment your father went through. Your grandfather's greed allowed those people to breed in your lands, and look where it got him."

And look where it got *me*. I'm frozen. Nothing about this meeting has gone the way I wanted it to.

As always this season, there is never enough *time*.

I follow her out of the castle. "What child? Where is it now?"

"Does it matter?" She turns with another thin-lipped smile. "Truly? You have lost your country, boy. Does it matter who the true heir to your father's throne is?" She climbs into the carriage, then stops her footman from closing the door. "When you flee, head north. I would give you a position among my castle staff. I believe my ladies would enjoy a new plaything."

"I will not flee." I bite the words out through clenched teeth.

"Then we will take you by force."

"You will not take Emberfall easily."

"No," she says, and any amusement drains out of her voice. "Lives will be lost on both sides. Regardless of whether you are the true heir to your father's throne, there is a key difference between your actions and those of a ruler. You know how to rally your people. You have built a force to stand against me. But you do not know you've lost. *They* do not know they've lost. It is one thing to build your people up. Entirely another to hold them together."

With that, she slams her door.

I want to order my soldiers to stop them. To set this carriage on fire and destroy her guards.

Anything I do to her will only hasten war.

Especially if there are spies among us.

"She could be baiting you, my lord," Grey says quietly.

"Of course she's baiting me." I watch her carriage bounce along the cobblestones. "It's working." I sigh. As with last night in my drawing room with Grey, I have no idea how to move forward from here.

Flee.

Fight.

I don't know what to do. I don't know what to tell my people to do.

After what Karis Luran just said, I don't even know if I'm the right person to tell them anything.

By nightfall, I sit alone in my father's strategy room. I've been staring at the maps of Emberfall all day, wondering if there's any way possible to arrange my meager army into a formation that will stand against a force from Syhl Shallow.

Harper called this a game once, and she's right. In a way it is.

A game I am destined to lose. Karis Luran holds most of the pieces.

"You look troubled, Prince Rhen."

Lilith speaks to me from the shadows.

I don't look at her. "I shouldn't be surprised that you would find me now."

"You've been too busy for me." Her tone of voice tells me she's pouting.

I ignore her. Harper's idea of luring soldiers into the mountain pass was a good one, an easy way to thin their ranks and pick them off more effectively. If Karis Luran hasn't sent the bulk of her army through the pass yet, it could be possible. Her existing soldiers would put up a fight. People would die. But if my army could survive enough to launch a second wave, we could eliminate her forces as they tried to move through the pass.

I could lead half my army to death on the hope of stopping Karis Luran.

And for what? I'll likely be a monster in a matter of hours.

Slender hands land on my shoulders from behind, stroking upward. "So troubled."

I whirl and smack her hands away. "You will not touch me again. Harper is gone. I have failed."

She steps away as if she meant to let go of me all along. "I found your meeting with Karis Luran to be quite amusing. Who knew your father's taste for random women could have left an heir languishing somewhere in your kingdom?" She puts a finger to her mouth. "A halfling! I must admit, the idea of a forgotten relative somewhere in Emberfall almost makes me want to save your poor country. Though it would likely be fruitless. The poor man probably has no idea what he is. And truly, stopping an invading army sounds like such a bore."

I hate that her comments burn at me. "Go away."

"But I have your leash ready, Prince Rhen. Do you care to see it?"

Leash. The word coils around my throat and jerks tight. "No."

In that moment, I realize what I have to do. Karis Luran was right: I've rallied my people. There is only one way to hold them together.

I turn away from Lilith and stride toward the door.

She follows me. "I should visit Karis Luran for a little chat, just to be sure I'm not misunderstanding. I'll bring you along on a chain to make sure she's forthcoming with information."

Grey is waiting outside the door and he looks alarmed when he sees Lilith following me.

"Ignore her," I tell him, and keep walking.

I head for the stairs.

She follows. So does Grey.

I bypass the third floor and head for the stone stairs leading to the turreted walkway at the top of the castle. A guard stands there: a lookout. His name is Leylan. I order him to stand down.

He hesitates, then glances at Lilith and Grey curiously.

"I gave you an order," I snap. "Stand down."

He obeys. We're alone at the top of the castle, standing under the stars. The moon shines a wide beam down on my lands. The air is cold, promising winter soon.

For the first time in three hundred twenty-seven seasons, snow may fall on Ironrose.

I think of my family.

"So very troubled," Lilith murmurs. "What are your intentions here, my dear prince?"

I turn to Grey. "Your sword, Commander."

As ever, he does not hesitate. His eyes are pools of black, dark and shining in the moonlight. He pulls the sword and lays it across his hands, offering it to me.

I take the weapon and hold his eyes. "Thank you for your service," I say to him.

Lilith claps her hands, delighted. "Have you promised to put Grey out of his misery before you change?"

"I have."

Then I turn and bury the sword in her chest.

She falls to her knees, impaled on his blade. Her mouth is working, whether from shock or pain I cannot tell, but she cannot speak. Her hands are scrabbling at the blade, trying to pull it loose.

"That will not hold her long," Grey says.

"I know. Send the generals to the towns. Have the people head south, away from the invasion of Karis Luran's army. Distribute the silver from the castle treasury. Tell them not to resist. The ships can carry people to the southern shores. They should be safe if we leave no ships. Take the seal. Tell them you act on my order."

"Yes, my lord."

I glare at Lilith. She's still choking, pulling at the blade. She is unable to draw breath to speak, which is an unexpected blessing. Her eyes are wells of evil anger.

"You may have won everything else," I snap. "But you will not win me."

I grab the edge of the parapet and hoist myself up. The wind is fierce, stinging my skin and burning my eyes.

I look at Grey. "My words were true. You have my thanks."

"As you have mine."

I look away. My eyes suddenly burn. "Once my people are safe, go for Harper, Grey. Escape all this."

"Yes, my lord."

My fingers grip the cold stone. I find I cannot move. I cannot breathe.

I am not brave enough, not even for self-sacrifice.

This is permanent.

This is forever.

I have failed.

Grey steps up to me. He holds out a hand.

I grasp it, and he grips tight. His eyes hold mine.

There are no choices left. Every path leads to destruction.

There is always a choice.

"For the good of Emberfall," Grey says quietly.

I squeeze his hand. My voice shakes. "For the good of all."

I let go.

I fall.

CHAPTER FORTY-THREE

HARPER

Jake gives Lawrence's men the necklaces. He says the gold bars and coins would invite too much question, but the necklaces can be explained away.

We're safe. For the time being.

An ambulance comes to take Mom's body away. I feel an emptiness when I watch the paramedics load her body onto a stretcher and zip a nylon bag closed around her.

I eventually succumb to exhaustion. I sleep fitfully at first, then wake late in the morning. So late that it's almost lunchtime.

I've grown so used to my room in the castle, to late-night chats with Zo, to the warmth of Rhen's body in bed beside me—that waking in a cold twin bed alone is jarring.

I don't want to be here. Jake doesn't want me here. I don't know why I came back.

For Mom.

I couldn't save her. I don't even think I gave her any peace.

I've told Jake everything. After the paramedics were gone, after Lawrence's men were gone, we sat in the living room and I laid it all out.

He doesn't believe a word of it. And seriously, who could blame him.

Then I said, "Why don't you go see Noah. Ask him what he thinks."

He froze. I think I actually saw the blood drain from his face. "Noah who?"

"God, Jake. You know I know." I hesitated. "I told you about the pictures on your phone. I told you about the curse." I shrugged. "I just didn't understand why you never told me."

He looked at his hands then. "I wanted something Dad's mess couldn't ruin."

I understand that. So I left it alone.

Grey is returning tonight. I thought I'd be uncertain about returning to Emberfall, that somehow my family would anchor me here, that I was obligated to play a role in their drama. I don't think I ever realized that I'm not trapped by their choices, any more than they're trapped by mine.

I am going to miss Jake. We're not close now—not like we were—but we could be again.

Once he believes the whole princess thing.

This afternoon, I pull on jeans and a long-sleeved shirt and head out for a walk. I'm sure there's some law against the concealed knives on my wrists, but I wear them anyway. I want to head toward Dupont Circle, where the sidewalks will be thicker with tourists and hipsters, but I end up heading south instead. Clouds cover the sun, the concrete buildings matching the sky overhead.

I remember hiding in doorways, so afraid someone would hassle me while I waited for Jake to keep us safe.

I'm not afraid now. I can keep myself safe.

I stay out all afternoon, buying dinner from a food truck, remembering the city that once felt too large to be comfortable. I walk along the dusk-darkened streets, my foot scraping lightly against the pavement because I'm tired, and think, *I'm ready to go home.*

Home doesn't mean here.

Home means Emberfall.

CHAPTER FORTY-FOUR

RHEN

There's a moment during the change when I'm aware of who and where I am.

It's a moment when I'm aware of *what* I am.

One moment I am falling into darkness, the wind a wild rush in my ears, death a welcome certainty at the bottom.

The next moment I am flying, powerful wings beating against the air current, catching my weight before I hit the ground. I swoop upward. A terrible screech pours from my throat. I fly upward, soaring high.

My keen ears pick up the sound of men shouting in sudden alarm as I am spotted.

Run, I think.

Then my eyes find the figures standing atop the castle. My claws extend. I feel each muscle and tendon. I fight the urge to attack and kill.

Run, I plea. *Run.*

And then I think of nothing but death.

CHAPTER FORTY-FIVE

HARPER

To my surprise, Jake joins me on a bench before midnight, saying he'll wait for Grey with me.

He thinks he's patronizing me. I'm not entirely sure what he *really* thinks is going to happen, but we curl onto a bench near the awning where Grey left me, as the city shuts down around us.

"Are you excited to be going back to fairyland?" Jake's voice is edged with a little mockery.

"Go to hell, Jake."

He says nothing, but eventually, a long breath escapes. "I'm not sure what to say, Harper."

"You don't have to say anything. Go back home."

He doesn't say anything. He doesn't leave, either.

"I was really worried about you," I say. "I can't believe what you were doing for Lawrence."

He shakes his head somewhat ruefully. "I didn't want to, Harper. I just . . . I just couldn't see another way out of it."

"I know." My voice is thin. I keep thinking of Rhen and all the choices he's had to make along the way.

I wonder what he's doing now.

Would it have been so hard to tell him I love him?

Was that even a choice?

Did I love him?

This is all so confusing. I've never been in love before, but I feel like it shouldn't be like this.

I look at Jake. "You could come with me. To Emberfall."

His face twists, like he's caught between believing me and wanting to patronize me before I vanish again. "Harper . . ."

"What?"

He rubs his jaw, roughened after two days of not shaving. His voice is low and quiet. "I can't leave Noah."

I hesitate. There's a note in his voice I've never heard before. "You love him."

He glances at me. His expression is almost shy. "I do." He pauses, and that shyness turns into sorrow. "Mom's the only one who knew."

I rise up on my knees and lock my arms around his neck.

He stiffens at first, but then he holds me, too. "I missed you so much," he murmurs against my shoulder.

"I missed you, too."

"Even if there's a part of me that thinks you've gone crazy."

I laugh a little, but he doesn't let go, so I don't either.

"I wish I could have met Noah," I say.

He draws back and grimaces. Late-night traffic rolls past us, but the sidewalks are empty. "I don't want him to get involved. I don't want him to know about any of this." He pulls his phone—a new one he must have gotten to replace the one I lost in Emberfall—out of his pocket and glances at it. "He's at the hospital tonight anyway. He said he gets off at midnight, which really means he'll be working until like six in the morning."

"How'd you meet him?"

Jake hesitates, but then a small smile finds his lips. "I was buying coffee once. When I was there with Mom. You know. He'd forgotten his wallet, so I picked up his coffee, too."

"He's a doctor?"

"Yeah, but he's still a resident."

"I don't know what that means."

"He's still learning. He's doing a rotation in a hospital. He's in the ER now."

"Sexy."

He grins. "Yeah."

My eyes burn again, for an entirely new reason.

"I can't believe you want to leave," says Jake. "You just got home."

I press my hands to my face. "There's too much at stake."

"In Emberfall." He hesitates. "There's a lot at stake here, too, Harp."

"Yeah." I pause. "Please. Please come with me."

"You know I don't really believe in this whole thing you're telling me."

"You do a little."

He blushes. "Yeah, the part of me that used to hide in my room with *Eragon* and *Harry Potter*. But they're not real."

"It is real." I hesitate, wondering what Jake will think of Grey. "You'll see. At midnight. You'll see."

"Even if this magical swordsman appears—"

"He's not magical."

"Fine." Jake rolls his eyes. "Even if this *completely mundane* swordsman appears, I can't just snap my fingers and leave home. It's nuts, Harper. Do you understand what you're asking me to do?"

"I understand that you're not going to be safe," I say. "You think Lawrence isn't going to hold what you've done over your head to make you do more for him?"

He flinches but doesn't say anything. We sit and watch the odd car roll down the road. Somewhere in the distance, a woman is shrieking at someone: a child or a boyfriend. No way to know.

Darkness eventually slips out of the sky to wrap us up. The store closes. I'm curled on the bench, leaning against Jake. So much about him is familiar. His scent. The pattern of his breathing.

"Harper."

I jerk awake. The street is pitch-black and I'm freezing.

"It's almost midnight," says Jake. "Do you have to do something special?"

Adrenaline hits me harder than a shot of espresso.

It's almost midnight.

Grey is coming. This is it. I'm saying goodbye to Jake . . . possibly forever.

My breathing is quick and rapid. I look at the darkened streets, at the narrow store doorway.

Jake must read my panic, because he says, "Harper. We can just go home. You don't have to go anywhere."

"What time is it?" I demand.

"It's eleven fifty-nine."

I swallow. Leave it to Grey to bring it right down to the minute.

I don't know what to do. Jake takes my hand. "It's okay," he says. "Whatever you decide."

I count to sixty.

Then I do it again, in case I did it too fast. And again.

Grey doesn't appear.

A strangled sound comes out of my throat.

"It's okay," Jake says again.

I punch him in the shoulder. "It is *not* okay."

Something happened.

Grey would show. I know he would.

"We need to wait," I say to Jake. "Just—we need to wait."

We wait all night.

Grey doesn't show.

CHAPTER FORTY-SIX

MONSTER

CHAPTER FORTY-SEVEN

HARPER

I had this moment in Emberfall, when I was in the stables behind the inn, when everything around me felt real, and my real life in Washington, DC, felt like a dream. A fantasy.

That's happening again. In reverse.

Two days have passed since Grey was supposed to return. I've spent so much time in the doorway of the shop across the street that they've called the cops and accused me of loitering. I've walked the streets Grey and I walked to get home. I've waited in the alley where we first appeared.

I should be helping Jake figure out what to do with Mom's body. I should be trying to find Dad. I should be going through Mom's things or praying in church.

By Thursday night, Jake finally agrees to invite Noah over. We don't have much food in the apartment, but we throw together macaroni and cheese and hot dogs, along with two cans of green beans from the cupboard.

If anything makes Emberfall feel like a fantasy my mind concocted, it's this food.

I can see why Jake loves Noah. I knew it from the pictures I could see on Jake's phone, but it's entirely different to meet him in person. We're playing cards, and his long, slender fingers flip them easily when he shuffles. His voice is deeper than Jake's, and he has a quiet, gentle manner that's soothing. He's also casually familiar with my brother, little touches and moments of warmth that take me by surprise. It's a nice counterbalance to the anxiety and sorrow that's been seeping through the walls of our apartment.

Noah sits across from me, and I'm not sure how much Jake has told him about where I've been, but it becomes painfully clear when he says, "Harper. Jake says you had quite the adventure."

"Yeah," I say noncommittally. I don't know if he's patronizing me or what, but I know he doesn't believe me. When Grey didn't show, I'm pretty sure I kissed Jake's belief goodbye, too. As I put together dinner, I heard Noah murmur things like *coping mechanism* and *escapist fantasy* and *you don't know what she's been through.*

Noah deals cards around the table. We're playing crazy eights, but I wish I had a deck of Grey's hand-painted cards so I could say, *Look. I didn't make it up. It was real.*

"Jake mentioned you fashioned an alliance with a false country," says Noah. "It's creative, I must say."

"It's nuts." Jake snorts. "Why would anyone believe that?"

I scowl and say nothing. Maybe it was a *little* nuts, but it was working.

"Maybe not," says Noah. "If the president came on television and said we were involved in a war with a country you'd never heard of, you wouldn't get on a plane to find out for yourself, would you?"

Noah shrugs. "Why do you think conspiracy theorists gain any traction?"

Jake considers this, then glances at me. "He's too smart for me."

"Probably," I agree.

He smiles and gives me a good-natured cuff on the shoulder. "Speaking of smarts, do you want to look at re-enrolling in school?" Jake says to me.

My hands hesitate on the cards. High school feels like a million miles away. Even when I was going, my mind was here, with Mom. With the mess Dad was making of our lives. I kept my head down and got my work done, but I doubt anyone was surprised when I disappeared. "It's the first week of April. You think they're just going to let me back in?"

"You need to graduate, Harper. We could find out what you need to do to take the GED. We can't rely on your bag of gold forever—if we can even figure out a way to sell it without looking like we stole it."

Like the food we're eating, nothing drives home the permanence of this situation like Jake talking about the GED and me needing to get a job.

Welcome home. I'd be laughing if it weren't all so pathetic. A week ago I was a princess trying to save a country. Now I'm wondering if the grocery store is hiring.

A heavy knock sounds at the door.

Jake is on his feet before the knocking is complete. A knife finds my hand.

"Whoa," says Noah. He flattens his cards against the table.

"Shh," Jake says fiercely. He makes a slashing motion against his throat.

Something shifts against the door again.

"Lawrence?" I whisper.

"I don't know," says Jake.

I tiptoe to the door and look through the peephole. All I see is dark clothing. Whoever stands outside is all but leaning against the doorjamb.

I tighten my grip on the knife and ease to the side so I'm not directly in front of the door. Jake is right at my back. Noah is sitting at the table, wide-eyed.

"Who's there?" I demand loudly.

Something shifts against the door again. Then a male voice says, "My lady."

My heart stops. I throw the lock.

The first thing I see is his face, drawn and pale and smudged with dirt—or worse.

Then I see all the blood: it's everywhere, on his armor, on his empty sword scabbard, on his cloak.

"Grey," I say. "Grey, are you—"

He starts to fall. He outweighs me by at least a hundred pounds, especially with the armor and weapons, but I drop the knife and step forward to catch him. Jake is suddenly beside me, lending his strength to the effort. Together, we ease Grey to the ground and get the door shut.

Blood oozes from everywhere. Under his armor, around his boots, through his sleeves. It's already on the carpet. His uniform is torn in several places. One especially deep gash cuts across his arm. His eyes are closed and he lies in a heap, breathing shallowly.

"Grey." I want to put my hand on his chest to shake him a little, but I don't want to hurt him. "Grey, please."

He doesn't respond. A small sound escapes my throat.

Noah drops to a knee beside me. He picks up the knife, and when he speaks, his voice is all business. "His name is Grey?"

I nod, and he says, "Grey, can you hear me? I'm going to try to find out where all the blood is coming from." Without waiting for a response—not that he gets one—Noah takes the knife and starts cutting through the leather buckles that hold Grey's armor on. Claw marks have gouged lines in the leather. The straps are slick with blood, but the blade is sharp and slices right through. The uppermost strap is already broken.

Noah's eyes flick up to Jake. "He's in shock. Call nine-one-one." Then he looks at me. "Get some towels."

"No." I swallow and look at Jake. "I mean—you can't. You can't call." I have no idea what a hospital would do with Grey, but I can't imagine they'd treat him and let him walk out the door. He has no identification. No insurance. There would be questions we can't answer.

Questions I can see in Noah's eyes right now.

"Please." My voice breaks. "Please help him."

"He needs a hospital." Noah slices through the straps on the opposite side of Grey's armor and lifts it away.

All the breath leaves me in a rush. Whatever attacked him found the vulnerable stretch of skin under his arm and dug four deep grooves into his ribs. A pink stretch of muscle glistens beneath all the blood.

"Clean towels," says Noah. "Now."

Jake goes. He comes back with three. Noah rolls one tightly and presses it against the injury. With his free hand, he puts two fingers against Grey's neck, looking for a pulse. "You need to call." His voice is grim. "He's breathing, but his pulse is weak. He's lost a lot of blood."

Jake is looking down at me. His eyes are wide. He's heard everything about Scary Grey and my stories from Emberfall, but hearing it and seeing it are two different things.

I don't want to think about what could happen if Grey woke in an ambulance. He once said he's somewhat familiar with this world, but there's a difference between snatching girls off the street and waking up in Shock Trauma. "He's not—he's not from here. He won't understand. The cops will be all over him." I look at Noah. "Can't you stitch him closed?"

"With what?" says Noah. "A needle and thread?"

When I nod, he looks exasperated. "Even if I could, he'll need antibiotics. A tetanus shot." His expression darkens. "Call, Jake."

Jake hesitates. "I think she's telling the truth."

"About what? That this is some prince from a fantasy world? That's real blood. Harper, hold this towel. Press hard."

I move into position and press it tightly against Grey's side. These cuts are deep, and my eyes flinch away. "He's not the prince," I say. "He's the prince's guard commander."

"Oh, that's better." Noah uses the knife to cut the sleeve away from the wound on Grey's arm. "This one needs stitches, too."

"Can't you—"

"No!" He sounds like he can't believe this is up for discussion. "I don't even have any supplies here!"

"I can go," says Jake quickly. "I can run to your place. Or—or the drugstore . . . ?"

"The *drugstore*? Are you kidding me?" Noah swears and uses the knife to tear a strip from another towel. "I can't do this. He could die. He could—"

Grey inhales sharply, then makes a low sound in his throat. His eyes flutter open. A hand lifts.

"It's okay," I say to him. I take his hand and press it between both of my own. His skin is tacky with blood. He's so pale. "It's okay," I whisper. I have no idea whether my words are true. "You'll be okay."

His eyes drift closed before I even finish the sentence.

I keep a tight grip on his hand and look across at Noah. "Please."

"I could lose my job. I could—"

"Please," says Jake.

Noah inhales like he's going to refuse, then lets it out in a rush. He moves the towels to the side to check the bleeding, then presses them back into place. "Jake. Get my keys out of my back pocket. My stuff is by the desk in the bedroom—"

"I know. I know where it is." Jake gets the keys and heads for the door.

Before he can pull it closed, Noah says, "Hey. Jake."

"Yeah?"

"You need to run."

Grey is stable.

At least, according to Noah. He and Jake moved him to the bedroom half an hour ago because Noah needed more light to stitch up Grey's side.

Grey's surviving pieces of armor are piled in a corner of the kitchen. After Jake left, Noah made like he was going to slice it all off, but I stopped him and started unbuckling. I have no idea what's going on in Emberfall or what Grey will have access to, but I don't want to destroy what he has left.

Noah sent Jake to the drugstore for more supplies, and I'm standing at the sink trying to wash the blood off the blades Grey still carried: his own set of throwing knives and the dagger strapped to his thigh.

Then I go still. If Grey is here, does that mean Rhen is dead?

I set the knives on a towel and go to the bedroom.

Grey is still unconscious, his skin nearly as pale as the sheets and towels beneath him, his hair dark and unruly against the pillow. I've never seen him look so vulnerable. Older scars decorate his torso, but nothing as severe as the wounds across his chest. He looks smaller, too, shirtless and injured, without all the armor and weapons. Scary Grey is nowhere to be seen.

The room smells like iodine and blood. Noah has completed the sutures along Grey's rib cage, four long arcs of neatly placed stitches. He's moved on to the slice across his arm.

When Noah speaks, his voice is low and quiet. "An inch lower, and this would have severed a tendon. I wouldn't have been able to fix that."

"Is he going to be okay?"

"His blood pressure is still low. He needs a liter of blood. IV fluids." His voice is still soft, but laced with irritation.

I don't know whether I owe him an apology or a thank-you. Probably both. Probably more.

"Is he going to survive?" I whisper.

"For the next few hours, yes. The bigger worry over the next few days will be infection. Right now, I'd feel better if he'd wake up and tell me his name."

Me too.

"Thanks," I say. "Thanks for doing this."

Noah doesn't say anything for the longest time, and I don't know him well enough to read his silence. I'm about to turn away when he says, "I didn't want to believe you. Jake's the one who loves all the superhero movies. My world is pretty concrete."

"Okay." I'm not sure where this is going and my voice shows it.

"He's got other scars." Noah glances over his shoulder to look at me. "None were treated in a hospital. I can tell." A pause. "Neither was that scar on your face."

I don't say anything.

"His clothing doesn't have any tags, either," says Noah. "And those weapons . . . they're not stainless steel, from what I can see."

"So what are you saying?"

"I don't know." He turns back to Grey's arm, and his voice is thoughtful. "I guess I'm saying I don't *disbelieve* you."

I can take that.

The apartment door slams. "I'm back," Jake calls. "I stopped for coffee, too."

"I only have one more stitch, and then I'm going to clean him up," says Noah. "I'll be right there."

I leave the bedroom to help Jake.

He's brought four coffees from the convenience store on the corner. Like he expected Grey to be all better when he got back.

My brother is such a dumb jock in some ways, but in others, he's effortlessly charming. I wrap my arms around him in a hug.

"What's this for?" he says.

"You brought four coffees."

"Yeah, well." He sounds abashed. But then he looks down at me and lowers his voice. "There's a car outside. I think it might be Lawrence's guys."

A chill takes grip of my chest. "Why?"

A sudden crash and a shout emit from the bedroom, then the light in the doorway flickers.

"Wait!" calls Noah, his voice strangled. "Jake—help—"

Jake and I nearly collide with each other trying to get into the bedroom. Grey is standing, and he's got a death grip on Noah's wrist, pinning his forearm to his chest. His other hand is wrapped around Noah's throat, forcing his head high.

Grey's still ghastly pale and panting from the effort. "You will—you will tell me where I am."

"Let him go!" Jake starts forward in a fury.

"Wait!" I grab hold of his arm and hang on while Jake drags me forward. Grey glances from Noah to me and then to Jake barreling down on him. He's unsteady and trembling, but he doesn't look ready to let go at *all.*

This is going nowhere good in a hurry. "He's scared. Grey—it's okay—"

"Easy," Noah grits out. "I was just—trying to help—"

"Take your hands off him," Jake growls. He pulls free of my grip and advances like he's going to throw a punch.

Grey tightens his grip. Noah makes a small sound.

"Commander!" I yell. "Release him."

He lets go. Noah stumbles back. Grey turns to face Jake. His eyes go between us as he tries to figure out who's a threat and who's an ally.

"I'm fine," Noah says quickly. He's rubbing the wrist Grey grabbed. "He woke up disoriented. He didn't hurt me."

Jake glances at him. Some of the tension drains out of his body. "Okay." He takes a step back. "Okay."

I move toward Grey, who's still watching the two men warily. His breathing is too shallow, and a bloom of sweat has broken out on his forehead. Adrenaline is probably all that's keeping him upright.

"You need to lie down," I say. "You've been unconscious for over an hour."

"Where are my weapons?" His voice is still thready.

"In the kitchen. I'll get them."

"The last thing he needs is weapons," Jake mutters.

Grey's stance stiffens.

"Stop!" I say. "Jake. Oh my god. Do something useful. Why don't you get him a T-shirt?" I consider the bloodstained trousers hanging on Grey's hips. "Maybe a clean pair of pants."

"Go," says Noah to Jake. His soothing doctor voice is back, and he begins picking up the supplies that must have scattered when Grey woke up. "We'll be all right."

Jake heads out of the room.

"Sit," I say to Grey. "Please. You're going to drop in a second."

He slowly eases onto the side of the bed. "I was unsure I would be able to find you."

"You did." I sit down beside him. My head is burning with questions about Rhen, about Emberfall, but he looks like a breeze would send him crashing to the ground, so I hold my tongue.

"Can I get your blood pressure?" says Noah. He already has a stethoscope plugged into his ears, the cuff ready in his hands.

Grey glances at me. When he blinks, it's too slow.

"He's a doctor," I tell him. "He stitched up your wounds. He won't hurt you."

He gives a nod. Noah shifts forward and reclaims his chair.

He slides the Velcro cuff around Grey's arm and begins inflating it. We all sit in silence and listen to the *whoosh* of air.

Finally, I can't take it. "Was it . . . was it the monster?" I ask Grey. I can't bear to say *Rhen.* "Is that what did this to you?"

He nods slowly.

"I thought he had a plan. A plan to protect his people."

"Too late."

Noah deflates the cuff. "Ninety-five over fifty. Still way too low." A pause. "But I can see why you didn't want to take him to the hospital."

I'm still stuck on what Grey said. "Too late?"

He shakes his head again, then has to take a long breath. "He tried to jump from the ramparts. He changed midair. He has wings . . . this time. He can attack from . . . from above."

"I'd really feel better if you could get him to lie down again," Noah says, his voice low.

He tried to jump from the ramparts.

Rhen tried to sacrifice himself to protect his people.

Even in his last effort to beat Lilith at something, he failed.

CHAPTER FORTY-EIGHT

HARPER

Grey refuses to lie down.

I can barely get him to stay seated, though his injuries are helping. Jake's presence seems to make him anxious. I don't know if this has to do with Jake's history or the fact that Grey's in no condition to defend himself, but he watches my brother like he doesn't trust him.

Jake doesn't help this effort, because he's watching Grey exactly the same way.

Earlier, Noah taped bandages over the stitches on Grey's chest and arm, then put a wide layer of ACE wrap over top of it all. He put three tablets of ibuprofen in front of the swordsman and said, "That should take the edge off. If you want something stronger, you're going to have to go to the hospital."

Grey took the tablets and said, "You have my thanks, healer." Before I could get him a glass of water, he crunched them like candy—then grimaced.

That made Noah look at him sideways, a musing expression on his face. It made Jake scowl.

Now we're all at the kitchen table, sipping the coffee Jake brought. Grey still looks shaky, but his color is a little better. Maybe the caffeine is helping. The borrowed green T-shirt is snug across his chest and arms, but the loose black pants fit him well enough. His dagger sits on the table beside his cup, but aside from the weapon, he looks like a college athlete with a hangover. I don't think I've ever seen his bare forearms. It's so hard to reconcile this figure with the strict, duty-bound guardsman I knew in Emberfall.

Jake sits directly across from him, his arms folded over his chest. Noah sits beside him, and his expression is more inquisitive. He's looking at Grey like he's someone he can't quite figure out.

I feel so stupid. I should have put it all together earlier. "Why didn't Rhen tell me?"

"What would that have changed?"

I don't know. I might have stayed.

Then I think of what Jake was facing. I wouldn't have been able to leave Jake or my mother. Rhen knew that. He was protecting me, even in the end.

Grey says, his voice low and rough, "You have heard stories of the damage the creature has caused. The lives lost. I believe he is ashamed." A pause. "*Was* ashamed."

The note in his voice makes me snap my head up. *"Was?"*

He nods. "He has no knowledge of himself when he is in this form." Grey shifts in his chair again, then puts a hand over his ribs as if he needs to hold himself together. "He has attacked the girls before. Some have not survived. I have learned to draw him away, to the less-populated areas of the kingdom, but . . ." A wince. "The castle is full of people now. They have taken shelter, but Rhen's creature is strong. He is pulling Ironrose apart brick by brick."

I think of Freya and the children. I think of Jamison. Zo. Everyone I've come to know and care for. "Has anyone died?"

"Yes." His voice is grave. "We are doing our best to lure him away from the castle. But he can fly and we cannot. Arrows do not pierce his skin. He has claws that grip and tear. He pulled me right off a horse. I put my sword through his wing and he fell, but it barely stopped him. He would have torn me apart."

"Would have?" says Jake. "What did you do?"

Grey glances at him. "I crossed over." A pause. "I came here."

"Why?" Jake's tone is demanding and I don't fully understand why.

"Because." Grey turns back to me. "We have no other hope."

"You want me to come back," I breathe.

"No," snaps Jake. *"No."*

We all look at him.

Jake presses his hands against the table. "Even if I believe all this—and I'm not saying I do—there is no way in hell I'm letting you go back with him, Harper. This guy *literally* fell through our door two hours ago. If Noah hadn't been here, he'd be dead right now. Did you listen to his story about being dragged off a horse and torn to shreds?"

Like I didn't see Grey collapse on the carpeting with my own two eyes. "Yeah, but—"

"But *nothing*. Are you listening to yourself? Are you listening to *him*?" He turns those furious eyes to the guardsman. "If you can't stop this thing, what makes you think *she* can?"

"You speak as though I seek assistance in battle. I do not."

"I don't care. It doesn't matter. He's a monster. She's not going to fall in love with him *now.* She's been through enough. She can't help you."

Nothing here has changed. I love Jake, but he'll never see me as anything more than little Harper who needs to be shoved into a back room and protected.

Perhaps he has a point. If Rhen is a monster, I don't know if there's any hope left at all. I can't fall in love with a murderous creature. "What about Karis Luran?"

"The queen came to the castle. The morning after you left. She was not fooled. She spoke of secrets known only to her and the King of Emberfall, then gave Rhen a week to have his people evacuate before her soldiers would begin to take Emberfall by force."

"But now the people are hiding from the monster."

"Yes, my lady."

"What about Lilith?"

"The enchantress," Noah says softly. He looks awed by this whole exchange. I'm not sure he believes any of it, either. But for all his talk of science and reason, he looks like he *wants* to.

"Lady Lilith fled. In this form, Rhen is a creature of magic and he *can* harm her."

That sounds like it should be an advantage—but if Rhen is determined to kill everything in sight, maybe not. "Do we still have an army? How many people have been killed?"

"So far the losses have been few. Several soldiers who were standing guard the night he changed. The people do not know the prince is the monster. Many fear he is dead." He pauses, and his voice is grim. "Many guards heard the queen's words. Rumors have spread that there is no alliance. That Disi has no assistance to provide."

All of our carefully laid plans have been unraveled in a few days.

"What do you expect Harper to do?" Jake snaps. "Ride in and play princess?"

"Yes," Grey says simply. His eyes are on me. "I would ask that you return to reassure your people."

My people. I stare back at him. He's still pale, but his gaze is clear.

I turn to Noah. "How quickly can Grey fight again?"

The doctor looks startled. "*Fight?* Not for weeks. He shouldn't even be sitting up in a chair."

"I can walk," says Grey. "I can fight."

I don't know about that, but if he can walk, he can take me back to Emberfall.

"You're not going!" Jake says.

I slide out of my chair and move across the kitchen to fetch the surviving pieces of Grey's armor. "I am. I couldn't—" My breath almost deserts me, and I turn back to the table with his bracers and greaves. "I couldn't save Mom, but I can do this."

When I drop them on the table in front of Grey, Jake grabs my arm and turns me around. His grip is almost painful. "You aren't doing this, Harper. I don't know where you think you've been or what you think you've been doing, but this sounds like an elaborate setup. If I have to drag you into your room and lock you in there—"

All of a sudden he's jerked away from me. Noah scrapes out of his chair in alarm.

Grey has Jake's arm twisted up behind his back and his dagger point sits at the soft bit of skin just below Jake's ear. "You will do no such thing," he says.

I look up at my idiot brother's wide eyes and sigh. "I wasn't lying when I said he was scary."

"Let me go," he grinds out.

My eyes shift to Grey. "Let him go before you hurt yourself. I'll help you put your armor on."

He does, and Jake jerks free. Grey eases back into the chair, trembling again.

"Keep doing that," says Noah, "and you're going to rip those stitches out."

"Harper," says Jake, his voice dark—though he doesn't touch me this time. "You can't do this."

"I can." I kneel and pull the boots over to Grey. "And I will."

Grey is sweating and pale and breathless by the time he's replaced the surviving armor. I want to beg him to wait. But he holds my gaze and I know he won't. If I won't come, he's still going back. If Rhen is gone, he has people to protect.

Jake hasn't said a word. He's silently fuming, watching all this from where he stands, leaning against the kitchen counter.

"At least wait until morning," says Noah. "One night. Six hours. Give the stitches time to set."

"I do not have a night, healer," says Grey. His voice is breathy. "Nor does Emberfall."

"How are you going to keep her safe?" says Jake. "What if you go back and you're attacked?"

"We will be cautious," says Grey. He grips the table to help push himself to his feet.

"Cautious? You're crazy. *All of this* is crazy."

A knock sounds at the door and we all freeze.

It's nearly midnight.

What did Jake say when he came in with coffee?

There's a car outside. I think it might be Lawrence's guys.

I look at Jake. "What do we do?" I whisper.

He doesn't have time for an answer. Wood splinters, men shout, and two men burst through the doorway, guns drawn and aimed. "Those necklaces were worth a lot. What kind of game are you playing here?"

Jake shoves me behind Grey. Noah's weight presses against my back.

"There's nothing," Jake says. "We don't have anything."

"Who's this guy?" says one of the men.

Grey moves. Drawing a weapon, I think. I can't see.

A gun is cocked. A bullet will beat a blade. This is all happening too fast. We need a plan. A course of action. We need—

The gun fires. I flinch.

And then we're in the woods, autumn warmth pressing around us. In the distance, torches hang at regular intervals, marking the castle territory. I'm still half ducking. My ears ring from the gunfire.

We're in exactly the same position we were before: Grey and Jake in front of me, with Noah beside me. Everyone is standing. Everyone is breathing. My heartbeat is so loud I almost can't hear anything else.

"What just happened?" says Jake. "Where are we?"

"Emberfall," I whisper.

"But—what *happened*?"

"Wait," says Noah. "Wait." He sounds like he's on the edge of panic. I remember that feeling.

Grey turns and looks at me. He's so pale, even in the dark. "We must walk. Karis Luran's soldiers have moved close. The castle could be . . ." He blinks hard. "We must walk."

Without warning, he's falling again.

Jake catches him like he did in the doorway.

"This feels *super* cautious," he snaps. But because he's Jake, and he does what needs to be done even if he doesn't want to, he gets Grey's arm around his neck and holds him upright.

"You there! Halt!" Three soldiers appear from between the trees. Bows are drawn, three arrows pointed at us from all sides. In the dark, I don't recognize any of them.

"It's the commander!" one yells. "Lieutenant!"

Grey is all but unconscious, most of his weight supported by my brother.

I don't know if they recognize me, but I'm in jeans and a sweatshirt—not exactly princess attire. They definitely don't know Jake and Noah. Our situation does not look good.

A fourth soldier steps out of the trees with a sword drawn. "Explain yourselves."

I recognize *him*. Thank god. "Jamison." I'm so relieved that I almost run forward to hug him.

He sees me and blinks. "Princess." I watch his eyes flick up and down my form, and then he looks at the soldiers. "Stand down."

They lower their arrows—but not all the way.

That alone tells me how far I've fallen in their esteem.

Mentally, I'm trapped between Emberfall and DC. I wasn't ready to snap right out of my kitchen into the role of Princess Harper. I need to get it together or I'll unravel whatever's left. "Commander Grey is injured. He needs assistance."

"We saw the monster seize him." A weighted pause. "We searched for his body. We thought he was dead."

He's looking for some kind of explanation.

Think, Harper. Think.

"I was returning to the castle when the monster attacked my entourage," I say. "My carriage was destroyed. We were forced to proceed on foot. We came across Commander Grey, and luckily my healer was with me." I glance at Noah.

He's staring back at me incredulously.

Please, I think. *Please don't mess this up.*

I imagine what Rhen would do in this same situation.

"Have your men carry the commander," I say. "I'll need a room and supplies for my healer. We're prepared to assist with those injured by the monster."

"Harper," says Jake, his voice low and warning.

The soldiers all turn to look at him. Arrow points raise a few inches.

"Who is this man?" says Jamison.

I look at the sword hanging in his hand. The arrows sitting nocked. Whatever happened with Karis Luran has deeply damaged any trust Rhen and I built.

"My brother," I say. "Prince Jacob. Heir to the throne of Disi. Captain of . . . of the Royal Army. We've heard of the lies spread by Karis Luran, and we are here to fight."

Jamison hesitates—but then he gives Jake a nod. "Forgive me, Your Highness. We are on alert. There have been rumors of soldiers from Syhl Shallow in the woods. And the monster, of course."

"Forgiven," says Jake. His voice is hollow. I reach down between us and squeeze his hand.

"Help the commander," Jamison orders his men. He gives me a nod as well. "We are pleased to have you return, Princess. We'll escort you to the castle."

CHAPTER FORTY-NINE

MONSTER

Harper?

Pain.

Sleep.

CHAPTER FIFTY

HARPER

The castle is darker than I've ever seen it, even at night—every window has been barred. Candles burn through suddenly claustrophobic hallways. Two of the soldiers have taken Grey to the infirmary, but Jamison personally leads us to my chambers.

The stationed guardsmen at the end of my hallway study me warily now, but Freya sweeps me into her arms when she sees me. "Oh, my lady," she says, her voice hushed because so much of the castle is asleep. "I've been so worried. The talk has been so troubling. How is your mother?"

She's so warm and soft and smells like home. I didn't realize how desperately I needed a hug until her arms came around me. I cling to her. My voice breaks. "Freya. She died. I barely made it in time to say goodbye."

"Ah. So sad." Her hand strokes up my back. "I am so sorry."

Then I see Zo, a short distance back. My guard. My *friend*. If she looks at me with distrust, I don't know if I'll be able to take it.

She strides forward and tackles me with a hug that nearly knocks me off my feet.

I hug her back. Tears spring to my eyes for a new reason. "I missed you so much."

"I thought I would never see you again," she says. "I asked the commander to allow me to come after you."

A man coughs behind me, and then Jake says, "Uh, Harp?"

His voice isn't unkind, but it's a reminder that they're stuck here with me—at least until Grey can wake up. I sniff and get myself together. "Sorry." I straighten. "Zo and Freya, this is my brother, Jacob." I force myself to speak without hesitating. It's one thing to play a role myself; entirely another to rope my unprepared brother and his boyfriend into it. "The Crown Prince of Disi. And Noah, the king's personal healer."

"Oh!" Freya offers a curtsy to the men behind me. "Your Highness. My lord."

"Welcome," says Zo.

Jake and Noah stare at both women and say nothing. They both still look shell-shocked.

"Our carriage was destroyed," I say. "We will rest in my chambers until Jamison can find rooms for Jacob and Noah."

"Yes," Freya says. "Yes, of course. I will have food brought." She heads for the staircase.

Zo studies me, then my brother and Noah. "Perhaps clothes as well?" She hesitates, a slight undercurrent of curiosity between her words. "If your things were destroyed?"

Freya believes the best of everyone, but Zo is more savvy. She doesn't distrust me, but she knows something is up. I want to tell her the truth, but it would unravel everything we've promised the people of Emberfall.

"Yes," I say to her. "Thank you."

She glances at my brother and Noah again. "Yes, my lady."

Once she's gone, I lead Jake and Noah into my rooms, then close the door. A fire rolls in the hearth, and every sconce on the walls is lit. They both turn in a full circle, taking it all in.

"I don't quite believe this," Noah says finally. "I need you to pinch me."

"I'm too busy pinching myself," says Jake.

Noah gives him a rueful look. "At least you get to be the prince. I got stuck with *healer*."

"Fine. Let's trade. You be the fake prince." Jake folds his arms across his chest. "When can your friend take us back?"

I frown at his tone. "Back into the house with the men who were about to shoot us? Maybe you should give it a few hours."

He flinches and looks away. "We can't stay here, Harper."

"Well, I can't take you home, and Grey needs rest."

Noah has moved to the fireplace. He runs a hand along the mantel. "Are we in the past?" He frowns and shakes his head. "That's a ridiculous question. That's impossible. But *this* is impossible—"

"Not in the past," I say. "They call it *the other side*. Or maybe *our* side is the other side—somehow our world runs parallel to theirs." I'm suddenly exhausted. I need to find out what rumors have been spread. The state of the army. What Karis Luran said.

I head into Arabella's closet and dig through the dresser until I find the doeskin breeches and knit pullovers I've grown accustomed to wearing when I spar with the soldiers. I pull the door halfway closed and speak around it while I change.

"Okay, look," I call to them. "Freya is going to come back with food and clothes. Put something on so you don't look like such outsiders. Have something to eat. Rest if you want. I don't care. But don't mess with what's going on here."

"What are you going to be doing?" Jake's voice is incredulous.

"I'm going to find out what happened while I was gone. I'm going to find out where the monster is. I'm going to talk to Rhen's army and see if we can figure out a way to save his people."

"Oh really?"

I pull a vest over the shirt and lace it up. "Yeah. Really. There's no one here leading these people. They're worried the royal family is dead."

"And you think you can lead them?"

No. I have no idea.

"Yes," I say. I yank a dagger belt out of the chest under the dresses and loop it twice around my waist as I come out of the closet. I lace the leather together in a practiced motion. "Do you think you can stay out of trouble for an hour?"

Jake sputters as he looks at me. "Harp—what are you—just who do you think you are?"

"Princess Harper," I say. "And you're my brother, the Crown Prince of Disi, so you'd better damn well act like it."

"How do I act like a prince? I don't even know *where we are*!"

"You're in Emberfall. And acting like a prince generally means acting like an arrogant know-it-all, so you shouldn't have any trouble at all."

The castle is packed with people who've taken shelter from the creature. Karis Luran's soldiers have moved east of the mountains, preventing any access to the passage to Syhl Shallow. Any who have attempted to engage in battle have been slaughtered. Messages are sent from city to city once per day—and messengers travel in packs of three. Many don't return. People fear that Rhen is dead, that the King of Emberfall is dead. Many of them thought that *I* was dead.

I learn of the rumors that say Rhen is not truly the heir, that Emberfall will fall to the armies of Syhl Shallow, that escape is impossible now that the creature has returned with a taste for blood.

I tell them that Disi has been attacked by the enchantress's creature as well, and that my traveling party was nearly all killed. Luckily I have returned with a skilled healer—and Grey's survival is proof enough of that.

We can't run without risking an attack by the creature. We can't stay here without risking an assault by Karis Luran's men.

Our people are tired and afraid, and looking for guidance. Even the most seasoned soldiers want orders, a chance to *act*.

Every story of the creature is more terrible than the last, and I don't know where truth ends and fear begins. All I can do is listen. And reassure.

And worry.

By the time I return to my chambers, I haven't been gone for an hour. I've been gone for four. Jake and Noah have fallen asleep in my bed. I can't remember how long it's been since I last slept. My leg is aching, but I ease out of the room and head to the infirmary.

It's empty aside from Grey. He's asleep on a narrow cot in the far corner, a thin muslin blanket thrown over him. We're in the basement of the castle, down the hall from the kitchens, and early-morning light streams down from windows near the ceiling.

I gently ease a stool over to his bed. The wood drags on stone just the slightest bit, but it's enough to startle him awake.

"Sorry," I say quietly. "I was trying not to wake you."

He squeezes his eyes shut and runs a hand down his face. Rough, dark stubble has formed on his jaw. "Forgive me." He puts a hand against the edge of the cot and forces himself upright. He's shirtless, but Noah's bandages are still tightly wrapped around his chest and upper arm. The blanket pools in his lap.

"You didn't need to get up," I say. "I really just came to check on you."

His eyes flick over my face. "You look as though you are more in need of a bed than I am."

"Probably." I can't sleep, though. Not knowing that everyone in this castle is living on borrowed time. "You said that Karis Luran gave Rhen a week to have his people leave Emberfall. It's been three days. Did Rhen have a plan to defeat her? What was he going to do?"

Grey shakes his head. "Sending our army to face hers would be sending our people to their death. We may be able to stop her front lines, but she would have replacements and we do not." He frowns. "His final order was to have the generals evacuate the people. To head south and then to board ships at Silvermoon, bound for the southern shores."

He was saving his people by giving up. Knowing Rhen, I understand how difficult a choice that would have been for him. "If we try to do that now, Rhen-the-monster will attack?"

"Or Karis Luran's soldiers will. An attack could come at any moment. I fear for those who live outside the castle territory."

"Will he attack her soldiers?"

"Maybe—but he would destroy ours as well. His attacks are quite indiscriminate. But he was injured when I drove my sword through his wing. That may have bought us a reprieve. There is no way to know until he attacks again." He looks back at me. "Have you spoken to anyone since arriving?"

"Yes, of course. I've talked to everyone. We're going to meet with the generals at mid-morning."

Some mixture of surprise and sorrow flickers across his face.

"What?" I say. "What's wrong?"

"Nothing." He shakes his head, then meets my eyes. His voice is low and quiet in the warmth of the sunlit room. "I could have chosen no one better, my lady. Truly."

A blush finds my cheeks before I'm ready for it. "Thanks, Grey."

"I was unsure you would return with me once you knew the truth." He pauses. "I am unsure what we can do, even now."

I give him a rueful smile. "I was kind of hoping you would wake up and have all the answers."

He gives me a sad smile in return. "The prince generally has all the answers. I simply follow his orders."

"What would Rhen do?" I say.

"He would likely order his soldiers to hunt this creature and destroy it. Or at the very least, lead it away from Ironrose so the rest of the castle can escape. But it is a mission of martyrdom either way—to lead the monster away from the people would mean heading directly into Karis Luran's forces."

A mission of martyrdom. Just like Rhen jumping from the parapet in an attempt to save his people. I swallow. "I'll do that. I'll take Will. He's fast and steady. You get them to leave."

His eyes widen in alarm. "I did not mean for you to—"

"It's fine." I take a steadying breath. "I've spent weeks convincing these people I would help them. It means nothing if I don't really do it. This is my choice."

"I will go with you."

"No! Grey—"

"This is *my* choice." Grey's tone is unyielding. "He will come after me before any other. I think even in this form he knows me—though he may not know *why*."

"You're hurt." I set my jaw. "I could order you to stay."

He sets his, every bit as intent in his own way. "In truth, you could not. Prince Rhen released me from my oath. I am sworn to no one."

I draw back. "Really?"

"Yes."

And still, he stayed. He came for me.

For a blinding moment, he is not Commander Grey, oath-sworn and duty bound to obey the Crown Prince of Emberfall. No uniform, no weapons, no men here to command. He's just Grey, and I'm just Harper.

His eyes, dark and intent, have not left mine.

"Do you think the curse can be broken?" I whisper.

"That is not a question for me to answer. Do *you*?"

Rhen is a monster. So far gone that he's attacking Grey. I wasn't sure if I was in love with him before. I don't see any way possible to move forward now. Can I be in love with a memory? I swallow. "I don't know."

His expression is resigned. "Then we must do what we must do."

CHAPTER FIFTY-ONE

HARPER

Jake is a problem.

No, maybe I'm the problem. My mind has been so focused on saving Rhen's people that I forgot about my brother waiting around to go home until he comes looking for me.

I'm in the armory with Grey, who moves stiffly, but he's not pale and sweating like he was last night. Some sleep did him good. I wish I could say the same for myself. He's stringing a sword belt around his waist when Jake appears in the doorway, the guardsman Dustan at his side.

Jake has changed into leather trousers and heavy boots, and he's buckled a jacket over his T-shirt. The clothes suit him—and the aggrieved expression on his face really does make him look like a rebellious young prince.

"Were you ever going to come back?" he demands.

"It's nice to see you, too." I glance past him, at Dustan. "Leave us. Please."

When he does, I push the heavy door closed, shutting Jake inside the narrow room with us. Grey barely spares my brother a glance.

"I did come back," I say to Jake. "You and Noah were sleeping. How did you get down here?"

"I told someone I needed to find you. You're not the only one who's read *A Game of Thrones*, you know. I can fake it, too." He seems to realize I'm buckling armor over my own clothes. "What are you doing?"

"We need to leave for a few hours. You need to lock yourself in the room with Noah. We'll be back by sundown. Grey can take you home when we can make sure it's safe."

Hopefully.

"No." Jake glares at me. "Now."

"This is important, Jake."

"So is *this*." He glances at Grey, who is buckling a dagger to his upper thigh. "Order him to do it. Right now. Or I'll tell everyone outside this door who and what you are."

Grey straightens and moves to face Jake. His voice is low and cold. "I would take you back this very instant, but your sister would worry about your survival. So I will return you when that can be assured, and Emberfall is not in immediate peril. Do you understand?"

Jake does not back down. "I'm not afraid of you."

"You need not fear me. But you will respect your sister, and you will respect me."

"Shouldn't that be the other way around if I'm the Crown Prince of Disi?"

Grey goes still. When he swings his head around to face me, his expression is almost murderous.

I cover my face and peek through my fingers. "Sorry?"

He sighs and turns those angry eyes back to Jake. His voice is clipped and full of venom. "Forgive me, my lord."

Jake's expression is dark with triumph. "So you'll take us back."

"I will respect the title your sister has given you." Grey looks away and pulls a shorter blade from the wall. "I am not sworn to serve you, and I need not act by your order." A pause. "A true prince would know this."

My brother inhales like he's going to argue.

"Jake," I snap. "We're wasting time. People could die. People *will* die. I'm asking you for twelve hours, okay? Twelve stupid hours to lock yourself in a room and eat delicacies and sit by a fire with your boyfriend. Can you just *do that*?"

"Not until you tell me what *you're* doing."

I hesitate. "We're going to see if we can distract Rhen—"

"You're *what*?"

"—so everyone else can escape to the boats at Silvermoon." His face begins to change, and I hurriedly say, "This is the only way to protect everyone. He knows Grey. I think he might know me, too—"

"Harper."

"You can't stop me," I say.

"Oh, trust me. I've gotten that memo over the last few days." He takes a breath, then glances around the room as if seeing all the weapons and armor for the first time. "Just . . . give me some stuff."

"Give you some . . . *stuff*?"

"Some stuff." He points at the wall. "You can be a total badass, Harper. But I've spent the last few weeks doing my best to survive, too. I'm not helpless either."

I'm not entirely sure what to say.

"You think I'm going to sit upstairs eating cake with Noah while you're out risking your life?" he snaps. "Quit staring at me. I'm coming with you."

The day is too beautiful for us to be hunting a monster. The sun shines down brightly on both sides of Ironrose territory. We've reached the point of the season where the temperature does not change when we pass through the woods, though the leaves change from the reds and golds of late fall into the vibrant green of early spring. I'm not sure Jake even notices.

We keep the horses at a walk for Jake's benefit. He took some lessons when I was riding—but he never kept up with it long enough to have any kind of proficiency. Considering how stiffly Grey sits his mount, I think the walking is somewhat for his benefit, too. I caught his grimace when he pulled himself into the saddle.

Earlier, Grey outfitted my brother with two daggers and a sword.

"Cool," Jake said, when Grey threaded the sword onto a belt for him.

Grey's gaze was dark, and he jerked the belt a little tighter than necessary. "It is in case I lose mine again."

It was hard to leave Zo—but I trust her to help get people out of the castle. She gave me a long look when I ordered her to watch out for the women and children, but she obeyed.

I want to tell her the truth. I just don't know how.

Just like that, I understand how he kept his monumental secret from me for so very long. Choices built upon choices. The thought tightens my chest. I need to think about something else. I look at Grey. "Do you think they'll have enough time to get people to Silvermoon?"

He lifts a shoulder in a shrug—then winces. "If the creature is grounded for the time being, yes. If not, he'll be able to pick them off one by one."

"So we're going to find this thing and kill it?" says Jake.

Grey's jaw tightens, but he says nothing.

"Sorry," I say again under my breath. "I'm surprised you let him come."

He sighs and glances my way. "Far be it from me to refuse a request from the 'Crown Prince of Disi.'"

His tone is pointed, and I scowl. "You were unconscious! I thought Jamison was going to tell the soldiers to shoot us! What else was I supposed to call him?"

He raises an eyebrow. "A servant? A footman?"

I open my mouth. Close it.

Grey's not done. "A slave, my lady. A *guard*."

"But she picked prince," Jake snaps. "Get over it."

Grey ignores him. "The healer's concubine?"

Jake snorts, but twin spots of pink find his cheeks. "Noah probably would have loved that."

We've been in the woods for ages, the trail wide and open. This is a major road, but all we hear are birds and small animals under the brush. No travelers. No people.

Everyone is hiding.

"We are close," says Grey. I'm not sure whether the silence worries him or encourages him. He points. "We fell just there."

I see the broken branches through the trees. A wide spray of brown along the bark—which I suddenly realize is dried blood.

A shimmer of white gleams between the leaves.

"There!" I point. "Grey, do you see—"

An inhuman screech splits the air.

That motionless bit of shimmer explodes off the ground, bursting through brush, becoming a monstrous four-legged creature. Another screech—and then suddenly it's galloping up the hill, charging right for us.

I can't register what it looks like. It's huge and glittering in the sunlight. Jake is screaming my name. Will is rearing. I'm falling.

Grey seizes hold of my arm and drags me onto his horse behind him. I grab him around the waist automatically and he cries out.

"I'm sorry!" I cry. "I'm sorry."

He's already driving heels into his horse's side.

"Take the reins," he says, breathless as he all but presses them against my hand before letting go to seize his knives.

I steer the horse toward the creature. I keep seeing it in flashes of terror from under Grey's arm as the horse moves. A massive four-legged body that must be ten feet tall, towering above us. A somewhat horselike head—but with black eyes and with fanged teeth that hang several inches below its mouth. Iridescent scales glitter along its hide, shifting into white feathers that sprout above its massive shoulders. One wing is tucked tight against its body, while the other drags alongside it. The front legs end in silver talons. The creature runs at us determinedly, screeching again when Grey shows no sign of slowing.

It's terrible and beautiful and somehow entirely Rhen . . . yet not at all.

When we near, it rears up over top of us, and I'm sure those taloned feet are going to come tearing down.

Grey is too quick. *Snick snick snick*, his throwing knives snap free of his hand. One bounces off the scales, but the other two stick true, driving into the skin at the base of a wing. I see dried blood under its wingspan and realize Grey was right.

The creature screams and throws itself back.

"Rhen!" I cry. "Rhen, please!"

"The wings," Grey breathes. "That's where he's vulnerable."

Rhen—the monster—crashes to the ground and scrambles for purchase. It's going to charge us again. I fight to get the reins in order.

I can't see—

I can't steer—

I can't—

This is too fast—

Jake grabs hold of our reins from the back of his horse. "Come on!" he yells. "I thought we were going to lead it away." He slams his heels into the sides of his horse, and then I'm nearly jerked off the back of Grey's as our animals bolt forward.

The monster's feet shake the ground as it runs after us. We tear through the woods, the horses side by side, hooves pounding into the turf. Grey has the reins again, and I cling tight to his armor.

"It's running," Grey says, almost panting. "It can't fly in the woods."

"It's still fast," yells Jake. His legs are swinging against his horse's sides, and he's got a fistful of mane. It's not going to take much to get him off the horse.

The monster shrieks again, the sound close enough to be right on top of us. I'm afraid to look. Grey's horse tucks its rump and springs forward. I grip tighter.

"It's going to catch us," says Grey. He's right. I duck my head and see flashes of white directly behind us.

"Hide her," yells Jake. "Get her to safety."

Before I can say a word in protest, Jake hauls hard on the horse's reins and loops back around to face the creature bearing down on us.

"Come on!" I hear him yell. "Come after me!"

"No!" It'll kill him. Rhen will kill my brother. "Grey—no! You can't—"

He makes no move to slow.

"Please," I cry. I try to fight him for the reins. "Please, Grey. Please—"

A clawed talon locks into the armor buckled around my rib cage. I'm lifted right off the back of the horse.

I scream. The horse disappears below us. Wind swirls around me. The talons are like steel against my back. One quick snap and my armor will be sliced in half.

Grey was wrong. It might be hurt—but it can fly.

"Please," I cry. "Please, Rhen. Please know me."

The creature screams and dives out of the air. I see Grey below us, driving his horse for more speed.

I have one arm free. I pull a dagger. I can't reach its wings, but I can reach the fleshy skin connecting the talons to its front legs.

"No!" I call. I stab with the blade.

The monster falters in the air and beats its wings against the current. I stab again. The talon loosens, just for a fraction of a second.

Then it tightens right up. The armor presses into me. I can barely feel my left arm.

"Damn it, Rhen!" I call. "Listen to me!"

We swoop and dive again, heading for Jake. My brother has a dagger in each hand, and he turns, ready to—

We slam into him. I'm wrapped in Rhen's talons, but I feel the impact. Jake and his horse go crashing into the ground.

Rhen rides the air current and we sweep upward, high into the sky. Suddenly, the ground is a blur, my brother and his horse a tiny motionless lump between the trees.

"No!" I scream. My voice is breaking. The wind freezes my cheeks. "No. Rhen. Please. I love you. I love you. I'll say whatever you want. Please just stop."

He doesn't stop. We dive again.

"Remember!" I cry. "You taught me how to hold a bow. You saved my life at Silvermoon. You taught me to dance on the cliff."

He doesn't hesitate. We send Grey into the ground. I hear him cry out. I feel him try to grab on to me, to pull me free.

It doesn't work. I'm in the air again.

"Please, Rhen." Despite my plea, I drive my dagger into the fleshy skin again. The talon slips and he screams, but he doesn't let go. "Remember me. Remember. Please. Remember when I came after you in the snow. After Lilith? Remember how we swayed?"

I'm choking on my own fear. Nothing changes.

Or maybe it does. It takes me a minute to realize he's been looping over the trees, diving down to threaten Jake and Grey, but then lifting high when they don't threaten him.

And he hasn't crushed me.

I stop stabbing at him. "Rhen?" My voice is broken. "Rhen. Please."

The air seems to pause.

Then Jake yells from below. "Hey! Let go of my sister!"

Rhen screams and dives. He doesn't know Jake. His fangs glitter in the sunlight.

"No!" I call.

He doesn't listen. The moment of recognition is gone. We're plummeting through the air. He's going to tear my brother apart.

"Please," I cry. "You said you would give me anything in your power to give. Please stop. *Please.*"

This last word is a desperate scream.

Rhen soars past my brother without touching him.

My breath almost stops. It worked. *It worked.*

We swoop low again—but without the speed this time. My feet drag against the ground.

He lets me go.

I stumble and fall and try to roll to my feet, but my body won't move that quickly. My shoulder feels like his talon is still embedded in my armor. I stagger and find my footing just as he lands a short distance away.

He's breathing hard, too. But he's still.

As before, he's beautiful and terrible. Part dragon, part horse, part something I can't even name. I can't stop staring at how fearsome he is. At how much damage he could cause. I have no idea how to break this curse. I have no idea how to save him.

But at least he's on the ground. He's not attacking.

From the corner of my eye, I catch motion. Jake is approaching, a dagger in each hand. His eyes are wide and determined.

Rhen drops to a crouch and screeches at him. His legs look primed to leap into the air again. Blood coats the underside of one wing, fresh from where Grey's knives drove into his skin and held fast.

"No!" I call. "Jake!" Then I get in front of Rhen and lift my hands harmlessly. "Stop. Rhen. Stop."

He blows out a long breath and paws at the ground. A talon digs a trench six feet long.

"It's okay," I say quietly. My voice shakes. I take a step toward him.

He screeches at me and I stop. I put a hand out. "It's okay," I whisper. "Rhen. It's me. It's okay."

He takes a dragging step forward. Grey is a short distance away, behind him, but he's absolutely still. His sword hangs in his hand, ready to attack if necessary.

When the creature draws close, I swallow. His fangs are the length of my forearm. His head is half the length of my body.

"Rhen," I whisper.

He takes another step. I look into the monster's black eyes and I see nothing familiar.

But I can almost *feel* him.

I move my hand forward slowly, like he's a dog and I want to let him catch my scent.

I say a prayer that he won't bite my hand off at the wrist.

He lowers his head, but he doesn't stop at my hand. I freeze. I stop breathing.

His face presses into my chest. He blows warm air against my knees.

I lift a hand and press it to his cheek, just below his eye. My other hand lifts to stroke the underside of his jaw. The scales feel like silk.

He leans his face against me and breathes a sigh.

I lean against him and do the same thing.

"Oh, Rhen," I say, and I realize I'm crying. He's here. He's not hurting anyone.

But he's still a monster.

The curse isn't broken.

CHAPTER FIFTY-TWO

MONSTER

Ah, Harper.

You've come back.

CHAPTER FIFTY-THREE

HARPER

As long as I stand there talking to him, Rhen-the-monster is as docile as a lapdog.

If Grey or Jake approach, he snakes his massive neck and screeches at them, but they've been keeping their distance, so he's settled. He drops to the ground at my urging so I can pull Grey's throwing knives from the base of his wing.

My fingers tremble with the aftereffects of adrenaline, and I nick my skin on the edge of his scales, but the knives come free. Blood streams down his body in narrow rivulets, but he doesn't seem bothered. He's so big that maybe these were more of an annoyance than anything else.

Rhen turns his head and presses his face against my body again.

Every time he does that, a wave of sadness washes over me.

He doesn't want this. I can't fix it. I can't kill him, either. Not like this.

I look up and call to Grey. "What do we do?"

The guardsman is pale again, leaning against his horse a short distance off. I wonder if he's reopened his stitches.

"I've never seen the creature settle," he says. "Not this season. Nor any others." He hesitates. "We do not know how long it will last."

"Well, we can't sit here in the woods forever." I'm scared to move away from him as it is, as if whatever keeps him at my side is a spell that can be broken by distance.

"In truth, my lady, I do not know what our next move should be." Grey sighs and straightens.

As soon as Grey takes a step toward me, Rhen-the-monster lifts from the ground and whirls to face him. A low growl rolls out of his throat, ending in that hair-raising screech.

The horses jump and shy back, prancing against the reins that keep them tied to the trees. Grey does not. He puts his hands up. "If a fraction of your mind exists inside this creature, you know I mean you no harm."

The low growl again, but without the same intensity.

"Harper just pulled your knives out of his wing," calls Jake from where he stands near the horses. "Might not believe you."

Grey doesn't look away from the creature. "I have a hundred stitches holding my chest together, so perhaps we are even."

Rhen paws at the ground, then takes a step back.

I have no idea whether that's a truce or what.

A loud sound echoes in the distance, like trumpets, but lower. Rhen's head snaps up and swivels in the direction of the sound.

"What's that noise?"

"The soldiers from Syhl Shallow," says Grey. "Their battle horns. They are advancing."

We have no way to know if everyone has been evacuated from the castle. We've stopped the monster, but we haven't stopped Karis Luran's men.

The horns sound again.

"We have to go back," I say. "We have to make sure. Can you tell how long we have?"

"If we ride fast, we could possibly beat them by half an hour. It takes time to move troops."

"What do we do with that thing?" calls Jake.

"I do not know." Grey hesitates, and there's an element of sadness to his voice that mirrors what I feel when Rhen presses his head against my chest. Grey looks up at the creature. "Do you wish to return to Ironrose? Do you wish to go home?"

Rhen crouches and leaps into the air, catching the wind with his wings, soaring high above before turning west. The scales glitter in a shimmering array of pinks and blues and greens in the sunlight. From here, he's all beauty. It's only up close that you see the danger.

"Hurry," says Grey. He turns for his horse and yanks the reins free. "If anyone is left, they may attack him."

Or Rhen may attack them.

I don't say it. I just limp across the small clearing and whistle for Will.

We ride hard and make good time. Rhen is faster, but he tracks with us, flying ahead before looping back to stay near. I keep worrying this docile tether is going to snap and he's going to pass over Ironrose, to find the people making their way toward Silvermoon and the waiting ships. He's large enough that he could easily destroy boats, crushing masts and sails. With his ability to fly, he could drown them all.

I need to stop thinking like this.

Especially when we near the lands surrounding the castle and he glides down to the ground to travel with us on foot. It's hard not to flinch away.

He towers over our horses. Will prances underneath me, and I keep a tight hold on the reins, but Rhen walks beside us like it's nothing.

I glance over at Grey. "What are we going to do with him at the castle?"

"Let him hide in the courtyard and wait for Karis Luran to drive us out, I suppose." He pauses. "Forgive me, my lady. I see no path to victory here."

The horns blow in the distance again. Rhen growls.

I glance back at him, and before I'm ready for it, emotion fills my chest. "I shouldn't have left, Grey. He needed me, and I was falling for him. But—my family—" I press my hand to my eyes.

Grey's voice is anguished. "He knows, my lady. I promise you. He knows."

"But he still let me go."

"Yes, of course."

When I look across into Grey's eyes, I realize.

Rhen fell for *me.*

I think of his voice when we stood on the cliff at Silvermoon. *I want to know it's real, too.*

It *was* real. For him, it was real.

He was waiting for me.

"I'm the one who failed here," I say, and my voice breaks. "It was me. Not him."

"No." Grey is stunned. "No. You have failed at nothing."

"I did—"

"No," says Jake, speaking for the first time in a while. "Harper, you didn't do this."

"But I could have stopped it. I couldn't get out of my own way—"

"No," he snaps. "And damn it, for once would you listen to me? You didn't curse him. You didn't bring yourself here." He takes a long breath. "You didn't—you didn't give Mom cancer. You didn't force Dad to borrow money from the wrong people—"

"You didn't, either," I say to him. "But you still went to work for Lawrence."

"I did what I had to do," he says. "To give Mom time. To protect you."

"Me too," I say.

We ride into the woods, and Rhen's creature drops back to follow. I should have known. I should have realized. Now we're going to ride back to an empty castle. Grey will return Jake and Noah to Washington, DC.

I don't know what I'll do.

As we ride through the trees, motion flickers ahead. Voices echo in the distance.

I draw up my horse. "Grey. Is it Karis Luran's army?" Have they gotten ahead of us somehow? But then the gold and red of Rhen's army's uniforms becomes clear through the trees.

"They didn't leave!" Confusion takes over the lump in my chest and squishes it into a new form. "They're still here! What happened? What's—"

"The monster!" a man cries. "The monster is in the forest!"

Men swarm forward. Shouts are all around us. I see bows raised. Horses trample the ground.

With a shriek, Rhen's monster unfurls his wings and tries to lift from the ground—but the trees are too dense here, and he's too large. They're going to attack him. He's going to fight back.

"No!" I yell. "Hold your charge!" Will prances, and I give him some rein so I can ride in front of the men who are leading the attack. "Stand down! Where is your general?"

Behind me, Rhen shrieks. Many of the soldiers fall back. Horses rear and prance in a barely contained formation. A few others push forward.

"Enough!" I call. "I said *hold your charge*."

Rhen's army stops. Grey is behind us, blocking the creature. I hope he's convincing Rhen to hold as well. We're trapped in a tense circle of fear and vicious loathing. Everyone wants to attack.

"My lady." Zo rides through the soldiers. Her face is fierce and lined with tension. She gives a worried glance at the monster behind Grey. "You have . . . *captured* the creature?"

Rhen's talons scrape at the ground. A low growl rolls through the woods. A nervous murmur goes up among the soldiers behind her.

"You were to evacuate," I say to her. "What are you doing here?"

"Everyone who was willing *has* evacuated."

"Everyone who was willing?" Several hundred men and women stand behind her. "Our orders were to evacuate all."

A man steps forward. His name is General Landon, a man who

once served Rhen's father. He stops his horse beside Zo. "My lady, if you are willing to risk your life to save us, we are willing to risk ours to save Emberfall. We did not form this army to run."

I'm not sure what to say. "General—the army from Disi has not been able to move." I feel tears form in my eyes and worry this will be seen as weakness. "Our numbers are not great enough to stop Karis Luran's soldiers. They are already advancing."

"If we can hold them until reinforcements arrive . . ."

Reinforcements.

"General." My voice breaks. "I do not—I do not have—"

Rhen screeches and paws at the ground. I turn and glance at him over my shoulder.

He might not be wholly himself, but he knows me. He knows Grey.

I swing my leg over the back of my horse and drop to the ground, then walk through the underbrush to get to the creature.

As soon as I stop in front of him, he stops glaring through the trees at the soldiers and presses his face against my chest. His warm breath blows against my knees again.

Another murmur goes through the soldiers again, growing louder as word spreads.

She's tamed it. The princess has tamed the creature.

I stroke the soft scales under his jaw and wonder if that's true. Rhen once told me that if we could get Karis Luran's army to retreat through the pass, we could station enough men there to prevent them from entering again. We just need to get her army to run.

Rhen is terrifying enough that they might run from him. I just don't know how to make him do it.

"We can't stay here. We're all in danger. Karis Luran's soldiers are coming." I put my hands on either side of his face and look into his night-black eyes. "Please. Do you understand?"

He butts his head against me, then paws at the ground again, stomping his taloned feet into the dirt, making the ground shake. The claws of his hind legs dig furrows into the path.

Soldiers shout and shift through the trees. "Don't let him harm the princess!"

Rhen roars and rears straight up. It makes him twenty feet tall. Maybe more. The growling screech he emits rolls through the forest and produces a visceral reaction in my body. I drop and cower.

He's going to crush me. He's going to kill them. He doesn't understand.

An arm grabs mine and jerks me back, out of the way. It's Zo, and her sword is up and in front of us. Rhen's taloned feet slam into the ground. He roars right in her face, and I shove her behind me.

"No!" I yell.

He stops—but turns on me. Fangs hook into the armor at my back. I'm jerked away from Zo. He's going to tear me apart. Men shout. I see a flash of steel as Grey unsheathes his blade. Jake yells, "Harper!"

I can't think. I take a breath. I wait for pain.

None comes. We're running, so fast the trees are a blur to the side. I'm hanging from his mouth like an errant kitten.

We break free of the trees and his wings catch the air. The ground begins to fall away below me. Someone's screaming.

It's me. I'm screaming.

All that's holding me aloft are these leather buckles keeping the armor on my body.

We're so high that I can see for miles. Ironrose Castle. The soldiers shifting to become a pack, the horses so tiny they could be rodents. I can see the inn, and Silvermoon in the distance.

We're so high that the air grows thin. My arms begin to go numb from the pressure of the straps against my chest. "Please," I whimper. "You're hurting me. Take me back. Please, Rhen."

He doesn't take me back.

He lets go.

CHAPTER FIFTY-FOUR

MONSTER

Destroy.

CHAPTER FIFTY-FIVE

HARPER

I fall forever. The wind is a wild rush in my ears, a freezing blast at my face. The ground races toward me.

Wings appear below me, white filling my field of vision. I expect to crash into him, but Rhen compensates for my fall, easing under me and swooping downward until my knees connect with the base of his wings, then leveling off. I wrap my arms around his neck, and the scales slice at my skin, but I grip tight.

I look down. The soldiers are following on horseback. We're faster, but they're following, turning into a tiny blur in the distance.

They won't be able to help me. He can fly anywhere. He can drop me again.

He could attack *them*.

I can't stop him. I can only hang on.

I was so stupid. Jake was right. We should have killed him.

In the distance ahead, a massive line of men on horseback are covering ground quickly. Green-and-black pennants flap in the wind. A horn rings out across the air.

Karis Luran's army.

They bear heavier artillery. Two catapults. They have crossbows.

I don't know much about military strategy, but I do know this army dwarfs ours. If Grey and Jake and everyone else are still following me, they'll be eviscerated.

As soon as Rhen and I draw near, we're spotted. Men shout, and their horses turn and shift, finding a new formation. Arrows sail through the air around us. I scream. "Rhen! We need to go back. We need to warn—"

He roars, the sound ending in that earsplitting screech. Rhen swoops low, dragging soldiers from their horses and dropping them onto each other. Men scream and grab for me, but Rhen in his monster form is too big, too powerful. Blood fills the air as he tears them apart and soars back into the sky.

He wasn't trying to kill me. He was doing what I asked. He was trying to stop them.

I don't want to see him like this. I don't want to watch these men die.

But I don't want to watch *our* soldiers die, either.

Rhen was so right about choices. There are no easy choices. None.

He swoops down through the soldiers again, cutting a swath through their ranks. Blood sprays, mixing with the tears on my cheeks. I'm safe between his wings, but it's a terrible kind of safety.

He strikes again. And again. And again. The soldiers are skilled, and they rearrange their formation to compensate for our attacks. I can't tell if his efforts are making any difference, and I want to bury my face against his neck, but I can't. Arrows fly around us, and my armor has kept me safe so far. I yank them from Rhen's wings when he's struck.

A loud *creak* and a *snap* sound from somewhere to my right, and it takes my brain too long to realize they've loaded the catapult.

"Duck!" I scream. I give Rhen's neck a wrench. A stone larger than my body barely misses us.

Rhen flies past the soldiers, catching an air current to soar, taking us too high for the catapult to reach. I'm gasping, choking on tears. Injured men scream below us. Swaths of blood coat the battlefield below, reminding me of the cursed room at Ironrose.

The soldiers are finding another formation. We have to do something. He's too indiscriminate, and there are too many of them.

Rhen spent a lot of time talking about battle strategy, but not with me. Always with his generals or the soldiers. I've only heard bits and pieces, but I do know the important people ride at the back.

I don't want to do this. I want him to fly me away from here.

As I have the thought, I'm already talking. "The back lines," I say to Rhen, and my voice breaks. I remember how broken he was after ordering the death of the man at Hutchins Forge. "We have to take out their officers." I swallow and force my voice to be strong. "The back line, Rhen. The flags. The officers. The *back*."

He loops around and dives.

I brace myself for an impact, clutching tight to his neck. He tears through the line at the back, shredding flags and bodies. The sound buries itself in my brain. Horses scream. Men shout and die. Boulders sail through the air and land with bone-breaking crashes.

Once we're airborne again, I lean out over his shoulder and survey the damage below us. My fingers are leaving bloodied handprints all over his gorgeous scales and wing feathers. He shows absolutely no sign of being winded.

Bodies decorate the countryside. Farmland is soaked in blood.

There's no sign of our army. I don't know if that's a good thing or a bad thing.

I pant against him. "Now the front," I say. "We can't let them move forward. The front, Rhen." I tug at his neck and point. "Do you understand?"

In answer, he dives.

These soldiers are younger. Smaller. Many are on foot. They die just as easily, caught by his talons or claws. The Syhl Shallow soldiers lose any sense of formation and they now run wildly, just trying to get out of Rhen's way. Men have begun to run west. We've completely stopped any forward movement toward Ironrose.

"We're winning," I cry at Rhen, though nothing about this feels like a victory. "It's working."

He gives a long shriek that drives more men to run. Especially when he flies at them, talons outstretched.

A *twang* and a whistle split the air.

The impact slams into Rhen like a tractor trailer. We fly sideways. He crashes into the ground.

His wings break my fall, but the impact gets me off his back. I go skidding along the dirt, feeling grit drive into the side of my face. The catapult finally landed a hit.

This is bad.

A boot kicks me onto my back. Arrows point down at my head. A loud *screech* echoes somewhere to my left.

One of the men aiming an arrow at my face lifts his head to yell. "Beast! We will destroy her! You cannot kill six of us at once!"

Another *screech*. The ground shakes as Rhen drives his feet into the dirt.

One man grabs hold of my armor and lifts his knife. My head is still recovering from slamming into the ground and my eyes blur. I'm sure he's about to stab me in the side, but he doesn't. He cuts my armor free. Under the steel-lined leather, I'm soaked in sweat, suddenly cold from the air that rushes across my chest.

Another screech.

The man standing over top of me lets his arrow fly.

The arrow slices right through my shoulder, driving into the ground below me.

Then he does it again.

It hurts worse than anything. I see stars. I see whole galaxies. My world is nothing but pain.

The monster screams again. His wings beat the air.

"Stay back!" the man cries. "There are many more places I can shoot without killing her."

Rhen must swoop close. *Snap snap snap.*

They're shooting at him. They're shooting at me.

This arrow goes through my upper arm.

I can't tell if I'm screaming or crying or both.

It's both. I'm going to pass out. I'm going to die.

The ground is pounding around me. More men are coming. I can't see anything.

"Don't stop!" I yell at Rhen. I'm crying. I'm babbling. I don't even know if he can hear me, but this can't all be for nothing. "Don't stop. Save your people. Let them kill me. Let them kill me, Rhen."

He screeches again, building into a fierce roar that shakes the ground.

Arrows fire. *Snap. Snap. Snap.* I wait for piercing pain.

It never comes. Sudden sunlight finds my eyes. The men around me are falling, arrows in their chests, arrows in their heads. Soldiers are fighting, swords swinging. I catch a flash of gold and red.

My army has arrived.

One of Karis Luran's soldiers makes it to me. He must know he's a dead man, because he draws back an arrow. It's pointed right at my face.

A bowstring snaps, and an arrow appears in his arm. His own shot fires wildly.

Sunlight flashes on silver. A sword swings.

The soldier's head disconnects from his neck. Blood flies. His body collapses.

I blink, and Grey is there with Zo. They're kneeling over me. My eyes fall closed. The scent of blood is thick in the air. Arrows are firing all around us. Steel clashes somewhere far off.

The creature shrieks and men yell.

"My lady." Grey's hand. My face. "Look at me. Harper!"

I blink and my eyes are open. "You never . . . call me Harper."

He lets out a breath. He's still so pale. Then he looks up, past me. "She will survive. I will keep her safe."

I think he's talking to Zo, but a blast of warm breath brushes my hair, and I realize it's Rhen. I go to lift a hand to touch his muzzle, but my arm is pinned to the ground.

I cry out instead. "Grey," I say. I sound like a child calling out for her mother.

"We need to cut them free."

I choke on a sob. "Okay. Okay."

He doesn't wait. He draws a dagger and snaps through the shafts below my arm. Then Zo pulls all three arrows in rapid succession. Before she's even done, I'm rolling onto my side to throw up into the blood-soaked grass. Once my body stops heaving, I shudder and open my eyes.

I'm staring into the lifeless eyes of the man who nearly killed me.

I scream and suddenly I'm lifted away. For a breath of time I think it's Rhen, and I don't know how I'm going to survive another trip through the air. But arms fasten under my knees and behind my back, and my head lolls onto a shoulder. My face is pressed into a neck.

"Easy, my lady." Grey's voice, low and gentle and somehow louder than all the fighting.

He shouldn't be carrying me. He's going to rip out his stitches.

I open my mouth to tell him so.

And instead I pass out.

I return to consciousness slowly.

For a long, slow, delirious moment, I think I'm in a hospital. There's a man barking orders about clean bandages. A feeling of harried movement around me.

My eyes open, and I'm in the infirmary. I recognize the ceiling, the shape of the darkened window above my bed. I'm in the same corner Grey once occupied. This morning? I don't even know. My entire left arm aches.

I groan and roll over.

The infirmary is packed. Every bed—sixteen of them—is occupied. Bloodstained sheets are everywhere. Men and women groan weakly.

Noah sits on a stool beside one of them. He's bracing a soldier's bloodied forearm to a board, wrapping it with lengths of muslin.

"I asked for clean bandages!" he says sharply.

A young woman near the door looks wide-eyed and almost panicked. Her name is Abigail, and she's been in charge of mending minor wounds since Rhen opened the doors to the castle. She's round and slow and motherly, but she's clearly not used to an ER doctor yelling orders at her. "Yes, Doctor." She says *doctor* like it's a foreign word. "Yes. I have sent for them."

"Noah." My voice croaks out of my throat.

He glances at me. His eyes flick over my form in less than a second. "Good. You're up." He rips off a length of muslin. "We need the bed. Abigail!"

The woman by the door jumps. "Yes—"

"Find Jake. Tell him Harper is up." He drags an elbow over his forehead.

"Ah . . . *Jake*?" she says.

Noah rolls his eyes and wraps another length of muslin. "Prince Jacob." She rushes off, and he looks at me. "You'll need a sling. Freya made one for one of the guys. I'll have her make you one, too."

My brain can't catch up this fast. Jake must be okay. My eyes flit across the bodies on the beds, seeking Grey. Seeking Rhen, just in case. I find neither. "Noah—"

"Jake said you two had to 'do something real quick' and then we'd be going home. Hilarious. Then he shows up with three dozen people with critical injuries. How do you not have a doctor here? You have an *army*. ABIGAIL!"

She flies through the door. "Yes, my—yes—"

"Have them bring in whoever is next. Make sure they're flushing those arrow wounds with *boiled salt water*. Not just plain water. Do you understand me? Do you . . ."

His voice trails off in my head. I fight to push myself upright. I have to pull my left arm against my body to keep it from aching.

"Harp." Jake is in front of me, his voice rough and exhausted. His eyes are shadowed and wounded, and his clothes are worn and dirtied in spots, but there are no bandages I can see.

"Jake." My voice breaks. "You're okay." I hesitate. "What happened to Rhen?"

Jake's face goes still, but he puts out a hand. "Come on. Noah is going to lose his mind if we don't clear this bed."

"Wait!" I scan the infirmary. "Where's Zo? Is she—"

"The girl with the braids? She's fine. She's bossier than you are. That Grey guy had to order her to go to sleep an hour ago."

Grey. I need to talk to Grey. I need to find out what happened to Rhen. With my brother's help, I get to my feet, and we make it into the hallway. I feel light-headed and grip tight to his arm. Men and women line the hallway, some I know, and some I don't. Some are injured, though many are not. The air is thick with lantern oil, sweat, and blood. They bow as we pass.

"Wow," I whisper to Jake. "You've really taken this prince thing to a new level."

"No," he says. "You have."

I look up at him in surprise. "What?"

"It's for you, Harper." His dark eyes flick down to meet mine. "All anyone can talk about is how you single-handedly fought the soldiers from Syhl Shallow. How you tamed the vicious beast and turned it against the enemy. How you saved their country."

"But—but I didn't—it was—"

"Shh." He puts a finger against my lips. "Not here."

"But it worked?" My heart lifts. "The army turned back?"

"They did." He grimaces. "It was brutal, Harp—and you know the things I've seen."

His eyes meet mine. I do know the things he's seen.

Thanks to the battle on that field, I've seen them, too.

"They ran," he says. "Anyone who could fight rode on to block the pass. We brought the wounded back here. Noah has been treating everyone as fast as his 'nurses' can get them cleaned up."

"Wow." I have no idea whether that will hold, if the soldiers will be able to keep Karis Luran's army from invading. But for the time being, we've been granted a reprieve.

I think we're heading back to my rooms, but Jake leads me through the castle until we find the doors from the Great Hall that lead to the rear courtyard and the stables.

"How long was I out?" I say.

"Most of the day."

"You've really found your way around."

"Crash course, I guess." He pauses. "It helps that everyone thinks my sister saved the world."

I'm not sure what to say to that, and he's pushing through the doorway anyway. It's twilight, and the autumn air is cold, tasting of burning wood and decaying leaves. Lit torches burn along the back of the castle, throwing long shadows across the courtyard.

Long shadows that stripe the monstrous creature standing near the trees, scales glinting in the firelight.

Emberfall is safe, but he hasn't changed.

Grey is out here, too. Fresh armor. Clean weapons. He stands at the base of the steps and turns when Jake pushes the door open. His expression is somber.

"My lady," he says. "You are awake."

"I am." I cradle my injured arm against my body. The bandages make everything feel tight and stiff. "Noah kicked me out."

"Your 'doctor' is fierce in his own way."

Jake snorts and leans against the door, closing the quiet of the courtyard in around us. "Don't let him hear you say that."

I swallow. "Are you—are you going home? Were you waiting for me to wake up?"

"Not yet." Jake kicks at the grit of the stone steps. "Noah won't leave until everyone is stable."

"That's amazing."

Jake shrugs, though it looks resigned. "He's not happy about it." A pause. "His parents are going to worry. His sister. He doesn't know what's going to happen if the cops came to the apartment. His cell phone was on the table."

I push my brain through the ramifications of that, and my thoughts go in a dozen different directions. Not many of them work out well for Noah. If anything happened with Lawrence's men and Noah is implicated in that . . . that could hurt his career. His family.

"I'm sorry, Jake," I whisper.

He shrugs again. "I'm going back down to help him." He glances at Grey, then at Rhen, whose large black eyes watch us from across the courtyard. "Are you okay?"

"Yeah. Of course."

He gives me a gentle hug, but before he pulls away, he looks down and says, "You really were amazing, Harp."

My mouth opens, but he shakes his head. "It wasn't all him. He wouldn't have done it without you. You deserve the respect." Then he smiles, a shadow of the old Jake, before life clobbered us all. "Mom would be really proud of you, Princess Harper." He kisses me on the forehead, then heads back through the doors into the castle.

I ease down the steps, gripping tightly to the banister while clutching my injured arm to my body.

Grey moves to stand in front of me. "You should likely not be walking down steps." He unbuckles his dagger belt, then slides the weapon free. "You should likely not be walking at all." With the remaining length of leather, he wraps it double around my forearm, then loops it behind my neck to fasten the buckle.

With the makeshift sling, I can relax my arm for the first time since waking. It's a relief I didn't know I needed. "Thanks, Grey."

A nod.

"You didn't pull your stitches loose?" I ask.

"Ah. Yes. The doctor says if I do it again, he will do me the honor of removing my arm."

"So he probably wouldn't be happy you're standing out here armed."

"Likely not."

I'm very aware of my breathing. Of his. Of the cursed creature in the back corner of this courtyard.

"Are you protecting the castle from Rhen?" I ask quietly. "Or the other way around?"

His eyes are dark and inscrutable in the twilit darkness. "Both, my lady."

"I hoped . . ." I sigh and look at my hands. I can't look at Rhen now.

"I believe he did as well."

A low growl comes from across the clearing. The darkness seems to part. I see nothing, but Grey draws his sword.

Then, beside me, a female voice says, "*Tsk, tsk, tsk.*"

CHAPTER FIFTY-SIX

MONSTER

Destroy.

CHAPTER FIFTY-SEVEN

HARPER

Rhen charges across the clearing when Lilith appears. His screech echoes against the walls of the castle.

Lilith steps beside me. "No, no, Prince Rhen," she says quietly. "I would hate to harm this lovely creature."

He skids to a stop in front of us, snaking his glittering neck in a threatening way. He snaps his fangs right in front of her face.

"Kill her," I say to Rhen. "I don't care if she kills me. Just do it."

He growls, that low, menacing sound that makes my insides curl—but he doesn't attack.

"He cares if I kill *you*," Lilith says delightedly. "Quite a bit, I would say."

"I said I loved him," I snapped at her. "I kissed him. I risked my life for him. What else do you want to break the curse?"

"You risked your life for Emberfall. Not for him." She sighs. "If you loved him, the curse would be broken. It is not something I must do. It is something *you* must do—or not do, as the case may be. True love is not about romance. True love requires sacrifice. A willingness to place another's life above your own."

"Then Grey should have broken the curse," I say. "He's been doing that over and over again."

"Grey was oath-bound to do so. Is that not true, Commander?"

At my side, Grey is very still, and very quiet.

"Do you know," she says, "I have been to see Karis Luran? She needed to know what you were doing to her soldiers." Lilith pouts. "She is very upset indeed. I was able to comfort her and learn a great many things about the late King of Emberfall."

Rhen growls again.

"Ah, yes," says Lilith. She strokes a fingertip down Rhen's face, and he flinches away. It's terrifying to see a creature like him flinch.

"A great many things," she says softly. "It turns out I sought the wrong prince all along. But you will be far more useful to me like this."

"Leave him alone." My heart roars in my chest. "What do you want?"

"Our dear prince knows what I want. He can submit, or I will destroy you. I do not even need a leash." She reaches out a hand to touch my cheek.

Fire explodes through my face. I'm on my knees, my good hand pressed to my cheek. I'm crying and I don't even know what happened.

I'm not bleeding. She didn't break the skin.

Rhen growls—but he falls back. An acquiescence.

"No," I say. "Please. Rhen. Don't." There has to be another way. I may have helped defeat the soldiers from Syhl Shallow, but he rallied his people. He formed this army. He is the ruler here, not me.

Lilith takes a step toward Rhen, and he shies away from her like a beaten dog. "Think of what we could do."

"Enough!" says Grey. His sword is drawn, but he hasn't taken action.

Lilith smiles and turns back toward him. "You cannot kill me, Commander. You know this." She takes a step toward him, and he takes a step back, his sword up in front of him.

Her smile widens. "I can use her against you, too, you know."

My mind spins. "No. Grey. No. Kill me. Just do it. Don't let her do this."

His breathing quickens, but he says nothing. He glances from me to Rhen and back to Lilith.

"Do it!" I yell at him. "You said I am welcome to any weapon you carry. Pull a knife and do it!"

He doesn't.

Lilith turns toward me. For the first time, the amusement drains out of her face. "What is it about you that inspires such loyalty?" She puts out a hand and I stumble back. "Truly, Harper, I find it mystifying." Her voice darkens, twisting into something that makes my chest tighten. "And frankly, quite irritating, you broken, worthless, little—"

"Take me instead," says Grey.

She stops and looks at him.

"I am no longer oath-bound. I am sworn to no one."

"No," I say, realizing what he's saying. "No. Grey. No—"

He speaks as though I am not there. "The prince is a powerful creature, but you would have to rely on his devotion to Harper, which would surely wane over time. He will one day turn on you."

"And you would not?"

"Once given, my word is good." He pauses. "As is yours, is it not?"

The creature growls again.

Grey does not look at him. "I am just a man, but I can go where a beast cannot. I can follow orders. I can do your bidding."

"I find your offer intriguing, Commander. I do not believe you know what you are offering."

He takes a breath. "I believe I do."

He kneels.

He lays his sword across both hands.

Offers it up to her.

"No!" I say. "No! Grey! You can't!" I move to rush forward to stop him, but Lilith catches my braid in one tight fist and jerks me back.

Rhen growls again.

Grey says nothing.

Lilith laughs. "The great Commander Grey, on his knees at my feet. They know I can still kill you, girl. I have not yet accepted his offer."

The sword still sits on his hands, solid and unwavering. "Do you accept?" he says.

"I do." She picks up his weapon. Releases my hair. I stagger back.

Rhen roars, rearing up to slam his feet into the ground.

Lilith whirls with the sword in her hand. "If I have him, I no longer need *you*." Then she steps forward, ready to drive the blade into his side. Right under his wing.

That's where he's vulnerable, Grey once said. *The wings.*

I don't think. I leap at her. I leap at the sword. I don't know what I'm doing. I just can't watch him die.

I have no armor. No weapons. Grey's sword is razor sharp. The blade bites into my skin like a million shards of glass. I fall—but Lilith falls, too. Where our skin connects, fire rages into my body. Rhen's roar coalesces into a screech that goes on forever.

Grey drags Lilith off me and throws her to the ground. His dagger is in his hand.

Her hand snakes out to grip his throat. "You swore."

"I did not." Grey drives his dagger into her chest. Blood flows around her hand at his neck and he makes a pained sound, but he shoves the blade down for good measure.

Her body jerks. "You can't—kill me—"

"I cannot kill you *here*. But I *can* kill you—"

They vanish.

I'm left gasping. The pain in my side is unimaginable. All-consuming. Time passes. An hour. A year. A second. An eternity.

A hand touches my face. Warm breath brushes my cheeks.

Before I lose consciousness, a male voice speaks. "Harper. Oh, Harper, what have you done?"

CHAPTER FIFTY-EIGHT

RHEN

This time, I do not keep a vigil alone. Zo sits with me. Harper's brother sits with me. The healer Noah spent hours stitching Harper back together.

When he was done, his voice was grim as he said, "I don't know. I don't know."

She's been given a dose of sleeping ether to make her rest, but even that made Noah grimace and fret about dosage and something called a coma.

So we sit. And we wait.

There are many things I do not know.

I do not know if she broke the curse with her action—or if Grey succeeded in killing Lilith and that set me free.

I do not know if Lilith succeeded in killing *him*.

It has been hours, and Grey has not returned.

Harper may not survive.

As always, my life seems destined to end in tragedy.

Jake speaks into the quiet, early-morning darkness of my chambers. “If she dies, I’m going to kill you.”

They’re the first words he’s spoken to me in hours. Since helping to move Harper to this room, in fact.

I wait for Zo to contradict him. She does not.

I sigh, then nod. “I will offer you my blade.”

CHAPTER FIFTY-NINE

HARPER

This time, my return to consciousness isn't gradual. I jerk awake with a shout and a cry.

Pain grips me from all sides, and I nearly curl in on myself. Sunlight burns my eyes. I'm lying in sheets soaked in sweat.

"Shh, my lady." Rhen's voice. His hand touches my cheek. "Another nightmare. Be at ease."

I blink and his warm eyes fill my vision.

He goes blurry as tears well up. "You're here." The pain takes my breath away, but I can't stop staring at him. "You're here."

"Yes. I am here." He uses his thumb to brush the tears out of my eyes. "Zo and Jacob will be quite relieved to hear your voice." His hand flattens over my cheek, then my forehead. "And your healer will be quite relieved to know your fever is gone."

"But—the curse—"

"Broken."

"Broken," I whisper.

"Yes." He brushes an errant lock of hair off my forehead. "It is quite nice to see you through these eyes again."

I swallow. "How long have I been unconscious?"

"Six days."

"Six days!" I struggle to sit up and regret it immediately.

"Easy." He pushes me back down. "You have many weeks of healing ahead of you."

"What about Grey? Is he okay?" I realize what he said about Jake and Noah. "He didn't take my brother and Noah home?"

Something in Rhen's eyes fractures. "Grey did not return."

"What?"

"Grey did not return. He disappeared with Lilith, and he did not return."

"Oh, Rhen." Tears find my eyes again. "Do you think—"

"I do not know what to think." He pauses. "He could be dead. He could be sworn to Lilith. He could be trapped on your side if he killed her there. I do not know."

I find his hand and grip it in mine, then watch his eyes flare in surprise.

He lifts mine and brushes a kiss across my knuckles. "I feel as though I have won and lost at the same time."

"Me too," I say.

Rhen frowns, then kisses my hand again. "I will send for your brother. I imagine you have much to say to each other."

Days pass.

Grey does not return.

The rumors of the evil enchantress and of the monster's

destruction of Karis Luran's army fly in wild directions. I hear murmurs of a halfling child who may languish somewhere—but many people have laughed this off as too far-fetched. Rhen does nothing to quell any of them. He is too popular. His alliance with Disi is seen as a victory that protected his people. He has regained the respect and support of Emberfall.

Jake and Noah are trapped here. They've fallen into a routine, and they seem happy enough, though I've heard Jake comforting an emotional Noah late at night, when the darkness is absolute and there are no patients to treat, and reality seems more profound.

Rhen is always busy. Always needed. He visits me often, but more frequently I'm entertained by Zo and Freya and the children. Even at night, Rhen gives me space and privacy, allowing me time to heal.

A week after I wake, Noah gives me a pass to go for a short walk outside in the sunlight. Rhen sticks to my side, and we're trailed by Dustan and Zo.

My abdomen aches, but the fresh air feels nice. We're in the back courtyard, near the stables, the trellis crawling with vibrant roses.

"The flowers are blooming!" I exclaim.

"Yes." Rhen smiles. "When the curse was broken, fall turned to spring. Overnight, the dried leaves curled up, new buds formed on the trees." A pause, and the smile slides off his face. "Though we faced many losses, our victory over Lilith and Karis Luran is seen as quite impressive."

A victory that meant the loss of Grey.

"I'm sorry," I say softly. "I miss him, too."

He shakes his head slowly. "He should have been a friend. I feel as though I still failed in so many ways."

He might come back. I think it, but I do not say it.

If Grey could come back, he would have.

"You didn't fail," I tell him. "You saved your people."

"I failed," Rhen says. "I did not save them soon enough. I did not prevent it from happening at all."

I'm quiet for a moment. "When Lilith told me my family was in danger, she said that Grey was the one who let her into your chambers. That first night. She bribed him for access. You never mentioned that." I pause. "But you knew, didn't you? You'd have to know."

He nods. "I knew."

"He once told me that he wasn't blameless for the curse."

"Perhaps not, but I allowed her to stay. I could have sent her back out." He pauses. "The responsibility was mine. The curse was mine."

"Do you remember when we played cards and you told me about how your father said everyone is dealt a hand and they have to play it all the way out?"

"Yes."

"I don't think he's right. I think you get cards, and you play them, but then you get more cards. I don't think it's all predestined from the beginning. All along the way, you could have made a different choice and this all could have ended up differently." I pause. "Failure isn't absolute. Just because you couldn't save everyone doesn't mean you didn't save anyone."

His expression has gone somber. The sun beams down and we walk in silence for a while. Eventually I reach out and catch his hand. His steps falter as if he's surprised, but I lace my fingers through his and keep walking.

"There is one area where I still do not know if I failed or succeeded," says Rhen.

"What's that?"

He stops me, then turns to face me. His hair is golden in the sunlight, his eyes intense on mine. "I do not know if you broke the curse—or if Grey did when he killed Lilith."

I study him. He hasn't asked a question, but his voice is weighted.

I suddenly realize he's asking if I'm in love with him.

My eyes drop. "I don't know."

Which I suppose is the wrong answer either way.

"Ah." He doesn't move, but I feel a new distance between us, as if he's taken a step back. His fingers unlace from mine.

I think of the nights we spent sharing secrets. How we'd sway to the music.

I think of Grey on his knees, offering himself, to spare me. To spare Rhen.

I think of iridescent scales and quiet nights and throwing knives and my mother.

I think of choices.

I think of who's in front of me, and who may never return.

Rhen is turning away. He's not going to push me—that was never his style.

I catch his hand. "Your Highness."

It's the first time I've ever said it without a shred of disdain, and it gets his attention. He turns back. "My lady."

I reach up and touch a hand to his face. Pull his mouth down to mine. "I'd like to find out."

EPILOGUE

GREY

The same dream plagues my nights for weeks.

Lilith on the gritty, wet pavement beneath me. Neon lights overhead.

"You can't kill me," she says. "Karis Luran told me the truth. You want the truth, don't you, Commander Grey? About Rhen? About yourself? About the true heir to the throne? About the blood that runs in your veins?" She gasped a breath as I pressed my sword against her neck. "Don't you want to know how you were the only guardsman to survive?"

"No," I say.

And then I cut her throat.

A woman is shaking me awake. "Grey. Grey. It's another night terror. Wake up."

My eyes slide open. My mother's worried eyes stare down at me. They've been worried since she found me half-dead in the stables, my throat bleeding from Lilith's last attempt to take my life, my stitches half-torn open under my armor. She kisses her fingers and presses them to my forehead—something she did when I was a child that I'd completely forgotten.

"There," she says. "That will chase it away."

I catch her hand. "You've told no one I'm here."

"You'll be telling them yourself if you keep shouting like that in your sleep."

"Mother." I sigh, then let her go.

If what Lilith said was true, this woman is not my mother at all.

"So serious." Her hand brushes across my cheek and I flinch away. I remember her touch. The thought that she may be nothing to me causes more pain than when I forswore them all. "They took my sweet boy into that castle and sent home a warrior." Her voice falters. "For so long, I've thought you were dead."

"No one can know I'm here." I swallow, and the still-healing wounds at my throat pull and ache. "You will tell people I'm your nephew. Injured in the battle against Syhl Shallow in the north."

"Why?" Her voice is hushed. "What have you done?"

"It's not what I've done. It's what I know."

And what I remember. Harper's eyes in the darkness.

The prince's grip on my hand as he threw himself off the castle parapet.

Lilith's words: *Karis Luran told me the truth.*

My blade cut true. I feel certain she died.

In truth, I am certain of nothing. I did not wait to be sure. She had no magic on the other side to save her.

But I fled before I was sure.

"What do you know?" my mother whispers. She touches my hand. Wraps it in both of her own.

I freeze. Pull my hand free. Open my eyes to look at her.

"No, Mother. What do *you* know? What do you know about my father?"

"Grey?" she whispers.

"What do you know about my mother?" I say. "My *real* mother."

Her face goes still. It's not an answer—but it's answer enough.

She reaches to touch my hand again. "It does not matter, Grey. It does not matter. I raised you as my son. I *love* you as my son. No one knows. No one. *You* were not to know."

I think of Karis Luran. "Someone knows."

Her face pales. "The king himself delivered you into my arms. I served in the castle. I lost a child at birth. He said that he and I were the only people to know, and if I told anyone, he would know that knowledge came from me. I have never said one word. Never once, Grey."

"You allowed me to apply as a guardsman. You *encouraged* it."

"We had nothing. After your father was injured—" Her voice breaks, and I know she is remembering the months—the *years*—of struggle our family faced. "I knew the king would not know you. He had never seen you since that day. He did not even know your name. You were so eager to apply. I could not take that from you."

We were desperate—and I *was* eager. I remember that, too.

"The prince is the heir," I say. "Not me." I swore my life because I believed that—I cannot unbelieve it so easily. It makes no difference who my father is.

"But Grey—"

I let go of her hand. "I cannot stay here." I shift to stand. "Enough has been said to raise questions. There is already doubt about the legitimacy of the prince. If anyone discovers my true birthright, I will be sought."

I have no desire to rule, but I have spent enough time at court to know my desire is meaningless. My very existence challenges the line of succession.

If anyone seeks me, they seek only my head separated from my body.

My mother must realize this at the same time. "No one knows." She swallows. "I have told no one. You can be my nephew, as you said—"

"I cannot." I already regret coming here. I have put her at risk.

"But—where will you go?" She stands, as if to stop me.

I step around her. It has been weeks, and my wounds have dulled to an ache. My weapons lie in a pile by the door—but they are all marked with the gold-and-red royal crest. "Bury those," I tell her. "Under the feeding trough, or the manure pile. Somewhere they cannot be found."

"But Grey—"

"I have remained here too long."

"Where will you *go*?"

"I do not know." Even if I did, I would not tell her. If she is interrogated—and it is likely more a question of *when* than of *if*—the less she knows, the better.

"But you have nothing."

"If I learned anything while serving in the Royal Guard, it is how to stay invisible and how to stay alive."

She swallows. "Grey. Please."

I turn for the door.

"Grey is dead, Mother. That is all you need to know."

AUTHOR'S NOTE

In *A Curse So Dark and Lonely*, the protagonist, Harper, has cerebral palsy. Much like a real-world individual who has CP, she is not defined by the condition; instead, it's something that is part of her daily life. I strove to create a girl who was strong, resilient, and capable—not in spite of any physical challenges she might face, but in addition to them. As Harper tells Rhen, cerebral palsy affects everyone differently. Capabilities will vary from person to person, so her story is just that: a story. Harper's experience may not be reflective of all people with CP, but hopefully her determination and tenacity will be relatable to everyone. I encourage readers to learn more about cerebral palsy at www.cerebralpalsy.org.

ACKNOWLEDGMENTS

If you've ever read one of my books, you might be used to my acknowledgments dragging on for two to three pages, and I'm just going to tell you that this time will be no different. This book has been a massive project for me. I began writing *A Curse So Dark and Lonely* years ago, and so many people have provided valuable input along the way that it's very possible (it's very *likely*) that I will forget to mention someone. If I forget you here, please know that I haven't forgotten you in my heart, and I'm so grateful for your help. Also, please remind me to buy you a cup of coffee. I owe you one.

Okay. Here we go.

First and foremost: my husband, Michael. When I was at a real low years ago, Mike said to me, "When was the last time you wrote something for fun? Not something under contract. Really just wrote something for yourself?" He was right—it had been a while. So I sat down, pulled out my notes about this idea of a cursed prince who turns into a beast over time, and started writing. A few weeks later, I showed it to my agent. A few months later, it was under contract. I often think back to that moment with my husband. It's a good reminder for me that the storytelling is the best part, and I should never lose sight of it. I'm lucky to have my husband along for this journey with me.

My mother, as always, is a constant inspiration. You would not be reading these words if not for her unwavering encouragement when I was growing up—and even now. She doesn't read many of my books, and she might not even be aware of what I write in the acknowledgments section, but she knows I love her, and I hope she knows what a profound influence her positivity has been in my life.

Bobbie Goettler is my best friend and has read almost every word I've ever written, since the beginning, when I was writing about silly vampires running around the suburbs. Thank you, Bobbie, for being such an amazing friend. Your support over the years has meant everything to me. I love that my kids call you Aunt Bobbie, and when they refer to their "cousins," they include your kids. For a friendship that started on a message board about writing, I think that's pretty powerful.

My amazing agent, Mandy Hubbard, is, like, *flawless* in her guidance of my writing and my career. From supportive text messages to amazing email GIFs to listening to me sob over Google chat—plus all the actual agent businessy-type stuff—Mandy is beyond compare. One of these days I'm going to build a statue of Mandy and put it on my front lawn.

I'll have to put it right next to the future statue of Mary Kate Castellani, my fearless editor at Bloomsbury. I don't know if I can put into words—hi, I'm a writer—how much I appreciate Mary Kate's influence on my writing. Whenever I think something is good enough, she pushes me to make it better. When it's better, she pushes me to make it the best. Mary Kate has a brilliant vision and always finds the story I didn't know I was looking for. Thank you, Mary Kate, for everything.

Speaking of Bloomsbury, I'm going to need to build a statue for Cindy Loh, Claire Stetzer, Lizzy Mason, Courtney Griffin, Erica

Barmash, Cristina Gilbert, Anna Bernard, Brittany Mitchell, Phoebe Dyer, Emily Ritter, Beth Eller, Melissa Kavonic, as well as Diane Aronson and the copyediting team—my yard is going to be really crowded, but it's fine—and everyone else at Bloomsbury who had a hand in putting this book into your hands. I wish I knew everyone's name so I could thank you all individually. Please know that my gratitude is endless, and I can't tell you how much I appreciate your efforts on my behalf.

This book took a tremendous amount of research, from Harper's cerebral palsy to Noah's medical training to Grey's skill at throwing a knife. Huge, tremendous thanks to Erin Kanner, my lifelong friend, for all her insight into cerebral palsy and what Harper could and could not do in a challenging situation. I think my favorite text exchange was when I said, "Could you leap off a galloping horse to tackle a guy, if you were trying to rescue someone?" and Erin wrote back enthusiastically, "I could!" Erin, I am so grateful for our years of friendship, and even though we're forty (!!!) and living on opposite sides of the country now, I hope we get another chance to careen around on horses like we did when we were young. Just don't tell Mike, because he'd worry.

Many thanks to my good friend Maegan Chaney-Bouis, MD, for insights into what Noah could do to piece Grey back together, as well as what he'd be able to do when he was stuck in Emberfall without the convenience of an ER. I owe you a drink. Bonefish Grill next weekend?

Additional thanks go to Claerie Kavanagh for doing an impressively thorough sensitivity read, and offering amazing suggestions for where I could add clarity about Harper's CP and her abilities. I'm so glad we were able to work together. Your feedback was invaluable.

Holy cow. I'm on my fourth page and there are still people to thank. Deep breath!

SO MANY PEOPLE read early drafts (or later drafts) of this manuscript and gave me feedback and input and insights. I joke that I wrote 300,000 words of this book to get it into your hands, but that's actually true. It might have been more. Special thanks to Bobbie Goettler, Nicole Choiniere-Kroeker, Joy George, Michelle MacWhirter, Alison Kemper Beard, Lee Bross, Shyla Stokes, Steph Messa, Sarah Fine, Tracy Houghton, Nicole Mooney, Sarah Maas, Jim Hilderbrandt, Jen Fisher, Anna Bright, Lea Nolan, Amy Martin, and Rae Chang. I couldn't have gotten to this point without you all. Thank you.

Tremendous thanks to book bloggers and bookstagrammers and book vloggers. I appreciate everyone who takes the time to talk about my books on social media. I still remember the first bloggers who spread the word about my debut novel, and I won't forget anyone since. Your support means everything to me. Thank you.

I also owe a debt of gratitude to Steve and Allison Horrigan at Stone Forge CrossFit. CrossFit helped me find a stress release I didn't know I needed, and a confidence I didn't realize I was lacking. I'm stronger and fitter than I ever thought possible, and I've met the most amazing community of people. When I say CrossFit changed my life, I mean that it literally changed my life. I'm a better person and a better writer because of it. Steve and Allison, thank you.

Finally, huge thanks to the Kemmerer boys, Jonathan, Nick, Sam, and not-such-a-Baby Zach. Thank you for being such wonderful boys, and for letting Mommy follow her dreams. I can't wait to watch you soar as you follow your own.